# HEART
# QUEST

HeartQuest brings you romantic fiction
with a foundation of biblical truth.
Adventure, mystery, intrigue, and suspense
mingle in our heartwarming stories of
men and women of faith striving to build
a love that will last a lifetime.

May HeartQuest books sweep you
into the arms of God, who longs for you
and pursues you always.

# Reunited

JUDY BAER • JERI ODELL

JAN DUFFY • PEGGY STOKS

Tyndale House Publishers, Inc.
WHEATON, ILLINOIS

Visit Tyndale's exciting Web site at www.tyndale.com

Editor: Kathryn S. Olson
Designer: Melinda Schumacher

**Library of Congress Cataloging-in-Publication Data**

Reunited / Judy Baer . . . [et al.]:
   p.  cm.
   Contents: Tell me no lies / Judy Baer—Scarlett dreamer / Jeri Odell—Mountain memories / Jan Duffy—The sound of the water / Peggy Stoks.
   ISBN 0-8423-0868-7 (soft cover)
   1. Man-woman relationships—United States—Fiction.   2. Christian fiction, American. 3. Love stories. American.   I. Baer, Judy.
PS648.L6R48   1998
813′.540803823—dc21                        98-21890

Printed in the United States of America

04   03   02   01   00   99   98
7    6    5    4    3    2    1

# CONTENTS

# Tell Me No Lies

### Judy Baer

# CHAPTER ONE

So sorry about your grandfather, Kirsti. He was a good friend."

"Jens Nord was the most generous man in three counties—no, five—no, in the whole state!"

"We'll all miss him, Kirsti. He helped more people in trouble over the years than anyone else I know."

Kirsti Nord nodded and offered a soft smile to each one of the mourners and friends who filed past her to the church basement, where the ladies were working their magic in the kitchen. Food was the answer to everything in Snowflake, North Dakota. It was prepared in bulk for weddings, funerals, anniversaries, and birthdays. Anything these Scandinavians couldn't say with words, they would say with food.

"It's going to be difficult for you living alone in that big old house," Adam Smith, the Nords' closest neighbor, commented. "Too bad your parents couldn't come home from Africa for a few months to help you through this." He was referring to Kirsti's missionary parents. The only child of only children, she did feel very alone right now. But she knew she was never really alone. God had been carrying her through this. She could practically feel the gentle lift of his hands when her spirits sank. His other gift to her was his promise of a peace that passes understanding. Even in this traumatic moment, she felt a stillness inside, a restful place where mourning might have been.

"He loved you very much, you know. He always talked about his beautiful, blond, blue-eyed granddaughter."

Kirsti smiled at the little woman before her. A neighbor of Gramps's and a dear friend.

"Thank you, Mrs. Keller. I appreciate knowing that. There was no one quite like my grandfather." Kirsti was having a hard time keeping her mind on the sincere sympathy and warm remarks she was gathering. Instead, her thoughts kept drifting to her grandfather.

He'd been her hero, that was for sure. Wise, witty, sharp as a tack when it came to business dealings and meddling in other people's lives. Jens always thought he knew what was best for others—and he didn't mind informing them of that fact. He was also the most sincere lover of the Lord that Kirsti had ever met. No day ever started without Bible study and prayer. And no night closed without the same.

His pew was going to be empty now. He'd sat in the same spot for eighty years, and now there would be no one to fill his place, for Snowflake's demise seemed imminent as well. Jens had always said that people in small-town churches went to their places just like well-trained horses to their stalls. And now his stall was empty.

It was Jens who had encouraged Kirsti in her faith and been her mentor and her guide. He'd been the one to encourage her personal relationship with Jesus Christ, both by his witness and by his words. Every evening since she was a tiny child, they'd read the Bible together, with Jens explaining each passage and Kirsti hanging on every word. Almost every day this past year, Jens had mentioned how exciting it would be to meet his Savior face-to-face, as if he knew that his time here was short and he was looking forward to the next step.

And that was why Kirsti couldn't feel terribly sad about

Jens's passing. He had gone to the place he wanted most to be. So Kirsti had chosen to sing only hymns of celebration and to release a handful of balloons over the grave. He would have liked firecrackers too, if she'd thought the pastor would allow it. Grandpa was fine. He had been old and had dreaded being ill and helpless. Neither had happened. It was better this way. Those who were left were mourning for themselves.

"Kirsti, dear, why don't you greet everyone downstairs?" A lady in an apron stood at her shoulder with a worried look. "You need to eat. Build up your strength."

It took all Kirsti's willpower not to smile. Food. The ultimate cure-all, social component, and staple of life. "Is that funeral hot dish I smell?" she asked.

"Of course. What else?"

*What else indeed?* It had been served at every such event at the church that Kirsti could remember. People didn't die in Snowflake without being sent off in a flurry of egg coffee and funeral hot dish!

She surveyed the crowd in the basement. People were laughing now and regaling each other with stories of Jens—like the Halloween prank in which he hitched seven cows into horse harnesses. When their owner came to the barn the next morning he found the befuddled animals patiently waiting to be milked but harnessed to the front of a plow. Or the story of when he and his friends dismantled a Model T Ford, hoisting it to the roof of a barn and reassembling it there. Jens had played tricks on, loaned money to, worked fields with, or prayed with every person in the room, and they had all loved him.

*Oh, Grandpa, what a great party you are throwing this time!*

For the sake of decorum, she suppressed a smile. The conversation was growing more boisterous as the Jens Nord stories began to be exchanged and exaggerated to epic proportions. The people of Snowflake were making valiant attempts to smile—Jens would have loved this, Kirsti thought. He'd been saying for a long time that Snowflake needed more parties.

"You are looking lovelier than ever, my dear," one of Kirsti's old piano teachers said, laying a gnarled and wrinkled hand on Kirsti's arm. Briefly Kirsti wondered if the woman could still play the piano as she used to.

"As are you, Mrs. Bentson."

"Nonsense. You were always sweet but never blind. I'm a wrinkled old crow. But it does my eyes good to look at you. What are you now? Six feet tall?"

"Five nine," Kirsti said with a laugh.

"Who'd guess that an ugly old troll like Jens could have a granddaughter who looks like you, with that blond, blue-eyed Nordic beauty?"

Kirsti didn't even flinch. Instead, she leaned over to give the woman a hug. "You were always in love with my grandfather, weren't you?"

Mrs. Bentson wiped a tear from her eye. "Was it so obvious?"

"He's the only one I ever heard you call a 'troll,' and in a tone so loving it sounds like a caress."

"I thought he might marry me, you know, after my husband, Ben, and your grandmother passed on, but I guess he was content just eating my apple pies and pot roast without more of a commitment."

"And your *lefse*," Kirsti pointed out, referring to the Norwegian equivalent of a tortilla, made with potatoes and served with butter and sugar. "He adored your *lefse*."

Mrs. Bentson launched into another story, but Kirsti was listening with only partial attention. A man stood in the doorway looking over the room, his dark-lashed violet eyes scanning every detail.

Kirsti's breath caught in her throat, and she felt a flutter in the pit of her stomach. What was Cade Callahan doing here? Wasn't he supposed to be someplace like London or Shanghai, designing those fabulous buildings for which he'd become famous? She hadn't dreamed he'd appear at Grandfather's funeral. He was one person she had expected—no, hoped—never to see again.

Her mind flashed back to the last time she'd seen Cade, ten years ago. The day she'd broken the tie with one of her best friends. It had seemed innocent enough at first, Cade and Cindy Mahon skipping school together for a day. Kirsti would have trusted Cade with her life, so she certainly had no qualms about his driving Cindy to an out-of-town photographer to get a passport photo taken. No qualms, that is, until she'd heard the rumors later.

"Is that who I think it is?" a voice whispered over Kirsti's shoulder, startling her back into the present. "And is it possible that he's even more handsome than ever? Isn't there a rule about that somewhere? If not, there should be. The man is gorgeous!"

Kirsti turned to see Natalie Johnson behind her. They'd been best friends since first grade when Natalie had managed to fall off the monkey bars and bloody both knees. Kirsti had helped her to the girls' bathroom, bathed the knees, and called the teacher for help. Natalie had reciprocated by being, from that moment on, the most loyal friend Kirsti had ever had. Her irreverence was a breath of normalcy in today's otherwise difficult scenario.

"Oh, Natty," she said, calling her friend by the nickname that had stuck since the knee incident, "I have no idea why he is here."

"At least you had the good sense to fall in love with someone incredibly good-looking. Remember my first love? Fred Owens? He was all teeth and bad hair. What did I see in him anyway? He did have a cute nose, though. Kind of Paul Newmanish. And he swaggered—"

"Hush, Natty. I can't think."

"You never could when Cade was around," Natty observed cheerfully. "Your hormones took over."

"Nat!"

"Oh, you know what I mean. Swooning, batting your eye-lashes, listening to his every word with bated breath."

"You make me sound like an idiot. I had a schoolgirl crush on him, that's all. We were pals. We caught frogs together, built tree houses, and played marathon games until we both fell asleep over the checkerboard. You know that."

It was true, as far as it went, but there was more. Much, much more. She'd loved him—or thought she had. She'd even engaged in the romantic meanderings of a schoolgirl's mind and peeked at the bride magazines in the drugstore and written *Mrs. Cade Callahan, Mrs. Kirsti Callahan, Cade and Kirsti Callahan* in secret places deep inside her notebooks, just to see how their names looked together. And they had seemed perfect to her. Back then, Cade was all she'd ever hoped for in a friend, a boyfriend, a—

"Right." Natty, in that inimitable way of hers, managed to create another reality check for Kirsti. "Then let's see you walk over to him and say hello. You wouldn't ignore your childhood playmate, would you?"

Kirsti felt trapped between her deeply inbred civility and the betrayal she still felt when she thought about Cade, even after all these years. For a while it had been almost an obses-sion with her to discover why he'd done what he'd done and lied about it. But Cade wasn't talking then or now. Cindy had gone abroad with her parents and never been seen again in Snowflake. The incident was insignificant history to everyone but Kirsti now. She alone had been unable to put it to rest.

"Look who's here!" Mrs. Keller gushed near Kirsti's ear. "That Cade Callahan just gets better looking every year." She laid a hand on Kirsti's arm and whispered conspiratorially, "We always thought you'd marry Cade, you know."

Once, Kirsti had thought so too.

Natty looked slyly from the corners of her eyes, oblivious to her friend's internal turmoil. "Or are you afraid?"

Bingo! Natty had hit the target straight on and dead center. Cade was handsome, charming, brilliant, witty, and all the other things a woman would choose were she to design her ideal man. But he had a dark side too. Maybe it was the curse of his Irish ancestors that he could be stubborn and melancholy and utterly frustrating.

But Natty was right. Kirsti had to greet him. He'd come for Grandfather's funeral, and no matter what remnants of the past hung between them, she must welcome him.

\ulli/

She took one step forward and then halted as Natty let out a long, low whistle. "No wonder he's here. Look who he's brought with him."

A sudden knot of pain tightened in Kirsti's throat, and the tears she'd been controlling all day sprang to her eyes. *Thomas Callahan.* Of course!

Cade would never allow his grandfather to attend Jens's funeral unaccompanied. Thomas and Jens had been best friends for over eighty years. If Kirsti had lost a grandfather, then Thomas had lost a brother.

"Does that man ever change?" Natty wondered as she gave Kirsti a little push toward the pair. "He's been wrinkled as a raisin for as long as I can remember."

"Hush," Kirsti ordered as she arranged a welcoming expression on her features. "He's an old darling, and you know it. And still spry as a leprechaun."

Now eager, she hurried toward the door.

"There's my darling gal!" Thomas Callahan greeted her. His blue eyes twinkled out from beneath wildly uncontrolled brows and a wealth of wrinkles.

*Child's eyes in an ancient's face,* Kirsti thought fleetingly. And how wonderful to see them.

She gathered Thomas into her arms to give him a gentle hug. He felt frail and bony beneath the too-large blue suit, circa 1975, that he wore, but his spirit was so dominant, so strong, that she might have been hugging Hercules. Thomas radiated presence, determination, and power.

"What was wrong with your grandfather anyway, dying like that? Rude, if you ask me! He didn't tell me he was planning to do it or even say good-bye!"

"Oh, Thomas, I think if he'd had any idea it was going to happen, you would have been the first to know."

"I certainly hope so. I'm still angry at him for leaving. Who am I going to play checkers with now? Those dolts at the café can't tell red from black. Pah!" He swung his cane like a weapon, and a lady carrying a coffeepot to a nearby table dodged out of his way. "All that I can say is that he'd better be having a good time right now because he certainly ruined my day."

This time Kirsti smiled, and it felt genuine and good. Leave it to Thomas to put things in perspective.

"I think he's having a wonderful time, and so do you. He's with the Lord, and you know how important that was to him. All we're doing here is feeling sorry for ourselves. That's what the funerals of Christians are all about, isn't it?"

Thomas digested that statement and nodded. "True. I never planned to play second fiddle to anyone, but Jens got me on that one." Then a grin split his creased and furrowed features. "And it took God to do it!"

Then all the humor left his face, and he reached with a shriveled, age-spotted hand to her. His fingers were twisted with arthritis, and his nails were split and chipped from the wood carving he still managed to do. "How are you, gal? Holding up? I know how you loved him."

"I miss him just as much as you do. But I'll be fine because I know he's happy now."

Thomas nodded briskly, as if glad that bit of business was out of the way. "Good. Now aren't you going to say hello to this reprobate of a grandson of mine? He came all the way from Zanzibar to bring me to this shindig. I suppose Norwegians don't have wakes like the Irish. Too bad. . . ."

"Hello, Kirsti." She hadn't changed much, Cade observed with pleasure. Only the best kind of changes had occurred—less baby fat, more chiseled features, more self-confidence and poise. How had he let her get away? Or, more correctly, why hadn't he been able to stop her? It was a question that had haunted him off and on throughout his adult life.

With dismay, Kirsti felt a thrill of pleasure at the sound of Cade's voice. Involuntarily, she remembered his singing Irish ditties and saying loving words . . . and breaking her heart.

With a mental snap, she shut off that train of thought and extended a graceful hand with long tapering fingers. "Cade. How lovely to see you. I didn't expect that you'd be here." She paused. "Especially from *Zanzibar.*"

"My grandfather exaggerates." His lip quirked in amusement. "I was in London and planning to come back to the States next week. This just made it important to come back early."

His eyes, blue-violet with black flecks and the thickest, blackest eyelashes known to man, studied her. "Besides, Jens was as much my grandfather as Thomas, here, is yours."

It was true. Kirsti and Cade had practically been raised together by the two old men. It had been a glorious and adventuresome childhood, filled with play, laughter, and teachings about faith that would never leave her. Thomas and Jens had never worried much about nutrition. If pizza for breakfast was requested, so be it. If a box of candy bars disappeared without a trace, no problem. But if they ever missed a Sunday school class, then watch out!

"Enough of this small talk!" Thomas announced and pulled away from the pair of them. "I smell hot dish. I hope it's the stuff with hamburger, elbow macaroni, and tomatoes. Haven't had that since Emmett Pierce decided to take up water-skiing and had the 'big one' trying to do acrobatics on one foot. Served him right, I say. A man in his seventies shouldn't water-ski. Nothing wrong with a hot tub or a lap pool at that age. Waterskiing. Old ninny."

Thomas caught Mrs. Bentson with the hooked end of his cane as she passed him. "Did you cook today?" he inquired, hobbling closer. "I hope so. Jens always said you were the best cook in Snowflake."

"Why, Thomas! What a lovely thing to say. And yes, I did cook. Homemade buns—and I even brought a little raspberry jam. Can I dish up a plate for you?"

Cade and Kirsti burst out laughing as the old pair made their way to the front of the lunch line.

"He's incorrigible. I'm sorry if his bluntness hurt you," Cade said.

"He's perfect. You always know what he's thinking. No guessing, no talking behind one's back. This would be a better place if there were more people like him."

"Meddling, manipulative, always positive he's right and everyone else is wrong? Those are his traits, too, you know."

Kirsti couldn't help but smile. "My grandfather was exactly the same way. I guess I grew to love those qualities. They are—and were—good men, Cade. God-loving, devoted family men who cared about their community." A twinge shot through her as she was reminded of Snowflake's current predicament.

Cade's dark hair fell toward one eye as he nodded. "And much easier to enjoy from a distance."

"Like London?"

"Zanzibar might be better," he said with a chuckle.

Kirsti was amazed at how quickly they had fallen into the easy conversation that had been so simple and comfortable in their past. Where had all the anger she'd felt toward Cade gone? Had it evaporated little by little with each passing year? Perhaps, more likely, her prayer had been answered. She'd begged God for the strength to forgive Cade for what he'd done to her and to her life. And now the anger was gone. She hadn't even missed it after harboring it, feeding it, and nurturing it for those dreadful years after high school. God did work miracles, Kirsti thought. Big ones.

Instead of the near hatred she'd expected to feel when she first saw Cade in the doorway, she'd felt—the thought stunned her—*attraction!* It was the last response she'd anticipated or wanted.

"And speaking of community, what's all this bad news I've been hearing about Snowflake?" Even concern looked good on Cade's features.

"We've made the international news?" Kirsti tried to keep her tone light. "Amazing."

"Hardly. But at least in my grandfather's mind it's important enough to do so." His somber expression created furrows in his brow that Kirsti yearned to wipe away. Instead, she wrung the handkerchief she was carrying.

"It's a mess, that's for sure. Ever since the fire at the Snowflake Snowmobile Plant, this town has been slowly but surely collapsing. The plant was our biggest employer—good benefits, fair wages, steady work. And it's getting worse. With the plant closed, other businesses are hurting as well. The hospital and several other institutions are cutting back on staff. So even the families who had a second paycheck from someplace else are beginning to feel desperate."

"So the place was destroyed entirely?"

"What was left was demolished for safety reasons. If the owners want to rebuild, they will have to start from scratch."

"*If* they rebuild?" The furrow between Cade's eyes deepened. "You mean Grandfather is right—there's a chance they'll lose the industry entirely?"

"It's not yet decided. After all, the fact that they built here once is fairly amazing. You know how small towns in the Midwest are faring. The investors may just take the insurance money and build elsewhere.

"My grandfather talked endlessly of creating a way to stanch the hemorrhage of people and money flowing out of this town with the loss of the plant. He thought he had a good idea not long before his death, but he didn't share it with me. He said it was too early. He wanted to perfect it before he said anything. And now, so quickly, it's too late."

Kirsti made a sweeping gesture toward the fellowship room, where people were lingering over their third and fourth cups of coffee. "Why do you think that there is still such a crowd here at three-thirty in the afternoon? Most of these people don't even *have* jobs to return to! People who never dreamed of taking help from anyone are standing in line for unemployment or thinking of tearing up roots and moving. Cities don't even notice new people. There are too many coming and going all the time. Snowflake *needs* and *loves* every single person. That's what a small town is—community. . . ."

Her voice drifted off, and she blushed, a charming pink glow on her creamy skin. "Sorry, I didn't mean to climb onto my soapbox and give you a lecture. It's just that it has been so difficult here lately."

"And the people of Snowflake are giving up hope?" Cade sounded surprised. "That doesn't sound like the place I knew."

"Everyone was extremely optimistic at first, but the longer no decision is made and the more sidestepping the investors do, the more our initial optimism is fading."

She glanced over the room, looking at the familiar faces she'd known and loved her entire life. "It's painful to watch hope turn quietly to desperation."

Then Kirsti forced herself to smile, and her blue eyes began to dance. "But look at it this way—today we're having a celebration of my grandfather's life. He would have loved that." Cade stared at her with those blue-violet eyes and shook his head in genuine amazement. "You are really something else, Kirsti Nord. Amazing. Phenomenal, in fact. You are able to find joy even here, even today." Impulsively he reached out and touched her cheek in the way that had once been so familiar, so special to her.

Something moved deep in the pit of Kirsti's stomach. When

she and Cade had parted, it had been on the worst of terms. And now he was telling her she was "amazing"—no, *"phenomenal"*? The irony was painful to consider. She'd never expected to see Cade again. And now this?

"Uh-oh, here comes trouble," Cade muttered. "I can tell by the look in his eye."

"Trouble" was Thomas Callahan heading straight for them with the purpose and determination of a locomotive. His spry step belied his eighty-plus years. He used his cane to clear a path before him, and people parted like waves on the Red Sea.

And he *was* trouble. Kirsti had seen that look before as well. Not only in Thomas's eyes, but in those of her own grandfather. They'd been the two most meddling, interfering, bossy, and impossible-to-redirect old darlings on the face of the earth. Thomas was wearing his meddling look right now.

"I see you two are finally coming to your senses. Took you long enough. Glad to see you're speaking again. Never could understand why you quit. Now that you're both back in Snowflake, you can start seeing each other again as well." The matchmaker in Thomas just never died. "You'll get to know each other again."

An aching stab of pain and anger slashed through her mind as an expression of amusement spread over Cade's handsome features. *See* each other? *Date?* Had Thomas Callahan gone mad?

Cade was watching Kirsti carefully and was not happy about what he saw. Her beautiful eyes dimmed, and the tension around her mouth intensified. Though careful not to show it to Thomas, Cade knew her well enough to know she was furious.

The idea didn't seem so bad to him, he mused. In fact, he rather liked the idea of reacquainting himself with Kirsti. Maybe, finally, he could get to the bottom of her rejection of him so long ago and put the issue to rest. Perhaps, with a little good fortune, they could even pick up where they'd left off. He'd missed Kirsti.

Why, though, did she appear so irate? Surely she couldn't *still* be remembering that ugly scene they'd had over Cindy? Not now, after all these years!

# CHAPTER TWO

Kirsti roamed about the white Victorian mansion she'd shared with her grandfather. Every room, every piece of furniture, every picture reminded her of Jens. He'd been born in this house, in the upstairs bedroom that overlooked the wide, quiet street lined with ancient oaks and elms. In the same ornate canopy bed in which her father—and Kirsti herself—had been born.

Their family history was so deeply woven into the fibers of this house that every nail, every board, and every pane of glass seemed a part of her. Still, it felt vast and empty now. She couldn't help waiting to hear the tap of Jens's cane on the stairs or—she smiled fleetingly—the uproarious pounding of it when he was trying to get her attention from the far end of the house.

She wished her parents could have come home for the funeral, but they were nearing the end of their last term as missionaries in Africa. What's more, she would have been forced to delay the funeral to accommodate their travel schedule. As her father had said to Kirsti when her parents had finally been reached by shortwave radio, "Dad would have wanted your mother and me to stay here and finish what we were called to do. We trust you to handle his affairs and make the correct decisions, honey. You know the Lord is with you and he'll never give you more than you can handle. Do your best."

*Her best.* And what exactly was that?

As was her habit when she was unsure, she took her well-worn Bible and carried it to the sunroom. Spreading it open on the table, she bowed her head and prayed quietly. "Now what, Father? Where do I go from here? Make me open and responsive to *your* will and not just my own. I know that sometimes what you have planned for your children seems difficult and confusing at first, but give me the faith to believe that your way is always best."

Then, as she sometimes did when she didn't know what she was looking for, she opened the Bible at random and began to read. It was the Psalms, one of her favorite books. It held so much wisdom, so much peace, so much comfort. As she thumbed through the pages, Psalm 48 caught her eye. "Go, inspect the city of Jerusalem. Walk around and count the many towers. Take note of the fortified walls, and tour all the citadels, that you may describe them to future generations. For that is what God is like. He is our God forever and ever, and he will be our guide until we die."

She sat back and smiled. Of course. Blunt, to the point, comforting. God wasn't going to leave her now to flounder in her new situation. He was hers *forever and ever,* her guide *to the very end!* And when God spoke, his word was true. *People* sometimes lied. She knew that very well, but *God* never did. His ways seemed mysterious at times to a mere mortal like her, but what he spoke was always true.

Feeling better already, Kirsti flipped backward a few pages until she found Psalm 32, where another verse leaped from the page at her. "The Lord says, 'I will guide you along the best pathway for your life. I will advise you and watch over you.'"

"If only I'm wise enough to listen," Kirsti murmured. "Help me to recognize your voice when you do speak. I get wrapped up in my own problems sometimes and think I've got all the answers. You know, Lord, that handwriting-on-the-wall thing you did once would sure be useful. Any chance you could start that again? It would help a lot. Especially for a stubborn Norwegian like me!"

Kirsti closed the Bible and stared thoughtfully out the window, feeling comforted. If she could stay close to God and discern his plan for her, she would be all right.

Feeling renewed, she decided that perhaps it was time she took a look at some of the papers in Jens's desk. It had to be done—and now, while she was feeling refreshed by God's Word, might be a good time to start.

Walking down the hallway, she stopped in front of a tall gilded mirror and stared at her reflection. Her hair, pale and gleaming as the most stereotypical of Scandinavians', was pulled severely away from her face in a silver clasp. The stark hairdo exposed her fine, straight nose, eyes clear and blue as the Norwegian fjords, and lips that were naturally rosy and full.

She'd taken no time with herself this morning. She wore jeans and a white long-sleeved shirt. Her only decoration was a small silver Norwegian pin over the top button of her shirt.

"How am I going to sort out an estate as complicated as Gramps's, God? You are going to be very busy teaching me." Though she had grown up around both wealth and philanthropy, she'd never been required to pay much attention to business matters. Jens had been shrewd enough for all of them.

Her talent was for teaching, not finance. She loved little children and each fall was overjoyed to welcome her newest kindergarten class of chubby cheeks and shiny faces. She understood Jesus' love and affection in the Bible when he said, "Let the children come to me." Children were her joy, her vocation and avocation, her fulfillment. But now that Jens was gone, would she have to set teaching aside to care for Nord family affairs?

Kirsti sighed in relief when the doorbell chimed, giving her an excuse to escape this painful evaluation. Her heavenly Father would bring her through. It was her exhaustion and the aching emptiness in the house that were affecting her now. She'd felt scared and alone, that was all. And, said an imp inside her brain, Cade Callahan's surprise return to Snowflake hadn't done a single thing to settle her nerves.

It was Natty waiting impatiently at the front door, arms crossed, foot tapping. "Were you in there moping?" she demanded as she breezed into the enormous foyer. "You promised me you wouldn't. I knew I should have stayed with you last night!"

Kirsti opened her mouth to speak, then stopped midprotest. "Maybe I was. It's weird around here without Gramps. I didn't realize how much his presence filled this house. He didn't move around much anymore, and he slept a great deal, but it's like an entire army has left this place!"

"An army's worth of personality, stubbornness, and unchangeable opinions, anyway," Natty observed matter-of-factly. "Have you had breakfast yet?"

"No. I wasn't hungry."

"Well, I am." Natty led the way to the kitchen, a gleaming white room filled with glass-paned cupboards, oak counters, and sunlight. "Orange juice, coffee, toast . . ."

"There are muffins in that container. Mrs. Olson brought them yesterday. I don't know what I'll do with all the food the neighbors have sent. They've been wonderful."

"Better yet—"

While Kirsti watched, Natty brewed coffee and filled a tray. She'd spent almost as much time in this house as Kirsti had over the years, and her comfort in the kitchen was apparent.

"Aren't you supposed to be at work today?" Kirsti asked. Natty was a loan officer at the Snowflake Community Bank.

"I said I'd be late. I wanted to check on you. Besides, the bank is so quiet, it's hard to stay awake. No one has money to deposit, and people are certainly not taking out business or housing loans. Everything is on hold. The 'wait and see' attitude is killing Main Street. If we don't get word on the plant soon, the only thing that will be happening is people closing out checking accounts."

With a flourish, she plucked one rose out of the assortment on the center of the table and dropped it into a bud vase. "Now, come."

They moved to a glass-enclosed porch off the dining area, filled with old wicker tables and chairs.

"Sit. And eat."

Grateful today for Natty's bossy ways, Kirsti was happy to let someone else think for her. Obediently she dropped into her favorite rocker and curled her feet beneath her. She took the steaming cup Natty handed her.

"Thanks, Nat. I guess I'm not doing as well as I thought I was." Kirsti sipped at the Colombian brew and closed her eyes to savor the aroma.

"Everyone does better with me around," Natty said complacently. "I'm a comfort zone."

"Right. And other things in your zone include poison ivy, ragweed, thistles, mules. . . ."

"I'm *your* comfort zone, then." Natty grabbed a muffin and devoured it with great satisfaction. "Want to talk?"

Kirsti smiled, knowing that for all Natty's bluster and goofiness, she was a true friend as well as a sister in Christ. If there was anyone to whom she could speak her heart and mind, it was Natalie.

"It's a good thing you didn't show up earlier. I was feeling pretty sorry for myself. Then I sat down with my Bible, and God and I had a little talk. He straightened me out." She shared the verses that had given her such consolation.

"Cool," Natty observed. "He has a way of doing that, doesn't he? But frankly I don't blame you for the way you're feeling. You're human, aren't you? Why wouldn't you be scared and alone when someone you loved as much as you loved Jens dies?

"I know you didn't take part in any of his business dealings and that your parents really didn't either. It was neat that Jens supported them in the missionary field, but that doesn't always make for a savvy businessperson. But you are one of the brightest people I know. You'll make it. Besides, you've got God on your side. Seems to me you got that guarantee just this morning: 'I will advise you and watch over you.' Cool. *Really* cool." Nat grinned at her, muffin crumbs dancing on her lower lip until she licked them away.

Then, totally changing the subject, Nat said, "So tell me every little thing you felt about Cade Callahan."

Kirsti nearly choked on her coffee. "I thought you came here to *comfort* me."

"Not really. I think it might be easier to *distract* you. And frankly there's nothing more distracting in this town right now than Cade." Natty picked at the paper surrounding her muffin. "The man must work out nonstop! And those eyes!"

If Nat had come to distract her, she was a roaring success, Kirsti thought. Now images of Cade filled her mind.

"Nat, please," she pleaded. "I don't want to—"

But Natalie was not to be stopped. "Your grandfather thought you'd marry him, didn't he?"

Kirsti rolled her eyes and surrendered to Nat's onslaught. "Yes. You know he did. As did Thomas Callahan. Those two old souls started planning our lives the day we were born. They used to drive my parents to distraction. Jens and Thomas would have coffee in the mornings and discuss the ages at which we should learn to ride horses and play tennis or golf. Together they decided which colleges we should attend and at what age Cade and I should marry."

Nat grinned. "They never did mind meddling in other people's lives!"

Laughter, the first real laughter in a long time, burst through Kirsti's lips. "They thought it was their role in life! And nothing my mild-mannered parents said could dissuade either of them. According to the grandfathers, Cade and I would grow up as childhood playmates, fall in love, marry, and obediently provide Thomas and Jens with great-grandchildren who shared the blood of both men. A perfect plan. Then they would be united in every possible way—shared friendship, shared history, shared blood."

"How convenient."

"Except for one small matter," Kirsti observed mildly. "Instead of growing to love Cade, I grew to despise him."

〰

The doorbell rang at that moment, cutting off any reply Nat might have made.

Relieved at the interruption, Kirsti hurried to the massive double doors at the front of the house.

Her relief was fleeting. Two people stood at the door—Ben Nordstrom, former manager of the now destroyed plant, and Cade.

Caught unawares, Kirsti first recalled her makeupless features and plain clothing. Then she remembered her last words to Natalie. If she despised Cade so much, what did she care how she looked? Besides, she was hardly a pride-filled person. What was going on here? Had Jens figured out a way to direct her life from heaven too? Otherwise, what was Cade doing here today? "Ben, Cade, come in. What can I do for you?" Her innate good manners overcame her dismay. She led them, back straight, head held high, to the formal living room.

It had been Jens's haven, full of down-filled couches, leather chairs, a massive fireplace, and walls of favorite books. A sob caught in Kirsti's throat as she noticed Jens's Bible still lying open on his favorite chair.

Ben stepped forward and rubbed her back with his big, calloused hand. "I couldn't make it to the funeral, so I wanted to come over today to see how you were doing."

"Minute by minute." Kirsti smiled through her unshed tears. She glanced up as Natty entered the room, rampant curiosity on her features. "Nat, would you get some coffee and juice for our guests?"

Nat bobbed her head like a well-trained maid and disappeared. First time, Kirsti thought, that Nat had ever acted like a well-trained anything.

They seated themselves awkwardly around a large game table near the patio windows, and when Nat arrived with cups, juice, coffee, and a basket of muffins, Kirsti parceled them out, glad to have her hands busy.

She turned to Ben. "Were you ill yesterday? I know you would have been there if you could have."

The man paled under his ruddy complexion and looked almost hangdog. "I had a job interview in Sioux Falls."

"South Dakota? But your home is here."

"It *used* to be here. Before the fire. Now I have no job, no resources to pay the mortgage on the house, and, the way things are looking, no future."

"Is it sure—that they aren't rebuilding?" Kirsti asked the questions; Cade listened.

"Not positive, but the prospects are bleak. I need an income. The sad thing is that we built our home here. If I stay, I lose. If I leave, I lose. I spoke to your grandfather not long before he died, and he talked as if he was formulating an idea that might help us out. But the idea—whatever it was—died with him."

Then Ben seemed to shake himself mentally. "I'm sorry, Kirsti. I came here to comfort *you*."

"Nonsense. We can't bring Gramps back, and he wouldn't want us to. But we can do some brainstorming to figure out a way to keep your family in Snowflake."

"You are an architect. You work with big corporations all the time." Ben's voice held enthusiasm for the first time as he turned toward Cade. "Maybe you could give us some ideas of how to encourage the plant owners to rebuild here instead of taking their investments somewhere else."

"I wish we knew what Gramps had in mind," Kirsti said. "He never said a word to me."

"I don't know. . . ." Cade's handsome brow was deeply furrowed.

Ben was oblivious to Cade's reluctance. Instead, he grabbed onto the first straw of hope he'd seen in months. His eagerness was so palpable, so almost pitiful, that Kirsti felt like weeping. Even she hadn't realized quite how devastated people were.

Ben's rapid-fire questions to Cade discouraged any other conversation, much to Kirsti's delight and Nat's obvious displeasure.

Nearly an hour passed before Ben stood up to leave. He was sweetly sympathetic to Kirsti and almost nauseatingly grateful to Cade for his input.

Natalie began to make herself useful by clearing away the dishes, but Kirsti put a hand on her arm and whispered, "I want to talk to Cade alone. I need to know why he came here today."

"I'll just be in the kitchen."

"Correct. The kitchen of your own house. Or the bank. Didn't you say you had to work today?"

"Aw, Kirsti! That's no fun. You won't even know I'm here."

"I'll be imagining you with your ear pressed to the door, salivating over whatever bits of conversation you 'think' you hear. If you're truly a friend, you'll leave. Please?"

"If I didn't love you so much, I'd argue with you about this," Natty said with a pout. "But you'll tell me everything later, won't you?"

Kirsti made no promises. There were some secrets that were hers alone.

Natty made a huge production of leaving. Her good-byes were long and dramatic but finally ended.

"Was she leaving for the Far East or just going to work?" Cade inquired as Nat waved her way down the drive. "Or did she want to drive home the point that now we are alone?"

"She's transparent, isn't she?" Kirsti agreed. "But always truthful, forthright, loyal . . ."

"Unlike others? Me, for example?" Cade was standing too close to her. She could smell his cologne, a spicy, leathery concoction that was purely male.

Kirsti backed away and nearly fell over a misplaced ottoman. Cade caught her arm. Putting his other hand around her body, he pulled her toward him. When she was upright, he reluctantly dragged his hands away.

"You are more beautiful than ever, Kirsti," he said. "I didn't think that was possible."

"Stop it, Cade. Flattery will get you nowhere—fast."

"Not flattery, truth. You look like a Nordic ice princess. . . ." Immediately he winced at his poor choice of words.

"Emphasis on *ice*? Do you feel a chill in the air? Then perhaps you should leave."

"Not so fast, Kirsti. Drop whatever it is that's been eating at you all these years. Let's try to pick up where we left off. I know we can do it. There was something so special between us that I've never been able to forget—"

"Why are you here, Cade?" she asked bluntly, determined not to let the old emotions get the better of her. Cade had disappointed her badly once, and she wasn't going to subject herself to another round of pain.

"I wasn't going to let my grandfather go to the funeral alone. Jens was more a brother than a friend. Frankly, I'm worried about Thomas. He's been very meek and quiet, both qualities I didn't know he possessed."

"I appreciate the fact that you came for your grandfather's sake," Kirsti said. "And I've worried about him, too. I know Jens would have been devastated if Thomas had gone first. But that wasn't my question. Why are you *here*? In my house? I thought we agreed a long time ago that you were no longer welcome."

"Why can't bygones be bygones? What about the old cliché 'Time heals all wounds'? Certainly enough *time* has passed!"

26

Kirsti squelched the feeling of longing inside her. It would be so easy. . . .

*Forbidden fruit.* That's what Cade was. Dangerous. Seductive. Capable of making her forget why she'd been so terribly upset—and how he had betrayed her trust. She didn't dare let down her guard.

Cade shook his head pityingly. "I still don't know why you flew into such a snit and threw me out on my ear. Kirsti, we were best friends for a lifetime until—"

Kirsti held her breath, waiting. Was he going to say it? Was he finally going to admit what he had done?

Then a flash of anger suffused his features. "What's the use? You're as stubborn as your grandfather. I can't read your mind, and I couldn't when we were eighteen. I'm not even sure I know what put the burr under your saddle, but I wish you'd get it out and get on with your life."

She felt herself sag with disappointment and immediately steeled herself against the pain. "You still haven't said why you came. Did Thomas send you?"

"Yes, although I'm not sure *why.* Some trumped-up idea about wanting to know when Jens's will was to be read. Said he wanted to be notified. He wants to be there, Kirsti, though I can't imagine why. He's got more money than he'll ever be able to spend in the years he has left. Besides, I doubt Jens would leave anything to him anyway, knowing Grandfather's healthy financial situation."

"I understand," Kirsti said softly. "It's the last he's going to hear from Jens. And he's probably hoping that my grandfather *did* leave something to him."

She moved gracefully across the room to a large oil portrait of two young men standing with a gigantic yet exceedingly elegant pair of Belgian draft horses. The horses' massive hooves and gleaming, muscled bodies were an awesome backdrop for the two handsome men in suspendered trousers and white shirts with full sleeves. Each man wore a snappy brimmed hat pulled low over his eyes.

"I've never seen that before!" Cade stared at the painting. "It's incredible!"

"Thomas and Jens when they were young. They shared that team to work their land. Thomas ran across an old photo three years ago and had it painted for Grandfather for Christmas. It was one of the few times I'd ever seen my grandfather weep for joy. It brought back every precious memory of that time, he said." She turned from the painting to look at Cade. "I have a hunch Thomas is hoping the painting was willed back to him. Frankly, I don't know. Grandfather was very closemouthed about his will—always changing and updating it depending on who pleased or displeased him at the moment. In fact, I think he was consulting with his attorney as late as last month. But if it's not mentioned, I plan to give it back to Thomas anyway. There's no one who'd get more pleasure from it."

"Then it's all right if he comes?"

Cade realized he was holding his breath. He hadn't known until just now how much all this meant to him as well. Kirsti and her grandfather had been in many ways *his* family, too, when he was young. Then somewhere along the line, he'd fallen in love with her. She had metamorphosed from little sister to the woman he loved. And shortly after, she'd pushed him out of her life. Though he'd never admitted it to another soul, he'd spent all these years wondering how a relationship so deep and precious could change so quickly—and why.

"Tomorrow at ten. Same attorney your grandfather uses. He'll know how to get there."

There seemed nothing more to say. Cade nodded and turned toward the door. As he walked away from her, Kirsti closed her eyes for a moment to gather her senses. This was ridiculous! Why was she mooning like a lovesick schoolgirl over a man she wouldn't—couldn't—be involved with ever again?

Handsome, charming, and familiar as Cade might be, their beliefs and values were too different. Their morals were light-years apart. Kirsti had learned that during one dreadful week long ago. Until then she'd been sure that Cade's faith was as sincere as her own. But now she knew better. And unlike Cade, she couldn't turn her back on what she believed to be right.

Tears welled in her eyes. She'd loved him. Then she had hated him. Now she had forgiven him. But she had to be careful. Cade Callahan was very easy to love, and she didn't dare chance that again.

He turned at the door and studied her face. With a gentle finger, he lifted a tear from her cheek.

"Whatever it is, Kirsti, we could work it out. What is it I have to do to prove myself to you? I've missed your friendship all these years. Thomas and Jens hated our falling out. Couldn't we try again? For them?"

Every fiber of her body screamed *yes, yes, yes!* but she shook her head. "It's better this way, Cade. I'm sorry."

She stood on her tiptoes and kissed his cheek. She could feel faint stubble on his skin and smell soap and expensive cologne and the indefinable scent that was all Cade. Then, before she weakened, she turned and ran up the stairs to the second floor and stood by the window until she saw Cade's Jeep leave the drive.

# CHAPTER THREE

Are you *sure* you want me to be here with you?" Natty fussed as she and Kirsti made their way into Holt, August, and Winston Law Offices. "The reading of a will is a very private matter. I'm not sure an outsider like me should . . ."

"You're *not* an outsider! You are more like family to me than anyone else I know. I need some support today, Nat, and you're it. Grandfather named me executor of his will since, I suppose, my parents are so rarely home."

Kirsti chewed nervously at her lower lip. "I've become accustomed to the life of a missionary's child, but today is one time I wish Mom and Dad were here. I've been praying all morning for wisdom."

"They have every confidence in you," Natty assured her worried friend. "And I do too. No one is expecting you to be Solomon, you know."

Then Natty's curious nature took over. "Who do you think he left his money to? You?"

"Natalie!"

"Well, you can't blame me for asking. Jens was not exactly a pauper."

"I'm sure he was very generous with the church and all his favorite charities. Even if I don't receive a dime, I wouldn't mind. Just knowing my grandfather was gift enough."

"I would. I think you are unhealthily noble and self-sacrificing. A little self-interest wouldn't hurt you a bit."

Kirsti smiled. That was more like it. She'd brought Natty along because her outrageous statements always kept Kirsti grounded.

"I *am* thinking of myself," Kirsti said mildly. "My grandfather changed his will the way other people change magazine subscriptions. He'd find a new charity or become disgruntled with mismanagement of an old one and call the attorney to re-write his will. Having no expectations frees me from worry. Besides, I have a good job. I can support myself."

Natty gave an unladylike snort that caused Kirsti to burst out laughing.

Much to their surprise, they were not the first ones to arrive at Mr. Holt's office. Thomas and Cade Callahan sat in two straight-backed chairs near a wall of books.

Thomas looked pale and frail, as if he'd aged ten years since Jens's funeral. Cade appeared edgy and out of place. He had eyes only for his grandfather.

Still, he jumped to his feet and came over when the two women entered.

"I'm sorry to be intruding like this" were the first words out of his mouth—"but Grandfather *insisted* on being here and I couldn't let him come alone. I'll wait outside if you wish." A lock of dark hair fell carelessly over one eye, and somehow Cade's apologetic look only made him seem more appealing.

Kirsti shook her head, not daring to speak.

"I'm an outsider too," Natalie pointed out as she looked around the room. "And we seem to be the entire crowd."

Kirsti sensed that Thomas was staring at her. She approached the old man with a gentle smile. "I'm glad you came."

"I couldn't stay away. Your grandfather and I shared a very

personal dream for the lives of our children and grandchildren. I feel as though you are my granddaughter, too, you know." Thomas reached out a gnarled hand and touched Kirsti's cheek.

The floodgates opened. Dropping to her knees, Kirsti wept, her head on Thomas's lap. When the tears subsided, she looked at him with a radiant smile on her face. "I've loved you two naughty old goats my whole life, you know."

"'Naughty old goat' am I now?" An odd expression passed over Thomas's features. "Maybe so."

The cryptic statement sailed right over Kirsti's head as Mr. Holt entered the room. She scrambled to her chair and took the tissue Natty held out to her.

"I'd like to welcome each of you here today," Mr. Holt began as he nervously fingered the legal document in his hands. Beads of perspiration were pooling on his upper lip, and his demeanor, usually one of utter calm, was agitated.

"This is a difficult day for all of us who knew Jens Nord. In many ways he was my personal mentor, as I know he was for all of you." Mr. Holt spoke without making eye contact with anyone but Natty. "And I want you to know that much time, thought, and love went into the writing of his will. As you know, Jens tended to be a bit . . . eccentric . . . where his will was concerned, but never for a moment was he miserly or mean-spirited in his wishes."

Kirsti shifted in her chair. Why was Holt saying all of this? Why didn't he just get on with the reading? Was he trying to prepare her for something? That Grandfather had left nothing to her or her parents? In spite of growing up wealthy, neither she nor her parents were enamored of possessions. They'd get along fine even if Grandfather had given everything away.

Mr. Holt cleared his throat again, took a sip of water from the glass on his desk, and stared down at the will. His hands were shaking.

"I would be happy to read this word for word if you wish,

but since there are so few of you here, if you like I can paraphrase Jens's wishes. . . ."

The first portion of the will held no surprises. There was money set aside to support the mission work Kirsti's father had begun, a generous gift to the church in Snowflake, and, as Kirsti had guessed, the giving of the portrait to his "dearest friend in all the world, Thomas Callahan."

Then, just as Kirsti was beginning to relax, Jens Nord dropped a bombshell—straight down, it seemed, from heaven.

"Your grandfather had some very specific wishes for the remainder of his estate, Kirsti, which involve you." Then Holt surprised them by turning to Cade and adding, "And also you."

The dumbfounded look on Cade's face matched that on Kirsti's. "Me? Why?"

"What? *What?*" Natty blurted, leaning forward in her chair as if she were watching a movie so suspenseful that she was about to fly into a thousand pieces.

"Jens's will states that he would like Kirsti to have his home—"

"The mansion? Cool."

Holt glared at Natty for interrupting before continuing. "And the bulk of the estate, minus some contributions to his favorite charities. In addition, he has set aside a sizable portion of the estate to be donated to the Snowflake City Development Fund to rebuild the snowmobile factory."

Kirsti gasped. Did her grandfather's generosity know no limits? That was exactly what this community needed!

"So he *did* get everything done before he died," Thomas muttered to himself. "Praise the Lord!"

"What's more," Mr. Holt continued, one eye jumping with a nervous tic, "he arranged that estate funds be made available to anyone who needs a loan—with no interest—to cover expenses until they are once again employed."

"Awesome!" Nat murmured. "He'd figured all this out and changed his will since the fire. What a great man."

"There is, however, one slight catch to this arrangement." Holt pulled off his eyeglasses and cleaned them with the hem of his suit jacket.

"Catch?" Kirsti felt a flurry of butterflies in her midsection. "What catch?"

"This document will go into effect only if you, Kirsti, agree to administer the monies given to the Snowflake City Development Fund in the way you see fit. Jens felt that if for some reason he could not do it himself, you would be the perfect one to do so. He said that you had the same sensibilities, values, and faith and would represent him well."

"Oh, Grandpa," Kirsti whispered, tears flooding her eyes. "So much trust! So much responsibility! What made you think I could do all that?"

"Jens's will is a document of unflagging generosity, Kirsti, but it was very important to him that you be involved. He truly felt you were an extension of himself in many ways. And—" Mr. Holt paused to clear his throat—"he knew that if you thought about it long enough, you would agree."

Kirsti remained silent, thoughtful. It was as if Grandfather were in the room, pushing her, encouraging her, egging her on.

"Jens also had one more very specific request," Holt continued. "He asked that you, Cade, work with Kirsti on this project."

Cade's jaw dropped.

"Since you are an experienced and rather renowned architect as well as a native of Snowflake, he thought it would be only appropriate if you and Kirsti worked together to make sure the town would 'get the most for the money.' Your decisions about the plant structure would guide Kirsti in administering the funds. Jens also felt that he could trust no one more than his friend Thomas's grandson to 'do right' by the project."

Cade was slowly shaking his head from side to side as Holt

continued. "He picked the people he trusted most, and I believe he chose well. Now it is up to you two to decide if you will take on this responsibility."

Holt looked squarely at the two of them. "Jens said you wouldn't disappoint him. He said he'd go to his grave confident of that."

"Now *that's* pressure," Cade muttered.

Natalie, however, was feeling anything *but* pressure. She leaped to her feet with a joyous whoop. "Snowflake can have its plant back! Isn't that wonderful? Why, it could be even bigger and better than before. Cade can do anything with designs. He's perfect for this! I heard they were considering building a line of personal watercraft before the fire. Wouldn't that be great? More jobs, more money into the community? Jens couldn't have done anything nicer for Snowflake or its residents."

"But what about us?" Kirsti choked. "Cade and me? Working together for months? I'd have to take a year off at school, and . . ." She looked warily at Cade as if he might gobble her up, but she left her fear unspoken.

"I have a business to run," Cade said calmly. "I can't be tied down here until this plant is rebuilt. I could draw up some plans, I suppose, but overseeing the operation is out of the question. I'm sure Jens had no idea how large or complicated my business has become."

"I'm sure he did." It was Thomas, looking outraged at the young people's response. "And he knew that the responsibility would terrify Kirsti. But he trusted you both, had confidence that you could and *would* do the job. For the town, for him—even for yourselves."

"So you think he did us a favor, Gramps?" Cade looked bewildered by all this bizarre logic the grandfathers had taken for granted.

"Snowflake is in trouble," Thomas said simply. "Jens created a way to put this community back on its feet. I don't know what could be more noble than that. Seems to me you all should be glad he got his gift down on paper before he died. Besides—" he gave Kirsti and Cade a stare—"he chose the two people he trusted most to carry out the benevolence if he wasn't able to do it himself. You should both be very proud—and very humbled."

"I think it's really cool," Natty said. "I've always thought Jens was great, but this is just awesome! He's going to save Snowflake!" Then a slight frown passed over her pert features. "Or, at least, you two will. Won't you?"

The enormity of the situation had finally begun to sink into Kirsti's consciousness. Her home, the city she loved, was dying a slow, painful death. Friends and neighbors were jobless, some almost destitute. She had within her grasp the means to save them all. The plant could be rebuilt. Interest-free loans could prevent people from having to leave town. Snowflake, instead of being on the brink of disaster, could survive.

And he'd left her the house, Kirsti thought gratefully. The only home she'd ever known would remain her own. The marvelous gazebo, where she so often drank her morning coffee and listened to bird songs. And the sunroom, where she and Natty discussed and solved world problems over the wrought-iron table.

And the attic! The wonderfully mysterious haven full of trunks of clothes that had belonged to her grandmother and great-grandmother; clothes she had tried on innumerable times over the years playing dress-up with Natty.

Her entire life was in this town. Her students, her home, her friends, her memories. And now she had the power and the means to save it.

But she would have to work with Cade. . . .

It suddenly occurred to Kirsti that she hadn't even given Cade's perception of this a second thought. She turned in her chair to speak to him and saw the black Irish fury suffusing his features.

"This is the most outrageous thing I have ever heard!" Cade towered over Mr. Holt, who sat meekly behind his desk.

"Why didn't you talk him out of this? There are others in this town perfectly capable and well equipped to manage this sort of thing."

"Jens was not the easiest man to talk out of anything," Mr. Holt reminded Cade. "I'm sure you know that as well as anyone. He was sure that the two of you would manage everything just as he himself might have. I promise you this—Jens wanted to help Snowflake himself, but he knew his own health was precarious. He signed this will the day before he died."

Tears sprang to Kirsti's eyes. She remembered Grandfather and Mr. Holt being closeted away for hours in the study that day. Grandfather had been exhausted and silent that evening— and passed quietly away the next day.

Cade blew out a frustrated gust of air and ruffled the curl that had fallen over his forehead. Then, unexpectedly, he began to laugh. It began as a chuckle deep in his chest and grew until he threw his head back and gave a great guffaw.

His shoulders were still shaking with mirth when Kirsti demanded, "I'd like to know what you find so funny here."

Cade wiped at his eyes, still chuckling. "He outsmarted everyone, that's what. He and my grandfather have been pushing us together since childhood. That's the 'very personal dream' to which my grandfather was referring earlier. You and I together. I've been hearing about it for years. 'Why don't you marry that Kirsti gal, my boy? You'd have fine wee ones.' Don't you see? If my grandfather wanted us together, yours did too. And now we have one more opportunity to figure out for ourselves that we'd be the ideal couple."

"I don't think Grandfather was devious, Cade. He wouldn't—"

"Not intentionally. Never. He was much too honorable a man. But I'm sure he thought it wouldn't hurt anything to give us this opportunity either."

Cade turned to his own grandfather, who was looking a bit shamefaced now. "I've hit on a little dream of yours, haven't I, Gramps? Getting Kirsti and me back together permanently?

And Jens accidently expedited the dream. The perfect breeding program for little Nord/Callahans—Thoroughbreds in the human world. Papered colts and fillies carrying Thomas and Jens genes."

"A fine way to talk about your loving old grandfather, boy," Thomas huffed. "But you *do* make a handsome pair."

Then, before anyone could respond, he stood, with all the dignity and military stiffness he could muster. "And now I'd like you to excuse me. I have a game of checkers planned down at the barbershop in ten minutes."

They all stared at the old man's proud back as he left the attorney's office. With a flick of his cane, he shut the door behind him.

Natalie giggled.

Kirsti did not see the humor, and she did not appreciate being compared to the mares that the Callahans had bred over the years. They were known as "the horse people" around Snowflake. Kirsti was sure she didn't want to become a part of the Callahan "stable."

Before she could verbalize her thoughts, Natty spoke. "Frankly, I don't see the problem. It was a wonderful thing Jens did. You can hardly blame the man for not discussing his requests with you. He was probably too concerned with getting things in order to do it beforehand, and afterward—well, the poor man *did* die!"

Leave it to Natalie to put things into perspective. "I think Jens picked the perfect pair to administer this project. You've known each other forever. When we were kids, I was always a little jealous of your friendship. You were practically able to read each other's minds. You seemed more like brother and sister then. And when we got to high school, I still remember how you wrangled over whom each of you should date. It occurred to me that you should have been dating each other, but neither of you was smart enough to figure *that* out."

Cade and Kirsti exchanged a startled glance.

Natty continued. "You two scrapped to be valedictorian of

our class, and it finally turned out that you *both* got equal honors. You even went to proms together because it was easier and more fun than having to find dates! And finally you dated for real until your big breakup. What's so wrong with people like that working together? You are two peas in a pod!"

Natalie sat back and crossed her arms, appearing satisfied to have had the opportunity to speak her mind. Cade and Kirsti stared at her.

"That was a long time ago," Cade finally managed. "We're different people now."

"Are you?" Natty challenged. "I don't see it."

"There are things you don't know . . . ," Kirsti stammered.

Cade spun to face her. "There are things *I* don't know. About why you quit speaking to me, about why you turned into an ice princess, about why—"

"Not here," Kirsti pleaded, well aware that Nat and Mr. Holt were a spellbound audience. "Not now. We need to talk business."

"All right," Cade said. "But this subject *will* come up again. We do have a history together, and we need to get it sorted out. You can't run away forever, Kirsti. If nothing else, this request to work together will give us the opportunity to put the past to rest."

With that, Cade spun around and left the office, leaving behind three shell-shocked victims of Jens Nord's atomic will.

Natalie, in a very tiny voice, murmured, "I think he just said he'd work on the project."

# Chapter Four

Y ou can't hide in the house forever, you know." Natty
peered through the ornate Victorian screen door. "I
know you're in there, so open up."

"Are you alone?" Kirsti's voice floated down from the second floor.

"Yes, but I won't be for long. Rumor has it that there's a
committee forming to come talk with you. They're convening
at the café right now. You can't hold off much longer. You've
got to give the community an answer. Will you administrate
the money or not? After all, Cade has already started his part
of the agreement. He's held two community meetings for input and has an initial set of plans in the works. And *he* isn't
even Jens's grandchild!"

An agonized groan came from the top of the stairs as Kirsti
relented and came to meet her friend. "Hurry up, get inside.
Although I suppose you'll just make me feel more guilty."

"Too bad they don't make a repellent for worried townspeople. You know, sort of like mosquito spray for bloodsucking humans." Natty rumpled her short dark hair. "I never
dreamed the town would respond to Jens's will with this
much enthusiasm."

"And pressure! People are just wild for me to get involved," Kirsti sighed.

"Desperate is more like it," Natty said bluntly. "And there's nothing else to talk about these days."

"They just don't understand how difficult it would be for me to work with Cade." Kirsti pleaded for her friend to understand.

"Of course not. You and Cade have been friends forever as far as this community is concerned. *I* don't understand it. Even *Cade* doesn't understand. I think he's been really gallant, considering the way you've been hemming and hawing around about this."

Kirsti's heart grew heavy. If Natalie wouldn't defend her, then she was pretty much sunk.

"I've been on my knees praying over this, Nat. I've been seeking God's wisdom for what seems to me like a monumental task. I don't want to explain to you why Cade and I shouldn't work together, but, believe me, it's true."

"Sorry. No can do. Your grandfather gave a beautiful gift, and now you are refusing to deliver it. It doesn't make sense, Kirsti, not to me, to Cade, to *anyone!*"

"I learned of something Cade did that made me lose all faith in him, Nat. I just don't feel like it would be morally right—"

"Isn't it for God to judge, not you?"

Kirsti threw back her head with a frustrated sigh. "Of course. But I don't feel comfortable—"

"*No one* is comfortable right now! This is your chance to ease people's pain. Isn't that more important than whatever personal snit you got into with Cade ten years ago?"

"Don't do this to me, not you, my best friend," Kirsti pleaded. "There are . . . reasons."

She was saved from elaborating by the slam of her screen door, which she'd forgotten to latch after Natty's arrival. Now Cade stood in the graciously decorated entry.

"Don't you knock?" Kirsti chided, not at all happy to see him.

"Don't you greet your newly appointed business partner with open arms?"

He wished she looked happier to see him. The last thing Cade wanted to do was bring more heartache into Kirsti's life. And until he found out how he'd hurt her, there was little he could do. He'd prayed about it, written and destroyed a hundred letters asking her why, and prayed some more. But God's time for answering questions was different from his. So far, all Cade had learned was patience—and he felt he had only a tenuous hold on that.

"Gotta go," Natty announced in a rush. "I can see that you want to share this tender moment alone."

"Stay!" Kirsti ordered.

"Go!" Cade commanded.

Natty went.

"I've never known you to lock yourself inside this house and pretend the world didn't exist, Kirsti." Cade's voice was soft, caressing. He held out his hand to her, led her into the living room, and settled her on a lush couch before dropping down beside her.

"I've never been in such a mess before, that's why." Tears came to her eyes. "When the plant was first built, people were absolutely giddy with excitement. Jobs. Industry. Life for this little town. Everyone began to have hope. Some built new houses. Others bought a long-overdue new car. Merchants expanded their inventory. We passed a mill levy to enlarge the school. All because we thought Snowflake would survive."

"And won't it?"

"Not without the plant. It was our last, best hope. And that's why I feel so terrible now."

Cade didn't speak. He just stared at her with those disconcerting Irish eyes. They were like one-way mirrors. He could see out, but Kirsti couldn't see in. His thoughts were a mystery.

"Don't you see? Now I feel responsible for the lives of dozens of families. Their futures, like a row of dominoes standing on end, are ready to tumble one way or another, depending on whether or not you and I can manage to work together so closely."

"And you think we can't? Give me a little credit, please. I'm able to work with huge corporations without giving them any problems! I think I can manage to put up a plant the size of the storage units some of my building designs need."

He sounded angry, Kirsti thought. Ironic, since *she* was the one who had the right to be angry.

"I didn't mean it as an insult. It's just that you and I are too different. Our values, our morals—"

"Wait a minute. You've said that before, and I don't get it. You've known me your entire life. Where did I go so wrong morally? I may have smoked a cigarette or two and done the things that high school boys think they have to do, but—"

The doorbell rang, and Kirsti flinched. Cade reached out a hand to calm her. And that was how the committee Natty had warned about found them—on the couch, Cade's hand on Kirsti's shoulder, tears in Kirsti's eyes. It made for an intimate and personal scene.

Ben Nordstrom led the pack. He was followed by Mrs. Bentson; Dr. Hale; Tessa Shannon, high school principal; and Ed Owens and Martin Marky, owners of Snowflake's grocery and automotive supply stores, respectively.

Ben looked red and embarrassed as he clung to the billed cap in his hands. He was thinner than the last time she'd seen him, Kirsti thought. And—was it possible—older, too?

Mrs. Bentson looked ready to burst into tears. Her kindly face sagged with unhappiness. Dr. Hale and Mrs. Shannon appeared to be all determination and business, while Owens and Marky looked as if they wished to be anywhere but here.

"We're sorry to barge in on you like this," Ben began, as the obvious winner—or loser—of the responsibility of being spokesperson. "It's just that there are a lot of rumors flying around Snowflake these days, and we thought that it would be better to come to the horse's mouth . . . er . . . to you, than to listen to all the speculation." A grimace passed over his features as though he had a sharp pain in his abdomen.

Mrs. Shannon, a teacher and born leader, had no such qualms. "Is it true that you are going to decline to administer Jens's gift? That's what everyone wants to know. With your knowledge of Jens's wishes and Cade's obvious expertise, the plant can be restored quickly, just as Jens wished. We don't have time to waste. Soon people will be leaving Snowflake like rats off a sinking ship! We've been treading water here for a long time, and this is the first positive bit of news we've had. People want to make plans. Do they move on or hold on? It's up to you now."

*"It's up to you now."* Kirsti glanced at Cade. She'd hoped never to see him again, and now this. What was she going to do?

It was Cade who rescued her.

"I realize that you are all very concerned about your homes and jobs and the provision Mr. Nord left in his will. But you must realize that Kirsti is grieving for her grandfather. I think it's fair to ask that you give her some time before pressuring her into important decisions." He looked large and protective as he stood between Kirsti and the group. "I'll proceed with my project until she feels ready to carry out her responsibilities. We have a little time yet, since the money is already in the bank."

"I told them we shouldn't have come yet," Mrs. Bentson murmured. "Poor girl."

"It's just that we're so desperate . . . ," Owens began.

"And the bank's getting nervous about my loan," Marky stammered.

"I apologize for coming this way," Dr. Hale said, "but you do need to know what's being thought and said around town. Our lives are in your hands now." He looked from Kirsti to

Cade and back again. "And I hope we aren't disappointed by some of our own."

They melted away then, leaving Dr. Hale's parting words lingering in the air. *"I hope we aren't disappointed by some of our own."* Kirsti. And Cade.

"What a lot of gall!" Cade growled as he closed the door behind the visitors and locked it. "How dare they think they can dictate what we do?" Then he began to chuckle. "I've got to admit, though, that this is definitely the weirdest situation in which I've ever found myself. Of course, there was that little incident in Saudi Arabia—"

"How can you laugh?" Kirsti demanded. "Those people were *serious!*"

"I meant what I said. You need time to heal, not to try to save an entire town."

Feeling exhausted both mentally and physically, Kirsti couldn't argue. She didn't even fight when Cade pressed her down against the pillows of the couch and covered her with a fuzzy knit throw. She was asleep even before he reached the front door, never knowing that he'd paused to stare at her and sent up a prayer for her over her sleeping form.

\\//

Finally, when the milk, bread, eggs, butter, and even flour were depleted, Kirsti decided she'd have to make a foray into the community. Besides going to the grocery store, it was time to pick up her mail. Natty had offered, but knowing that necessity was the only thing that would force her out of the house, Kirsti had declined her help.

Her hopes that the furor had died down were dashed before she'd even managed to separate a cart from its companions in the cart stall at the grocery store. Mrs. Shannon came bearing down on her like a jumbo jet to a landing strip. She pulled her full cart up just short of a collision.

"Glad to see you out and about. You must be feeling better." The implication of her words were clear. *Now you can get started.*

"Not better, just hungry." Kirsti tried to maneuver away but found her way blocked by half a dozen folks listening intently to the conversation. When they realized they'd been caught, each nodded pleasantly, greeted both women, and scattered.

Kirsti escaped in the confusion and, without making eye contact with another soul, rushed through the store picking up supplies.

When she finally got to her car, she closed her eyes, leaned back in her seat, and prayed aloud. "I don't get it, God. What am I supposed to do?" I know my grandfather must have wanted this, but if he'd lived, he would have understood my reluctance. I don't care about money for myself or even the house, but I *do* care about this town. But *Cade,* God? It wouldn't be right, would it?" A tear dripped from beneath Kirsti's closed lids. "You know my heart, Father, and you know I've always loved him. He was like a brother to me. My best friend. Then, when I thought we were growing to care for each other in an even more special way, he let me down. With your help I've forgiven him, but I'm afraid to let myself get too close to him again."

A tap on the window snapped Kirsti back to the present moment. Natty was peering in the window of the sport utility vehicle, her nose and lips pressed to the glass so that her features were comically distorted. She stepped back when Kirsti rolled down the window.

"What are you doing in there? Sleeping? Don't you have people talking enough already?"

"Hop in," Kirsti ordered. "You can run into the post office and pick up my mail for me."

"Coward," Natty muttered as she obeyed. "Then people will ask *me* what you plan to do."

"How did this get so out of hand?" Kirsti moaned. "What *am* I going to do?"

"Well, you'd better do *something,* and do it fast. The pressure is mounting."

"But what *can* I do?"

"Talk to Cade, for one thing. In fact, you can do that right now. He's just coming out of the post office."

Before Kirsti could stop her, Natty rolled down her window and yelled, "Hey, Cade! Come here!"

He looked surprised, standing there in well-washed denims and a deep navy sweatshirt that somehow managed to bring out that devastating blue-violet color in his eyes.

Natty opened the door of the Explorer and slid out as Kirsti came to a stop. "Get in." She gave Cade a little shove toward the vehicle.

"What is this? A kidnapping? Shouldn't you put a bag over my head so I can't see where you're taking me?"

"Maybe we should put one in your *mouth,*" Natty retorted cheerfully, "but then you and Kirsti couldn't talk about this situation and how you're going to resolve it."

"I'm not *in* a 'situation.' Jens did the best he could. We both know how much he would have loved to see Snowflake rebuilt with his financial gift. And I'm sure he didn't understand Kirsti's attitude toward me any better than I do myself," Cade said calmly. "Besides, my grandfather will be waiting for me."

"Hah! He's playing checkers right now, and you know it. Get inside."

With a dramatic show of false submission, Cade slid into the vehicle.

Natty slammed the door and ordered Kirsti, "Now, floor it and go someplace where no one can find you. Then *talk.*"

Almost automatically, Kirsti did as she was told. She knew they couldn't stay there, in the middle of Snowflake, like a centerpiece on a table.

Without even thinking about what she was doing, she drove to a grove of trees outside of town. It was a place where she and Cade had played as children, picnicked as teenagers, and had their last hurtful conversation before they parted ways.

"Some things never change, do they?" Cade said quietly. "The trees are a little bigger, but otherwise we could have stepped back ten years in time."

Kirsti's head snapped up as if she'd just realized where she'd taken them. "We'll go somewhere else."

"No. I like it here. *Most* of my memories are good ones." Cade slid out of the vehicle. Before Kirsti could move, he walked to the back door and opened it.

"Just as I thought. Always prepared." He explored the interior of a rubberized container and pulled out a blanket. "Snow gear, candles, matches, coffee can, toilet paper . . ." He referred to what all sensible people carried in their cars during the winter in North Dakota in case they were trapped by a storm while traveling.

"I meant to take it out for the summer. I just never got around to it."

"I'm glad you didn't." Cade took the blanket to the base of a large cottonwood and spread it on the ground. Then he came back to Kirsti, took her hand, and led her to the tree. He dropped onto the blanket, situated himself against the tree, and beckoned her to follow.

How many dozens of times had they done this before? Kirsti wondered. How many times had it felt so right? Her body automatically folded down beside his. At first she didn't even realize that tears were streaming down her cheeks.

He let her cry, offering up a pristine white handkerchief from his back pocket, and waited patiently until the well of her tears was empty. Then he tucked her beneath his arm and waited for her to speak.

"You know me too well," she muttered in complaint. "You know just what to do."

"Years of experience," he responded with a chuckle. "I have you to thank for everything I know about women. Well, almost everything."

She punched him in the ribs and felt satisfaction at the little grunt of surprise he gave. They sat together for a long while, neither speaking, neither needing to.

Kirsti realized that she must have fallen asleep when the squawking of a grackle in a tree made her jump. Cade's body was warm and comforting next to hers.

"Feeling better?" His mouth was very near her ear.

"Yes. No. I don't know."

"That's what I like, a decisive female."

She straightened so that she could look him in the eye. "Oh, Cade, what are we going to do? There's all of Snowflake to consider."

Cade grinned widely, flashing his perfectly white, perfectly even teeth. "What a kick it is too. Crazy. The more I think about it, the more I like it—you and me, together again. Besides, I've been thinking about it. I've got ways to cut weeks off our building time—"

Kirsti stared at him. "You think this is *funny?*"

"What else *can* I think?"

He looked long and hard into her eyes. "I know that I'm in no danger of ending up stealing your heart. Your words to me ten years ago were perfectly clear on that account."

He began to repeat the phrases that Kirsti had thought he'd long forgotten. " 'We don't have the same values, Cade. Apparently you don't share my faith. Whether you will admit it or not, you have done things I cannot abide. There is no future for us. Our friendship was a childish thing. We're adults now. Our childishness must remain in the past.' "

As he spoke, he stared at her with eyes that looked like chips of violet ice. "I never really understood where that little speech came from, or why, but I certainly didn't forget it."

He never understood? Couldn't he even remember what he'd done? Shaking herself mentally, Kirsti refused to go down that path. They had to address the problems of the here and now.

"We have the opportunity to save an entire community,"

Cade continued. "I must have fended off a dozen questions about the 'upcoming partnership' in the post office alone. People are thinking of themselves, Kirsti. Understandably so. Let's just do the best thing for both Jens and the community. Give them their dream."

"I can't imagine why people think we'd even want to collaborate now," Kirsti mused, more to herself than to Cade. "We haven't seen each other for years. Our paths have been so separate. . . ." She gave a disparaging laugh. "What do I know about anything? After college I came home to Snowflake while you traveled all over the world. I teach tiny children how to count and tie their shoelaces. You design buildings for millions to see!"

"So you are just a sweet little dormouse and I am a big bad cat?" He stroked her cheek, and somehow it did feel predatory and threatening.

She looked at him steadily. He had a dark, sometimes unpredictable Irish humor. It didn't really surprise her that Cade was not taking this problem as seriously as she. He rarely took things seriously. That had been part of the problem.

"I'm just saying that you are savvy, street-smart, credible. . . . And what do I know about this sort of thing?"

"I sound like the perfect choice—and so do you. Jens knew it; Snowflake knows it. He trusted you to fulfill his dreams no matter what you thought of me."

"Cade, don't. There are people all over town wishing that we'd do this, but I don't feel right—"

"Sacrificing ourselves for the good of the whole? That's scriptural, Kirsti. It's been done on a much bigger scale than this," he said.

Kirsti ignored him, not wanting to hear the truth of his words. She was beginning to feel desperate, feeling her resolve slipping. "How can we make them understand that the situation is impossible?"

"Show them, I suppose." Cade leaned against the tree and crossed his legs at the ankle. He carelessly plucked a blade of long grass, positioned it between the balls of his thumbs, and blew a tuneless, reedy whistle.

Kirsti scrambled to her knees and clapped her hands together. Her pale blond hair circled her face like a cloud. She finally felt a ray of hope. "That's *it!* You are absolutely right. We'll *show* them it can't work!"

# CHAPTER FIVE

Cade lifted one lazy eyebrow and looked at Kirsti as if she'd gone mad. "What are you talking about?"

"Showing Snowflake that we're very different people now than we were ten years ago. If we try to spend time together—and fail both publicly and miserably, it will become obvious that we simply can't agree on anything! The people of this town are desperate, but they are also reasonable and compassionate. They'll realize how unfair it is to you to take time away from your work and for me to attempt to make huge financial decisions that could affect the city forever."

"I'm *not* going to have a fight with you in the middle of the town square just to prove we can't get along," Cade said. "Things are bizarre enough already."

"That's not what I meant. You'll be you, and I'll be me, and everyone will see that it won't work."

"Well, I *am* pretty good at being me," Cade acquiesced. "I've done it quite a long time now."

He was baiting her, of course, but Kirsti chose to ignore him.

"We'll be seen together around town. At least that way people will know we're making the attempt to get along. We just have to point out our weaknesses, not our strengths, our differences and not our similarities—"

"You're a woman, and I'm a man. There's a start. Of course, I don't think that's going to further your plan very much. What else did you have in mind?"

Nothing, really, but Kirsti didn't say that to Cade. She was desperate. This had to work. The people of Snowflake were sensible. They'd come to realize that no one could force a couple to work together on a project of this magnitude. If Cade and Kirsti obviously couldn't get along, surely they'd have to find someone else to fill one pair of shoes or the other. *It could work,* Kirsti thought, feeling optimism for the first time in what seemed like ages.

And she wouldn't have to feel guilty, either. Jens hadn't known what Cade had become or he never would have requested his expertise.

*But would Cade cooperate?*

⋇

"How are we doing so far? When you ordered chicken, did you notice that I told our waitress I hated chicken? Of course, that left me with pork chops, which are not a favorite either. . . ."

Cade had been impossible all morning, but Kirsti was determined not to let him wear her down. People would at least see that they were trying to make a partnership of this but failing miserably. And that would have to be enough.

"If you don't mind, I wish you'd order bread pudding for dessert. At least that way I can have the cheesecake. I really do despise bread pudding—soggy toast with raisins. Horrible."

"This might begin to work very well, Cade," Kirsti said through clenched teeth, glaring at him with steely blue eyes, "if I decide to throttle you here and now. Please start behaving yourself." People's heads *were* beginning to turn and eyebrows to raise.

"OK." With a twinkle in his eye that spoke of pure mischief, he reached across the table, took Kirsti's hand, and stared lovingly into her eyes. "How's this?"

He flinched when she kicked him under the table. Though she hadn't meant for it to happen, it was seen by one and all. After a painful silence, the other patrons of the restaurant began buzzing conversations in low tones.

Cade rubbed his shin and frowned. "Very effective. Why didn't I think of it?" Then the sour look melted into a heart-stopping grin. "I don't suppose next time it could be my turn?"

She laughed in spite of herself. She'd forgotten how much she'd missed Cade—their banter, their endless talks, their comfortable silences. He was a big part of her life—her *past* life. She hoped it wasn't too obvious that she had to convince herself as well as the good people of Snowflake that this alliance couldn't work.

"Well, well, well, look who's here!" The Irish brogue was unmistakable. Thomas Callahan, dressed in a green knit sweater and brandishing his cane, looked like he'd just stepped off the leprechaun boat from the Emerald Isle.

So overjoyed was he at the sight of them together that Kirsti was afraid he might break into an Irish jig or try to click his heels and do himself some bodily harm. And that was something she felt like doing to him herself, she thought with some amusement.

"Join us?" Cade moved so that his grandfather could sit down.

After he'd ordered tea and a plate of sticky buns and made enough noise to make sure everyone in the café had seen Cade and Kirsti together, Thomas studied the two faces he loved so much. "I knew ye'd be gettin' along better than you thought. You're a mighty fine lookin' pair, you know."

"Don't get your hopes up, Gramps. This isn't working out," Cade told him.

Thomas snorted like an old stallion. "Blarney! That's what

you're talkin' now, laddie. Me old friend Jens had a fine idea. You two do belong together—on Jens's project and for the rest of your lives. It's apparent to all but you. Coming upon you as I did when I entered the café, you were pretty as a picture, staring lovingly into each other's eyes. It was enough to make an old man die happy."

*Seeing me kick your grandson in the shin?*

Kirsti watched Thomas tuck away the tea and buns and didn't know if she should laugh or cry. Thomas rarely fell so deeply into his Irish brogue. The old imp was too pleased with himself by far. She felt a weighty load of responsibility and concern descending upon her slim shoulders as she listened to Cade and Thomas swap tall tales.

Then, as she sat there, tuned out to the world around her and attuned only to the turmoil within, Kirsti began to realize that the enormity of the problem was beyond even her.

She felt rather than saw Andy Macaboy come to their table. His breathing was rough and agitated, and he smelled, as usual, of diesel fuel and gasoline.

"Kirsti? I need to talk to you."

"Not now, Andy. Later?" The last thing she wanted was to have Cade see an exchange between her and Andy.

Andy was the owner/operator of Macaboy's Garage. He ran a tidy and efficient business, could repair anything with wheels, and was, by his own admission, head over heels in love with Kirsti. That she didn't return the emotion had never seemed to matter to Andy.

He glowered at Cade with unrelenting fury in his pale green eyes and put a hand on Kirsti's shoulder as if to protect her. She felt a hysterical laugh bubbling up inside her. Protect her from what? A geriatric Irishman, a plate of sticky buns, and a man who had as much business being here in Snowflake with her as a polar bear in South America?

"A friend of yours?" Cade asked of Kirsti when he finally noticed Andy's presence and his scowl. "A *good* friend?"

"What right have you to come back here and tamper with

56

Kirsti's life now?" Andy asked belligerently. "She was doing just fine without you."

"Andy!" Kirsti hissed, taken aback by the vehemence in his words. They'd dated once or twice and then fallen into a friendly companionship that Kirsti had never taken seriously. But Andy had. He looked like a knight in oil-stained jeans ready and willing to fight the dragon for his ladylove.

"I'm sure she was. I was too. This was not exactly what I had planned for my vacation, you know. Death, business collaborations, saving a town. Until I came back to Snowflake, I was thinking something more along the lines of the Caribbean. You know, surf, sand, and sun?"

Andy blinked, not knowing how to respond. Kirsti was sure Cade's sarcasm was above him, and she would guarantee that he didn't have a clue about Cade's reference to the Caribbean.

She was right. Instead of responding to Cade, Andy turned to her. "Don't do it, Kirsti. I know you don't want to work with him. It's all over town. Send this guy back to where he came from. You're better than that. It doesn't matter if I have to close my garage because of lack of business. I'd rather do that than have you get mixed up with him if you don't want to." His unspoken meaning came through loud and clear: *Because I want you for myself.*

Kirsti, however had caught on three other words. " 'Close your garage'?"

"The banker isn't sure yet, of course—it all depends on the plant." Andy gave her the most tender of looks. "What's most important is your happiness. Don't let people pressure you into something you don't want to do."

Overcome with emotion and having spoken more than Kirsti had ever before heard him speak, Andy scowled at Cade one last time, spun on his heel, and stalked out of the café.

"Your boyfriend?" Cade asked mildly.

"A friend, that's all."

"Not from his point of view. That was love making his hands shake and his knees knock."

"You don't know what you're talking about!" Kirsti's eyes narrowed. "You don't know anything about love."

"I did once. Or thought I did. But I was mistaken, I guess, because the girl I loved turned on me."

Thomas's head swiveled back and forth on his scrawny little neck, and his eyes bulged as he listened to the pair. "Now, now . . ." His age-spotted hand waved over the dishes on the table.

"Oh! You are the most impossible man I have ever known!" Kirsti pushed away from the table to flee.

"I doubt you've known many," Cade retorted sardonically. "Not in this rabbit hole of a town."

"Now, now . . . ," Thomas quavered.

"You disgust me!" Kirsti turned and stormed out. It wasn't until she was across the street in the town square, sitting on a park bench and doing slow breathing exercises, that she began to calm down. Then a smile spread across her features. She and Cade had had a fight in the Snowflake Café, right in front of everyone. If that didn't tell the town they were mismatched, nothing would!

\\//

"I heard some very interesting gossip today," Natalie said with annoying delight. "Juicy."

"I don't gossip." They were standing in Kirsti's kitchen deciding what to have for supper. Natty usually ate with Kirsti two or three times a week. Tonight she'd brought chocolate-fudge almond ice cream for dessert.

"I heard that Cade and Andy had a fight over you in the café."

" 'Over' me?"

"Yeah. That Andy came in and tried to tell Cade that you were his woman and Cade put him in his place. Everyone thinks it's really cool how he stood up to Andy for you and that he must be really in love with you. Everybody's guessing that by the time the plant is running, you and Cade will be a romantic item."

"But what . . . how . . ." Kirsti sank into the nearest kitchen chair with a cry. "That wasn't how it was at all! Cade was a jerk to Andy. Andy was trying to save me from *Cade.*"

"That's not the way I heard it," Natty said complacently. "Now everybody is more sure than ever that you two will not only honor Jens's will but probably get married, too! The excitement quotient has risen fifty points around town. Rumor is Ben Nordstrom held off putting his house up for sale once he heard about the fight."

"It wasn't a fight! Well, it was, but not about what everyone thinks!" Kirsti felt as though she might burst with frustration. Though she'd lived in a small town all her life, she'd never completely embraced the accepted notion that everyone's private business was semipublic property.

"Don't people have enough to do around here?" she stormed. "Why do they have time to sit around gossiping and speculating about my love life?"

"Because they don't have jobs." Natty said bluntly. "Because they feel that their own lives hang in the balance. Because they all want for both personal and public reasons for you and Cade to get along. And because this town loves you both, they want you to love one another, get married, have kids, and save the town, that's why!" Natty grinned with satisfaction. "I didn't realize until now what a romantic little place Snowflake is."

"I'm living a real-life soap opera," Kirsti grumbled. "And I'm ready for a commercial break. I can't live with being responsible for letting my hometown wither and die. But Cade? You just don't know what he did, Nat. And what he did to me was nothing compared to what he did to someone else. What am I going to do?"

"I'd sure like to know what this big dark secret is," Natty mused. "Must be a doozy to keep you so upset for so long. Funny that Cade doesn't even seem to remember it."

"Oh, he remembers, all right. But he's not going to admit—"

The doorbell chimed, and Kirsti looked askance. There wasn't a single person she could think of that she wanted to see right now—especially Cade or his gleeful grandfather.

"Kirsti?" a tentative voice called.

"Tiffany? Is that you?" Tiffany Marks was a former high school classmate. She'd spent a lot of time with Kirsti and Natty, sharing slumber parties, cheerleading practice, and girlish secrets. Tiffany had grown into a quiet, serious woman who'd married her high school sweetheart. They were raising three children on her husband's salary from the plant.

"It's me." She entered the kitchen, and Kirsti had to suppress a gasp of surprise.

"Tiff? What's wrong? You look horrible."

Natty hurried to pull out a chair so the woman could sit down.

"I've just had some bad news," Tiffany murmured. "I know I shouldn't have come, but I didn't know what else to do."

"It's not Roger, is it?" Natty referred to Tiffany's husband. "Has he been hurt? Or one of the kids?"

Tiffany looked startled at the question. "Hurt? Oh, no. Nothing like that." Then realization crossed her features. "No one is ill. I'm sorry if I frightened you. I've just been so focused on this problem that I've forgotten about everything else."

Kirsti set a glass of water in front of her friend and pulled out the chair across from her. "Want to talk about it?"

"Yes. No. I don't know. It's *you* that won't want to talk, I'm sure."

"Uh-oh," Natty muttered.

Kirsti felt a knot in her stomach. "If it's about Cade and me . . ."

Tiffany held up her hand. "Let me say something first. If I

don't, I'll lose my courage, and it took me all afternoon to build up enough of it to come here."

She took a deep breath and began. "Roger and I were very excited when he got a management position at the plant. Too excited, I guess. We believed all the kind words about his 'leadership potential' and his 'promising future.'

"Anyway—" Tiffany took a sip of water before continuing—"we did something stupid on the assumption that he was on the fast track at the plant."

Natty and Kirsti exchanged a worried glance.

"As you know, we sold the house we were living in, the one my parents gave us when they moved to Arizona. With that money and what we had in savings and, of course, what the bank loaned us, we built the new house."

"It's spectacular," Natty interjected.

"And now we're going to lose it." A sob caught in Tiffany's voice.

"What do you mean, 'lose it'?" A cold feeling inched its way into Kirsti's belly along with that nervous knot.

"They have to foreclose. We haven't been able to keep up the payments." Tears began to slip down Tiffany's pale cheeks. "It's partly my fault. I made the decision to stay home with the children. If I'd been working, then maybe . . ."

"This can't be happening!" Kirsti jumped to her feet and began to pace the length of the kitchen. "It's a bad dream, and I'm going to wake up soon. I *have* to!"

"Roger told me not to come," Tiffany continued, "but we've been friends a long time, and I needed to tell you what was happening to us—to all of us."

Tears welled in her eyes. "I don't want you to do something you aren't comfortable doing, Kirsti, but I don't want to lose my home, either! The longer you delay accepting the terms of your grandfather's will, the more danger we're in of being foreclosed upon! We need the plant *now*. You and Cade might have had a falling out—I remember back in the spring of senior year when you quit spending time with him. But you

are both Christians, and I know you can work it out. You are
the dearest, most forgiving woman I know." She stuffed the
knuckles of her fist into her mouth to push back a sob. "I've
done this very badly, and I'm sorry. Do what you have to do,
Kirsti, to be happy." And Tiffany fled, leaving Kirsti and
Natty frozen to the spot.

Natty was the first to thaw. She led Kirsti into the sunroom
and settled her into a chair as if she were a small child. "Can I
make some tea? Coffee? Can I do anything?"

Kirsti shook her head despairingly. "There's nothing anyone can do. Not even me. I can't, won't, explain why I feel the
way I do because there is someone else involved who doesn't
deserve to be part of public gossip. I wouldn't wish this on
anyone else! I'm beginning to have real sympathy for those
poor people who find themselves in the tabloids. Gossip is a
hideous sin, Nat. It does so much harm and so little good."

Natalie flushed. "I know. It's the weakness I'm always
fighting. I've got all the gossip verses memorized and I still slip
up. 'Do not spread slanderous gossip among your people. Do
not try to get ahead at the cost of your neighbor's life,' Leviti-
cus 19:16."

"What about 'A troublemaker plants seeds of strife; gossip
separates the best of friends'? That's what's happening here."

" 'Fire goes out for lack of fuel, and quarrels disappear
when gossip stops,' " Natty quoted, looking as though she
might cry. "I know, I know. I'm as guilty—no, guiltier—than
the next person. But I do love both you and Cade. And I can't
help wondering what makes you so wary of him. I think you
are more vulnerable to Cade than you are willing to let on.
Under what circumstances *would* you reconcile with him?
What would have to change?"

Kirsti laughed humorlessly. "Cade. His values. His faith, or
rather, his lack of it. You know, little things."

"You can be very sarcastic when you choose," Natty observed. "Ouch."

"Exactly. Ouch. Everywhere I turn I feel more pain."

"You still love him, don't you? In spite of whatever it was that made you leave him." Natty's voice was soft.

"Oh, I suppose I do—at least a little," Kirsti admitted reluctantly. "Although I've tried to fight it. But I also know we're totally and utterly mismatched. We'd probably botch up everything for Snowflake."

"You do have a problem," Natty said with supreme understatement.

"And what problem is that?" Cade's voice made them both jump. Neither had heard him enter. "I let myself in since no one answered my knock and I could hear you in here. Is something wrong?"

Both women looked at him in disbelief. Everything was wrong! Couldn't he see that?

*Of course not,* Kirsti realized. Cade still thought this was a slightly amusing, fairly annoying predicament Jens had brought down upon them.

"Tiffany Marks was just here. They're losing their new home and will have no place to live."

A frown passed over Cade's handsome features. "I'm sorry Jens asked this of us, but I know his intentions were the best. We *could* make a great team, Kirsti, if you'd let go of whatever is holding you back."

Kirsti was surprised by Cade's response. He was taking this more seriously than she had thought.

"You look as though you're about to have a nervous breakdown," he muttered unhappily. She'd alarmed him the moment he'd entered. This pressure was too much for her. "I'll try to take care of everything alone if that will help you."

"You'd do that?" she whispered. Then she straightened. It was as though a revelation had taken place at that moment in her heart. "No, I can't let you. We can settle what's between us later. I *will* work with you, Cade, for Grandfather." She drew a determined breath, hoping she wouldn't regret her decision. "And for Snowflake."

# CHAPTER SIX

Kirsti's newfound determination had flagged some-
what by the next afternoon. She'd spent the morning
at the bank and the lawyer's office, poring over the
papers that outlined Jens's funding for the new plant. Her
head was spinning, and she'd forgotten to eat lunch, so she
was feeling both light-headed and overwhelmed by the time
she had even the remotest idea about the extent of the project
she and Cade were undertaking.

Tucking a sheaf of papers under her arm, she made her way
to her Explorer. There was no way she was going to sort this
out alone.

Cade's rental car was in the driveway of the Callahan
home. Kirsti pulled in behind it, determined not to let him get
away until she'd made sense of a few things.

But it was Thomas who met her at the door. He was wearing old baggy pants, worn slippers, and a flannel shirt so well
washed and ancient that tiny holes were popping out in the
fabric. When he saw who it was, his face split into a wide grin.

"Look who's here! It's been too long, honey." He turned
toward the stairs. "Cade, you have company!"

Then he glanced in the mirror and looked askance at his attire. "I didn't expect guests."

"My grandfather did the same thing. He wore his favorite, most worn-out clothing every chance he got. It was only my nagging that kept him from looking like a homeless person most of the time."

Thomas nodded sagely. "Once you lose your natural beauty, I guess you just don't care anymore."

Kirsti burst out laughing and gave the old man a hug. "You're still a beauty, Thomas. You are beautiful inside."

"A lovely liver and a handsome heart?" Cade sounded amused as he stood on the stairs. "I'm not sure I want to know any more about this conversation."

Thomas winked broadly at Kirsti and vanished into the study, leaving her alone with his grandson.

"This is a surprise," Cade said mildly, though his heart was pounding unusually hard in his chest. How long had it been since Kirsti had sought *him* out?

"I'm trying to get up to speed on the project. You'll have to help me. I assume you have an idea of the numbers—how much of what needs to be ordered, how much it will cost, etc."

Kirsti felt odd standing in the foyer of this grand old house with its wood-paneled walls and ancient ancestors hanging in gilded frames. The parquet floor was perfect as ever, as though it were hardly ever stepped upon. Kirsti knew that Thomas had a woman come to clean every week and that he was most particular about this floor.

Memories came rushing back. The photos they had taken on prom night right on the stairs on which Cade was now standing. The hide-and-seek games they had played as children, scrambling behind sideboards and that old suit of armor . . .

"Kirsti? Kirsti? Have you heard a thing I've said?"

She snapped to attention. "Sorry. Guess I'm a little woozy. I missed lunch."

"And I haven't eaten mine yet. You're in luck."

Cade led her to the vast kitchen that had fascinated her as a child. Highly polished pots and pans hung from big round racks dangling from the ceiling. A deeply scarred chopping block sat in the middle of the room. In the bay window were a table and chairs, the same ones at which she'd eaten as a child.

"This is a trip down memory lane," she finally murmured.

Cade nodded, understanding. It had felt that way for him when he'd come home this time as well. Maybe they were finally growing up and beginning to appreciate the special world they had enjoyed as children.

He opened the refrigerator and began piling sandwich fixings onto the chopping block. Ham, sliced turkey, tomatoes, cheese, mayonnaise, pickles, lettuce, and horseradish, with thick slices of bread made from a recipe Thomas had brought with him from Ireland.

Kirsti laughed out loud. "You still cook the same meal you always did!"

"When you've achieved perfection, why tinker with it?" Cade began to slather mayo and horseradish on the bread and stack everything else on top. When he'd made a sandwich twice the size of Kirsti's mouth, he handed it to her. "Teapot's on—as always. Want some?"

She never turned down tea in this house. It was always made to perfection through a ritual that involved a certain little black teapot, boiling water poured through it to make the pot warm, and tea leaves in an infuser ball. Cade knew the steps as well as Thomas himself.

It was more wonderful than she'd expected to see Cade working around this big old kitchen as he used to when they were in high school. He'd always been capable at everything he'd tried. A wave of longing passed over her. *Oh, Cade, I loved you. Why did you do it?*

"Don't look so grim," he chided, seeing the expression on her face. "I haven't poisoned anyone in, oh, six months."

*What is wrong with her, anyway?* he wondered for the hundredth time. She looked so *sad* every time she looked at him. He had to get to the bottom of this one way or another, but obviously now was not the time. Business first.

"What did you learn from the lawyer and the bank?"

"That my grandfather was a genius with numbers and that I'm an idiot. When he left the funds, he had guesstimated how much would have to be allocated for building materials, payroll, equipment, etc. He even suggested a few design changes that he thought would be more economical and practical. And I didn't even know he paid attention to that plant!"

"Those grandfathers of ours paid attention to *everything*. Have you forgotten? They could smell candy on our breath within an hour of supper at sixty paces.

"I'm glad you've got Jens's numbers. The blueprints are in the refining stage, and I want to start ordering materials. If you're finished with your sandwich, just grab your tea and come upstairs. I've been working in the study."

As they passed Thomas, he gave them a cheery wave before going back to his newspaper. When they were out of sight, Cade whispered, "My grandfather is quite a talented guy. Did you notice? He was reading that paper upside down."

Kirsti had to put her hand over her mouth to keep from laughing. *Inquisitive old darling,* she thought. His ears would probably be stretched all the way to the staircase trying to hear their every word.

\\\\\

The study was walnut paneled and held every sort of electronic video gadget and screen imaginable—quite a surprise for the home of an eighty-year-old man. But of course it was Cade who saw to it that Thomas had everything he might enjoy. The study also housed an impressive and eclectic array of books, everything from pricey art books to paperback mysteries. The chairs in this room looked well worn and comfy. The artwork here had none of the decorator look of the main floor. Instead, one wall was covered with framed photographs. Kirsti saw herself there as a child with Cade. Jens and Thomas were a theme echoed again and again. Even a photo of Kirsti's parents graced the wall.

"This is the time we went looking for the pot of gold at the end of the rainbow and got ourselves stuck in that huge puddle." Kirsti laughed out loud. "Look at that mud! I remember Grandpa hosing us down with ice-cold well water before he'd let us near the house. Why weren't you wearing any shoes?"

"Because that mud sucked them right off. I had rubber boots on, if you remember, and when I tried to lift my feet, I couldn't do it. I thought I was going to be trapped in that muck until the dry season." Cade pointed at another photo. "Remember this?"

"How could I forget? Tammy and Tommy." Kirsti referred to two old fat ponies glaring stubbornly out of the picture. "Why the grandfathers gave us those two old reprobates of animals, I'll never know. Some days we couldn't even get them to leave the yard, remember? Once, when I was giving Tammy a particularly motivational kick in the side, she turned around and bit me!"

"I don't think the grandfathers *wanted* us going anywhere. Those rotten little ponies kept us entertained, and there was little danger of our getting hurt because they usually refused to move.

"It couldn't have been a completely negative experience, though, since I still have a horse today." Cade picked up a loose photo of a magnificent Thoroughbred. "I don't have time to ride much anymore, but we get out for a run occasionally."

"I feel as though my past just flashed before my eyes," Kirsti murmured. "It's all here on this wall."

"Your past is my past," Cade said, his voice carefully flat. "And, according to you, what's past is past."

Kirsti felt a little lurch in her stomach. If that was what she wanted him to believe, then why did it hurt to hear him say it?

He pulled a second chair to the huge desk at which he'd been working. Without hesitation, he lifted a thick list of materials to be ordered. "Let's see how close Jens got to my estimates."

For the next two hours, they were both lost in a world of figures, but when they were done, it appeared that Jens *had* allocated the right amount of money for nearly every eventuality.

Cade leaned back and stretched. "He was a genius, Kirsti. I went to school for a lot of years to figure out what he did in his head from just common sense and experience."

"I didn't even know he was interested in such things," Kirsti admitted sadly. "He talked about building a lot, but it was always based on the verse 'Don't you realize that all of you together are the temple of God and that the Spirit of God lives in you?' But, then again, Jens always surprised me. Why should he stop now?"

As Cade leaned forward again to pore over the papers, his arm brushed Kirsti's, and a jolt of awareness shot through both of them. Here they were, side by side, working in complete harmony, just as if ten years had disappeared without a trace.

And the feelings were back.

Kirsti wanted to close her eyes and lean into Cade's strong arms and rest there until her head stopped spinning and her heart stopped hurting.

Cade longed to gather her up and carry her to the big old rocker across the room and press her head to his shoulder and comfort her and chase away whatever it was that haunted her.

*You are so beautiful, Kirsti,* he thought to himself, *and so vulnerable and so kind. What have I done to you? And why won't you discuss it?*

But Thomas's cane on the stair held them both in place until he popped his head through the door and announced that it was time for more tea and a hearty bowl of his famous Irish stew.

Sadly, for both of them, the tender moment passed.

"So how's it going with you and Cade?" Natalie asked. "I hear the plant is coming along nicely now that you two finally got your acts together. He's a pretty cool guy, don't you think?"

"I think as little as possible," Kirsti said. "It works best that way."

"I just don't get it," Natalie fumed. "Cade is a good guy. Why, yesterday, I saw him playing kickball with a bunch of kids he'd had to chase from the building site. Instead of making them mad at him for ruining their dangerous fun, he had them all right in his pocket. When I left, they were making plans for a rematch!"

"Cade has always been very athletic," Kirsti responded mildly.

Natty rolled her eyes. "And he must have visited a dozen people at the rest home—old friends of your grandfathers. And he brought every one of them something—flowers, candy, a book. The nurses were very impressed."

"I'm sure they were."

"*You* are the only one who *doesn't* seem impressed. In fact, the more Cade does, the *less* impressed you seem. I don't get it, Kirsti. This is not like you."

Tears flooded Kirsti's eyes. "I know. And I'm so disappointed with myself. Last night, as I was doing my evening devotions, I read Proverbs 3:5: 'Trust in the Lord with all your heart; do not depend on your own understanding.' It was speaking to *me*, Nat. I'm finding myself trying to depend on my own understanding of something I should have turned over to God long ago."

Natalie lost her flippant attitude immediately and grabbed Kirsti's hands in her own. "We've got to pray about this, kiddo."

Kirsti nodded, and they both bowed their heads.

"Father," Natalie began, "your child Kirsti is really mixed

up right now. She's having a hard time dealing with something that happened years ago. Release her from this, please. It is separating her from you and from people who are important to her. You know the problem, and you know the solution, Lord, so we leave it in your capable hands. Amen." Natty squeezed Kirsti's hands before releasing them.

Kirsti wiped away a tear. "What would I do without you, Nat? You really are a gift to me."

For once, Natalie was serious. "You've been given many gifts, Kirsti. Start being grateful for them, and begin enjoying them."

***

Natalie's words haunted Kirsti for the rest of the day. It was becoming very clear to her that she'd been afraid to work with Cade because she didn't trust herself not to lose her heart to him again. But she needed to trust the Lord to work that out, especially since she had been given the opportunity to do so much good for so many people. She remembered the passage she'd read a few days earlier from the Psalms: "I will guide you along the best pathway for your life. I will advise you and watch over you." She knew now that she had to trust the Lord to watch over her; she couldn't do it by herself.

# CHAPTER SEVEN

Kirsti dragged herself to the front door, wishing that whoever was persistently ringing the bell would go away and come back when she'd finished her nap. Sleep had become a precious commodity these days, and her head still felt fuzzy.

That feeling was doused by a furious tirade that began as soon as Kirsti opened the door.

"Sleeping? In the middle of the day? With so much to be done? No wonder things are moving at a snail's pace. You might have plenty of money, little lady, but the rest of us don't. My unemployment is going to run out before you and Callahan can make up your minds about who your decorator will be!"

The sarcasm was heavy in Willy Metcalf's voice. Kirsti barely knew him, just that he'd worked at the snowmobile plant, that he lived in a trailer at the edge of town, and that he seemed to have little control over his emotions. She'd seen him at the grocery store once raving over a head of lettuce with some brown-edged leaves.

Kirsti opened her mouth to speak, but Willy wasn't finished yet. "Those fancy new ideas of Callahan's are what's holding this up, aren't they? You're in charge of the money. Don't let him waste time. We aren't building a skyscraper, you know."

"Cade's plans aren't holding things up. We're waiting for a shipment of steel beams that should be in this week. . . ."

"Another week? What kind of incompetents are you? Who's going to pay my bills? What was Jens thinking when he left this in the charge of a fancy-pants Irishman and a skinny, washed-out, barefoot Norwegian, anyway? I'm going to the mayor. Maybe he can get something done." With that, Willy stomped off, his heavy work boots leaving tracks of mud and dirt across Kirsti's freshly swept porch.

She stood in the doorway, stunned. There had been an occasional complaint about delays but 99 percent of the population had been incredibly supportive. And now Willy.

"We're doing the best we can!" Kirsti called to the retreating back of her visitor.

Then her eyes narrowed. " 'A skinny, washed-out Norwegian,' am I? Well, let's just see what we can do about that!"

When Kirsti was upset—very, very upset—she cooked. Fried ham and eggs. Biscuits and gravy. A fudge cake. Macaroons and a large pot of soup.

Cade found her in the kitchen, surrounded by a veritable feast.

"Who are you expecting for dinner, Henry VIII?" he asked, surveying the heavily laden countertops.

"No, but Marquis de Sade stopped by. Or was it Attila the Hun? Someone very crabby." She described Willy's visit. Her stomach hurt, and for some reason, so did her heart. If only Jens had left well enough alone!

"What time was that?"

"I don't know. How long does it take to cook everything in a refrigerator?" Kirsti looked at Cade apologetically. "I'm sorry Willy made me so angry. Much of the delay *was* my fault. And he called me a 'skinny, washed-out, barefoot Norwegian'!"

Kirsti sounded so insulted that Cade burst out laughing.

"I can't help it that I'd scrubbed off all my makeup and taken off my shoes. I'd been napping, and I know I wasn't at my best—"

"Kirsti, darling, you *are* a willowy, fashionably pale, earthy Scandinavian. I didn't think Willy had the good taste to notice."

"I am?" She looked at him in dumbfounded amazement.

"You have never given yourself credit for your beauty. How many guys did I have to threaten, bribe, or injure to keep them away from you in high—" He stopped short.

"You did that? Who gave you permission to . . . Oh, it doesn't matter now." *So Cade had tried to keep her for himself!* She found the fact rather sweet. She could feel herself softening toward him. But then, who could resist a gorgeous Irishman with brains, talent, and a smile that could melt granite? *Not her.*

"Kirsti, are you all right?" There was concern in Cade's voice. "You just got a very strange expression on your face."

"I . . . guess all this food is making me lose my appetite. Excuse me." And she fled to the living room. She couldn't let Cade see her eyes right now. He had always been able to read everything she was feeling in her eyes.

To her dismay, Cade refused to leave it at that. He crossed the room and sat on the edge of the couch on which she was curled, his weight making the firm cushion sag slightly. Gentle fingers brushed the golden length of her hair.

"I came over to ask you out for dinner, but I have a hunch you aren't interested anymore."

Kirsti nodded into the pillow, refusing to look at him.

"Then how about something else? A movie? A show?" He looked at his watch. "If we hurry we can drive into Fargo. I noticed that *My Fair Lady* is there right now. It's community theater, but if you don't mind . . ."

"I've always loved that play," Kirsti said wistfully. She felt her mood perk up immediately.

"Then climb into some shoes, comb your hair, and we'll go."

"Oh, no. I'll have to put on some makeup and change."

"Not for me, you don't," Cade said softly. "You're lovely just the way you are."

She shooed him out of the house anyway and told him to come back after he'd changed his clothes too.

She'd been trapped in Snowflake for so long that she didn't even know if she owned anything appropriate to wear. As she put away all the food she'd prepared in her fury, she mentally sorted through her meager wardrobe. Sunday morning church in Snowflake did not have a demanding dress code.

But there was always the black dress. Kirsti finished up in the kitchen, headed for her bedroom, and pulled the garment from the back of the closet. Its soft lines fell into place, and the fabric felt soft and silky in her hands. She'd purchased it on a whim, 50 percent off at Snowflake's dress shop.

"Most of us don't have a place to wear a dress so fancy," the shopkeeper had said, "but I ordered it anyway just because it was so beautiful."

And it was beautiful—especially on Kirsti. Since she was model tall and slender, anything she put on seemed to fit, but the black dress was especially flattering. It was sleeveless and held together over the shoulders and back by a complicated-looking arrangement of tiny, rhinestone-studded straps. And, to date, she'd never worn it out of the house.

Should she or shouldn't she? Kirsti debated. Her only other choices seemed much too casual in comparison.

Decision made, Kirsti slipped into the dress, did a hasty but effective job of her makeup, and rolled her hair into a loose French twist, which she secured with a row of rhinestone-studded hairpins. Satisfied that she didn't look too bad considering the time she'd had to prepare, all the tears she'd shed recently, and all the food she'd eaten, she went to find Cade. He'd rung the doorbell moments earlier and was no doubt entertaining himself downstairs.

She found him in the living room reading the *Wall Street Journal*. He'd changed into black trousers and a pristine white shirt. A suit jacket was thrown carelessly over the chair next to him.

"Ready?" he glanced up from the paper. "I guess you are. You look fabulous!"

"For a 'washed-out Norwegian'?" she asked weakly, genuinely appreciating the compliment.

"For anyone."

The look he gave her nearly stopped her heart. Kirsti, both thrilled and alarmed, averted her eyes. She'd seen that look before in high school. It meant Cade was attracted to a girl. She'd seen it time and time again when he'd become intrigued with someone new. But this time there was no one in the room but her.

⋰⋰⋰

The doors were minutes from closing when Cade purchased two tickets for the ninth row, center.

"Someone is missing great seats," he commented as they squeezed by the people already in their seats, who were trying to curl themselves into fetal positions so Cade and Kirsti could pass.

She'd had time only to smooth down her dress and settle her body into the cushiony seat before the program began. She didn't even notice Cade's arm slipping protectively across the back of her chair.

The first half of the show passed quickly, and at intermission Cade offered to get her something to eat or drink.

"Mineral water would be fine." Kirsti said, squirming in her chair. "But if you don't mind, I'll come with you. I'd like to stretch."

The lobby was swarming with people, and lines began to form outside the restroom doors. Cade steered her toward a quiet spot and hailed a tall, dignified-looking couple.

"Kirsti, I'd like to you meet someone I used to work with. In fact, Gabe was part of my firm before he decided to go solo. This is Gabe Miller and his wife, Ellen. Gabe, Ellen, this is Kirsti Nord, my—"

"So you're the one? The high school sweetheart—the lost love?"

Kirsti turned an inquiring eye toward Cade, but he was already negotiating his way toward the beverage bar. When she turned back to the couple, they were studying her with undisguised curiosity.

"We weren't sure you existed," Gabe said, his eyes looking at her with amusement. Kirsti wasn't sure she liked him.

"Oh?" *What an odd statement!* "Why?"

"We thought Cade made you up to keep women at arm's length," Ellen continued. "I can't tell you how many conversations we've had that included his saying, 'When Kirsti and I did this or that.'"

"We grew up together and were best friends for many years," Kirsti said. "I don't see why—"

"Women love Cade. They flock to him. And when he invariably refers to another woman somewhere in the conversation, it's a bit like dousing a flame, that's all." Ellen smiled with affection. Kirsti sensed immediately how fond the couple was of Cade.

Gabe chuckled and furtively moved a bit closer. "To be perfectly honest, Ellen and I began teasing Cade about his 'imaginary friend.' We'd accuse him of inventing you just to keep other ladies on their toes. They could never be too complacent around Cade, we said, because you were always lurking in his background."

Kirsti glanced around the room. There were so many lovely women here in low-cut gowns; trim, tailored suits; and elegant dresses. Suddenly she felt like a country girl in her single party dress. Because she *was* a country girl, that's why!

The bright lights and glittery people dimmed considerably as she listened to Gabe and Ellen talk about their travels and experiences with Cade. They thought they were amusing her, but what they were really doing was breaking her heart.

The lights had already begun to dim when Cade returned with her mineral water. "You've kept her entertained, I presume?" he said to Gabe.

"Just telling her a few little stories about you, that's all," Gabe said slyly, giving Cade a thump on the back.

"Don't pay any attention to him," Cade admonished Kirsti. "He's a bag of wind, and Ellen encourages him."

Ellen's response was to give Cade a kiss on each cheek and murmur, "Come for dinner sometime, darling." She gave Kirsti a dismissing little wave.

Kirsti trailed Cade back to their seats feeling more and more depressed and disgusted with herself for even caring about Cade's life. *She'd* been the one to end their relationship, after all, not Cade!

Cade settled her in her seat and searched her face just as the theater darkened. "Gabe is a gifted architect, but he and Ellen are both serious social climbers. You can't give too much credit to what they say. Their points of view are pretty skewed to the social scene. They think it's hilarious that I grew up in a place called Snowflake."

"Deliriously funny," Kirsti said weakly. "Uproarious."

She sat through the rest of the performance seeing and hearing nothing. The chattering inside her own skull was much too loud.

Gabe and Ellen thought her a cute little joke, a "blast from the past."

Well, she *was* a joke! That much was true. A skinny blond with one good dress and a grandfather who had done all the wrong things for her by trying to do the right one. What an inviting package she was.

A tear leaked from beneath her lid and slid down her cheek. Her grandfather had been the wisest man she'd ever known. But he would have been heartbroken to know how he'd complicated her life this way. If only he hadn't specified Cade in his will! All the old feelings were coming back, both good and bad—and Kirsti feared them both.

\\\\//

"I don't understand what's wrong," Cade said as they drove home from the plant site. They had been checking the construction progress and were pleased to see that it was coming along nicely. "Last night was supposed to be a treat for you, a time away from pressure. And you look worse than you did before we went!"

Kirsti didn't answer.

"Kirsti, look," Cade continued, "I've been trying to let this play out your way, but I think it's time I told you that—"

Cade was about to finish his statement when he slammed on the brakes. "Is that Thomas's car in front of city hall?"

"Looks like it."

"I wonder what that old schemer is up to now." Cade's eyes narrowed to suspicious slits. "This is the time of day he usually plays checkers. Something is up."

They were startled to find several people in the mayor's office—Ben Nordstrom, Dr. Hale, Tessa Shannon, Ed Owens, and Martin Marky—all wearing big smiles. Thomas Callahan and Mayor Grange were at the crowd's center.

"And here they are now!" Ben called out.

"Uh-oh—trouble," Cade muttered as he pulled Kirsti close to himself.

That protective move was exactly what the group wanted to see.

"Looks like they're still getting along, eh, Thomas?"

"Good news for all of us."

"And a bonus besides!"

"Bonus? What bonus? Gramps, what have you done now?"

Thomas looked up at the handsome grandson towering over him. "You look a lot like your father, but those eyes belonged to your mother. Why, when he brought your mother home to meet me for the very first time, I just *knew* they were meant to be together." Thomas gave a disapproving snort. "Took them long enough to figure it out, though. Young people just aren't as bright as they used to be about affairs of the heart." He scowled a bit at Cade. "And it seems that each successive generation is getting just a little bit more simple-minded about the whole thing."

"What have you done?" Cade's voice was a controlled roar. The happy group around Thomas froze.

"Something I should have thought of long ago." Thomas flicked his cane and made Cade jump aside. "Now I have to leave. I have a checkers game waiting to be played. The good mayor can give you the details."

Thomas toddled toward the door like the gleeful old leprechaun that he was. When he reached it, he turned around and gave Cade and Kirsti a beady-eyed stare. "Now don't you two go messing things up. I know what I'm doing."

"Mr. Mayor, may Kirsti and I speak to you—" Cade eyed the staring audience—"alone?"

The others melted away as Cade and Kirsti entered the inner office. Building plans and pages of bids were scattered all over the mayor's desk. He swept them aside.

"Well, ah, er . . ."

"Just tell us what he's done." Cade's voice was controlled. "I won't hold you responsible. I know how my grandfather can be."

"He's been very generous, Mr. Callahan. *Very* generous."

"Fine. He has money. He has a right to be generous. Now what did he do?"

"He called it 'sweetening the pot,' if I recall correctly. Another phrase he used was 'encouraging the obvious.' " The mayor was sweating now. Beads of perspiration were standing out all over the top of his head. He mopped it with a limp gray handkerchief.

"And exactly what did he mean by that?"

Kirsti saw Cade's knuckles growing white on the arms of

his chair and then realized that she was wringing her own hands. She forced them to lie flat on her lap.

"Thomas has very generously offered to build a community center here in Jens's honor. The 'Jens Nord Family Center.'"

"How sweet," Kirsti blurted, touched by the idea. "My grandfather would have been deeply honored."

The mayor's face flushed a deep, rocketing-blood-pressure sort of red. "There is one string attached. Only one, mind you, and it's a very generous offer—"

"And what is that 'string'?" Cade's voice could have cut a diamond.

"That you and Kirsti make your 'partnership' permanent." The mayor shuffled the plans on his desk.

"According to Thomas, he's been observing you together and has decided that without a push you'll never 'tie the knot and raise wee bairns' as you should. He knows he has no business pushing you this way, but he says 'the only way to prevent a stalemate is with a bold, dramatic move.'"

"And I thought my grandfather preferred checkers to chess. This is certainly both 'bold' and 'dramatic,'" Cade said grimly. "And ridiculous and preposterous and—"

The mayor timidly held up a finger. "Just one more thing. He has a timeline. Thomas wants ground broken before freeze-up."

# CHAPTER EIGHT

Kirsti gasped. Cade slumped forward and put his head in his hands.

"If you would like to discuss this, I'd be happy to leave my office—"

"Thank you, Mr. Mayor, but I think Kirsti and I need a place slightly more private." Cade rose and took Kirsti by the arm. Half pushing and half carrying her, he propelled her out of city hall and into his car. Neither of them spoke until they were inside the Nord mansion. Kirsti put on the kettle while Cade, still remembering where everything was located in the big kitchen, took out cups, saucers, and spoons.

When the instant hot cocoa was made, Kirsti sat down at the table across from him. "I'll never be able face anyone in this town again," she said with resignation. "I've heard there are openings for preschool and kindergarten teachers in South Dakota and Minnesota. If I get an application in now, I might have a chance at this fall's openings."

"You're giving up? Just like that? Because Thomas embarrassed us? He did impulsive things all the time we were growing up, and we lived through it. His heart has always been far bigger than his brain where we're concerned."

Kirsti laughed in spite of herself.

"I always believed you were a fighter, Kirsti, but then you changed—almost overnight."

She knew he was referring to that last horrible week they'd had together, and she didn't want the subject to come up.

Cade, however, would not back off. "We have some very old business to attend to, Kirsti, and until you explain to me what happened between us back then, I'm never going to understand your attitude toward me since that time."

He leaned back in the chair and watched her closely. "You have never asked me what I'd like to do about this situation, you know."

"You said it was 'ridiculous' and 'preposterous.' That's pretty clear."

"But you never assumed for a moment that I might *want* to marry you. Maybe Thomas *is* right. We would raise 'fine wee bairns.'"

Kirsti could not have been more shocked had the ceiling fallen in on her head. "You? Marry me?" Her voice cracked, and she hated herself for the weakness. "But I couldn't—"

"Then tell me *why*. One day ten years ago, everything changed between us, and I've never really known the reason . . . although I can't be faulted for not trying to find out." His perfectly proportioned features were perplexed. "You just stepped out of my life and never came back."

"And you couldn't figure it out?" she said in disbelief. "After knowing me and my values your entire life?"

"What's with this 'values' thing anyway? You keep hammering me over the head with it, and I don't get it. What did I do?"

Kirsti steeled herself before speaking. "You took our classmate Cindy Mahon out of town to get an abortion."

Cade paled. "How did you—"

"And you lied to me about it." Kirsti's face crumpled, and the tears came. "I trusted you! I thought you believed as I did about the sanctity of life. Instead, you borrowed your grandfather's car and drove her wherever she needed to go. When I asked you where you'd gone, you had some stupid story about Cindy needing a passport photo taken before a trip with her family."

"Kirsti, I—"

"Let me finish. I've been so hurt and so confused about you for so long that it needs to come out. Cindy let it slip to Tiffany that she thought she was pregnant. She asked Tiffany if she knew of someone who could 'take care of the pregnancy' for her. When Tiff told her she had no ideas about that sort of thing, Cindy told her she was going to ask you because 'Cade's family is rich and travels all the time. Surely a Callahan would know about these things.'"

Cade slipped down in his seat and stared at Kirsti with horror-stricken eyes.

"Tiff told me what Cindy was planning to do. I defended you and said that you would *never* be a party to something like that. That you couldn't approve of taking the life of an unborn child. You'd always said you liked children as much as I do, that you wanted some of your own someday. And then you took Cindy away."

"The passport photo—"

"Don't try to lie your way out of it. You helped Cindy find an abortionist. That's why you refused to say anything when I asked you about that day. Finally, when I persisted, you *lied* to me!" Kirsti started to cry. "Everything inside me broke then, Cade. I *loved* you, and you chose to do something dreadful—and you weren't even man enough to tell me to my face! *That's* why I can't marry you even though I love you. I don't trust you anymore. And I don't know if you really share my faith in God or if that's just been a lie too."

Cade didn't speak for a long time. The wind whipped around the mansion, rattling windowpanes and adding to the already frantic mood. When he raised his head, his eyes were startlingly dark, like storm clouds gathering before a tempest.

"I did take Cindy out of town that day," he admitted. "And

she did have an appointment with a doctor to do the . . ." He couldn't say the word. "But it wasn't like you thought, Kirsti. She was desperate."

"So Cade, the wealthy knight on a white horse, saved the day." Kirsti's sarcasm hurt, and he grimaced.

"I wanted to tell you, but Cindy made me promise never to say a thing to anyone. She said she'd considered taking her own life and would do it if I told anyone what we'd done."

"So you stayed with her through the whole grisly thing?" Kirsti felt like throwing up. She'd *loved* this man. She'd *trusted* him!

"Not exactly. We talked—and I prayed—all the way to the clinic, and when we got there, I could see that she was getting scared, so I told her that if she'd reconsider, I knew someone who would help her."

Kirsti stared at him. "Who?"

"My grandfather. I told her that I knew he'd support her till she had the baby and gave it up for adoption, that it would be our secret."

"And?"

"She cried a lot, but she finally agreed. We got back to Grandfather's house about two in the morning and woke him up. Without a question, he gave her the name and address of a friend of his, a doctor who could do prenatal care and find a home for her. So, when Cindy's family went abroad, she stayed behind at a home for unwed mothers. Gramps footed the bill. We both agreed never to tell another soul. That's why I couldn't say anything, Kirsti. I'd made a *promise*. I'm sorry if it hurt you. It was just that Cindy was so distraught that I didn't know what she might do if she thought she'd been found out." Cade grimaced. "I guess it didn't matter—if you already knew back here in Snowflake."

Kirsti stared at him. Had she been mistaken for ten entire years? "So you didn't take her for an abortion?"

"No, of course not! I went because I wanted to try to talk

her out of it. I wasn't sure if I could, but I thought it was worth a try. You know how I felt—and still feel—about abortion."

She sat, stunned. "So you didn't . . . She didn't . . . ?"

"You mean that's what's kept you so angry all these years?" An array of emotions passed across Cade's features: disbelief, anger, regret.

"You were lying to me, Cade. I knew that. How could I *not* know? We spent eighteen years together. You were always a lousy liar."

"I'm sorry I lied to you, Kirsti. I wanted to tell you. I asked Cindy if I could, and she nearly went wild. She said if I told *anyone,* she'd kill herself. That's a pretty big burden for an eighteen-year-old kid. I know how much God values honesty, but I was scared. If Cindy had actually done something foolish, I would have felt I was to blame for the rest of my life."

Kirsti was silent, trying to process what he was saying.

Cade took her silence for disbelief. "Ask my grandfather if you'd like. He'll tell you that what I'm saying is the truth. Now even *Cindy* would tell you. She still writes to Gramps and tells him how grateful she is that she didn't go through with the abortion. She has a couple of children now and has realized that life is more precious than she ever imagined." His eyes were violet pools, his chiseled jaw tense. "I see now that my silence came between us, Kirsti. Maybe I should have trusted you enough to confide in you back then. I just wasn't sure what was the right thing to do." He cast his eyes downward.

"I have to think." Kirsti could hear the panic in her own voice. Her hands fluttered to her cheeks. "This is all so sudden, so surprising. Leave me alone for a while, Cade. Please?"

He rose slowly to tower over her, his face grim. "I'm sorry, Kirsti. I should have told you, but I was young and afraid. It never dawned on me that you'd find out or that you'd think I'd encourage a girl to—"

"Please leave. Please?" She couldn't breathe. She was suffocating with confusion, grief, and remorse.

He nodded then and turned to the door. "I'll be around for a few more days if you need to talk to me."

And he was gone. She heard the engine start and the purring drone of the motor disappear down the lane. She sat there until the gong of the grandfather clock startled her from her reverie.

The house felt so empty without Grandfather—and without Cade. It was too early for Natty to stop by and fill the place with her chatter, and Kirsti knew that she didn't want to seek out company uptown. She couldn't stand the beseeching and hopeful eyes that followed her wherever she went.

Not knowing what else to do, Kirsti retreated to the one place she had relied on as a child when the world seemed too much for her—the attic.

It had always seemed a magical place to her, filled with everything from rocking horses to ancient military uniforms, from old movie magazines to unused furniture. The air was hot and stuffy and smelled of dust. Kirsti opened a window and sat down by the old chest that housed all the photos taken over the years. She pulled out a shoe box and plucked a picture from the center.

It was her grandfather and grandmother looking very much like the couple in Grant Wood's *American Gothic,* but Gramps was holding a rifle, not a pitchfork, and Grandma was dutifully holding a trophy bird in her hand.

The next was of her parents during one of their visits. Although she loved them very much, they seemed distant to her now, involved with a life and a people that she could barely comprehend. It would have been good to have them nearby to confide in and to comfort her, but she was proud of them for serving the Lord so wholeheartedly.

A sigh escaped her at the next photo. It was her and Cade standing by those two stubborn ponies. Kirsti was smiling into the camera with a wide, innocent expression, unaware that Tommy had one of her long blond braids in his mouth. Cade, sturdy and handsome as the man he would grow to be, stood with legs spread wide apart in a defiant stance. He scowled into the camera as if he were willing it to break.

There were other photos of the two of them. Kirsti in a sundress pouring imaginary tea for her dolls with Cade sitting, disgruntled, between Raggedy Ann and Winnie the Pooh. Cade swinging upside down from a tree branch with Kirsti lifting her arms to him, pleading for him to return to earth.

There was a theme here, Kirsti realized with a weak smile. In every photo and in every memory, she and Cade were polar opposites—dark and light, sun and shadow—two halves of one itchy, prickly whole. Together they were complete.

She set the box down and stared out the window, wondering why it hadn't occurred to her before—most likely because she'd been so consumed with the fact that Cade had lied to her, not to mention the unconscionable deed she had thought he had taken part in. They *were* best when they were together. Complete. Whole. A unit. A team. And now that she no longer had blinders on, she could see plenty of evidence that Cade was truly the godly man she'd always thought he could be.

Grandfather and Thomas already knew. Was it possible those two had hit upon the truth that had escaped both her and Cade? That they actually knew what was best for their grandchildren? *And* for Snowflake?

Gathering several of the telling photos, she put the box aside and dusted off the front of her shirt. Moving quickly so she wouldn't lose her courage, she ran downstairs to the telephone and dialed Thomas Callahan's number.

"Callahans'. Cade here."

"I need to see you."

"Wasn't I just kicked out of your house an hour ago?"

"I needed to think."

"You're very quick."

"Quit being sarcastic, Cade. Can you come over?"

"I promised I'd pick up my grandfather at the café in ten minutes."

"Then I'll meet you there. Try to get the last booth. It's most private."

"Should I worry? Have you got plans to do me bodily harm?" he teased.

"Only if you don't quit being difficult. Snowflake Café. Ten minutes." And Kirsti hung up the phone.

It occurred to her as she pulled her Explorer into an empty spot in front of the café that this probably wasn't the wisest place to have chosen to talk. The coffee crowd was milling about much later than usual today.

Cade had obeyed her orders and secured the back booth. Holding her head high, Kirsti walked past the table where Thomas was playing checkers and pretending not to see her. She slipped into the booth feeling as though a hundred eyes were staring straight into her.

"What can I get you?" Rosie McGrady asked. "Pie's fresh. Couple donuts left."

"Just coffee for me," Kirsti said.

"Apple pie and coffee," Cade ordered.

Rosie nodded but didn't leave. "I know it's none of my business, but I'm glad to see you two together," she blurted, her face flushing. "You two are a good team—always have been—and you are doing a lot for our town."

She swept a hand toward the rest of the room. "We're full of people, but nobody buys anything but coffee. Nobody knows where their next cash is going to come from, so they're careful. Some days we serve only ten full meals. Can't keep a business running that way. That plant can't open too soon for me." Then, as if realizing that she'd probably spoken out of turn, she spun on her heel and left.

After Rosie, it was as though a parade had organized to pass by the table. People expressing thanks, encouragement, and support for the town, and concerns about Cade and Kirsti's much-examined relationship—or both—streamed by. There were a few careful, cloaked comments about the community center and Thomas's off-the-wall idea. Kirsti was grateful when Rosie returned with their order, forcing people to leave them alone to eat.

"I never realized people thought we were quite this important," Cade said lightly. "I'm waiting for someone to ask me for my autograph. And, if I'm not mistaken, the third table by the window is taking bets on the outcome of our conversation."

"Exactly what about this seems funny to you?" Kirsti groaned.

"Everything. Thomas planning this misguided mission for Cupid, Jens's unintended part in the whole thing, and now, the town actually thinking something might come of it—of us."

"I think I need a good laugh too," Kirsti said, her head spinning with the sudden turn of events.

"We've been fighting our grandfathers' wisdom for our entire lives. Didn't you ever notice? 'Don't play with fire,'" they said, and we promptly hid in the trees to play with our contraband matches. . . ."

"And the fire department had to come and put the brushfire out," she finished for him.

"And 'Don't lay those wet leather gloves so near the stove to dry. . . .'"

"But we did and ended up with two pairs of shriveled gloves that wouldn't fit no matter how we stretched them!"

"Or 'Don't feed those ponies too much. . . .'"

"And they both ended up with colic because we didn't listen." Kirsti sighed. "You're right. We never listened to them and always had to learn the hard way."

"Smart men, our grandfathers. They knew how to listen to their hearts—and to God."

"'We can make our plans, but the Lord determines our steps,'" Kirsti quoted. "Proverbs 16:9. All the time we've been planning our lives, God's been leading us in the direction he knows is best for us."

He leaned back in the booth, shaking his head. "You know,

Kirsti, it really drives me crazy when those grandfathers of ours are right."

"Is that a proposal or an analysis of your mental state?" Thomas popped around the corner of the booth grinning like a jack-o'-lantern. "Frankly, my boy, I think you can do better than that."

With a theatrical sigh, Cade heaved himself out of the booth and dropped to his knee at Kirsti's feet. There, in front of not only God and Thomas Callahan, but a goodly share of the population of Snowflake, he asked Kirsti Nord to marry him. "Kirsti, I've loved you ever since I can remember. Will you do me the honor of becoming my wife?"

And her quiet yes was nearly drowned out by the joyous roar of the crowd and the clapping of hands. Sometimes grandfathers do know best.

# RECIPE

〜

Lefse *(pronounced LEF-seh) is a pale, flat circle of dough marked by dark fry spots that could be called "the Norwegian tortilla." A staple of the traditional Scandinavian community, it is made with potatoes, flour, and cream, rolled flat, and fried on a round* lefse *griddle. I like to cut my* lefse *into quarters, add a thin layer of butter and sugar, and roll it into a cone to eat. My mother (the Irish side of my family) prefers to eat it without the sugar and in place of bread at a meal.*

*Enjoying* lefse *comes naturally to me because I grew up in a pocket of* lefse-*making ladies (and gentlemen—my father does the rolling while my mother is in charge of the griddle).*

*My grandfather homesteaded land in 1882 when he emigrated from Norway. He was one of the founding fathers of a little country church still in operation today. Those faithful men actually built the church before finishing their own homes.*

*My father, a full-blooded Norwegian, was confirmed in the Norwegian language. As a child, I never appreciated (or learned) it. It was always used when my grandmother and father wanted to talk about something they didn't think a child should hear! My mother was also cut out of these conversations. I wish now that we'd learned enough to know what was being talked about!*

*Some of my most vivid childhood memories of that church are the aromas—egg coffee and hot dish. Still a staple in the church I attend today, "funeral hot dish" can be made in large amounts in roasters and doled out with finger rolls with lots of butter, Jell-O, and either cake or bars. Comfort food without compare!*

—Judy Baer

## LEFSE

10 cups hot mashed or riced potatoes (which were salted while cooking)
1 cup cream (or half-and-half)
1 cup oil (butter flavored is good)
3½–4 cups flour

Mix hot potatoes, cream, and oil. Cool. Mix in flour. Roll very thin on floured pie-crust cloth or counter. Fry on a griddle (or a special *lefse* maker) just until light brown spots appear, turning once. Serve with butter and sugar.

## FUNERAL HOT DISH

5 lbs. ground beef
5 lbs. elbow macaroni
1 large can tomato juice
2 large cans tomato soup
2 small cans cream of celery soup
2 8-oz. cans tomato sauce
1 pkg. dry onion soup
1 12-oz. can tomato paste
1 small pkg. spaghetti sauce mix

Brown ground beef and drain off fat. Add all the other ingredients (except macaroni) and simmer to blend flavors. Meanwhile, cook macaroni according to package directions. Mix cooked macaroni into sauce. Keep warm in large roaster until serving time.

## ABOUT THE AUTHOR

Judy Baer lives in North Dakota, where she raises buffalo and horses, (quarter horses and paints) and keeps sled dogs. A novelist and freelance writer with more than sixty books to her credit, Judy is a member of numerous writers associations and frequently speaks at writers conferences as well as at local schools and churches. She has taught adult Sunday school and has served on her church council for several years.

You can write to Judy in care of Tyndale House Author Relations, P.O. Box 80, Wheaton, IL 60189-0080.

# Scarlett Dreamer

## JERI ODELL

This book is dedicated to Dean,
my husband of twenty-five years.
Many of the qualities found in Rick are qualities
I've found in you.

\\\\\//

Also dedicated to Pat Z,
my trusted critique partner and valued friend.
Without your help, I don't think this book would be in print.
Thank you.

And to Mercy Ministries of America
P.O. Box 111060
Nashville, TN 37222-1060
615-831-6987
www.mercyministries.org
Though Katie is a fictional character,
Mercy Ministries reaches out to numerous girls just like her.
My thanks to God for your work in furthering the cause of Christ.

# CHAPTER ONE

*"Come now, let us reason together," says the Lord. "Though your sins are like scarlet, they shall be as white as snow; though they are red as crimson, they shall be like wool."*
ISAIAH 1:18, NIV

Rick Laramie settled into the third pew, feeling himself relax. "Welcome, welcome," a familiar-sounding voice spoke into the microphone. "I'm Scarlett, and joining me is Forever His. We'll lead worship this week during the tenth annual spiritual-growth retreat here at the Glorieta Conference Center."

Rick tore his eyes from the stained-glass window and focused on the woman at the podium. "Dear God," he whispered aloud, "it's Katie." *Katie Scarlett O'Malley,* his mind supplied the missing piece of the puzzle. She continued her welcome speech, but the words didn't penetrate his stunned mind. He blinked, making sure his imagination wasn't deceiving him, but she still stood behind the microphone at center stage.

His mind whirled. How many times had he begged God to bring her back into his life? For four years he had prayed diligently for her. Now the cry of his heart stood before him in the flesh, and he struggled to breathe, to think.

"November in Glorieta is like heaven on earth." He refocused on her voice. "Now let's worship the Creator, our King and Savior, Jesus Christ."

He noticed a tiny southern drawl in Katie's speech that hadn't existed when he knew her. He tried to concentrate on the songs and on God, but only Katie filled his mind.

Her hair still resembled black coffee, only now she pulled it up and it fell in curls behind her. The once long, straight locks looked styled and updated. Her large brown eyes shimmered as she sang to her Lord. She looked thinner and more mature. His Katie had grown into even more of a beauty than he had expected.

His mind reeled back to another time, another place. His younger sister, Lanae, and Katie had decided to form a band. Katie played the keyboard and sang lead. Much to his mother's dismay, they practiced daily.

*"Rick, come listen. We're really good." Lanae dragged him by the hand into the family room. Even as a junior high student, Katie had talent; unfortunately, she was the only band member who did.*

Now her contralto voice rang clear, rich, and pure. The sweet sound pierced his soul. *Katie, my love, I've longed to see you, to know you've found Christ, and to possibly take up where we left off. You stole my heart and have carried it with you these past six years. I can't forget you. God knows I've tried.*

The worship team left the stage, and Harv Samuelson stepped up to the podium. "It's wonderful to be here and to have the privilege of sharing with you this week. Spiritual growth is a challenge and concern as each of us strives to be more like Christ. I come before you not as an authority but as a fellow striver. . . ."

Rick took out his notebook, hoping that writing would keep his attention on the message and off the brunette seated two rows in front of him. Though his intentions were honorable, he failed miserably. Another memory surfaced.

*He and Katie were in the barn unsaddling their horses after a moonlight ride. He knew something had changed between them, for new feelings and emotions surprised him at every* turn. *The very air they breathed exploded with unseen currents of electricity.*

*"Let me carry the saddle for you." His heart increased its pace at her nearness. He stood directly behind her, but instead of stepping away, she turned, and they were mere inches apart. Her doe eyes looked into his, and her lips invited his kiss. Slowly, reverently, his lips found hers. She wrapped her arms around his neck and shyly returned the kiss.*

*"Katie," he whispered her name.*

*"Shh, don't spoil it with words." She laid her index finger against his mouth to quiet him. Instead of talking, he held her close for tranquil moments. Both seemed content to cherish the memory of their first kiss.*

*Rocket grew impatient with their dallying and nudged them with his nose. They laughed and finished the jobs at hand. When the horses were fed and groomed and the tack put away, he and Katie walked hand in hand up the hill to the big house.*

Looking back, he realized that on that very night he'd wrapped his heart in love and placed it in Katie's hands. She was his first love, and as it turned out, his only love. He had had no idea she would run away, leaving him heartbroken and hurting.

⁂

Katie focused her eyes on the gray-haired man preaching, but her mind wandered to Texas Hall, where DeDe and Kasey waited in the room the three of them shared. They had stayed behind because Kasey hadn't felt well. Katie hoped it wasn't the flu, or she and DeDe might catch it too. She couldn't even consider the possibility, not here, with this opportunity before her.

The worship had gone well, and once they began singing, her nerves had calmed. Honored to be here, she felt grateful to God for the chance. She loved Holcomb Auditorium. Her eyes lovingly admired the rich wood of the ceiling, walls, and stage. Glorieta—a place of peace . . .

Before Katie realized it, the sermon ended. The other members of Forever His rose, and she followed them back up onstage. She felt annoyed with herself, having no idea what Harv had spoken about because she'd let her thoughts wander.

After the closing song, Katie, Forever His, and Harv gathered in the foyer to greet people and shake hands. A sea of faces swarmed before her, endless comments, hugs, and nods. Her face ached from smiling, and she wanted to check on DeDe and Kasey. She wasn't good at this part of her job. Onstage her confidence soared, but down here, she hated the limelight.

"Katie."

She turned toward the voice, her mind vaguely registering that no one in the music business, except DeDe, knew her first name. Here, in this world, she was Scarlett. Her eyes focused on a square jaw, warm gray eyes . . . Rick. She felt her head spin and her knees go weak. He grabbed her by the upper arms to steady her, then led her back into the auditorium and guided her to a back pew. Squatting in the aisle next to her, he asked in his familiar, deep voice, "Are you all right?"

Katie nodded. *What is he doing here?* She felt her life unraveling as she looked into his tender eyes. *Remember, Katie, you were just a summer fling. He never loved you. He only used you.* . . .

"You found Christ." His smile touched her deeply, and she noticed he still had the dimple in his left cheek. She only nodded, and he continued, "Me, too. Four years ago, and I've prayed every day that you'd give your life to him too. Now here we are together at a spiritual-growth retreat!"

He seemed ecstatic that their paths had crossed. She felt trepidation. Her life lay neatly packaged and figured out, except for Rick. She'd locked him in the closet of her mind, refusing to deal with him. Now he stood before her, and somehow she knew that nothing in her world would ever be the same.

"Katie, you haven't said a word. Are you OK?"

"I'm surprised—stunned."

"I hoped you'd be glad to see me. I'm thrilled to see you."

*You're a bad memory back to haunt me. How can you expect me to be happy?* "I'm sorry. I'm in shock. I never expected to see you again, especially at a Christian conference center."

"And here we are. Can we have dinner—catch up?"

How could she say no? Lanae had been her best friend growing up; she and her parents had lived on the Laramie ranch as caretakers for seven years, and for one sweet summer, Rick had been hers too. Her heart responded with a pang of pain. The intense longing in his gaze beckoned her. Tomorrow she'd probably regret her decision, but tonight she would allow Rick to share her life once more. Just tonight . . .

⸎

Rick waited for Katie in front of the Chuck Wagon snack bar. Part of him doubted she'd show up. He'd seen fear in her eyes when she recognized him. What he didn't understand was why. She'd nearly fainted upon seeing him, and renewing their friendship seemed like the last thing she wanted to do. He sighed, then spotted her walking toward him from Texas Hall.

His mood lifted at the sight of her. He knew he'd never gotten over Katie, but he was still surprised at how quickly and strongly his heart responded to her. "Hi." He walked out toward her, and they met in the middle of the parking lot.

Her smile turned his insides to Jell-O. "Hi, yourself." She shivered and drew her coat tighter around her. "Autumn in the Rocky Mountains of northern New Mexico is colder than I'm used to."

"Where's that?"

She paused, appearing to debate with herself whether to answer the question or change the subject. "Nashville."

*Nashville.* When Katie disappeared, Rick had hired a private investigator. He traced her to the airport in Nashville but could never pick up her trail again. He noted the fear filling her eyes again. What troubled her?

"How long have you been there?" he asked.

"Can we talk about something else?" Her voice shook with emotions that he didn't understand.

"Sure. Let's walk." He turned and started down the road toward the dining hall. After several minutes of silence, Rick decided to find a safer, less volatile topic. "I love this place. Have you been here before?"

"Yes. How about you?"

"This is my fourth spiritual-growth retreat."

"It's my first, but I came for Worship Week last year."

"I feel God here. And peace."

"And it's incredibly beautiful."

"Especially compared to Arizona." He poked fun at his home state, and they both laughed. He knew that she, too, was picturing the dry, brown, desert land.

"How are things on the ranch?" she asked a moment later.

"Good. Tucson's grown so much the houses almost reach our place in Catalina. Can you believe it?" She shook her head, and he continued. "We've had a couple of hard years with drought. Lost almost a hundred head of cattle because of the heat the last two summers. Do you miss ranch life?" He glanced over at her, but the night was too dark to read her expression.

"I do. Especially horseback rides on warm summer nights. And I miss Lanae. How is she?"

"She's fine." *Except her best friend disappeared without a word and never once tried to call.* "She never finished college, couldn't decide on a major. She fell in love with a rodeo man and travels with him. He rides bulls and broncos, and she runs barrels. They seem happy enough, but neither has a relationship with Christ. She thinks I'm some religious nut."

"And your parents?"

"They think I'm a religious nut, too, but they're well. Dad retired completely, and I run the ranch. They have a motor home and travel about nine months a year. Mom likes having all of Dad's time and attention."

They'd circled the lake and were back to New Mexico Hall. "Let's go into the Chuck Wagon since I promised you dinner." Rick took Katie's elbow to guide her to a table. He felt her tense at his touch, and that hurt. "What can I get you?"

"I'm not hungry, but coffee would be nice."

Rick returned minutes later with two coffees and a hamburger. "What about you, Katie? Fill me in on your life while I eat. I don't want to talk with my mouth full." He tried to sound casual, knowing she was trying to avoid talking about herself. Immediately, he saw her stiffen.

"There's not much to tell. I live in Nashville, work as a secretary, and I'm trying to break into the contemporary-Christian-music arena." She scrunched her empty sugar packet into a little ball.

"Are you married?"

"No."

"Engaged?"

"I don't even date."

"Why?"

"It's not worth the pain." Her voice sounded lifeless. Her eyes never left the wadded sugar wrapper.

"Someone hurt you?"

She only nodded, offering no explanation.

His heart ached with the realization that Katie had loved another and he'd hurt her. Rick knew it had been naive to hope she'd loved only him, but he had held on to that hope nevertheless. Now it lay shattered at his feet.

"Why, Katie? Why did you leave?" He could no longer put off the question that was uppermost in his mind.

# CHAPTER TWO

Katie wondered why she had agreed to meet with Rick, knowing it was inevitable he'd ask her for an explanation of her actions so long ago. "I can't explain," she told him, "but I did the right thing." Rick sighed and ran his hand through his medium brown hair, a gesture she remembered well—he did it whenever he felt frustrated.

"Katie, you owe me an explanation."

"I can't. Not now. I'm sorry." Following a pattern she had set for herself years before, Katie rose and left Rick alone. She didn't look back, couldn't look back. Tears streamed down her face as she hurried away into the night, fleeing toward the prayer garden.

Had she done the right thing? For the first time, she questioned her decision. Confusion and uncertainty assaulted her. Katie ran faster. When she arrived at the prayer garden, breathless and spent, she faced the inevitable. "I can't outrun the demons of my past." Her whispered statement shattered the silence of the night and left her chilled to the bone. She fell to her knees in front of a park bench, laid her head on the wooden seat, and wept.

*Lord, please get me through this week. Give me strength*

*and courage. Help me to know the right thing to do. Should I tell him the truth, or are some things best left unsaid?* Katie's tears finally subsided, but the agony in her heart remained.

She trudged up the hill toward her room. Even the quiet peace of this crisp night did nothing to relieve the pain. She hoped DeDe and Kasey were sound asleep so she could avoid playing twenty questions. When Katie had gone back to her room before meeting Rick, Kasey was feeling better and playing a game with DeDe, so she had avoided the interrogation she'd seen in DeDe's eyes.

Upon entering the room, Katie realized her luck had run out. Kasey lay curled in sound sleep in the middle of the double bed they shared, but DeDe was stretched out on her twin bed across the room, reading her Bible.

"Hi," Katie whispered.

"Time to 'fess up. What's going on? You look horrible."

Katie placed her coat across the desk chair and laid the back of her hand against Kasey's cheek. "She feels cooler. Thanks for watching her for me." She bent and placed a kiss on the sleeping child's cheek. Kasey's honey brown hair fanned out over the pillow.

"Katie?" DeDe's voice held a note of exasperation.

Katie sighed. "Please, let me shower first. Then we'll talk." She hated the fact that no matter how long she put off the unavoidable, it never disappeared. *And neither will Rick.* The thought kept rattling around in her brain. Katie took the longest, hottest shower she could stand, but when she finished, DeDe was still waiting to hear the story—all of it.

"Who is this mystery man you met tonight?"

"Rick."

"*The* Rick?"

"Kendrick Colin Laramie the third." Katie noted DeDe's shocked expression.

"The father of Kendra Colleen O'Malley the first?" DeDe knew the whole sordid story.

"Yes, Kasey's dad."

110

"Did you tell him?"

"No."

"That *no* sounded too final. He has a right to know."

"You've always said that. I think he lost his right when I found out he only used me." Katie removed the towel from her wet hair and walked to the bathroom to rehang it.

"Katie, we all make mistakes. He's obviously a Christian now and, like all of us, has probably asked God's forgiveness for past choices. Katie—he *is* her father." Tears formed in DeDe's eyes. "Please tell him."

"I can't!" Fresh tears rolled down Katie's cheeks. "What if he takes her from me? I'd die. She's all I have!" Katie sat next to DeDe on the bed. They cried together.

"Katie, pray about this. It's no mistake that he's here. Kasey needs her father."

"I'm so afraid, DeDe. I don't know if I can do the right thing."

"I'll pray with you. God can bring healing to your hurts. This could have a happy ending."

"I don't see how." Katie hugged DeDe, turned out the light, and crawled into bed next to Kasey. "G'night, De."

"Night, Katie."

Katie held her daughter close and thanked God for her, as she did each night. She knew she'd been fooling herself in thinking she could keep Kasey's father from learning of the child's existence, and deep down, she knew she had been wrong to try. But as she had told DeDe, her fear was almost paralyzing. Sleep eluded her for a long time. And when it finally came, she dreamed of Rick's stealing Kasey away.

\\\\//

Rick spent much of the night in prayer, struggling to make sense of Katie's reaction, then and now. He rose with the sun and carried his Bible to the prayer garden. *Father God, surely it's no accident that Katie and I are both here. Obviously I've caused her an enormous amount of pain and somehow need to make things right. I don't even know why she ran away. I thought she understood how much I loved her. Please show me the next step, God. Bring healing and restoration to Katie's heart.*

The morning class Rick chose to attend was on evangelizing unsaved family members. He sat near the window, and his eyes wandered over the pine-covered hills. He needed to listen but had lost his concentration. Again, his mind returned to the past.

Katie had come into his life as the livestock foreman's step-daughter. She was Lanae's age and nothing but a pain if you asked him. "Could you ride with Lanae and Katie? I don't want them out alone." "Could you drive the girls to town to see a movie? They're bored today." His parents' requests were endless and always involved Lanae and Katie.

First she had been a thorn in his side, then an accepted member of the family, and when Katie turned sixteen, they had become friends. Lanae had planned a surprise party for Katie and needed Rick to divert her attention. Rick had grumbled but finally agreed to Lanae's plan.

*The day of the party he drove his pickup down to the mobile home near the barn. He knocked on the door, hoping her mom and stepdad wouldn't think he wanted to date their daughter. He felt silly allowing his sister to put him in this position.*

*Katie's mom answered the door.*

*"Is Katie home?"*

*"I thought Katie lived with your family up at the big house," her mom joked. "Come in. I'll get her."*

*He stood just inside the front door.*

*"Rick!" Katie's surprised voice drew his gaze toward the hall.*

*He cleared his throat, feeling uncomfortable. "Hi."*

*"Hi, yourself."*

*He just stood there, terrified that she'd misunderstand his in-*

*tentions. Most of his life Lanae's friends had developed crushes on him and become giggly and annoying in his presence.*

*"So—what brings you down the hill?"*

*"I thought you might like to ride to town with me. Lanae's sick. I'm running errands for my dad." He wondered if he looked as stupid as he felt.*

*"Wait a minute. You've spent every day of your life since I met you complaining whenever you had to drag Lanae and me along, and now you expect me to believe that you want me to go with you?" Katie shook her head, apparently not making sense of this scenario. "What gives?"*

*"Nothing," he insisted. "Now I'm just so used to having you girls around that I don't want to go alone."*

*Her eyes looked doubtful, but she said, "Sure, why not?"*

*He found himself enjoying Katie and their day together. They ran the errands for his dad, saw a movie, and stopped for ice cream on the way home. When he dropped Katie off in front of her house, she leaned across the seat and planted a kiss on his cheek.*

*"Thanks for being the big brother I never had, and thanks for keeping me out of Lanae's hair so she could decorate for my party tonight." Katie winked and hopped out of the truck.*

*He shook his head. They hadn't fooled her for a minute.*

Class ended, and Rick didn't remember one point they had discussed. He closed the notebook cover over the blank lined paper. Slipping into his jacket, he headed out the door and into the nippy morning breeze. Something about the wind always lifted his spirits.

Having skipped breakfast, he decided an early lunch sounded good. Walking past the lake toward the dining hall, he hummed an old country-and-western song Katie had taught him. She used to joke that it was "their song." He remembered the tune, but the only words he recalled were, "Yes, I'm a Scarlett dreamer, and I keep dreaming Scarlett's mine." Could the dream he had thought long dead be resurrected?

Rounding a corner, singing to himself, Rick nearly collided with Katie, a blond woman, and a little girl. They stood on a wooden footbridge, watching fish swimming in a clear stream that fed into the lake. "Yes, I'm a Scarlett dreamer," he sang, looking at Katie. Their eyes locked, and for the briefest of moments he thought he saw longing in hers.

"Rick!" He'd never heard his name said with such panic before.

"Hello, Katie."

"Hi," the blond lady said, sticking out her hand in a friendly gesture. "I'm DeDe, Katie's manager."

"Rick Laramie. I used to be an old friend." His eyes moved to Katie, wondering what she considered him now. "Katie, I'd like to treat you to lunch in Santa Fe, if these lovely ladies will excuse you."

"I . . ." She appeared to grope for an excuse.

"Go, Katie. Kasey and I'll be fine."

⁂

"OK," she agreed quickly, wanting to get away before Kasey called her *Mommy*. "I'll meet you later in the room," she said to DeDe. "Bye, Kasey."

"Bye." Thankfully, Kasey was watching the fish so intently that she barely looked up.

Neither spoke on the walk to Rick's hunter green Ford Explorer nor on the drive to Santa Fe. Katie tried to relax and concentrate on the beauty of the surrounding countryside but couldn't. Her stomach knotted, and her palms felt clammy and sweaty. She tried taking deep, slow breaths to calm her insides, but nothing helped.

"This place was recommended for its Mexican food," Rick said as he pulled into a semicrowded parking lot. "I hope it's OK."

Katie nodded and swallowed hard.

The restaurant had a dim interior. A candle sat on each table. The decor was southwestern, and a mariachi band strolled throughout, playing loud Spanish tunes.

"Can we have a quiet corner?" Rick asked the hostess.

Once seated, they placed their orders. As soon as the waitress left, Rick said, "Katie, I want to apologize to you for our past. Now that I'm a Christian, I understand that as the man, it was my responsibility to protect your purity."

He paused and looked deep into her eyes. Katie felt her face heat up. She wanted to look away, but in light of his humility, she didn't. He seemed to expect some response from her, so she nodded.

He continued, "I loved you, Katie." He swallowed hard. "Even though now I know that what we did was a sin, I want you to understand how much I loved you. I never intended to hurt you. In my carnal state, it was the most natural thing in the world to make love to you." His voice cracked with emotion. "Please forgive me. I know I stole the most precious gift you had to give your future husband." His eyes looked watery to Katie, and his sorrow melted her heart. "I'd do anything if I could change the past, but I can't. I've long since confessed this to God, and in his grace he has forgiven me. Now I can only ask for your forgiveness."

Tears ran down her cheeks of their own volition. Katie wiped them away with her napkin, but more fell in their place.

"I don't know why you left, and I don't understand why you can't explain it to me. But I do realize that I've hurt you deeply. I'm sorry for everything, except the fact that I fell in love with you. I don't regret that for a minute, but I do regret the pain you feel because of me. Will you try to forgive me?"

Katie nodded just as the waitress brought their food. Lunch was a silent affair, and Katie used the time to try to make sense of everything. The things his mother had told her didn't match his words today. She felt more confused than ever. One thing did make sense: Rick felt deep remorse for their past choices, and he took full responsibility, even though she had played a willing part.

When the table was cleared, he asked, "Where do we go from here?"

Katie shrugged her shoulders, knowing she had to tell him about Kasey.

"I'd like to spend some time with you this week. Not anything romantic—I just miss my friend Katie."

She smiled ever so slightly, and he reached across the table and squeezed her hand. "What do you say?" he asked, and she heard the note of hope in his voice.

"Sure. Just give me some time, and don't ask questions. I'll try to help you understand why I left when I feel ready to talk about it."

"Deal." Again he reached across the table, but this time he shook her hand to seal their agreement. They rose and returned to his Explorer.

Katie longed for the simplicity of their summer romance. Why did life become difficult upon reaching adulthood? Her mind carried her back to the summer she had graduated from high school.

*"Good-bye, Lanae." She hugged her dearest friend in all the world. "See you in September."*

*"I wish you were coming with us," Lanae said sadly.*

*"Me, too. But you'll have a great time in Europe with or without me."*

*Katie watched Rick hug his sister and parents good-bye. "It's wonderful, Son, to leave the ranch in your hands. Enables me to enjoy this time off with my girls." Rick's dad shook his hand and moved forward with Lanae and his wife to the airline employee taking the boarding passes. Soon they were out of sight.*

*Katie sniffed, trying not to cry. Rick wrapped an arm around her shoulders, and his gentle gesture caused a wall of tears to break loose. He stopped right there in front of everyone and held her in his bear hug. She soaked the front of his*

*T-shirt. When her sobs turned to quiet hiccuping sounds, he loosened his hold.*

*"You ready now?" asked with a smile.*

*She smiled, too, feeling silly.* "Sorry. Three months just seems like forever. I'll be so bored and lonely."

*"Me, too. We can hang out together."*

That was the first time she found comfort in Rick's arms. As the summer progressed, they became her safe haven from life. In those strong, rock-solid arms, Katie found the comfort and love she needed—if only for that brief span of time.

"Looks like we're late for the first afternoon session," Rick commented as they drove up to the deserted-looking campus. "According to my watch, it started fifteen minutes ago. Do you want to walk until the next session begins?"

Katie nodded, climbing out of his vehicle. "Where to?"

"How about the prayer garden? It has some benches."

"Tell me how you came to know Christ." Katie wanted to steer the conversation far away from herself and Kasey.

"Well, after you left—" *After your disappearance devastated me, I started drinking to forget you,* he wanted to say. But Katie seemed so upset whenever he mentioned their past that he didn't want to bring up her part in what had happened to him. "Well, eventually I started drinking. I spent almost two years in a drunken stupor. My dad ended up firing me because I could no longer run the ranch. My parents asked me to quit drinking or move.

"I had no job, no money, and nowhere to go. Curly, a man we hired after you left, was a Christian. He found me in the barn, sitting on a bale of hay, crying my eyes out. He sat down next to me and told me about his own fight with alcohol. When he asked Jesus to forgive him and take over his life, the habit ended.

"I asked how I could know Christ. He told me I needed to repent, which isn't just feeling sorry but actually turning away from my sin. Right there on that bale of hay, I told God how sorry I was about you, about drinking, and about the mess I'd made of my life. I invited him to take charge, and a peace washed over me. I felt clean, free, and loved. Then I wept with joy.

"Curly bought me a Bible, started discipling me, and took me to church with him every week. I never touched another drink. As I grew in the Lord, I felt terrible about you and me and what we had done. I kept asking God to give me a chance to make things right. And here we are."

"Yes, here we are." Her conscience prodded her to share her testimony about getting saved at a home for unwed mothers—not to mention the fact that he had a daughter he'd never met. *Tomorrow, God. Let us have one nice day. I'll tell him tomorrow.* The old adage "Tomorrow never comes" echoed through her mind.

# CHAPTER THREE

Do you remember when I taught you to rope?" Rick sensed Katie's withdrawal and aimed for a lighter topic to draw her back.

"Yes." She laughed at the memory. "I never did get the hang of it."

"Somehow you always got yourself or Rocket tangled up in the rope." Now they both laughed, and the mood brightened by degrees.

"I wasn't much of a ranch hand. Though you do get an A for spending the summer patiently trying to teach me."

"You did OK. You already knew how to ride well and soon became a natural at herding cattle."

"I sure missed Lanae that summer. I would have died from boredom if you hadn't donated your time to teach me the ways of the West." Katie's eyes held a faraway, wistful look.

"Hey, if I remember right, you fed this poor old cowboy more than one home-cooked meal, and how many loads of dirty jeans did you wash on my behalf?"

"I hardly think grilled-cheese sandwiches count as home-cooked fare."

"Well, you made my mom's sour-cream enchiladas several times."

"That was the best recipe. I still love those things."

"Me too." *But not as much as I love you, Katie.*

"Do you remember when we trailered the horses to Sabino Canyon and rode all the way to Mt. Lemmon?"

"I remember you were a little freaked-out at times."

"I hated heights, and there we were on a narrow trail with a cliff on one side and a steep mountain on the other."

"You missed so much of the beauty because you refused to look around." Rick laughed at the memory of her sitting ramrod straight on Rocket's back, barely daring to breathe lest she cause her horse to slip.

"You kept talking, trying to calm my nerves, but in reality, you made me more tense."

"Finally you said, 'Rick, please, just shut up.' I didn't say another word until we reached the top."

"But you did whistle, which was even worse!"

They both broke into laughter. Rick glanced at his watch. "Wow, we'd better head back or we'll miss the next session too. Can I buy you dinner tonight?"

"I really need to spend some time with DeDe. Why don't I meet you after evening worship, and we'll go for coffee?"

"That'll work." He hoped his disappointment didn't seep into his voice. Since he had found her, he wanted to spend every moment with her. If he didn't get his mind back on this conference, his desire to get to know God better this week wouldn't be fulfilled.

As they walked together toward the conference rooms, Rick realized that falling for Katie had been the easiest, most natural thing in the world. Reliving the past served only to fortify his feelings in the present.

"Rick, thank you for lunch—" she paused—"and for everything. I'll see you tonight."

He nodded and smiled, watching Katie walk away. Her dark hair shimmered in the sunlight. He knew the "everything" meant his apology. Katie had always struggled to put serious topics into words. He had told her he loved her weeks before she worked up the courage to say it back, but that was Katie.

The afternoon session passed quickly. Rick spotted Katie, DeDe, and the little girl in the dining hall, but he respected Katie's desire to spend time with her friend and didn't approach them. Somehow he couldn't help watching them from afar, though.

Katie seemed more attentive to the child than her own mother did. He remembered how much she'd loved the baby animals on the ranch. She had nursed more than one calf or colt with a baby bottle. She had also stepped easily into the nurturing role of wife, even though no marriage had existed between them. And he would have married Katie in a quick second, if she'd given him the chance.

Rick made his way to the evening worship service, settling into the pew he'd sat in the night before. Had it been only twenty-four hours since Katie dropped back into his life? *God, please let her be part of my future. I want to make up for all the hurt I've caused her. I want to fill her life with joy, happiness, and love.*

Katie and Forever His led the worship. She seemed distracted and not as focused as last night. Then Harv Samuelson stepped up to the podium. "Tonight we'll discuss what I believe is the very key to spiritual growth: forgiving others. We're told to forgive as we've been forgiven, which means everything done against us, both the intentional and the unintentional."

Tonight Rick found it easy to listen to the message. He kept wondering if Katie listened intently too. Was this message meant for her? Was God asking her to forgive Rick for the pain he'd left in her heart? Would she be able to? Only the future would tell the story.

✶

Katie listened purposefully to Harv's message. God's timing never ceased to amaze her. Meeting Rick again after six years, and now the sermon speaking about forgiveness. After Rick's tender apology at lunch, her heart had softened and forgiveness had seemed possible, even easy. But the question nagged her, *Will Rick forgive me when he learns about Kasey?*

"Hi." At the sound of his voice, Katie turned to find Rick waiting for her in the emptied-out foyer. Her heart responded to the sight of him. She smiled, taking note of his rugged good looks. For a moment neither said a word; they just looked at each other. Rick's warm eyes told Katie he liked what he saw. She wondered if her eyes conveyed the same message to him.

"So—coffee—where? Here or Santa Fe?"

"Either. You choose."

"Let's drive to town, then." He took Katie's elbow to guide her out the door and toward the Explorer. His touch sent a shiver up her spine. The old feelings still lived in her heart; she'd buried them, but they were definitely not dead. After tomorrow, she doubted he'd want to renew their friendship, so this could be their last time together.

They chatted about trivial information regarding Santa Fe. The town held much history and charm. Then Katie asked, "Did you know Glorieta was the site of a very bloody Civil War battle?"

"No. I had no idea." Then he pointed out the window. "How about the Aztec Street Café? It's a coffeehouse."

"Looks great."

After parking the vehicle, they made their way inside to a quiet table. Rick stuck with his old favorite, black coffee. Katie ordered a café mocha.

Once they were settled with their drinks, Rick turned the conversation in a more serious direction. "You said you don't date. Don't you ever want to get married and have kids?"

Katie swallowed the hot liquid wrong and choked. "Wh-what?" she sputtered.

"I noticed you tonight at dinner with DeDe's little girl. You're so good with her, so nurturing. Don't you want any of your own?"

Katie nodded without verbalizing her answer. Surely that didn't constitute a lie. She did want more kids someday. She loved being Kasey's mom and would have a dozen kids if it didn't involve a man. "How about you? Do you want children?"

"At least a dozen," Rick said with a smile. Katie felt like he'd read her mind.

"A dozen? I hope you marry someone who feels the same way."

Rick nodded his agreement.

"Is there anyone special in your life? A future Mrs. Laramie?"

"I hope so. There is someone I'm crazy about, but I have no idea how she feels about me." His eyes lit up as he spoke.

Katie's heart dropped. That's why he had said he'd like to spend time with her but "not anything romantic." She found herself staring into her cup, wishing she hadn't asked. "I hope she likes kids. . . . Tell me about you, your life now." *Tell me about anything but your girlfriend.*

"Besides God, church, and the ranch, I don't have much life."

"What do you do for relaxation or entertainment?"

"I still enjoy ranch work tremendously. For me it's relaxing. I read a lot. I try to soak up a few Christian books each month besides my regular time in Bible study."

"Who's your favorite author?"

"I like the classics: Spurgeon, Chambers, Murray."

"Obviously your relationship with God means a lot to you."

"It means everything. When you've been as low as I have, you truly understand his incredible love and grace. My heart's desire is to be Christlike and to really know him. I want to be salt and light in my parents' dark world. Only if I live the truth of Christ before them do I stand a chance for them to listen to my words."

"A picture is worth a thousand words." Katie understood that from her days at Mercy Ministries of America.

"And someday," Rick got a yearning look in his eyes, "I

want to be a godly husband and father. I want to be the man God intends for me to be, for the woman he created to share my life with me."

Katie felt choked up by his admission. That was exactly what she desired for Kasey, a godly father. "Can we go?" Katie knew her request sounded abrupt, but she couldn't keep listening to his dreams and plans. She stood, grabbed her coat, and walked to the front door, hoping he didn't notice the tears pooling in her eyes.

\\\\//

It took Rick a minute to catch up. One moment he was answering her questions and honestly sharing his heart, the next Katie appeared agitated and stormed out. He grabbed his coat, tossed a ten on the table, and followed her to his Ford. He walked to the passenger door, placing the key in the lock.

"Katie—" he lifted her chin with his index finger—"what just happened?"

"I'm really tired and didn't sleep well last night." Her eyes were glassy with unshed tears, so he didn't press the issue.

"I'll take you back."

No one spoke on the drive back, and Rick pulled up right in front of Texas Hall to drop her off. "Katie," he said just before she closed the door, "I'm sorry. For what, I don't know, but I'm sorry."

She only nodded and shut the door. Would he ever figure her out? He parked in front of the Hall of States, but instead of going to his room, he walked toward the lake. Rick walked for what seemed like hours but drew no conclusions about Katie, life, or God's will.

\\\\//

The next morning Rick found an unoccupied table in the dining hall. Not in the mood for conversation, he avoided human

124

contact. He read Psalm 77 as he ate and felt as discouraged as Asaph had.

> *I cry out to God without holding back.*
> *Oh, that God would listen to me!*
> *When I was in deep trouble,*
> *I searched for the Lord.*
> *All night long I pray, with hands lifted toward heaven,*
> *   pleading.*
> *There can be no joy for me until he acts.*

"Rick?" Katie's tentative voice drew his eyes away from his Bible. She looked colorless and afraid. "May I join you?"

He nodded, sensing her trepidation. She sat across from him, taking a deep breath. Her brown eyes lacked their usual sparkle, and her face looked tight and drawn. She seemed to have something important on her mind, so he waited for her to speak.

"Kasey is my daughter." Her eyes didn't quite meet his.

"I beg your pardon?"

"Kasey—the little girl—I'm her mother."

Rick's heart jolted at her announcement. *Was he the father?* "How old is she?"

"Five."

No, he couldn't be her father. It had been over six years since he and Katie were together. Katie must have met someone within weeks of leaving him.

"What did you do, go straight from my bed into someone else's?" His voice sounded harsh, accusing.

"No." Hers sounded weak and ashamed.

"I don't understand. While I grieved the loss of you, you'd already met someone else? You slept with another man and bore his child? I thought we loved each other. I thought what we shared meant something to you. Then you just go out and find someone else?" His voice quaked with deep pain.

"No. That's not how it happened." Tears streamed down her cheeks, and the words were spoken in an agonized whisper.

"So how did it happen, Katie? Is that why you left—because you found something better?" Anger coursed through him at the reality of the situation. He had spent years mourning the loss of a myth. "Did you marry the guy?"

Katie only shook her bowed head. She apparently couldn't even look at him. He needed air. Breathing was difficult. He couldn't remember ever feeling this furious, except maybe when she had disappeared. He wanted to slam his fist into a wall. Maybe he hadn't really been her first at all. Maybe that was a lie too.

Rick grabbed his Bible and walked out. He didn't even glance back at her. He'd never walked out on anyone before, but he'd watched Katie, the pro, do it often enough.

\|\|\|/

Katie had expected Rick's anger, but his reaction measured about ten on the Richter scale. Usually the cool, unshakable one, today he'd shown her a different side. Her head ached from all the crying she'd done last night and this morning. Rising from the table, Katie dumped her untouched food into the trash.

Dragging herself back up the hill to her room, she kept her eyes on the ground. She prayed that no one would stop her to chat, for visiting with a friendly stranger was more than she could handle right now. She longed to curl up in a ball of misery on her bed and cry until no tears remained.

DeDe had volunteered to take Kasey to child care this morning so Katie and Rick could talk. When she unlocked the door, the room sat empty. Katie fell onto her bed and gave in to the sobs. Sometime later she heard DeDe enter.

"I passed an angry-looking Rick and wondered if I'd find you here. I assume things didn't go well."

"No," Katie said, sniffing.

DeDe handed her the box of tissues off the dresser. "What happened?" She walked over to her bed and sat down facing Katie. Katie sat up on the edge of her bed.

"He's really mad. He thinks I left him for another guy."

"You didn't tell him Kasey is his?"

"I couldn't. He never gave me a chance. Besides, he has a girlfriend. I don't want him to feel obligated to us. He really likes this girl, and I don't want him to resent Kasey." She remembered the way his eyes had lit up last night when he spoke of someone special.

"Katie," DeDe sounded exasperated, "those are all just excuses. You have to tell him the truth, all of it."

Knowing DeDe was right made Katie angry, and she lashed out at her friend. "That's easy for you to say! Maybe you should try a day in my moccasins before you give advice!"

"I'm sorry. You're right. I don't know how tough this is, but Rick is a nice man. Give him a chance."

"I planned to tell him I had a daughter and hoped he'd want to meet her, get to know her. Then when he realized he adored her, I proposed to mention that she was his. I envisioned him joyfully receiving the news and becoming the godly father he dreams of someday being." Her voice choked over her dying hopes.

DeDe came and sat next to her, wrapping her in a hug. "I'll keep praying. I know you'll tell him when you're ready."

The problem was, would she ever be ready? Katie knew she never embraced difficult situations but fled from them.

# CHAPTER FOUR

The brisk morning air did nothing to relieve the ache in Rick's heart. He walked fast, his anger propelling him forward. Dead, crumpled leaves crunched under his feet as he walked through the prayer garden. The bare trees, towering among the pines, looked as desolate as he felt.

*Father God, I'm so mad, so hurt. How could this happen?* After pacing through the prayer garden, reliving the scene between him and Katie just minutes before, he finally sat down on a short stone wall. He bent and picked up a dry, curling leaf. It crumbled in his hand just as his hopes for a relationship with Katie had crumbled in his heart.

*"Forgive as you've been forgiven."* Harv's words from last night's sermon returned to him now. "How, God? How can I ever trust her, ever believe anything she says?" This betrayal hurt even worse than her running away six years before had.

Rick's mind recalled the many things God had forgiven him for. How could he not forgive Katie? Yet he didn't want to. "Forgiving is a choice," Harv had said, "not a feeling." Would he make that choice? Could he make that choice?

Rick bowed his head and poured out his heart to God. *I don't want to forgive her. She doesn't deserve it—yet neither did I.* The thought kept nagging him. Forgiveness wasn't earned or deserved but freely given by a loving God and by his loving people.

*Help me, God. Give me the strength and courage to do the right thing.*

Rick let out a long sigh and wearily ran a hand through his hair. Life was never easy, but he'd always found God to be enough.

Rick rose and walked back toward the meeting rooms. He felt battle weary, and it wasn't even noon yet. As he passed the lake, he spotted DeDe sitting at a picnic table, watching the ducks. She glanced up just as he hoped to sneak by.

"Hello, Rick."

He smiled at her and nodded, not in the mood for chitchat.

"Do you have a minute?" she asked.

Reluctantly he joined her on the opposite bench, wishing he'd taken another route. He looked into DeDe's blue eyes, expecting a lecture. He knew his posture appeared defensive, but he didn't care.

"I know you and Katie had a misunderstanding, and I wanted you to know I'm praying for both of you."

Her honest, nonjudgmental statement took the edge off his attitude. He smiled slightly. "Thanks." His eyes roamed across the lake, envying the ducks for their free, uncomplicated lives. He looked back at DeDe, noting the compassion reflected in her eyes.

"You still love her, don't you?" she asked softly.

"Am I that obvious?"

DeDe nodded and chuckled. "I'm a romantic. I can spot a man in love a mile away."

"I never got over her. I tried to shake the memory, but she haunted me."

At his long pause DeDe finished his unvoiced thoughts aloud. "Now you feel betrayed."

He nodded, amazed by her perception.

"Remember, nothing in life is ever as cut-and-dried as it first seems."

"Meaning . . . ?" *Here comes the lecture.*

"You've brought this down to one simple choice of right or wrong, but there is so much more to it. You assume Katie willfully betrayed you, but you don't even know the whole story. You must know how she struggles with facing issues in her life. Give her a chance to tell the whole tale before you send her to the gallows."

A stabbing sensation hit his heart at her words. "Touché. I did immediately assume the worst."

"Please be patient with her, Rick, and don't tell her we had this conversation. She'd kill me for interfering." DeDe got up and strode away, leaving Rick to contemplate her words and Harv's message on forgiveness. He chuckled at his own vain assumption last night that the sermon was for Katie. He obviously had much to learn himself on the topic of forgiving others.

Looking back, he suddenly understood Katie's bizarre reaction to last night's conversation on children. Now her walking out made sense. He'd led her to a topic that was extremely uncomfortable for her because she obviously didn't want to tell him the truth. Being an unwed mother must have brought Katie a great deal of pain. The realization softened his angry heart a tad.

※

Katie dreaded evening worship. Not only were she and Rick at odds, but tonight it would be her turn to share her testimony. She'd carefully wade through the beginning, so Rick wouldn't figure out the truth. She'd start with her days at Mercy Ministries of America rather than when she left the ranch.

Her heart reminded her that she must eventually disclose Kasey's parentage to Rick, but she wouldn't do it in an auditorium full of people. Maybe she'd tell him on the last day of the conference. Yes, that would work.

After dinner, Katie kissed Kasey good-bye and waved to DeDe. As they walked back toward the room, she strolled in the opposite direction to the prayer garden. She needed time alone with the Lord to prepare for tonight.

Katie snuggled into her coat, buttoning the top button against the chill. As she roamed through the prayer garden, a spectacular sunset caught her eye, reminding her that God was still in control and that he still loved her completely. Peace flooded her soul. "Thank you," she whispered, never taking her eyes from his palette in the sky. Slowly the brilliance was replaced by night, and Katie made her way to the evening service.

"Welcome to our third night of worship!" Rejuvenated in the prayer garden, Katie greeted the congregation enthusiastically. "Did you all see God's handiwork in the sky tonight? What a sunset! I couldn't help thinking of the words Job penned so long ago: 'Where does the light come from, and where does the darkness go?' Only God could put those hues in the sky. Only God . . ."

With reverence, Katie and Forever His led them in a resounding chorus of "I Stand in Awe of You." Then they sang several other worship choruses before Katie stepped up to the podium.

"Tonight I want to share with you my journey to Christ." She paused, looking out over the crowd. In the third pew, center section, sat Rick, his eyes fixed on her. Katie swallowed hard, noticing that Kasey and DeDe shared his pew. Kasey's face beamed up at her mother. Katie sent a smile in her direction.

"First I'd like to introduce you to my daughter. Kasey, would you stand up on the pew for a minute, so everyone can meet you?" Kasey had not a shy bone in her body, so she happily obliged. She stood on her tiptoes in the pew next to Rick. He reached out a hand to steady her balance. Kasey grinned and waved in Miss America fashion to the crowd's oohs and aahs.

"Thank you, sweetheart." When Kasey returned to her place on the pew, she sat much closer to Rick than before.

"Kasey is a precious gift from God. But when I discovered I carried a child in my womb, joy was not my first reaction. Terror was. As an unmarried teenage girl, the thought of becoming a mother frightened me. I had no one to turn to, nowhere to go.

"By God's divine providence, someone I knew had just heard about Mercy Ministries of America. Mercy runs two homes—one in Monroe, Louisiana, and one in Nashville, Tennessee—for unwed mothers as well as girls with eating disorders, drug or alcohol dependency, or any other life-controlling problem.

"I went to the home in Nashville the day after I found out I was pregnant. I feared going to what I imagined would be a horrible place, but I found a beautiful home with grass, trees, and even four dogs. My first impression when I arrived was this incredible peace that seemed to surround the place, and I felt warmth and hope. It wasn't an institution, as I had expected, but a home, and the other girls became my family.

"At Mercy, I experienced unconditional love. It was easy to grasp God's love because the people there loved me with their actions. I knew I was a sinner—and they obviously knew it too!—but I felt no judgment or condemnation. They loved me and accepted me from day one. It was awesome!

"Eventually I came to understand and accept God's forgiveness through Jesus Christ—not only for my sexual sin but for every sin I'd ever committed. New life in Christ is the greatest gift I've ever received.

"I thank God that he took my liabilities and made them assets. He used my precious unborn daughter to lead me to Jesus. He redeemed my mistake. Kasey is the bright spot in my life. She reminds me daily of God's mercy, of where I've been and where I'm headed. His love is incredible, just as the life I experienced at Mercy was incredible.

"Now I'm a secretary at their corporate office. I have the privilege of seeing God change lives on a daily basis. I want to encourage those of you who are feeling overwhelmed by your own circumstances—God can turn your liabilities into assets too. Though people may use you or hurt you, God can and will get you through."

Katie paused, her eyes settling on Rick. Kasey now leaned her head against his side. *She's never met a stranger,* Katie thought lovingly. Rick's arm draped around her in casual fashion. The picture pierced her heart with incredible longing.

"Harv will now continue to challenge us to grow as Christians." Katie smiled at Harv and left the podium.

Unsure where to sit, Katie paused a moment just offstage. DeDe motioned her to them, so she sat between Kasey and DeDe, leaving Kasey between her and Rick. As she listened to Harv's message on unconditional love, an awareness of Rick and Kasey filled her. She realized this was the closest they would ever come to being a family, sharing the same church pew.

To the unknowing eye, they looked like a family unit, the daddy, the mommy, and the little girl. Kasey laid her head in Katie's lap and her feet in Rick's. Katie leaned over to remove them, but Rick stopped her. His touch sent wild currents pulsating through her arm. He smiled and whispered, "She's fine." His eyes had warmed by at least a hundred degrees since this morning. Dared she hope?

\\\\//

Harv's take on spiritual growth surprised Rick. First Harv spoke on striving toward Christlikeness, then on forgiving others, and now on unconditional love. Harv believed that much of a person's spiritual growth came out of interaction with other people.

"Our connection with God is much easier to maintain, but growth lies in our relationships with other people, in the challenge of not reacting to people who hurt, mistreat, or use us. Growth in Christ comes when we, like him, choose to unconditionally love that person in spite of the pain, disappointment, or sorrow they've caused us. Only in forgiving and loving can we come close to being like Jesus."

Harv's words penetrated Rick's remaining anger, and he knew that he must find it in his heart to forgive Katie. He looked at the sleeping child between them, a beautiful little girl with Katie's eyes and an exuberant personality. The question was, would he allow her to remain between them as a liability to their future, or could he allow God to make her an asset in their relationship?

When Harv began to pray, Rick lifted the sleeping child into his arms so Katie could return to the stage. As he held Kasey against his heart, he acknowledged that she'd be easy to love; after all, he loved her mother.

After the service ended, Rick remained seated with Kasey. "I'll take her so you don't have to wait around for Katie," DeDe offered.

"I think I'd like to wait, if you don't mind." DeDe nodded, so he continued, "By the way, I took your words to heart this morning. Thanks."

She smiled, touching Kasey's cheek tenderly. "She'll steal your heart if you give her a chance."

"Are you talking about Kasey or her mother?"

"Both." DeDe winked.

"One already has." He traced the shape of Kasey's pug nose with his index finger. Her slightly pudgy cheeks appeared highly kissable. "The other looks like a viable possibility."

"I'm glad. Nobody deserves happiness more than Katie. She's a jewel."

"You two are close?"

"She's like a sister to me. If you hurt her, you'll have me to answer to—got that, buster?"

"Got it." He saluted her with his left hand because his right arm remained full of little girl.

"Thanks for inviting us to sit with you tonight. I think I'll disappear now so you and Katie can talk. I'll let her know you and Kasey await her company. See you later."

"OK, and thanks, DeDe—for everything."

Rick thought back over Katie's words during her testimony. This little girl, however she was conceived and whoever her father was, was the tool God had used to draw Katie to himself. How could he resent her? How could he be angry? How could he not love her? Without her, he and Katie might have never met in this place, at this time.

"Hi." Tears pooled in Katie's eyes as she gazed upon him holding her daughter.

His heart lurched at the sight of her. "Hi." He slid over and patted the pew next to him, and she settled there. "I'm sorry about this morning. Please forgive me. As I listened to your testimony, I realized what an idiot I am. I reacted like a jealous nut. Once again I throw myself upon your mercy. Can you forgive me?"

Katie nodded, and tears ran unchecked down her cheeks.

"I also seem to cause you to cry quite often." He placed his free arm around her shoulders and drew her against him. She laid her head on his chest, and his heart constricted. He rested his cheek against the top of her head. Holding Katie in one arm and Kasey in the other felt really right to him. For several minutes he enjoyed the privilege of freely hugging them both.

"Are you soaking my shirt? That seems to be a habit of yours," Rick joked to lighten the mood.

"One of my worst." Katie wiped her damp cheeks with her fingers. Kasey squirmed in Rick's arms. "I'd better get her to bed. Thanks for watching her for me."

"I'll carry her up to your room. She must be pretty heavy for you, especially trudging up the hill to Texas Hall."

Katie smiled. "Thank you."

They walked in quiet contemplation. Rick wondered if Katie felt all the crazy things he did. After she opened the door, Rick carried Kasey into the room, laying her on the double bed. He sat on the edge and removed her shoes.

The look of tenderness on Katie's face made him want to

kiss her. Instead he quickly made his way to the open doorway. "I'll leave so you can get Kasey into her pj's." He reached out his hand, laying it against her cheek. "Good night, Katie." Before he weakened, he quickly closed the door.

# CHAPTER FIVE

Katie touched her face where Rick's hand had just lingered. She leaned back against the wall, not sure her legs were steady enough to hold her up. Her heart pounded in her chest, and her emotions whirled within her like a tumbleweed caught up in a dust devil.

What was happening? Sitting in the pew with his protective arm around her earlier, a contentment had filled Katie that scared her to death. She found herself wanting to spend a lifetime in those arms.

The way he looked at her, hugged her against him, and touched her left Katie filled with questions. These were not the overtures of an older brother or someone who was just a good friend. His actions spoke of a man attracted to a woman, but what about his girlfriend? And what about their past? Perhaps God offered them a new beginning as Christians and none of those things mattered.

Katie floated through her prebedtime routine, including getting Kasey undressed and into bed. She loved Rick, still. Her first and only love held her heart in his hands. His tenderness and humility had torn down the walls that stood between them. Nothing that happened could change the feelings of love her heart declared to be true.

A smile lingered on her lips long after she turned off the lights and crawled under the covers with Kasey. She'd fallen hard for Rick all those years ago, and as much as she'd tried to hate him and get over him, neither had happened. Even feeling damaged and fearful of men, she still loved him. Even losing her heart and her ability to trust because of him, she loved him still. Every time she held their child, a part of him, of them, she realized again that she loved him. Despite the pain of their relationship, he had given her Kasey, and for that she'd always love him.

\|\|\|/

A knock at the door woke Katie. The clock showed seven in the morning. At first she wondered if it was DeDe, but DeDe lay sleeping in the twin bed across the room. Katie grabbed her robe, realizing she had slept like a rock last night, not even hearing DeDe come in.

She pushed her tousled hair out of her face and opened the door. "Rick!" she whispered, surprised. A smile lit his face and eyes. He stood before her, looking better than she could ever remember, holding a red rose that he offered to her.

Suddenly the fog of sleep lifted, and Katie's brain kicked into gear. She took the extended bud and lifted it to her nose, enjoying the sweet fragrance. A single red rose—didn't that mean "I love you"? She smiled at Rick; a tender expression on his face echoed back at her.

He took her arm, pulling her into the hall and closing the door behind them. "Will you and Kasey spend the day with me?" he whispered. "I feared if I waited until a decent hour, you'd be gone."

It touched her heart deeply that his invitation included Kasey. "We'd love to."

"When should I come back for you?"

"Give us half an hour." Just like the night before, he laid his hand against her cheek for a moment, looking into her eyes. Then he turned and left.

*Lord, please protect my heart. I love this man, but what are his intentions?*

\\\\//

At the knock on their door half an hour later, a perky Kasey answered. "Hi, Rick. Mommy says we're spending the day with you. Did you see the miniature golf place they have here?"

His eyes rose to meet Katie's as she stood behind Kasey. "That is her polite way of letting you know her desires without actually asking," Katie explained, laughing at her daughter's antics.

Rick squatted down to Kasey's level. "Do you like golf?" At her nod, he continued, "Well, then, you and I have a date later today, but let's feed your tummy first, OK?" She nodded again and smiled up at her mom.

He rose, took Kasey's hand, and led her down the stairs and out into the cool morning air. "Where to?"

"McDonald's." Kasey supplied the answer.

"McDonald's it is." Rick led them to his Explorer.

"Are we ditching the whole day?" Katie asked.

"Is that OK with you? Being with you two seems more important than anything else today."

"Just so I'm back for evening worship." Her heart rejoiced at his declaration.

"I thought we'd let Kasey plan the day. I want it to be fun for her."

At McDonald's, Katie and Kasey found a table while Rick ordered. After they finished eating, Kasey went to the playground and they moved to a table next to the window to watch her play.

"She's a great kid." Rick reached out and covered Katie's hand with his. "About yesterday—"

"You don't need to explain," Katie cut in before he could continue.

"Yes, I do." He turned away from the window and looked deep into Katie's eyes. "I said some horrible things. I was jealous. You see—" he paused, glancing at Kasey—"I'm still in love with you."

Katie closed her eyes, reveling in his words. "You are?" Her voice sounded weak, yet hopeful.

"I am." His smile seemed brighter than the sun shining through the windows. "I never got over you."

"What about your girlfriend?" Katie had to ask the question uppermost in her mind. The question that had nagged her since that night at the coffeehouse.

"I don't have a girlfriend. I haven't dated at all since I became a Christian. I kept asking God to bring you back to me."

"But at the Aztec Street Café when I asked if there was anyone special in your life, a future Mrs. Laramie, you said, 'I hope so. There is someone I'm crazy about.'"

Rick patted her hand and smiled. "That was you, Katie. I was talking about you. I am crazy about you. I had planned to marry you someday, but you disappeared. I never canceled those plans."

She could scarcely keep up with all he said. But her heart celebrated his words of love.

"I nursed this hope that you had waited for me, too, and learning that you hadn't drove me into a jealous fit. Can you forgive my behavior yesterday?"

Katie nodded. This was the time to tell him the truth. He loved her, and he would be glad to learn that there had been no other man, ever.

"Do you mind if I go out and play with Kasey?" Rick asked after a short pause.

"No, I'll finish my coffee and join you." Katie felt relieved that the moment to tell him had passed, but she vowed to do it today.

∿

Rick joined Kasey, feeling disappointed that Katie hadn't expressed her feelings for him. He reminded himself that that was her normal mode of operation. *Be patient. You can see it in her eyes. In time, she'll say the words aloud.* Rick tried to reassure himself, but he really needed to hear those three special words from Katie's lips.

Katie joined him and Kasey, and they buried her in the plastic balls. After enjoying the McDonald's playground for a while, Rick asked, "What do you want to do next?"

"Golf," Kasey answered, her expression hopeful.

"And then what?"

Kasey looked to her mom and then shrugged.

"OK, listen to my idea and tell me what you think. The Santa Fe Children's Museum is supposed to be lots of fun. We could go there next, then have lunch wherever you say, then go back to Glorieta to golf and ride bikes. How does that sound?"

Her brown eyes lit up, and a smile shone bright. She jumped up and down, "Yes, yes, yes! Is that OK, Mommy?"

"Sure, honey." Katie bent down to retie Kasey's shoelace.

Rick held out a hand to each of his girls. *Father God, I pray that one day they will really be my girls.*

At the museum, Kasey had a wonderful time. Their "Do Touch" policy was every child's dream. Rick and Katie followed Kasey from one display to another. She stopped at a magnet table, mesmerized by the magnets' force.

"Is her dad a part of her life?" Rick wondered aloud as he watched her play. Glancing at Katie, he saw that her face had gone pale. "Are you OK?"

"Yeah, I'm fine," she said, but her voice sounded unconvincing. "No, she never sees her dad."

Kasey must have overheard the conversation. She looked up from her seat at the magnet table and announced, "I'm named after my daddy. He lives far, far away, but someday he might visit us."

"Kasey," Katie snapped, "Mommy's hungry. Can we go now?"

Surprise etched itself on Kasey's features.

*She must not hear that tone from her mother very often.* Rick made two mental notes: *Katie is extremely uncomfortable talking about Kasey's father, yet she named her daughter after him.* Those two items seemed contradictory in his mind.

"Hey, pumpkin, what does your tummy say it wants for lunch?" He lifted Kasey into his arms and spun her around, hoping to erase the hurt look from her little face. He wouldn't repeat the mistake of mentioning her father, especially if Kasey was within earshot.

"Pizza." Her smile returned. "Maybe *you* could be my daddy."

"Kasey!" Katie's expression was nothing less than horrified. Her face lit up like Rudolph's nose when she looked at Rick. "I'm sorry. She's recently become aware of daddies and the fact that hers is missing. She's noticed that most of her classmates have what she lacks. It's been on her mind lately."

"It's really OK." He impulsively kissed Kasey's cheek. "It's the nicest request I've heard in a long time." He took Katie's hand, changed the subject, and led the way to the car. *Maybe I could be her new daddy, Lord.*

After pizza, the trio drove back to Glorieta. "Next stop, the golf course," Rick announced.

Kasey again jumped up and down, smiling and cheering. After they picked up their clubs and balls, Kasey took the first swing. She enjoyed Rick's attention and looked to him for approval after she hit each ball.

"Great job, Kasey." He cheered her on. Looking at Katie, he said, "You asked about my goals the other day but didn't tell me yours." She had been very quiet since the daddy conversation, and Rick wanted to draw her out.

"I want to enjoy every moment I have with Kasey and raise her to be a woman who loves God. She's pretty much my whole focus right now."

"And you avoid men." He jokingly reminded her of another goal she'd mentioned previously.

"At all cost."

"What about the music business? DeDe's your agent, and you said something about trying to break in."

"That's really an exaggeration. I realized that giving Kasey a stable home life appealed to me more than traipsing all over the country. DeDe is really my best friend, and because she is an agent, she occasionally gets me a gig, like the one here, for example."

He removed their three balls from the hole, returning each one to its proper owner. They followed the arrows to their next shot. "So you're not really aiming for the big time."

"No. I like being home with Kasey too much."

"Tell me about home."

"We live in an apartment on the third floor with a great view overlooking the Cumberland River."

"Do you like Nashville?"

"I love it. It's incredibly green compared to Arizona. Kasey and I go to a wonderful church. I sing in the choir, and she's in Awana."

"My church has Awana too. I work with the junior high boys."

"You're kidding!" Delight filled her voice. "I work with the Cubbies."

Spontaneously, Rick hugged her tight and kissed her on the forehead. "Providence," he said with a smile.

"What?" Katie looked skeptical.

"Divine providence. We both work in Awana. We're meant to be together."

He watched a blush spread over Katie's face. He kissed her

nose, winked, and got back to the game of golf. After an exhilarating finish, which Kasey won, they returned their balls and clubs, then rented bikes. Rick's had a child's seat attached for Kasey.

They rode all through the Glorieta grounds, even the roads back by the private facilities. They didn't talk much but just enjoyed the scenery and being together. Rick felt high on life. At this moment, he lived his dream. He smiled over at the rider next to him. *Katie, oh, how I love you.*

\\\\\\/

Katie smiled back at Rick. The look in his eyes nearly sent her toppling over on her bike. She'd avoided all thoughts of him these last six years because the pain that accompanied those thoughts had proved unbearable. Now she couldn't stop thinking about him, his eyes, his smile, and that adorable crease in his left cheek. And his arms . . . How she loved those rock-solid arms, especially when they were wrapped around her.

Evening approached as they returned the bikes. "What a day! Thank you, Rick." Katie wanted to say more, but that was all she could muster. He sent her a smile, and she watched him tenderly lift their daughter from the child's bike seat. Instead of setting her down, he wrapped her in those incredible arms. Kasey wrapped hers around his neck. Their faces were inches apart.

"How about you, pumpkin? Did you have fun?"

Her eyes sparkled, and her yes left no question of how much she had enjoyed the day. Rick held her close for a moment, kissed her cheek, and placed her on her feet.

He looked at Katie. "How much time do you have before you need to get ready for tonight's service?"

Looking at her watch, she said, "Less than an hour."

"How about a burger at the Chuck Wagon, then?"

Kasey answered with a wholehearted, "Yes!"

Rick's eyes met Katie's again, and they chuckled over Kasey's reply. "She doesn't care for the dining-hall food," Katie informed him.

After dinner, Rick walked them back to their room. At the door, he lifted Kasey to tell her good-bye. She gave him a hug and a kiss, then ran inside to tell DeDe about her day.

Katie and Rick stared at each other for endless moments. "Can I see you later tonight?" he finally asked.

"You mean you're not sick of me yet?" Katie joked, hoping to keep the conversation light. Even though she longed to hear his words of love again, she wasn't prepared to respond to his proclamations yet. First she must get things out in the open.

"Never, but I'd like to spend a lifetime figuring out if I ever could be." His eyes danced, and her heart reacted. "Tonight?" He raised one brow and plastered a pleading look on his face.

Katie nodded, not trusting her voice. He leaned forward, placing a kiss on her cheek just as he had done with Kasey. His warm breath sent a shiver down her spine. She watched him walk away, and everything in her wanted to call out to him, *Rick, I love you!* Instead she whispered a prayer to God. "Please don't let him hurt me. I don't want to feel that much pain again, not ever. Please, God, let us be OK."

# Chapter Six

The day had gone far better than Rick could have imagined. "Thank you, Lord," he whispered with a grin. He wondered if he'd ever stop smiling again. All those years of earnest prayers had paid off. Katie was close, very close, to being his again!

Sitting in the pew tonight next to Katie and with Kasey's head in his lap brought to the forefront his desire for them to become a family unit. He sensed a real contentment in Katie as well. Finally the crowd died down in the foyer, and she approached him.

Her faced glowed with what he hoped was happiness. Her eyes sparkled, and a smile lit her face when their eyes met. Rick's heart flipped over itself when he saw the expression in her eyes. His "hi" sounded husky.

"Hi, yourself." Their eyes communicated secrets that neither put into words. "DeDe offered to watch Kasey, so we can enjoy some time alone."

"Sounds promising." He lifted an eyebrow.

Katie blushed and broke their cow-eyed stare. "Where to?"

He took her hand, leading her out the door and into the

cold night. "Do you want to walk for a while? We'll have to keep moving to avoid freezing to death."

They strolled along in silence.

Finally Katie said softly, "This was a really nice day, Rick. Thank you."

"For me, too."

"You stole my daughter's heart. She talked about you non-stop while we got ready for the service tonight, and I noticed how she cuddled right up against you on the pew. You even got the privilege of holding her head instead of her feet tonight."

"She's something else. You're a lucky woman, Katie O'Malley." The thought of Kasey brought a smile to his lips and a stirring to his heart.

"You're very good with kids. I hope God gives you the dozen you dream of."

"Just think, if you're in God's plan for my future, we have a head start." He heard Katie's sharp intake of breath, but she made no comment, so he let the subject drop. *Don't rush her,* he reminded himself. *Katie wades into life more slowly than you do.* "Tell me more about Mercy Ministries of America. It sounds intriguing." He felt Katie relax at his change of subject.

"God gave Nancy, the president and founder, an incredible vision to reach the hurting for Christ. She believes that, regardless of their sin, we, as Christians, must extend the unconditional love of Christ to them. She says nothing else will work. I believe she's right.

"She operates the homes debt free, by faith, and there is no cost to the girls. If there had been, I could never have gone. Over fifteen hundred girls have passed through Mercy's doors in the past fifteen years, many, like me, whose lives were irrevocably changed by the love of Jesus Christ.

"They even offer a private adoption service for the girls who choose not to keep their babies, and they educated us on the pros and cons of both single parenting and adoption. Each girl prayerfully makes the right decision for herself, with no outside pressure whatsoever."

"Did you consider giving up Kasey?"

"No," she replied emphatically.

"Not even for a minute?"

"Not even for a microsecond."

"I'm glad you didn't."

"So am I."

They ambled for what seemed like hours, sometimes in a comfortable silence and sometimes in easy conversation.

"It's late. I should get up to my room," Katie finally said. He thought he heard regret in her voice.

"Sure." He would have walked all night, even though his feet were dog tired, just to stay in her company. "What's on your agenda for tomorrow?"

"DeDe arranged a meeting with the conference coordinator here. She's hoping to get me a few engagements next year as part of a worship team. Would you like to pick Kasey up from her classroom, just in case my appointment runs late? Then DeDe and I could meet you for lunch."

"I'd love to," Rick answered with a smile.

Katie informed him of the time and place to fetch Kasey and told him she would clear it with the teacher. She and DeDe would meet them at the Chuck Wagon as soon as they could get there.

When they arrived at Katie's room, she said, "I enjoyed tonight. At least all of me but my feet did." She stood facing him, her hand on the doorknob. Her smile, her eyes, her creamy ivory skin all looked beautiful to him. He swallowed hard. Katie looked away. "Good night, Rick."

His hand reached out to her, his index finger drawing her chin up until their gazes connected. "Good night, Katie," he said in a low whisper. Then his lips found hers in a tender, reverent kiss.

He heard Katie sigh when the kiss ended. He smiled at the contented sound of it.

"Rick?" Her voice sounded tentative. "I need to tell you about Kasey's dad."

Her chin still rested on his finger, and he raised his thumb to cover her lips. "Not right now, Katie. It's late, and this day was too perfect for us to spoil." He kissed the tip of her nose. "Tell me tomorrow. That's soon enough."

She nodded, a ghost of a smile touching her lips. He drew her to himself, in what Katie used to refer to as his bear hug. He whispered, "I love you, Katie," near her ear and kissed her cheek.

She opened the door, and just before it closed, he heard her soft, "Me, too." It wasn't those three little words his heart ached to hear, but it was close enough to make him race down the stairs and kick his heels together when he reached the bottom.

\\\\\

Rick slept better than he had in years. He awoke and found the most beautiful day before him. The sun shone, the birds sang, and Katie loved him. Katie loved him! He longed to shout it from the mountaintops and tell every person he saw. Instead he just repeated it over and over to himself.

Rick found Kasey's classroom at the appointed time. "Kasey O'Malley," he said to the woman at the door. As promised, Katie had arranged with the teacher for him to pick her up.

"Rick!" An excited Kasey ran into his arms.

"Hey, pumpkin, did you have a good morning?" He felt as happy to see her as she seemed at seeing him. After a warm hug, they turned to walk away, hand in hand.

"Kasey," the teacher called after them, "don't forget your artwork."

Kasey ran back and returned carrying a rolled-up poster. "Here, Rick, I made this for you."

He took her extended gift. "Why, thank you. I'll treasure it always."

"It's a picture of me," she announced proudly. "Do you want to see it?"

"I sure do. Let's go up to those tables so I can unroll it."

He examined Kasey's self-portrait while she stood on the bench watching and smiling. Someone had traced an outline of her, and she had colored in the details. At the bottom of the paper, Rick spotted Kasey's vital statistics written in an adult hand.

He read them aloud. "Name: Kendra Colleen O'Malley. Nickname: Kasey. Age: Five and a half. Birth date: April 16, 1993."

A pain knifed through Rick's heart as realization dawned: He was Kasey's father. He leaned against the table, tears blurring his vision.

"Don't you like it?"

He looked at Kasey's puzzled expression. Gently he enfolded her in his arms. "I love it, pumpkin. Nobody's ever given me a better present." His voice sounded husky and emotional. He rerolled the picture and pulled himself together. He must act normal for Kasey's sake. "I really love it." *My precious daughter*. He hugged her again and set her on the ground. They walked together, father and daughter, to the Chuck Wagon.

Rick had never felt so torn in his life. On the one hand, he was moved to tears at the knowledge that this beautiful, precious child was his—a part of him, a part of the woman he loved with all his heart. And yet he was devastated at what Katie had done. The love of his life had not only vanished without a trace but had also kept from him the most incredible gift a man could ever receive—the news that he was a father. Shock, confusion, and finally anger washed over him as he considered what he would say to her.

\|\|\|/

"Well, that went well," DeDe stated as they left the meeting.

"Yes, I was pleased," Katie agreed, but she felt more

pleased about the prospect of seeing Rick in just a few minutes.

"You are positively glowing. Is there something you want to tell me?"

"No." Katie felt a blush creep up her cheeks. "I have no idea what you mean." She raised her chin higher and walked toward the Chuck Wagon with purpose.

"You're in love with him, aren't you?"

Katie glanced at DeDe. "As a matter of fact, I am."

"Does he know?"

"I think so."

DeDe groaned. "You haven't told him?"

"Not exactly, but I think he knows."

Katie spotted Rick and Kasey as soon as she entered the café. She also realized immediately that something was wrong. Rick sat stiff and unnatural; his smile at Kasey looked forced and didn't reach his eyes. A fear crept over Katie. Had their bliss ended so soon?

"Hi," she said, striving to sound normal.

He looked at her and nodded but didn't speak. His eyes were cold, even angry. "Hello, DeDe. I wonder if you'd mind spending the afternoon with Kasey? Katie and I need to talk." Though worded as a request, it sounded like an order to Katie.

"Sure, not at all." DeDe appeared taken aback by his mood as well.

"Is that OK, pumpkin?" The question he posed to Kasey sounded gentle and loving.

Kasey nodded, looking up from coloring her place mat. "Hi, Mommy. Hi, Aunt DeDe. I made Rick a picture."

"Hi, sweetheart. That's nice. Will you eat lunch with Aunt De?"

Kasey nodded, intently working on her creation. Katie threw DeDe an apologetic look and shrugged.

DeDe smiled. "Take as long as you need. I'll see you at tonight's worship service, if not before."

"Thanks. Bye." Rick grabbed Katie's arm just above her elbow and escorted her to the door. His grasp was unusually tight. He didn't say a word, even when they were in his Explorer, speeding down the highway.

Katie struggled to pinpoint what could have changed between their tender good-night scene last night and today. Her heart pounded out the message of impending doom, and fear gripped her mind. A few miles later, he exited the freeway and stopped along the side of a small road.

"Kasey's my daughter! How could you lie to me?" A mixture of agony and anger laced his words. He shoved the art project at her, but Katie already knew what it revealed. Kasey had made a self-portrait in Sunday school just the week before and had proudly insisted that her teacher record all the details of her identity.

Rick's jaw clenched tight as he stared at her, his eyes cold and accusing, waiting for an explanation.

"I'm sorry." Her voice sounded small and pathetic.

"You steal a man's daughter from him for the first third of her childhood, and all you say is, 'I'm sorry'?" With a clenched fist, he hit the dashboard. "Did you ever plan to tell me?"

Katie nodded meekly. Physical violence frightened her, having grown up with an ill-tempered and sometimes violent stepfather. "Remember last night, I—"

"Last night was the first time in over five years that it occurred to you to tell me that I'm a father?" he asked incredulously. Stated that way, she had to admit it sounded unthinkable.

"I—I—," she stammered. Suddenly none of her excuses seemed valid.

"Katie, she's mine. My child. My flesh and blood. You had no right." Rick grasped the steering wheel tightly, looking like he needed all of his control not to shake her.

Tears streamed down Katie's face. Loud, uncontrollable sobs echoed through the vehicle. "I know. I'm sorry. I'm so sorry." Katie repeated the words again and again.

Rick laid his head against the steering wheel, and she realized that he, too, felt broken over her choice. Both caught up in their own grief and pain, a long time passed before either spoke.

"Rick . . ." Katie's dull, lifeless voice finally broke the silence. "Please listen to me. I need you to hear what I have to say." The look of anguish he carried on his face tore at her heart. She'd caused him more pain than she ever could have imagined.

"I was wrong to run away. I realize that now." Her voice cracked, but she forced herself to forge ahead. "I was a frightened teenage girl. I didn't want a marriage of convenience or pity."

The muscle in Rick's jaw contracted at her words. "I loved you. How would that constitute pity? Did you think every time I said those words, I lied to you?"

Katie couldn't speak. Had he really loved her? Had she been wrong to leave as she did?

"And like always, your standard answer was to run away. Maybe just once, Katie, you ought to stick around and work something through to the end."

His accusation stabbed her heart with truth. She stared at the hands folded in her lap. "I'm sorry."

"You cheated me, Katie! You cheated Kasey. Those are years and memories you can never give back to us." He sighed and ran his hand through his hair. "What have you told her about me?"

Katie felt her face heat up but said the words anyway. "I told her we loved each other very much and that's why I named her after you. I told her you were wonderful and handsome and a cowboy. That held lots of appeal to a little girl. I told her that we had lost track of each other and that you lived on a ranch far, far away."

"What are you going to tell her now?"

"The truth."

"Well, that's something new for you, isn't it?" Rick's sarcasm cut her to the quick. He sighed again. "I'm sorry. That was uncalled-for."

"But not undeserved." Katie stared out the window to avoid looking at Rick.

He started the car and drove back toward Glorieta. "I'd like to be there when you tell her."

Katie nodded, keeping her gaze on passing scenery but seeing nothing. She knew Rick wasn't going to let her get out of the task before her.

"Just for the record, Katie, I would have been overjoyed at the news of being a dad." His announcement only added to her guilt, sentencing her to a life of self-recrimination.

Rick and Katie spotted DeDe and Kasey on the swings as they drove toward Texas Hall. Rick stopped and picked up Kasey. He offered DeDe a ride, but she declined. After parking, they walked to a picnic table down by the lake. Luckily, Kasey chattered incessantly, so neither Katie nor Rick had to speak.

# CHAPTER SEVEN

M ommy, look at the ducks!" Kasey squealed with delight as they waddled around her.

"They hope you'll feed them some bread or popcorn," Rick told her. He watched her eyes light up just like Katie's used to. *Why, God? Why did she do this to me—to us?* He doubted he'd ever understand.

"Kasey, let's sit over here." Katie pointed to the picnic table. The very same table at which DeDe had urged him to give her another chance. *Nothing is ever as cut-and-dried as it first appears.* Thinking she'd slept with another man now seemed less devastating than the truth—she'd stolen his right to know his own child.

Kasey obeyed her mother, but her eyes still watched the ducks. Rick found himself both anticipating and dreading Kasey's reaction to the news of finding her own daddy. His eyes met Katie's red, watery, swollen ones; they begged him to understand, but he just couldn't. He looked away.

Katie cleared her throat. "Kasey, can you look at Mommy? I need to tell you something important."

Kasey turned around on the bench, facing her mom, who sat directly across from her. Rick sat on the other end of

159

Kasey's bench. *God, please help this to be happy news for her. Help us to bond and to build a relationship.*

"Honey, remember Mommy telling you that Rick was my friend from a long time ago?" Kasey nodded, and Katie continued, "Well, what I didn't tell you was that Rick is your daddy."

Kasey's eyes lit up like she'd just found a treasure chest full of toys. Her smile filled her entire face. She looked from her mother to Rick. "You're my daddy?"

At Rick's nod, she dashed into his waiting arms, hugging his neck tightly. His heart swelled with love for his little girl. He wrapped her in a tight embrace. *Thank you, Lord.* He felt tears running down his face. As he hugged Kasey against him, he noticed that her hair was the same shade of brown as his own.

Kasey held on tight, and he wondered if she was afraid to let go because she might lose him again. He glanced at Katie, and she, too, was crying.

Finally he loosened Kasey's grip around his neck and held her back far enough so he could look into her eyes. They still sparkled, and her smile remained.

"Why are you crying, Rick?" A puzzled look crossed her features.

"Because I'm so happy. I'm glad I found you."

"I knew you would." Kasey stated matter-of-factly.

"You did?"

She nodded. "Every night when I prayed, I asked God to find my daddy."

"The faith of a child." Rick drew her into another tight hug.

After a minute, Kasey pulled back slightly and looked into his eyes. "Can I call you Daddy?"

"Only if I can call you pumpkin." *Daddy.* It had a wonderful sound.

"OK!" Kasey giggled, and he kissed her nose.

"Mommy," Kasey turned her face toward Katie. "Can

Daddy live at our house?" Katie looked at him, horror filling her face.

"Daddy lives on a ranch and has to take care of the horses and cows." Rick explained the situation to Kasey.

"Then can we live with you?"

He saw Katie bite her lip, waiting for his reply. "Your mommy has a job in Nashville, so that wouldn't work either. Maybe you can live with me sometimes, though."

He heard Katie's sharp intake of breath and figured she hadn't thought about sharing their daughter. Well, she'd just better get used to the idea, and maybe now was the time to plant a seed or two.

"Katie, I'd like to take Kasey into Santa Fe for McDonald's and a movie—G-rated, of course."

"Of course," was her only response, but he spotted fear in her eyes.

"Do you mind?" He didn't really care if she did or not. She hadn't cared about his right to know his own daughter. He asked only out of politeness. If she said no, she'd have a fight on her hands.

"That's fine. I know you need time together."

The three of them walked to the Explorer. He watched Katie struggle not to cry as she told Kasey good-bye. Her chin quivered as she watched him strap Kasey into her seat. She forced a smile for Kasey's sake and waved as he locked and closed the door.

"Please don't take her away from me," Katie pleaded softly, once the door slammed shut.

"Why not, Katie? You took her away from me for all these years." Though he kept his voice low, he knew it sounded cold and harsh. He couldn't help himself. But he knew in his heart he'd never do that, even if she deserved it.

A sadness filled him as he looked at her. Tears, almost resembling a waterfall, streamed down her face. "It could have been so different for us, but honesty and trust mean everything. Once they're gone—" he paused—"there is nothing left, not even hope."

\\\\//

The slamming of his car door gave finality to his words, and to Katie's hope for a future with Rick. She stood in the middle of the parking lot sobbing. As she watched Rick whisk their daughter away, the incredible pain made her feel physically sick. She longed to curl up in a fetal ball right there but turned toward Texas Hall instead.

\\\\//

DeDe sat cross-legged in the middle of her bed. Katie ran into her arms, accidentally knocking the book she read onto the floor. "Oh, DeDe, he hates me!" Katie cried. She wept until her head felt as if it would explode.

DeDe rocked her back and forth. "Shh, it'll be OK," her soft, southern voice drawled over and over.

Finally Katie rose and found the box of tissues. She dabbed her face and blew her nose.

"What happened?"

"Kasey made a picture of herself for Rick. On it she had the teacher put her whole name, age, and birth date. The rest is history."

"Rick's upset?"

"*Furious* is a better description. I've never seen him like this! His eyes were so cold and hard."

"He'll work through it. Give him some time."

"No, he won't. He hates me. I saw it in his face. He'll never get over my deception. I made a big mistake, but I can't undo it."

"Did you tell him that? Did you apologize?"

"At least a hundred times. He feels like I stole his rights from him."

DeDe was quiet for a moment. "Katie, why *did* you run away without telling him about the pregnancy? You've never told me the whole story. Was it only casual sex, and you didn't want to rope him into unwanted responsibility?"

Katie got comfortable on her bed, placing a pillow between her back and the wall. "What have I told you so far?"

"Just that he was your best friend's brother, and while spending the summer together, you became sexually involved. You avoided discussing your past, so I never pressed the issue."

"No, it wasn't casual sex. I fell in love with him, and sex seemed the natural progression of things. I thought he loved me too; at least he said he did. By the end of the summer, I thought I might be pregnant and bought one of those home pregnancy tests. The test came out positive. I was thrilled and couldn't wait to tell Rick. I assumed we'd get married, have the baby, and live happily ever after.

"I was in Lanae's room helping her unpack. Sofia, his mother, asked if we could talk for a moment. I remember thinking it seemed strange but followed her into Rick's dad's office. She closed the door, and I knew something troubled her by the look on her face.

"She said, 'Katie, I know you and Rick are having sex.' She paused, but I said nothing—I was too stunned—so she continued. 'You're pregnant, aren't you?' I only nodded. 'Katie, you're like another daughter to me, and I want only the best for you. It breaks my heart to tell you this, but Rick doesn't love you.'

"I remember feeling weak-kneed, so I sat down on the leather couch. 'But he said he does,' I told her. Then she said something like, 'Katie, men say all sorts of things when they want to get a woman into bed. Rick is a young, virile male, and you are a beautiful young woman. He confused lust for love.' She said he was sorry, but he didn't know how to tell me. He considered me a summer fling and was ready to move on.

"I remember I started sobbing. She walked over and sat next to me, wrapping her arm around my shoulder. She said even though it hurt her to tell me, she wanted me to know the truth. Then she said that I should get an abortion and tell Rick I didn't want to see him anymore. She didn't want Rick or her husband to know about the pregnancy.

"I remember firmly telling her no to the abortion idea. I loved Rick and wanted his child whether he did or not. Then she said, 'Well, dear, let's put our heads together and find another way. Don't you agree that a marriage of pity is worse than no marriage at all?' I nodded again. 'If Mr. Laramie finds out, he'll force Rick to marry you and fire your father. We can't have that, now, can we?'

"I shook my head, feeling my life spinning out of control, but I knew I didn't want Rick without love between us. She told me about a home in Nashville that a friend had told her about, for unwed mothers—Mercy Ministries of America. She offered to pay my airfare to get there. Since the home doesn't charge, she said I'd be fine once I got there.

"She suggested that I go home pretending not to feel well and pack my things. At three in the morning she'd send a taxi to the other side of the barn to take me to the airport. She'd arrange for someone to meet me in Nashville. She was doing me an enormous favor by taking care of all the details. Her only request was that I tell no one. I did write a note to my parents, explaining that I was running away because I could no longer tolerate my stepfather's abusive behavior. Mrs. Laramie said it would be best if I left without a word to Rick or Lanae.

"Now I'm so confused because Rick keeps talking about how much he loved me."

"Do you think she lied to you, Katie? Maybe she didn't want you to marry Rick."

"She always said she loved me. Why would she lie to me?"

"I don't know, but you need to fill Rick in on these details. Maybe he'll better understand why you left."

"I can't. He already hates me. I can't destroy his relationship with his mother, too."

"So you left your family, your best friend, and the love of

your life because one woman said it was the best idea?" DeDe sounded skeptical.

"It all happened so quickly; I never had time to think." *And I've been trying hard not to think about it ever since,* she silently admitted to herself.

"What about your mom? How do you think she felt?"

"Rick's mom got her a post-office box and gave her my address. We write, and I send her pictures of Kasey. Mom knew my stepdad would kill me, so she thinks it all worked out for the best."

DeDe shook her head and sighed, and Katie felt certain she questioned whether this truly was the best. "Where are Rick and Kasey now?"

"Dinner and a movie." Katie rubbed her temples. "I feel horrible. Do you think you could get me out of leading worship tonight?"

"Yeah, no problem. You take a relaxing shower and go to bed early. I think that's what you need for the moment."

Katie didn't argue. An escape sounded wonderful, even if it was only for an evening.

\|\|\|

Rick spent a glorious evening with Kasey. She already held the title of Daddy's little princess, and this was only her first day as his daughter. Every time she called him Daddy, his heart rejoiced. Just the knowledge that she was his caused an overwhelming love to flood through him. He found it amazing to learn that parental love was immediate.

He glanced over at her sleeping form, with her head resting against the car door. He felt a smile touch his lips. She seemed to love having a daddy as much as he loved being one.

Glancing at his watch, he realized the evening worship service would be ending soon. He hoped to catch DeDe before she left and deposit Kasey with her. His emotions couldn't take another run-in with Katie. Just seeing her made his blood boil.

After parking, he scooped the sleeping child into his arms and walked toward Holcomb Auditorium. The session had just ended, and people were making their way toward the back. Rick felt like a fish swimming upstream. He saw DeDe and fought his way toward her.

"Can you see that this bundle finds her way to her mother?"

DeDe turned toward him. Her blue eyes reflected compassion. She nodded and took Kasey.

"Thanks." He turned and left without another word. He couldn't face DeDe's advice right now.

Rick spent most of the night pondering the fact that he had a daughter and the fact that Katie had never told him. He wondered if she ever would have had he not stumbled onto the information on his own. Why would Katie think he didn't love her? Well, he didn't anymore, but he had. . . .

Sometime during the night he decided he'd spend all day tomorrow with Kasey as well. He had a lot of lost time to make up for. They could play miniature golf again and ride bikes, and he'd take her on the paddle boats. After he reached this decision, a peaceful sleep finally claimed him.

Rick knocked on Katie's door at eight the next morning. A pajama-clad Kasey threw it open.

"Daddy!"

She ran into his arms, where he twirled her in a tender embrace. When he stopped, Katie stood in the doorway with a toothbrush in her hand.

"Rick."

"Katie." She looked terrible. Her eyes were swollen and puffy, her nose red, and her voice sounded lifeless. A tiny twinge of guilt pricked at his conscience, but he reminded himself that she deserved to feel horrible for what she'd done.

She broke eye contact and stared at the floor. After a sigh she asked, "Did you come for Kasey?" He heard raw pain in her voice. It bothered him that he was intentionally causing her hurt, but she had brought it on herself.

"She's my daughter. I have a right to spend time with her."

Katie only nodded, looking at their daughter. "Yes, you do have the right." Her dull brown eyes met his. "Let me get her dressed first."

Something inside him stirred. Something stronger than the anger. Something that made him want to take her into his arms and tell her it would be OK. But would it? How could it be after what she'd done?

# CHAPTER EIGHT

Katie clamped her mouth tightly shut, trying to smile and act brave for Kasey's sake. Inside, her throat ached from the ball of tears lodged there. Her stomach churned, and nausea assaulted her. Her heart splintered into a million pieces as she watched Rick and Kasey leave together in joyous laughter.

She felt her lip quiver as they disappeared down the stairs. The tears then rolled freely down her cheeks, dropping onto her robe. She closed the door and fell into a heap of misery on her bed. She grabbed Kasey's bear and clutched it against her heart.

The thought of many lonely holidays and summers without Kasey caused her to cry harder and louder. Rick had made it clear that he expected his equal share of their daughter. How could she endure the days ahead?

"Katie?" DeDe came out of the bathroom with a towel wrapped around her wet tresses. "What's wrong?" She sat next to Katie on the bed, pushing her hair back off her wet cheeks.

Katie wondered if DeDe could even understand her words. They came out in sobbing, jerking sounds. "He—took—Kasey."

"For the day?" DeDe's voice held an edge of concern.

Katie nodded. "She'll spend holidays with Rick and her grandparents, and I'll be alone. I'll always be alone." Katie sobbed harder. DeDe tried to comfort her, but nothing helped.

Finally, Katie stopped weeping and took a shower. She decided to walk to the prayer garden and talk things over with God. On her way, she spotted Rick and Kasey paddling around the lake. She stood on a hill and watched from afar. At least he loved Kasey. He would make a good father, something Katie had never had. How could she begrudge her own child that?

Maybe God had planned all along to provide just a dad for Kasey, not a spouse for her. She'd let feelings and emotions carry her into a world of hopes and dreams about husbands, wives, and a dozen children. In truth, none of that was possible.

Katie spent much of her day in the prayer garden, finding the peace and strength to survive. She held tightly to the promise that she could do all things through Christ. Tonight was the last worship service, and tomorrow they'd all go home around noon. Sometime between now and then, she and Rick must discuss sharing Kasey.

God gave Katie the strength to lead the worship, though she knew her sparkle was missing. Kasey again shared a pew with Rick and DeDe. Katie kept her eyes averted, trying to forget how badly she hurt. After she finished leading worship, she sat in the front with Forever His.

Harv's sermon spoke directly to Katie. He said, "Don't live in the 'if only's.' They will destroy your life and ministry. 'If only' never happened, so move forward. Live in the *truth* rather than the *facts*.

"The *fact* is that Sarah was too old to have a baby. The *truth* is that she's the mother of the nation of Israel. The facts bring us down. The truth sets us free. Live in God's truth, and overcome the facts of your past."

During the prayer time, while walking back onstage, Katie

committed to live in the truth rather than in the facts of all her bad choices. In the truth, she knew she'd find freedom.

◊

Rick woke with a heavy heart. Glancing out the window and finding a blanket of snow covering the ground did nothing to lift his spirits. He let out a sigh and ran his fingers through his hair. Somehow his heart felt as cold as the snow fluttering from the sky.

" 'And the truth will set you free,' " he quoted aloud. His eyes roved over the mountains, the trees, and the sky, seeing their beauty but feeling no appreciation for it. He'd let the truth condemn Katie. He'd forced her to live with the fact that she'd made a bad choice, and he didn't want her to ever forget it. God, on the other hand, removed people's bad choices as far as the east was from the west in loving forgiveness.

From the window, he saw DeDe and Katie loading their luggage into the trunk of a blue Prizm. Kasey danced around with her head tilted back and her mouth open. He smiled at their daughter, his and Katie's. He grabbed his coat and headed out to say good morning.

◊

DeDe and Katie laughed at their antics as they tried to stuff another suitcase into an overfull trunk. "How did we get it all in here when we left the airport?" DeDe wondered out loud.

"Good morning, ladies. Need a hand?" At the sound of Rick's voice, Katie dropped her overnight case to the ground. She turned to find that the hardness in his eyes had softened a tad since yesterday. He actually smiled at her. The sight of that dimple caught her heart off guard, and she surprised herself by smiling back.

"We'd love your help," DeDe replied emphatically.

"Daddy!" Kasey paused from catching snowflakes with her tongue to hug him. He lifted her and kissed her rosy cheek.

"Hello, pumpkin." He set her down and faced the task at hand. He unloaded and reloaded their luggage, somehow getting it all to fit and the trunk closed. "Are you leaving before this morning's classes?"

"No, we just wanted to get everything loaded in case this snowstorm gets worse." DeDe filled him in on their plans.

He nodded, sticking his gloved fingers in the front pockets of his jeans. He cleared his throat. "Katie, could we have coffee and talk?" His voice had lost the hard edge she'd grown accustomed to these last couple of days. Her heart dropped at the thought of battling it out with him again. She nodded and swallowed hard.

"Why don't I take Kasey to breakfast?" DeDe suggested. Again, Katie only nodded.

Once she and Rick were settled at a table in the Chuck Wagon, Rick spoke. "I'd like to take Kasey home with me to the ranch."

Katie made a gasping sound as she sucked in a breath of air. She felt her mouth go dry and panic rise in her chest.

"Only for a week," he assured her. He must have sensed her terror. "I want her to see the ranch, meet her grandparents, and get to know me better."

Katie nodded and bit her lower lip. "What about later? Then what will you want?" Her voice sounded anguished, and she fought tears.

"Katie, my goal isn't to hurt you. Well, maybe it was—but not anymore."

She wondered what had changed. "I'm not ready for this. She's never been away from me for more than one night. I can't send her home with a stranger."

Katie noticed how tightly Rick clamped his jaw shut. After

several seconds his words poured forth in quiet anger. "Frankly, I wasn't ready to miss all these years with her, either, and I wouldn't *be* a stranger if you'd done the right thing in the first place. You'd better get ready, Katie, because I *will* spend time with my daughter, even if I have to take you to court to make it happen."

Rick rose and walked out, leaving her to contemplate his threat. The determination in his voice, the set of his jaw, and the anger shooting from his eyes left her with no doubt that he meant exactly what he said.

Katie dried her tears with a napkin and looked out the window. The snow still floated through the air toward the ground. She remembered God's promise to cleanse his people of their sin, making them white as snow. If only Rick could forgive her as God had.

⟞⟋⟍⟞

At noon, Katie waited by Rick's Explorer, hoping to speak to him before he left for home. She tried to look composed and brave, acknowledging that what little strength she had came from spending much of the morning in prayer.

She watched him approach and longed for the freedom to run into those strong, protective arms. She knew in her heart that Kasey would be fine with him, but like everything hard in her life, Katie chose to put this off as long as possible. She noticed the anger still residing in his eyes.

"I thought you might want to say good-bye to Kasey before we leave, and I wanted to give you our phone number." Katie handed him a slip of paper. "You're welcome to call anytime—every day, if you want." She waited for some response, but he made none. "I thought maybe Kasey could visit for three days at Thanksgiving, and we'll see how that goes before I send her for a week."

Rick nodded, but she remained uncertain of whether he appreciated her offer or felt angered by it. His stance made him seem unapproachable.

"Kasey and DeDe are waiting over there in the car." Katie turned and led the way.

Rick opened the passenger door, squatting down to Kasey's level. "You be a good girl, and Daddy will call you tomorrow." The emotion Katie heard in his voice wrenched her heart.

"I will, Daddy. I promise." Kasey planted a big loud kiss on his cheek.

"I love you, pumpkin." After a long hug, Rick placed one last kiss on the top of Kasey's head. Katie swallowed a lump in her throat, noting the tears glistening in Rick's eyes as they held hers for a moment. Then he turned and walked away without a word.

Would either of their broken hearts ever heal? Katie watched Rick leave, and it was all she could do not to follow him. A desire to once again beg for his forgiveness overwhelmed her. How could they ever share their daughter amicably with so much hurt and emotion between them?

※

Even in the midst of feeling furious at Katie, a need to protect her from pain almost drove Rick back to her. Only by sheer determination of will did he avoid that response. He tried to remind himself that she deserved to feel bad, but it didn't lessen the ache in his own heart for her and for them.

He gripped the steering wheel so tightly that his hands ached. He drove away from Glorieta, and Katie drove toward Santa Fe. As he put miles between them, he couldn't seem to outrun the picture haunting him. He saw Katie shrouded in sadness, shoulders hunched from the weight of her sorrow, watching him tell Kasey good-bye.

The truth was that he'd never get over Katie. Even if he couldn't trust her, he'd always love her. *Oh, God, please help us both to get through this time of pain and sorrow. May we each look more like Jesus when we get to the other side of all this heartache.*

Loving Katie wasn't enough. Without trust there was no foundation for a relationship or a marriage, but hopefully they could learn to be friends for Kasey's sake. Once again, he found himself facing the need to forgive Katie. How do you forgive five and a half years of silence?

\\\\\\/

Katie climbed into the passenger seat of the rental car after moving Kasey to the rear and helping her put on her earphones to listen to her Psalty tape. As they drove away, Katie's cyes were drawn to the cream-colored steeple towering above the pines. It stood tall and proud, beckoning people to come, come and find peace, come and find Christ. Katie sighed as they sped away from the tree-covered hills.

She glanced back over her shoulder, her eyes straining for one last look at Glorieta. "I love it here. I wonder if this pain-filled experience will taint my joy at being in this place. I wonder if I can ever go back without reliving these last few days."

DeDe reached over and patted her hand.

"I love the ranch, too. It's hard to think of sending Kasey there without me."

"Why don't you think about going back for a visit yourself? Maybe it's time to face the demons of your past, including Mrs. Laramie. There's nothing to hide anymore since Rick knows the truth."

Katie sighed but made no comment.

"Why should you spend the holidays alone in Tennessee when your parents live right there? Go with Kasey, and even if she stays at Rick's, you can still see her every day."

Katie smiled slightly. "Always the optimist, aren't you? I don't know if I can bear being so close to Rick, yet so far."

"Still love him, huh?"

"So much it hurts. I'll be lucky if he can ever stand the sight of me again."

"Maybe he still loves you, too, and that's why your deception made him so angry."

"I doubt it. No matter how much I wish things were different, or how stupid my choices look now, I can't change them. Rick is gone, DeDe, gone from my life forever. . . ."

Fresh tears spilled over her cheeks as she voiced her fears aloud. Katie knew he'd never forgive her this time.

# CHAPTER NINE

Night settled in around him. In the quiet, Rick found
his thoughts straying to Katie. His anger now some-
what dissipated, his own heart ached thinking about
the pain in hers.

His thoughts carried him back to their summer together.
That last morning, he had awoken to Katie bending over him,
kissing his lips.

"What time is it?" he asked in a groggy state.

"Almost six, sleepyhead. I made you a surprise. Sit up." She
helped prop pillows behind him and set a tray filled with
breakfast foods in front of him.

He grinned up at her. "The bacon smells wonderful. A man
could get used to this."

"That's what I'm counting on." She sat next to him on the
bed while he ate. "This is our last morning together." A sadness filled her voice.

"You don't think my mother would appreciate you waking
me each day with your sweet kisses?"

He watched Katie's face turn pink. "What will happen to us
now, Rick?"

*"I think for a while we should keep this relationship between us."*

*"You mean I can't even tell Lanae?"*

He kissed her nose. *"Eventually. I just need time to break this to my mom gently."*

*"Do you think she'll be mad?"* Concern brought frown lines to Katie's forehead.

*"I think she'll disapprove of our dating at first, until she gets used to the idea."* He set the empty breakfast tray on the nightstand, taking Katie's hand in his own.

*"Why?"*

*"She'll say you're too young for me. But I say you're perfect for me."*

*"Next week Lanae and I are supposed to move into the dorm at the U of A. When will I see you again after that?"*

He wondered why Katie suddenly seemed so insecure. He'd never seen this side of her. *"This week I'll meet you in the barn every night at eleven, after your parents and mine are asleep. Once you move, we'll find ways to be together."* He kissed her nose again.

*"I've never kept a secret from Lanae before."*

He sensed her apprehension at hiding their relationship.

*"Katie, my love, it will only be for a few weeks, a couple of months at the most. You can last that long."*

She hadn't shown up at eleven that night. The next day she was gone. For the first time he realized how callous he'd been during their last morning together. She had needed reassurance, and he'd made their love sound like a cheap affair to be hidden and lived out in secret. Why hadn't he told her of his plans to propose within the next few weeks? He'd hoped to surprise her, but instead she had surprised him by running away.

As Rick drove up the hill to the big house, he wondered how his parents and Katie's would respond to the news of their illegitimate grandchild.

〻〻

Katie ran to the phone, knowing she'd hear Rick's voice. He called Kasey each evening about this time. She appreciated his thoughtfulness, and she was beginning to feel that they could amicably share their child because underneath it all, Rick was a good man. It wasn't in his nature to be vindictive.

"Hello!" She was breathless from her race to answer the beckoning ring. She also sounded excited to hear from him.

"Hello, Katie. I didn't expect such a warm greeting." Rick's tender teasing sent chills up her spine. Katie drew a deep breath at his words. She couldn't keep up with his moods. She felt more comfortable with his anger—at least then she knew where she stood.

"Katie, are you there?"

"Yeah."

"I've been wondering how you are. You've been on my mind a lot."

"I'm fine." Her voice sounded more emotional than she wanted it to. "Thank you for showering Kasey with all these calls and letters the past couple of weeks. It means the world to her."

"She's a great kid. You've done a good job with her."

"Thanks."

Rick cleared his throat. She thought his voice sounded emotional too. "Katie, I was thinking, why don't you come with Kasey for Thanksgiving? I'd like to buy your ticket, and your mom really wants you to come."

"I can't. I'm leading worship at Mercy that day. Maybe Christmas."

He paused a minute before suggesting, "What if I came there for Thanksgiving? I mean, if you wouldn't mind. I just don't want you to be alone." His thoughtfulness touched her deeply. "Then you and Kasey could come for a week or two at Christmas. Maybe by spring you'd feel comfortable letting her come alone. And, Katie, I'm sorry I was so hard on you at Glorieta. I'm trying to see this from your perspective."

Katie swallowed hard. "Thank you, Rick, for understanding. This is very hard for me." Could he tell by her voice that she was crying? "If you want to come here, that will be fine. Now a certain little girl is dancing around me, dying to speak to her daddy, so I'll say good-bye for now."

"Bye, Katie. See you next week." She thought she heard a wistful tone in his words.

Katie found her feelings in turmoil. From the warmth of their conversation sprang a new hope in her heart. He cared at least a little. . . .

\ıllı/

After talking to Kasey, Rick went back out to the barn to check on a new foal that wasn't thriving as he expected.

"Hey, Curly. You checking on the little guy too?"

"I think he's getting a little stronger each day. He just started slow for some unknown reason."

"Watching him this week has reminded me of everything I missed in Kasey's life—her first step, word, laugh, tooth."

"But look at all that's to come," Curly reminded him.

"And I'll be two thousand miles away for most of it. I'll see her some each summer and every other holiday. I don't want to be an absentee father. I want to be the one who tucks her in at night. I want to look across the breakfast table and see her little face." Rick heard the longing in his own voice.

"Don't have to be like that. It's up to you." Curly chewed on a piece of hay that dangled from his mouth.

"How's it up to me?"

"Marry her mama. You still love her?"

"Never stopped, but I don't trust her. Not much hope without that." Rick watched the mare nuzzle her foal.

"God could change your heart—if you let him."

Those words pierced Rick. Was his own stubborn pride

what prevented him and Katie from moving past this? He wanted to blame her, but was that the truth? Could God rebuild the broken trust in their relationship? He pondered that thought long after he crawled into bed that night.

\||/

"You're sure quiet this morning," Rick's mom pointed out at breakfast a few days later, the morning he was due to leave for Nashville. "Are you all packed?"

"Yeah."

"What time does your plane leave?"

"Two."

"She's a lovely child," his mother remarked, glancing at the picture of Rick and Kasey hanging on the refrigerator. She looked intently at Rick for a moment before continuing, "You still love Katie, don't you?"

"I never stopped."

His mom's eyes filled with tears. "Now that you're a parent, do you understand how fierce and protective parental love is?"

He nodded, wondering where this was leading. He sensed by his mother's tone that they were embarking on a serious discussion.

"Remember the day we got home from Europe?"

Again he nodded, pushing his empty plate away from him.

"It was the summer Katie left. Anyway, I immediately noticed the looks and grins you and Katie exchanged and knew something had developed between you two while we were gone. When I found out Katie felt ill, I figured out how things were."

Rick felt his heart increase in speed. He was all ears, feeling a dread rising from the pit of his stomach. "Go on."

"I want you to try and understand that I loved Katie. She'd been a wonderful friend for Lanae. She was bright, charming, and vivacious. But the thought of you marrying a girl like Katie, in a shotgun wedding, was more than I could stand."

"Mother, what are you saying? And what do you mean by 'a girl like Katie'?" *God, please help me not to react in anger. I want my mom to see Christ in me.*

"Katie came from a poor family with an alcoholic, abusive stepfather. I desired you to marry a girl from a socially prominent family. Someone whose breeding matched your own."

"You make me sound like a horse!" Rick accused. "Are you telling me you sent Katie away?" Part of him felt relieved by this possibility. For the first time, Katie's disappearance was beginning to make sense.

"For your own good."

"How could you think denying my rights as a father was for my own good? She carried your grandchild in her womb, and you sent her away?" Rick's voice reflected the stunned disbelief he felt. "What gave you the right to play God in our lives?" Rick asked, shaking his head.

"I was ashamed. Ashamed of what my friends would think, and worse, what they would say."

"You sold out your own grandchild because of what someone might think or say? I feel sorry for you, Mother. How tragic to care more about others' opinions than your own flesh and blood." Rick blew out a long, slow breath. He looked into his mother's teary eyes. "So how did you convince her to leave?"

"I lied to her. I'm sorry, Rick." She dabbed her eyes with a napkin. "I told her you regretted getting involved with her. I told her it would be best never to mention the baby because she wouldn't want a marriage of pity."

Everything was suddenly clear. Katie had left not of her own accord but because his own mother had manipulated her. "And how do you feel about everything now?"

"I made a mistake. That's why I'm telling you the truth, so maybe you and Katie can have a fair chance. You said you still love her. No one wants her to live halfway across the country." She looked down at the napkin that she had been wadding and unwadding. In a barely audible whisper she asked, "Will you forgive me?"

He walked over to his mother's chair and held her in a tight hug. "I can forgive you, Mom, because of all the times God's forgiven me. To tell you the truth, I'm relieved about this news because so many things between Katie and me make sense now. But I hope you'll never interfere in our lives again. This could have ended much differently."

# CHAPTER TEN

Katie nearly had to run up the escalator to keep up with Kasey. They had plenty of time, but her anticipation of seeing her daddy after three weeks apart drove her onward. Kasey had missed Rick more than Katie had ever thought possible.

Katie had spent extra time with God this past week, preparing for Rick's visit. She'd be OK. The times when Kasey was away with Rick would be tough, but nothing she couldn't handle with God's help. This was now her lot in life, and she could either buck up and find joy anyway or wallow in misery. She decided to opt for joy.

Katie found a chair and tried to read the magazine she had brought with her, but she couldn't keep her mind on the words. She walked to the window where Kasey stood watching the planes come and go. Finally, Rick's plane arrived. Kasey stood as close as she could to the door that her daddy would pass through, acting like a child waiting for Christmas. Standing still proved impossible, and she danced with excitement.

As Katie watched the passengers disembark, her eyes locked with a pair of familiar gray ones. Rick. Emotions surged through her—joy, love, fear, panic.

"Daddy!" Kasey leaped into his arms, diverting his gaze.

"I hope it's really OK that I came," Rick said to Katie, taking her elbow to steer her out of the main line of traffic.

She nodded, feeling like a liar. She faced the next four days with fear and trepidation.

"Katie, I promise you, I'll be on my best behavior." He lifted Katie's chin to establish eye contact. "Please don't be afraid. I came to see her life here, so when I think of her playing, I can picture her room. And I came to work things out between us." He said it so matter-of-factly.

They each took one of Kasey's hands as they walked toward the baggage-claim area. Katie wondered how they'd work things out. How much time did he want with Kasey?

Katie acknowledged to herself that having him visit would be bittersweet. Seeing him brought back feelings and memories like his kiss, his bear hug, and the tender words of love he once whispered to her.

As they waited for the luggage carousel to start moving, Rick asked, "Is there a hotel near your place?"

"Actually, there's an older gentleman who lives in my building who's out of town this week. I'm feeding his cat, and he said he didn't mind if you crashed in his guest room. I imagine you'll spend most of your awake time with Kasey anyway."

"That would be great. Are you sure he won't mind?"

Katie nodded, and he grabbed his suitcase as it passed by. "Did you eat?" she asked.

"Just peanuts."

"Kasey's favorite place is an Italian restaurant downtown called the Old Spaghetti Factory. It's really quite good. Sound OK?"

Rick nodded, wishing the time would come when they could talk alone. Not that he wanted to get rid of Kasey, but he longed to get things straight between the two of them. He grinned at Katie and enjoyed watching a blush darken her face.

Just as they were about to exit the airport, he grabbed her arm. "Wait, do I need to get a rental car?"

"You can use mine, if you need one." Her eyes sparkled, warming his heart.

The three of them had a lot of fun at dinner, laughing and cutting up. It was the first time since he'd learned the truth about Kasey that it had been comfortable to be together. Katie seemed relaxed and more like her old self.

Kasey chattered during most of the meal. She described her bedroom, their apartment, their church, her Sunday school classroom and teacher, and her school classroom and teacher. She told him about the toys in her room, what they looked like and what they did.

Rick enjoyed hearing all the details of her life; it made him feel more a part of it and less like he'd already missed so much. He thanked God that Kasey wasn't shy; otherwise getting to know her could have proved difficult. He smiled at her narration of life from a five-year-old perspective.

Kasey filled him in on her church friends, her school friends, and her mommy's friends. Rick listened more intently as she named off Katie's friends. He noticed that there wasn't one male in the lot, and that information brought a sigh of relief.

Often his eyes met Katie's across the table. She had never looked more beautiful to him than she did tonight. He hoped this trip would provide a happy ending to his dream for the two of them.

Finally, they drove to Katie's apartment building. "You'll have to come up to my place so I can give you the key to Mr. Kingsley's," she informed him.

Kasey ran ahead so she could push the buttons on the elevator. Katie seemed to tense up when they entered her apartment. *She hates serious conversations and knows one is coming,* Rick concluded.

"Nice place."

"It's nothing fancy, but it's home. I'll get the keys."

"Daddy, come see my room." Kasey tugged on his hand. He followed her to the first door on the left.

Her room was very girlish. "Wow, Kasey, this is great!"

"Kasey, let's walk Daddy over to Mr. Kingsley's, so he can drop off his luggage." Katie spoke from the open doorway. "Then he can come see your stuff." The last sentence surprised him. He had assumed Katie was trying to get rid of him for the night and was glad to hear that he was welcome to come back.

Mr. Kingsley's ended up being just two doors down. Rick wasn't a cat lover, but he'd survive in order to be this close to Katie and Kasey. They took him on a tour, and Katie said, "I'll lend you towels and sheets so we don't have to use his stuff." She placed the key in his hand as they exited. He felt electricity when their fingers brushed; her eyes told him she felt it too.

"It's past Kasey's bedtime. Do you want to read her a story and tuck her in?"

"You don't mind?"

"No, I've had a lot more turns than you have." The compassion in her eyes touched him. He longed to draw her into his arms and hold her there forever, but he wasn't sure how she'd respond.

"Thanks. Oh, by the way, both mothers sent letters for you." He pulled them from his shirt pocket. "You read these, and I'll handle bedtime duty."

〰️

As Katie took the letters from Rick, she noticed a slight tremble in her hand. What could his mother have to say to her after all these years? Katie felt disappointed in Sofia's response to her own grandchild. Katie had thought Sofia would at least check on them from time to time, but she never had.

Kasey led Rick to her room, and Katie grabbed her coat and went out onto the balcony, leaning against the railing. She

wanted to be as alone as possible when she read these. She
opened her mother's first, not sure she wanted to face the contents of Sofia's letter.

> *My dearest daughter,*
>
> *It was wonderful to hear that Rick finally knows
> about his child. I long to meet my only granddaughter,
> to hold her, laugh with her, and hug her tight. My
> heart longs to hold you as well.*
>
> *Rick will make a wonderful daddy. He loves Kasey
> so very much and glows whenever he talks about her. I
> believe he still loves you as well.*
>
> *Katie, it's time for you to come home. Please con-
> sider it. If not for good, then at least for a visit.*
>
> > *Love from Mom.*

Katie pulled a tissue from her pocket, wiping the tears.
How her heart ached to return to the ranch, but could she face
the constant contact with Rick? She pulled out a chair at the
outdoor table, sat down, and opened Sofia's letter.

> *Katie,*
>
> *My reason for writing is threefold. First, I write to
> let you know that I have confessed to Rick my part in
> sending you away. I was stunned that you had not told
> him yourself during your week together in Glorieta.
> You behaved quite honorably to guard our secret after
> all these years, but it is no longer necessary.*
>
> *My second reason for writing is more difficult to
> admit. I lied to you when I said Rick had grown tired
> of you. Rick and I never spoke of you at all. I figured
> out what was going on between the two of you on my
> own and did not want my son involved in a scandal. I
> can only hope that as a mother you can understand the*

*extremes to which a woman may go in order to protect
her offspring. I realize now that I made a mistake, and
I am truly sorry.*

*Last, Katie, I beseech you to come back to the ranch,
where you and Kasey belong. Had I not interfered,
you'd both have been here all along. Kasey is a darling,
and I understand you've done remarkably well on your
own, but wouldn't it be nice to be surrounded by the
love and support of family?*

*I could name another reason for your return but
promised my son never to interfere in his life again, so
I shall not mention how much he needs and wants you.
Please consider my plea for you to rejoin us in Arizona.*

*Sincerely, Sofia Laramie*

Katie looked up to find Rick watching her. She sniffed and
wiped her eyes. "I didn't hear you come out."

"Kasey fell asleep before I got to page 5."

Katie felt uncomfortable under his scrutiny, so she walked
over to the railing. She felt more comfortable with her back to
him. *Does he need and want me?* Somehow she doubted it.

"Katie?" His voice came from right behind her. She shivered, both from the cold and from his nearness. He drew her
back against him and wrapped his coat around her.

She closed her eyes, afraid to hope. Maybe this was just a
chivalrous gesture to keep her warm. "Why did your mom
think I was so bad for you that she had to protect you from
me?" She tried to sound nonchalant but failed miserably. Her
hurt resounded loud and clear.

Rick withdrew his arms from around her and turned her to
face him. He used his thumbs to dry her tears. "I'm ashamed
to tell you—peer pressure."

"What?" Katie was astounded.

"She was afraid of what her friends would say and think."
His hands still held her face, and for the briefest of moments,

she thought he might kiss her. Instead, he dropped his hands to her shoulders. "Katie, I'm sorry I overreacted at the news that I'm Kasey's dad."

"I think your response was understandable. I was wrong. I never should have kept Kasey's existence a secret from you. I know that now." Katie walked to the other end of the balcony, needing to escape his closeness. "My mistake affected so many lives, and I can never change that fact. I can't give you back the things you missed in Kasey's life. I can't give Kasey early memories of you or her grandparents. I can't ever make it up to any of you." Her voice rose slightly with each sentence.

"You can make it up to me." He'd followed her and stood near once again.

"How?" She knew her voice sounded hopeless.

He again turned her to face him. "Give me eleven more just like Kasey." His husky words caused her heart to jump. She searched his eyes, and the warm glow she saw there told her she'd been forgiven.

"Katie, I realized the other day that what my mom meant for bad, God used for good. We both found Christ because of the loss of each other. If we'd gotten married and had Kasey, we probably wouldn't be Christians."

"So you see this as a good thing?" She doubted that.

Rick smiled at her. "Well, it no longer looks quite so bad. Katie, I know you'd never have left if my mother hadn't interfered."

"That's true. It was so easy for me to believe her because just that morning when we talked, I felt like you were ashamed of me. You didn't want anyone to know."

"Never," he reassured her emphatically. "I planned to get you a ring and tell everyone, once you said yes, that you'd be mine forever."

"Oh, Rick . . ." Katie sighed at how confused their lives and love had become.

"I hurt so bad when you left that I thought I'd die."

"I hurt so bad leaving you that I wanted to die."

"And now I never want to live without you again." Rick bent down on one knee. "Katie Scarlett O'Malley, will you be my wife? Will you come home and live on the ranch and ride with me and rope with me, as long as we both shall live?"

The look in Katie's eyes stole his breath away. She pulled him up to his feet and wrapped her arms around his neck. He felt her fingers tangle into his hair just like she used to do once upon a time.

"Rick . . ." She paused, and her doe eyes invited him to drown in them. "I love you. I always have. I always will. I want to be your wife more than anything, but I have to know, is this about us or about Kasey?"

"If there were no Kasey, if there had never been a Kasey, I'd still be standing here asking you the same question. I loved you before Kasey, and I'll love you long after Kasey is grown and gone." Rick pulled a ring box from his jacket pocket.

"I bought you this the day after you left. I wanted to have it in case you came back. I've held on to it all these years. Will you wear it?" He lifted a small solitaire from the velvet bed where it lay. He smiled at the tears on Katie's face, certain somehow that these stemmed from joy. He slipped the ring onto her outstretched finger and drew her into his embrace. She laid her head against his heart. He wondered if she could hear it pounding out their song. *"Yes, I'm a Scarlett dreamer, and I keep dreaming Scarlett's mine. . . ."*

# RECIPE

\\\||//

*Katie made these enchiladas for Rick, using his mother's recipe. I have made them for many people over the years, and almost everyone requests a copy of the recipe. I got the original recipe from my friend Rhonda, but it has evolved over the years.*

*Some turn up their nose at the sour cream, but I've never had anyone taste them and still claim to dislike them. They make a wonderful potluck dish, a quick dinner entrée, or a great meal for company with a side of beans and rice. I hope it becomes one of your favorites as well.*

*Just as God provides food to nourish our physical bodies, he gives us the Bible to nourish our souls. My prayer for you is a deeper hunger for the Word of God in your life. May you, like Katie and Rick, find that he is enough—enough in life's hard times and enough when the sun is shining. Because, I promise you, he is.*

*—Jeri Odell*

## SOUR-CREAM ENCHILADAS

16 oz. sour cream
2 cans cream of chicken soup
7-oz. can diced green chilies
1 pkg. medium-sized flour tortillas
16 oz. shredded cheddar cheese

Heat oven to 350°. Mix sour cream, cream of chicken soup, and green chilies together over low heat. Spoon enough soup mixture into 9x13" pan to cover the bottom. Spoon soup mixture onto tortillas, cover with cheese, and roll.

Place rolled tortillas in pan. Cover with remaining soup mixture and top with remaining cheese. Bake 20–30 minutes, or until cheese melts and enchiladas are bubbly.

# ABOUT THE AUTHOR

Jeri Odell discovered a love for writing in the sixth grade and is now living her dream. As a writer, her personal goals are to exalt Christ, edify the believer, and point the unsaved to Jesus. She hopes to reach beyond entertainment and challenge women to walk more closely with the Lord.

Besides *Scarlett Dreamer,* she has written greeting cards, devotionals, short stories, and articles for *Focus on the Family* and *Parent Life.* She is happily married to her high school sweetheart, and they recently celebrated their twenty-fifth anniversary. She and her husband live in Arizona and have three grown children.

You can write to Jeri in care of Tyndale House Author Relations, P.O. Box 80, Wheaton, IL 60189-0080.

# Mountain Memories

## JAN DUFFY

To Cathy, my lifelong sister-friend and
prayer partner

# CHAPTER ONE

The quick swipe across the ear took Mikaela by surprise and upset the precarious balance she was trying to maintain on the toes of her hiking boots. "Griffin!" she yelled as chunky dog food poured from the overturned bag across the kitchen floor. She landed with a thump on the seat of her Levi's. "See what you've done!"

The huge golden retriever lay down on the floor beside her, rested his head on his giant paws, and gave her a sorrowful stare. The smaller female sat on her haunches with a look that said, "Are you yelling at me, too?" Her half-grown pup, Theodore, skittered through the unexpected feast and began to munch with joyous delight.

Mikaela wiped the slobbery dog kiss from her ear with the sleeve of her flannel shirt and shook her head. "This mess is the last thing I need right now."

The remorseful dog looked at her with big, warm eyes and placed a paw on her leg, pleading for forgiveness. She huffed a sigh of resignation and rubbed his silky, blond ear. "It's OK, boy. Things aren't working this morning." He wagged his tail and stood up, all forgiven.

She'd been planning for a month to start renovating the old

cabin today. Now everything was on hold because *he* was arriving. She got up off the floor and dusted her hands on her jeans.

"Go on, Sally. You might as well dig in with the boys while I clean this mess up."

Mikaela took the dustpan from the broom closet and used it as a shovel to scoop dog food back into the bag. After dropping a panful into the dogs' bowls, she stretched and brushed back a strand of flyaway blond hair that had escaped her ponytail.

*Lord,* she prayed, *you know I want to be in your will. I'm thankful for your provision through this job, but I'm worried. How am I going to turn a two-hundred-year-old cabin into a gift shop while I'm playing nursemaid to Daniel?*

Her old friend's offer of good money to manage his mountain property and care for his dogs had been an answer to prayer. She figured taking care of Daniel's business and working her four-to-midnight shift at the ranger station would help her save up a decent down payment toward the $200,000 she needed to buy the one hundred acres of land that adjoined the old settlers' cabin. Getting the land was the last big hurdle she needed to overcome to fulfill her dream of a wildlife sanctuary, a place of healing for injured animals and birds, many of which were close to becoming endangered species in the Appalachian Mountain chain.

But now an unexpected wrinkle had developed in her well-laid plans. Daniel's leg had been broken in three places when a drunk driver ran a stop sign and smashed into Daniel's car while he was returning home from a music-industry party. He had sounded so pitiful when he called and asked if she could help him out while he recuperated in the mountains that she couldn't bear to turn him down. She looked heavenward and whispered, "God, why didn't I say a firm no when he asked me to help him out while he recuperates? I must be out of my mind."

Shaking her head, she walked into the crisp mountain air and fetched an armload of firewood from the cord of split oak stacked on the back porch. In less then ten minutes she had a roaring fire going in the massive fieldstone fireplace in the great room.

The homey and nostalgic smell of burning oak gave her a sudden craving for her mom's reunion bread pudding, seasoned with cinnamon and plump raisins. She sat on the hearth's edge, letting the fire warm her back and thinking back to the many times her parents and their college friends had had annual reunions during the fall at Smoky Mountain National Park.

The memories filtered back bittersweet. She could almost hear the sound of giggling and crunching as the children buried themselves in a huge pile of leaves they had spent the cold afternoon gathering. They sat there talking well past dusk while the adults played cards by the campfire.

Her brother Jonathan was going to be a lawyer like their dad. Daniel said he wanted to grow up and play his guitar in honky-tonks. Cynthia was going to be a nun with good habits. Little Jessie would be a ballerina and have twelve children. Bartlet, who wore shoulder pads to the reunion three years in a row, planned to become a college football coach. Gloria stood in the center of the pile of leaves and declared that she would someday be very wealthy but would not forget the rest of them. She graciously promised that she would allow them to take turns driving her around the mountain in her limousine.

Mikaela thought for a moment. What was it she had wanted to be? Then it came to her, the faces of her little comrades rolling around in the leaves and laughing, "Did you hear what Bug just said?!" She, Bug, had declared to one and all that someday she was going to marry Daniel.

Griffin padded in from the kitchen and looked expectantly at Mikaela, then at the ceiling. "What is it, boy? You still hungry?" Suddenly the distant thumping of rotating helicopter blades filled the air.

Mikaela opened the French doors leading out onto the wraparound deck and shielded her eyes from the bright morning sun. The surrounding mountainside was bursting with glorious gold, burnt umber, and a whole spectrum of reds painted from God's autumn palette.

The air ambulance came into view over a ridge of the Great Smoky Mountains and hovered like an eagle adrift on a high mountain current. Even from this distance, Mikaela could feel the gusts of cold, mountain air washing over her from the force of the helicopter blades slicing the air.

The helicopter landed with a gentle bounce in a field of mountain heather below the cabin. Two paramedics dressed in red flight suits emerged from the side door.

"How did I ever let myself get talked into this?" she said to her canine companions. But she was talking to herself. The bouncing trio of golden fur had left her side and was now charging down the hill toward the helicopter.

*I hope you know what you're doing, Lord,* she prayed as she watched the dogs running in circles, barking furiously at the strange, giant bird invading their property. *This wasn't exactly what I was expecting when I said I needed to earn some extra cash.*

The paramedics carried Daniel on a stretcher up the path to the big log house. The dogs bounded and barked ecstatically beside their master. Despite her apprehension, Mikaela found herself grinning.

A sense of excitement warmed her cheeks as old feelings, long ago tucked away, began to resurface. What was Daniel going to be like now? He was "city" now, a noted Nashville songwriter, with a couple of awards under his belt and the number one single, "Forever and for Always," dominating the charts. Daniel's days were full of record deals, power lunches, and television interviews.

She was "country," a hometown girl, a forest ranger, spending her days helping lost tourists, caring for injured wild animals, and spreading the word about the dangers of forest fires.

His life was full of excitement, hers the mundane.

She spied his muscular frame on the stretcher. He definitely was not the adorable, towheaded boy who had been her brother's best friend. On the stretcher smiling up at her lay a handsome stranger.

\\\\//

The rich fragrance of perking coffee drifted in from the kitchen. Roused from a light sleep by the smell, Daniel stretched and yawned as he readjusted himself on the soft maroon leather couch and wedged another pillow under the heavy cast covering most of his right leg. The events of this past week had left him physically and mentally exhausted.

The homey sounds of breakfast being prepared in the kitchen gave birth to a smile in his soul that eventually broke out across his face. It felt good, so good, being here in the quietness of the mountains. He had come to the mountain cabin only twice since purchasing it and the surrounding acres.

When the surgeon told him he'd be out of commission for eight to ten weeks, he had grumbled sarcastically, "Oh, great! You mean I'll be flat on my back for two months or more? I'll miss the award show. My publisher will be thrilled about that." With a good chance of winning Songwriter of the Year coming up, the push from his public for another big hit song weighed heavily on his shoulders.

The doctor heard him out before handing him a prescription. The paper simply said, "Rest, no stress for eight weeks."

Rest *and* no stress? Impossible! *God,* he prayed right then and there, *every time the phone rings, my publisher is on the other end of the line wanting to know when I'll be finished with my next song. You've been gracious, Lord, to give me three top-ten songs in the past two years, but the words won't come anymore. All this pressure has sucked the joy right out of my songwriting.*

He spent the first few days after surgery angry and depressed, until a young cancer patient he met caused him to rethink his priorities. Finally realizing he had been living for himself and not for the Lord, he began to think about how he could put God back in control of his life. Then it came to him: Go to the mountains. That's where he would find the Lord again. He could breathe in some fresh mountain air and take the time needed to heal his body and soul.

Only one problem remained: How was he going to find someone he could trust to take care of him while he recuperated? Suddenly it became crystal clear. There was only one person who knew the mountains, was familiar with his house, and loved his dogs. Mikaela.

\\\\//

"Hey, Bug! How about sharing a cup of that great-smelling brew with me?"

He could hear a fresh pot of coffee brewing in the kitchen. Mikaela appeared in the doorway with fire in her eyes. The sight of her brought an unexpected tightening to his chest. There she stood, tall and willowy. Her sun-streaked blond hair was pulled back in a ponytail reminiscent of childhood days. But this woman standing before him was no little tomboy. She had grown into a natural beauty. Her makeup-free cheeks looked soft and fresh as baby's skin. The red flannel shirt, blue jeans, and hiking boots only added to her appeal.

Her deep indigo blue eyes held an unexpected fire. "Don't call me Bug. For your information, I'm all grown up now."

Her sudden outburst made him laugh out loud. "Hey, settle down, little lady. I called you Bug because I figured since you're a forest-ranger lady, you still carry an insect collection or two around in your pocket."

"Let's get something straight, OK? I'm here to assist you during your recuperation. But as soon as you are on your feet, I am out of here." Her cheeks took on a rosy hue as she appeared to fight for control. "Don't mess with me, and I won't make your life miserable. Got it?"

The fine lady was a real spitfire, no doubt about it, he

thought with sudden pleasure. "Please don't look at me like that." He gave Mikaela his most charming smile. "I'm sorry. So Bug is no good. It's a shame, really. I've enjoyed calling you that since the first time you showed me your worm collection. You must have been four, five maybe? But since I'm completely at your mercy, I certainly want to keep you happy. Hmm. Let's see. Ms. Davonport maybe? Or Madam Forest Ranger? I've got it! I just thought of the perfect solution that will make us both happy. Since you're all grown up now, I'll call you *Lady*bug!"

"I should have known you haven't changed," Mikaela said as she disappeared back into the kitchen. "You are still impossible to deal with."

Was there a tinge of affection in her voice? Maybe not. Just to be on the safe side, now was a good time to change the subject.

"Can you believe that all the times I've been to the mountains in the last few years our paths have never crossed? You've done a great job with the house and dogs for me. If I've never thanked you, thanks!"

"You're welcome. I've really enjoyed doing it—and the extra money is great to have."

"I really appreciate your agreeing to help me out while my leg heals up too. I know you're really busy with your job and your life. It'll be great getting to know you again. I've even been thinking I might move here to the mountains and buy up a chunk of land."

"Why would you want to do that?" she asked as she came around the corner with two steaming mugs of coffee.

"Well, it's always been a dream of mine to have a place for up-and-coming musicians to showcase their talent. The way I see it, a thousand-seat amphitheater ought to do it."

"Great! That's what we really need around here. Another tourist attraction to use as an excuse to destroy more of the mountains." She narrowed her eyes as she approached with the coffee.

He slipped his head under the gray tartan flannel blanket. "You're not going to dump that hot coffee on me, are you?" he asked, his voice muffled.

"Daniel. Look. Your coffee is on the table beside you."

He picked up the mug and took a careful sip. "What's wrong with wanting to help the people in my hometown? God's blessed me. New development creating new jobs would be a good, Christian thing to do, don't you think? I want to give something back to the people who've had a hand in my upbringing. I would make sure whatever I built would help put a dent in the high unemployment in the area."

"That's fine, but isn't it also your job as well as mine to save and preserve the flora and fauna of our mountains for future generations? Developers come through here all the time with their big ideas. Hack and burn for the greenbacks, that's their motto. Who cares if in the process they destroy the habitats of endangered animals?"

"Oh no," he said with a look of mock horror. "I've got one of those save-the-whale activists right here in my own house!"

"I can see you are still an immature pain in the backside." She turned and stomped into the kitchen, her hiking boots sending resounding vibrations across the waxed pine floor.

Daniel peered over the top of the blanket. "I take it that last statement was meant as a compliment," he called after her. She answered with a slam of the refrigerator door.

He leaned back on his pillow and took a slow sip of coffee. "If you don't talk to me the rest of the morning, that's fine with me. I happen to have the patience of a saint," he called out. Still no answer.

Daniel tried to catch a glimpse of her over the kitchen bar, but she was staying well out of sight. He set the empty coffee mug down on the table and smiled to himself. Yes, this was certainly going to be an interesting recuperation.

# CHAPTER TWO

Mikaela stretched and yawned before she closed the door of her Jeep. The first day Daniel was home, she had worked with him to rearrange his schedule, send faxes, place calls, and generally reorganize his life. The following days she had spent running errands, going grocery shopping, and trying to cheer him up. All that and she still had her evening responsibilities at Ranger Station #3.

The man had been full of himself his first day home, teasing her and irritating her just for the fun of it. But by the second day, marooned on the couch, Daniel had grown quiet. She had laid his guitar on the coffee table so it would be close by in case he wanted to write or sing. When she left yesterday, he still hadn't picked it up.

A gust of cold mountain air whipped about her, carrying with it swirls of fall color. She shoved her hands deep into the pockets of her corduroy coat and stood for a moment listening to the call of the mountains. *Lord,* she prayed, looking skyward, *Daniel is driving me crazy! Give me an injured black-bear cub or a barn owl shot full of BBs and I'd know what to do. Bring me a man with a broken leg and I'm lost. I honestly don't know which way to turn. Please show me what it is you need me to do.*

A sudden movement in the blue sky above caught her eye. The unexpected sight of an endangered peregrine falcon gliding high aloft in an updraft warmed Mikaela's heart.

Worn wooden steps squeaked as she ascended to the back porch of the house. She opened the door and was nearly knocked over by an excited pup. Griffin and Sally joined in the welcome by nudging Theodore aside with cool, wet noses to get their greetings in. She let them out the door and laughed as Theodore tumbled and tripped on his oversized paws in his haste to chase a young wood squirrel playing among the cedars.

Mrs. Bloomgarten, the night nurse, sat at the kitchen table with her brown wool coat buttoned up to her chin and her purse hanging from her arm. The tapping of her sturdy walking shoes said it all.

"You are seven minutes late," she huffed. "Please inform your employer he can expect to be billed for overtime."

"I'm sorry. I had an early morning emergency," Mikaela said. "A call came in before dawn about an injured logger on the other side of Otter Creek. Thank God he's going to be all right, but the call put me behind schedule."

"I do not tolerate tardiness no matter what the excuse." The dowdy woman pulled a cotton hanky out of her purse. She honked loudly as she marched out.

Mikaela looked over the bar into the great room. A good fire was going in the fireplace. A lump under the blanket and a profusion of pillows scattered across the floor were all she could see of human occupation on the couch. The guitar remained on the coffee table in the same spot she had left it in yesterday.

She turned to start some coffee when a deep, sleepy voice called out, "Hallelujah! You've finally decided to rescue me." His voice held a decidedly sarcastic tone.

Mikaela leaned over the bar once again. This time she could see Daniel pulling himself up into a sitting position.

He caught sight of her and pulled a pitiful look. "Ladybug, that woman is scary. She browbeat me all night. It started when she turned out the lights at ten. She said I had to go to sleep because she was going to watch a rerun of *Star Trek* on the TV in the kitchen and didn't want me bothering her. Sweet little me! And do you know what she said when I asked for eggs and bacon for breakfast this morning? She said she couldn't give me eggs and bacon because the cholesterol combined with my inactivity would kill me, and she preferred to do the job herself!" He smiled at her expectantly. "Then she brought me this." He pointed to a small plate with a plain bagel and some orange slices. The muscles in his thick neck flexed as his mouth twitched with boyish amusement, and then he winked.

Old childhood feelings, long forgotten, flooded her with unexpected sensations. From the first time she had laid eyes on Daniel at the age of five, his dimpled smile and boyish charm had warmed her heart. She had forgotten the excitement she used to feel at reunion time each year as she had awaited the arrival of Daniel's family from Chattanooga. Now she consciously brushed the unwelcome feeling away. There was no room for even small thoughts of romance in her busy life. Besides, he had always been a terrible flirt. Flirting, she chided herself, was all he was doing with those gorgeous dark brown eyes. Still, she could not keep the heat from rising up her neck and, as she well knew, leaving bright pink spots on her cheeks.

A loud bark at the kitchen door saved her from the unexpected reaction she was having. The three dogs trooped in, panting from their romp on the mountainside. Mikaela followed the excited retrievers into the great room.

Daniel tried to save himself from the adoring Theodore by ducking under a large goose-down pillow. The puppy, encouraged by the action, took two loping strides and landed with a tumble on top of the helpless man.

Mikaela watched the dogs lick and slobber on their master while he fought to come up for air. She could see how they had outgrown Daniel's apartment in Nashville. He had sent them here to the mountains so they would have room to run. The dogs had adjusted so well after the move that Mikaela hadn't realized until now how much they had missed him. She laughed out loud as the man playing with his dogs brought to mind the little boy she used to tag after. A warm glow filtered through her, and it didn't emanate from the fire at her back.

"Save me, Ladybug! Please!" He extended his hand through the tangle of dog. She wanted to call the dogs off, but instead she reached out to help him. His large hand engulfed hers in a tight clasp.

Sally jumped playfully at Mikaela, knocking her off balance. In an instant she had tumbled forward. Daniel reacted quickly and caught her firmly by the shoulders. She found herself close enough to smell Old Spice and golden retriever. He reached up and gently cupped his hand under her chin. She trembled at the unexpected roughness of his fingertips against the softness of her skin.

Griffin pushed a wet nose between them while Theodore wiggled across the pillows onto his back, begging for a tummy rub.

Mikaela pushed away, then stood quickly in an attempt to disperse the charge in the air. This was not what she wanted at all. Not now. "Here," she said, picking up the guitar and handing it to him. "Why don't you start working on a song while I make you a plate of artery-clogging vittles?"

He picked a few chords and then laid the instrument down. "I've been having a hard time getting the words to come. It's like I've lost something from here." He laid his hand over his heart. She turned to look at him, surprised by his confession.

Mikaela sensed that he needed a sympathetic ear. Fixing him something to eat could wait. She chose instead to sit down on the arm of the overstuffed chair, a safe distance from the couch. "No one on this earth can take away the talent God has given you, Daniel. Any person who could write a song as beautiful as 'Forever and for Always' has a very special gift. Hey, you've even been nominated for Songwriter of the Year. Now that's a real accomplishment."

Daniel leaned over and rubbed Griffin's ear. He rapped the top of the cast with his knuckles. "I won't be able to attend the awards ceremony in Nashville, not that it matters really."

But Mikaela could see that it did matter. "Is that what's been bothering you these last few days? Do you want to talk about it?"

His jaw flexed as he gave her a thoughtful look. "God started dealing with me while I was still in the hospital. I've been putting my career first, above everything. I've let God ride in the backseat." He looked down at the floor as he spoke. "Not a very nice picture, hey?"

"I think all of us try things our own way sometimes. The important thing is that you listened to what God was telling you."

"This accident has really made me reevaluate my priorities. I think it's about time I left the fast life in Music City and moved here to the mountains. I could use a simpler life."

Mikaela watched the red, glowing embers of the fire for a moment. "What if choosing a simpler life isn't what God has planned for you? After all, he is the one who has blessed you with the talent and success you have."

"But what if I'm not doing what God wants me to do with my life? I could have easily been killed in the car accident. It made me start to wonder what good I've accomplished for the Lord. Who have I really helped?"

"Me, for one. I know 'Forever and for Always' is supposed to be a love song between a man and a woman, but ever since the first time I heard it on the radio, I have felt it's really a heart praise song to God. Now every time I hear it I feel like praising God. I have a feeling other people are affected the same way, and if you think about it, that is pretty incredible."

Daniel looked intently into her eyes. "You are amazing, Mikaela. Do you know you are the first person who has ever realized what the song really means? I wrote 'Forever' as a love song to God. The studio execs thought it would go over bigger as a love song than a religious song, and I just went along for the ride."

"That's no reason to throw it all away. Keep praying about it. God will show you what he wants you to do." They sat in silence for a while, listening to Theodore snore from his warm spot, wedged between Griffin and Sally on the rug in front of the fire.

"You know what you need, Daniel?" Mikaela said softly. "You need something to keep you busy and get your mind off your troubles. Got any good ideas?"

The flames from the fire danced and flickered in reply.

"I could start working with Theodore," he finally said, giving the sleeping pup an affectionate look. "He's a real nuisance with all the teething he's doing. Did I tell you he chewed up my new leather CD case last night?"

She laughed. "No, you didn't, but I think training him is a good idea. Teething isn't his only problem. He's been getting into everything. I found two rolls of toilet paper spread down the hall this morning. I should have been working with him before now, but I've been too busy. I've got a couple of good dog-training books at home. I'll bring them to you if you want. And I've got another idea," she added. "I hate that you have to miss the awards show. How about renting a big-screen TV and inviting a bunch of your music buddies here to watch it with you? It would be a lot of fun. I'll help you pull it together."

"Mikaela, you're the greatest! What would I do without you?" Daniel was brightening. "We could order up some barbecue to feed the crowd."

"You think about how you would like to handle it while I

make you some breakfast." Mikaela helped Daniel lift his cast and prop it on a pillow on the coffee table beside the guitar. He gave her a dimpled smile before she turned and went into the kitchen.

"Ladybug," he called out, "I've got an even better idea. Since most of my music buddies will be attending the awards show anyway, how about inviting the old reunion gang? Except for your brother, I haven't seen any of them in ten years."

"Everyone?" Mikaela asked with an edge of irritation to her voice. "Including Gloria?" A picture of Gloria poking her in the chest on that last reunion in the mountains came back to her clearly. The older girl hadn't liked the way Mikaela had been joking around with Daniel. "Stay out of my way, Mikaela, or I will squash you like the *bug* you are." She could hear Gloria's threatening words as if they had been said yesterday.

"Gloria will be the first one we call!" Daniel replied with the sudden sound of excitement in his voice. He obviously hadn't noticed her reaction to Gloria's name. "Put that foxy lady at the top of the list. Do you think she'll come? I wonder if the old sparks will fly."

"Of course she'll come," Mikaela answered with more than a twinge of annoyance. *Keep your opinions to yourself, girl,* she thought. She had to bite her tongue to heed her own advice. *Lord, please forgive me for all these hard feelings I still feel toward Gloria even after all these years. I hadn't realized until now how strong they still are.*

Mikaela glanced over the kitchen counter while she cooked bacon and eggs and sprinkled sugar on the cinnamon toast. She could see Daniel, his eyes closed, his head resting against the back of the couch. She listened closely and thought she could hear him humming their old high school fight song.

# CHAPTER THREE

I can't believe your love for me will be always and forever...." Mikaela hit the high note on the last verse of
Daniel's hit with gusto as she climbed the steps to the back
porch. Sally lifted her head and yawned. Griffin looked up but
didn't bother lifting his big head, as though he were afraid any
movement might make the warm sun spot he was occupying
disappear. Both dogs thumped the warm porch planks with
their thick tails.

"Good morning, friends!" Mikaela sang out as she leaned
over to give the soft, warm heads a pat. "Where is that little
rascal of yours? Off chasing field mice and butterflies again?"

In response to the question, Sally laid her head on her front
paws and sighed.

"I know how you feel, girl. I have a fellow I look after that
makes me feel exactly the same way."

The back door opened, and Mrs. Bloomgarten stepped out
onto the porch with a light blue scarf tied tightly under her
chin and a shopping bag hung over one arm. She gave neither
a nod nor a glance acknowledging Mikaela's presence before
she headed down the steps.

When she spoke, she talked briskly and without turning

around. "He has been a very good boy for once. I gave him a special breakfast of eggs and ham and homemade biscuits with strawberry jam. Please see to it that 'The Leg' bathes before I return this evening. My back is acting up, so I won't be able to assist him."

Without so much as a good-bye, the woman got into her Ford Escort and drove away.

Mikaela considered a few things she would like to say to the pompous woman but decided the day was too beautiful to let the likes of Mrs. Bloomgarten hang a storm cloud over it. It was one of those rare fall days that God blessed with spring-like warmth and glorious sunshine.

She peeked around the corner, expecting to see "The Leg"—as Mrs. Bloomgarten had taken to calling her charge—up, dressed, and pleasingly plump from such a hearty breakfast. But all she could see, as she had seen every morning since his arrival, was a big jumble of pillows and blankets spread over the leather couch and spilling onto the pine floor.

Mikaela put her hands on her hips and marched into the great room. The fireplace stood cold. She wouldn't start a fire today. Instead she threw open the French doors to let the fresh, cool mountain breeze wash away the stale night air. A stream of sunshine spilled through the room and across the hardwood floor, stretching fingers of warmth to the tousle of blankets and pillows covering the couch.

"This is the day that the Lord has made, rejoice and be glad in it! This morning shouldn't be wasted hiding under the security of flannel, Mr. —" Mikaela leaned over and jerked back the blanket. Theodore's head popped out beside a big, white cast. In an instant he dragged his wet, slobbery tongue across her nose. "Ahh!" she yelled in surprise.

"*Arp!*" Theodore yipped happily in response. It took a good swipe of her sleeve to remove the wet puppy kiss from her face.

Daniel's rumpled head popped out from under the blankets at the other end of the leather couch. "Do you always holler like that when you see a man's feet? An invalid can't get any peace and quiet around here." He pulled himself up on one elbow and gave her a cute, grumpy smile. How could he look so handsome so early in the morning?

Mikaela felt an urge to place a soft kiss on his rough cheek, still red with sleep. Instead she leaned over and gently smacked him on the top of his head. "What are you doing going back to sleep on such a fine morning? The best half of the day has already flown by. It's time to get up and soak in some of God's gift of warm sunshine."

Daniel picked up his wristwatch from the coffee table and squinted at it. "What are you rambling on about? I haven't been up yet. It's only seven-thirty in the morning!"

"Mrs. Bloomgarten told me on the way out that you had been a good boy and she had fixed you a nice breakfast. I thought that was a very sweet gesture, considering what a crotchety woman she is. Was it good?"

"Was what good?"

"The ham and eggs and biscuits she fixed you."

"Ask him." He pointed an accusing finger at the pup, who she noticed *was* looking extraordinarily content this morning. "He's the one she fixed the feast for." Theodore sat panting happily on the floor beside the couch.

"Why, you little scoundrel!" Mikaela said as she scratched the plump, contented pup on his belly, which was as fat and round as a roasted hen. "You've been flirting with the hired help again!"

"Would you scratch *my* belly?"

"In your dreams." Mikaela gave the covers a good yank, this time sending them over the back of the couch.

"Hey! I'm not properly dressed," Daniel cried out as he tried, unsuccessfully, to hang on to the blanket.

"You're right about that! I'm tired of seeing you in those disgusting black jogging pants every single morning I come in here. It's time you took a bath and got moving," Mikaela ordered. "Put 'The Leg' in that wheelchair, now. March!"

Her charge protested all the way to the bathroom. Mikaela didn't listen for one minute. She wheeled him into the spacious bathroom, bright with sunlight from the skylight above the whirlpool tub. She filled the sink with warm water, placed a fluffy white towel on the counter, handed him a bottle of shampoo and a bar of soap, and closed the door on her way out.

She could hear him grumbling, then splashing, then singing. She chuckled at the sound of his deep voice singing "Row, Row, Row Your Boat" as she fixed a ham-and-cheese omelet. The coffee finished brewing as she sliced a tomato and laid it carefully on the plate. She found two extra biscuits Mrs. Bloomgarten had hidden away and added them to the plate.

"Ladybug!" Daniel yelled out, "Throw me a pair of jogging pants and a shirt, will ya?"

Daniel emerged from the bathroom looking as clean and sharp as the air after a good rain. The fresh white T-shirt he had pulled on outlined the bulk of his broad shoulders. He wore a pair of bright orange University of Tennessee jogging pants slit up one leg to accommodate the cast. His short, thick, damp hair was slicked back, highlighting his strong cheekbones and deep brown eyes.

Mikaela wanted to tell him that despite the sandy brown color of his hair, he looked surprisingly like a Cherokee Indian brave. She decided against such a familiar comment because he might mistakenly think she was flirting with him. She could smell the sweet musky scent of his freshly scrubbed skin as she wheeled him through the French doors, onto the front deck, and into the sunshine.

When she reemerged from the house with his breakfast on a tray, Daniel was gazing out over the mountains. "In Nashville I think about these mountains almost every day. There have been times in my life recently when I wanted to drop everything I was doing and hop on a plane and come home. It's incredible up here in the fall." They both looked out over the autumn foliage. "I love Indian summer, don't you?"

Mikaela took the second glass of fresh-squeezed orange juice from the tray and pulled up a deck chair next to Daniel's wheelchair. "This is certainly a rare day. On days like this, I'm sure thankful God has allowed me to do my work in such a gorgeous place."

The smell of breakfast brought Theodore out from behind a large wild hydrangea bush. He stopped at the bottom of the stairs, looked like he was contemplating the energy required to make it up to the deck, and, thinking better of it, flopped down on the grass.

Mikaela and Daniel both laughed. "Theodore, is your little belly too full to make the climb?" Mikaela asked as Theodore rolled over on his back and wriggled around to find a comfortable spot.

"Good boy, Theo! Stay right where you are. You wouldn't share your biscuits with me, so I won't give you a single bite of mine," Daniel mumbled as he stuffed a large forkful of omelet into his mouth.

Griffin and Sally came around the side of the house, curious as to what their master was up to. They joined the pup on the sun-warmed ground. For a while the dogs and their people sat in companionable silence enjoying the treasure of the day.

While Daniel ate, Mikaela closed her eyes and enjoyed the warmth of the sun on her face. If it were a little warmer, she would abandon her hiking boots and thick socks and run barefoot through the grass. For now she would have to content herself with rolling up the sleeves of her chamois shirt.

In the silence of the morning, she dozed. She was walking hand in hand with someone through a field of wild mountain flowers. The fragrance of yellow violets and lily of the valley followed them. They sat in the soft grass, and he handed her a bouquet of bishop's-cap, morning glory, periwinkle, and sweet cicely.

"Mikaela." The sound of a male voice startled her awake. She quickly sat up. "Did you say something?" *I must be more worn out by all this extra work than I realized,* she thought to herself.

"I said it sounds like we have a fax. Can you go see? It might be one of the old gang getting back to us about the reunion." Daniel was leaning over the back of his chair and looking through the open French doors expectantly.

The electronic age was a complete nuisance on days like today. She loved and depended on her computer, but she'd be happier living in a simpler era. Mikaela approached the fax machine with a certain amount of trepidation. She mentally said a little prayer. *Father, I hope this one is not from Gloria.* She took the paper from the fax machine.

"Who is it from? Is it from one of our old friends? Hey, don't read it without me."

"I'm coming." She paused briefly to read the sender's name, breathing a sigh of relief as she carried the fax out to the deck. It was good to hear from Jessie Moorland.

# CHAPTER FOUR

Daniel watched with amusement as a smile skittered across Mikaela's face and landed with a twinkle in her deep blue eyes. How could he not have noticed her all these years? She was a willowy beauty in nature's best sense of the words. He had found himself listening for the sound of her voice while pretending to be asleep when she came in to relieve Mrs. Bloomgarten early in the morning.

The woman was a mystery to him. She could be sweeter than her mama's bread pudding one minute and downright ornery the next. And her temper? Boy, did the woman have a temper! He would just as soon wrestle a mountain lion as get on her bad side. Although he would have to admit that he did enjoy getting a rise out of her on occasion. No doubt about it, she was a real spitfire, especially early in the morning.

Just yesterday, when he had been trying to get the hang of maneuvering in and out of his wheelchair, he had seen a soft side of her so gentle and kind that it strummed the chords of his heart. She worked with him patiently until he got the hang of it, all the while offering encouragement every time he faltered while trying to move his large, cumbersome cast back and forth. After Theodore got underfoot, causing him to lose his balance and whack his broken leg on the edge of the coffee table, she had helped him back onto the couch, placed ice bags around the cast where his knee was throbbing, and put on his favorite CD.

The woman touched his heart every time she laughed or hollered or hugged on the dogs. He wished she would hug on him like that! But so far no such luck. It was possible she wouldn't ever have any interest in him; she had known him too well, too long.

As he watched her work, he wondered if she was involved with anyone. He never asked because he didn't want to know.

ᒪᒪᒪ

"Read the fax from Jessie again," Daniel asked as he leaned forward in his wheelchair. He looked as intent as a little boy listening to his mama read him his first birthday-party invitation.

Mikaela pushed back a stray wisp of blond hair and squinted in the sunshine. " 'Hi, gang! It was wonderful to get your letter. Are you two married?' " Mikaela looked over at Daniel as he laughed aloud. " 'Of course I will come to your house in the mountains for a reunion. What a great idea! I must warn you, though, I am expecting my fifth child anytime now. Hopefully he won't arrive too early and ground me at home base! I'll bring my mama's famous baked beans—the ones she used to bring to our reunions in the mountains that everyone liked so much. Will call soon. Yours truly, Jessie.' "

"Jessie always said she wanted twelve kids, remember?"

Mikaela nodded. "She's definitely well on her way." She couldn't imagine skinny little Jessie as the mother of such a large brood.

"Do you want to have kids someday, Ladybug?"

"Sure. I like kids."

"How many?"

"First tell me how many *you* want."

"Hey, I asked you first! You want eight, ten, twelve?" Daniel asked solemnly.

Mikaela sat thoughtfully for a moment before she answered. When she was twelve or thirteen, she had decided she wanted four kids, two boys and two girls. At that young age she had decided she would raise her children in the mountains so they could run barefoot in the summer and build snowmen in the winter.

There was something about Daniel that made her want to take the plunge and tell him about her dreams. But every time she started to, her heart held her back. She considered herself a private person. For as long as she could remember it had always been hard for her to share her inner self with others.

"Well? Have I asked you to divulge a great state secret or something?"

Mikaela could feel the warmth of a blush spread across her cheeks. "If I tell you and you laugh, I'll have to kill you." She gave him her best serious look.

"That's what you want to do to me most days anyway. If it makes you feel any better, I'll go first. I'm gonna have a couple of boys and a couple of girls."

"Two boys and two girls?"

He grinned and nodded.

"Funny. That's what I've always wanted."

He flashed her a dimpled smile that caused the natural blush of her cheeks to deepen.

Daniel reached over and touched the back of her hand. "You're the first person I've ever told that to. Do you think it's weird for a guy to admit something like that?"

"No. I think it's great you are in touch with your feminine side," she teased.

"My feminine side? I don't have a feminine side!" Daniel backed his wheelchair to the far side of the deck. "No guy with a girlish heart could do this!" He pulled back with such force his biceps bulged.

Mikaela couldn't believe her eyes. The guy was going to try

to pop a wheelie! "Don't do that! You could kill yourself. I was just kidding—you have no feminine side," Mikaela said in alarm, gripping the side of her chair, as if that act would keep the wheelchair from falling over backward.

Despite Daniel's best efforts, the cumbersome wheelchair refused to lean back more than a few inches. The wheelchair landed with a vibrating thump on the deck's surface. The force of the landing caused the large wheels to spin like one of the rubber-band racers they had played with as children.

At that moment it was as plain as feathers on a falcon that Daniel hadn't paid one bit of attention when she'd explained the braking mechanism to him. Griffin, who had lifted his big head off the warm wooden planks to see what all the commotion was about, found the reflexes to hop to one side. Even then the wheelchair only missed the startled dog by half a tail.

Daniel's cast, sticking out like the lance of a charging knight, rammed against Mikaela's lounger, and he came to a vibrating stop. This was followed by a loud, pained yell from the knight in question. Mikaela sat there in silence for a moment with her long legs pulled tightly under her.

"Serves you right, Daniel. It's a wonder you didn't run over poor old Griffin, not to mention mashing me like a bug!"

She had to push the wheelchair back to stand up. Despite her irritation, she inspected the speed demon closely. Except for bumping the previously broken leg, which he now was complaining was throbbing unmercifully, he appeared to have escaped the accident unscathed. His face and neck were a dark red—whether from the sun or from embarrassment, she couldn't tell.

Sally, Griffin, and Theodore stood at attention in a neat row beside the wheelchair like little soldiers waiting for their orders. Mikaela shook her head and chewed on her lower lip to keep from laughing out loud at their questioning gazes.

"Let him try to explain that one at the next doctor's visit," she called toward the trio as she turned to go inside. And in Daniel's direction she said loudly, "I can't stay out here put-

ting my life in danger all day. I've got work to do." She was re-
warded with a sheepish grin.

*Dear God,* she prayed, *please bless me with patience!*

While Mikaela organized Daniel's medical records, he remained in his wheelchair on the deck with the dogs at his feet.
He hadn't moved an inch since she had gone inside. But she
was pretty sure he hadn't bruised more than his ego.

As she worked she caught herself watching him through the
open French doors, noticing the gentle rise and fall of his
chest. There was something about him that was sweetly innocent, like a little boy who had fallen asleep in soft green summer grass waiting for the fish to bite.

*What is it about him that makes me want to share my
dreams with him?* she wondered. *Even though he talks about
developing the land around here, I know he cares about these
mountains.* If she told him about the animal sanctuary, could
she change his mind about tearing down more forest? She
could tell him about the near extinction of the red-cockaded
woodpecker and the northern river otter or the Appalachian
sedge and how they very well might not be around for the children of future generations to enjoy. After hearing about their
plight, was it possible that he might even want to find a way to
help? She smiled as she looked at Daniel with his hand on
Griffin's big, furry back. He certainly had a soft heart where
animals were concerned.

\\\\\//

Mikaela had been so busy trying to enter Daniel's unorganized
files into the computer that she hadn't noticed him come back
inside. At the creak of the wheelchair on the hardwood floor,
she turned. She started to ask him if his leg was still throbbing,
but when she saw what he was doing, she kept quiet. For the
first time since he had arrived home, Daniel had picked up his
guitar.

Her heart thumped quickly. "How about playing one of

your songs? I would love to hear you sing something you wrote." As he turned to look at her, she added a big smile as an extra encouragement.

He ran his fingers over the wood, lovingly caressing the smooth, shiny surface. He picked at the strings with his thumb and forefingers. The twang echoed in the air as he laid the instrument down. "I was just wiping the dust off the base." His face clouded over before he turned his back to her.

Mikaela could feel the heat rush up her neck and across her cheeks. Every time she suggested he get his mind off his troubles by writing music, he pulled back from her. There had been a couple of times he hadn't spoken to her for hours afterward.

Sally, the sweet mother dog that she was, seemed to sense her master's pain. She left the warmth of the sun on the deck and came inside and laid her big snout on his good knee. Mikaela watched Daniel give Sally a halfhearted rub behind the ears. His mind was on his songwriting career, not the dog at his side.

A sudden chilly gust blew through the open French doors and whipped the papers on the small desk where Mikaela was working. She stood up and took a breath of the sweet fall breeze. The distant mountains had taken on a deep bluish haze.

*Father,* she prayed silently, *thank you for this day. Show me how I can be an encourager to Daniel.*

Putting on her biggest smile, she suggested, "How about working on the plans for the reunion?" She waited for Theodore and Griffin to come inside, then closed the doors to the deck.

"What's left to do? Aren't we just waiting until everyone tells us if they can come or not?" He rolled himself into the kitchen and grabbed a green Granny Smith apple from the old dough bowl on the kitchen counter.

Now Mikaela was stumped. Daniel had been so excited about the reunion only an hour ago. If he didn't want to talk about it, how was she going to get his mind off his musical slump? "We need to get a smile back on your face," she half teased. Theodore took her advice and playfully tugged on the throw cover Daniel had across his legs.

"You think I'm feeling sorry for myself, don't you." It was more a statement than a question. "Well, you're right." His big brown eyes looked as soulful as Theodore's when he wanted attention. "Let's talk about something else. What do you do in your spare time?"

The question took her by surprise. He hadn't asked her many questions about herself since his arrival. Oh, they had covered some safe ground about the past. It was easy to talk about her brother and his wife, who were now living in New York, about her parents and his mom, and about how everyone's life had changed over the span of the past fifteen years. But that was as personal as it had gotten.

Mikaela had made a point not to pry into his personal life. If he wanted to share, it would be up to him. As far as she was concerned, it was not her place to ask. She had to admit, though, that there had been more than a few times she had wondered about the status of his love life.

"We've talked some, but I don't know a thing about the grown-up Bug."

Mikaela felt like she had swallowed a butterfly. He wanted to know more about her!

"Of course, if you're really a CIA undercover operative, then tell me to mind my own business," he teased. "As your boss, it's my duty to find out if you, my employee, are satisfied with your life."

Mikaela's heart sank quicker than a river otter diving for crawdads. Her *employer* wanted to know about her as an *employee*. She swallowed hard, but she couldn't find her voice.

"I really doubt you are an undercover agent. You're much too pretty." He laughed, an infectious laugh. Mikaela joined him in spite of the fact that her heart was yo-yoing from her chest to the heel of her boot and back.

*He's doing it to me again, Lord. One minute the serious
employer, the next a boyish flirt. I know I shouldn't ever take
him seriously.*

The man didn't know when to quit. "Well, class, it's time
for Mikaela Davonport to come to the front and give her report on 'What I did on my summer vacation.'" Daniel seemed
revived to his earlier good mood by their banter. He was acting like Theodore playing tug-of-war with a wet dishrag, and
he wasn't about to give up. Daniel paused and gave her another dimpled grin as he wheeled closer.

"You are good. I'll give you that," she grudgingly admitted.

He looked at her expectantly.

"What can I tell you? Aside from being a forest ranger and
taking care of you, my life is pretty boring." She wrinkled her
nose at him. *Where are my great comebacks when I need
them? Should I tell him about the wildlife sanctuary?* she
wondered. *Will he make a joke out of my hopes and dreams?
Will he think I've lost my mind like everyone else does?*

Would he agree with Aunt Gladys, who liked to say, "How
would you raise the money, dear? People like to give money to
projects like 'save the elephants.' I doubt most people would
bother sending money to someone trying to save the wood
cricket or some undistinguished mountain moss."

Mikaela went into the kitchen to avoid further questions.
Making a fresh pot of coffee was much easier. Daniel wheeled
right along behind her.

"Do you follow Mrs. Bloomgarten around like this? No
wonder you get on her nerves. You're better than Theodore at
getting underfoot."

Daniel polished the bright green apple on the front of his
shirt, then pitched it into the air. It made a soft thunk as it
landed in the large palm of his hand. Mikaela could hear the
loud crunch as he bit into the juicy apple.

"It's fun being a pest, if that's what you're asking. Do you
do anything for fun besides locking away litter bugs and finding lost children?"

For some reason the question and the tone of his voice hit her the wrong way. Who did he think she was, anyway? A country bumpkin? She would pretend he wasn't there. The coffee was now brewing, so she took her anger out on the day's dishes as she rinsed them off and stacked them in the dishwasher.

He didn't seem bothered in the least by her cold back. Finally the apple crunching got to her. Forget ignoring the man. Without turning around, she let loose. "I'm about as close to being a hick as you are. I'm proud of what I do as a forest ranger. I worked hard to get my master's degree from the University of Tennessee." A small pan clanged as it hit the tray of silverware. Mikaela was so intent on letting her anger loose that she didn't realize that Daniel had come up behind her. The creaking of the wheelchair on the floor behind her made her jump. Daniel reached over and placed a warm palm on her cool arm.

He looked up at her in honest concern. "I didn't mean to offend you, Ladybug. I was just fooling around." He handed the apple core to Theodore, who had been following closely on his master's wheels. Daniel knew the little guy had a taste for fruit. The pup took the treat eagerly and crawled under the old harvest table in the kitchen to enjoy the treasure.

Before she could say anything, a loud noise at the back door made them both turn around. Mrs. Bloomgarten stood there with the look of a tyrannical jailer catching them in the act of planning a breakout. Or worse, Mikaela realized in horror. The two of them were in such close proximity that it appeared they were having an intimate moment.

Embarrassed, Mikaela tried unsuccessfully to come up with a quick, logical explanation for why "The Leg's" wheelchair was pressed up against her. The stormy flashes shooting from Mrs. Bloomgarten's eyes and the mischievous glee in Daniel's expression told Mikaela her shift was over and it was past time to go.

As she headed out to her Jeep, she wanted to cry—but the

tears wouldn't come. *What's wrong with me, Lord? I used to love the teasing. I could give better than I ever got. What is it about Daniel that makes me so crazy? I've become so sensitive these past few weeks that it's become downright embarrassing.*

Thank goodness she hadn't told Daniel about the sanctuary. He would have laughed, and that would have turned into a complete fiasco. What she needed right now was time to think.

# CHAPTER FIVE

Mr. Pitkins grunted as he creaked his way into a standing position. Mikaela supported him the last few inches with her hand under his elbow. "You back here for another book of stamps already, Mickey? You trying to support the United States Postal Service all by yourself?"

The postmaster had been old as far back as she could remember. Mikaela figured the community fixture had to be close to ninety. He had first delivered mail to the Appalachian community as a young man on horseback. The United States Postal Service had retired his horse long before Mikaela was born. It was a running joke around Sugartree that as a baby, Isaiah Pitkins had fallen off a covered wagon when the first settlers began to move west.

He brushed the soil from a wrinkled, brown bulb and pitched it into the grapevine basket at his feet. Mikaela knew he would store his bulbs under the postal counter until it was time to plant them again next spring.

She smiled down at the tiny, frail man. "My new boss does like to send out a lot of letters, but today I don't need stamps. I need a handful of metered postcards." She winked at the man she loved like a grandfather. Her old friend was the best prayer warrior she knew. He had a knack for spreading sunshine. After his wife had died the previous spring, Mikaela had taken to joining him on the back row of Good Faith Baptist Church every Sunday. He was good company in and out of church.

Mr. Pitkins strained to hold the post office's heavy door open for Mikaela. She held back the urge to take ahold of the door herself. Although he was on the high side of frail, he remained a true Southern gentleman.

The postmaster disappeared into the back room, and Mikaela could hear the soft shuffle of his worn shoes on the yellowed linoleum as he slowly made his way to the back of the mail boxes.

"A couple of bills, the Clearing House Sweepstakes, and a large envelope that smells funny. Gotta be for that singing feller you're working for. Wait a minute, here's two more letters. Yep. This one's from the phone company, and this one's from a preacher fellow." He was shaking as he came back behind the counter with the stack of mail. "You asked that rich feller you're working for if he would build that animal hospital of yours?"

"No, and I don't plan to. And it's not a hospital, Mr. Pitkins, remember? It's a sanctuary," she patiently explained once again. "You know, a place where injured animals on the endangered-species list can stay while they recuperate from injuries, or live out their lives if need be. Do you remember the baby horned owl you found shot full of BBs a couple of years ago? I had to take him all the way to Knoxville, to the university. He died shortly after I left him there. That little owl might have lived if I could have kept him here in the mountains."

Mr. Pitkins sighed. "Child, you remind me of one of them wrestlers I like to watch on television. You don't let up till you know you're gonna win. Don't get me wrong," he added brightly. "I like you just the way you are. I probably wouldn't be alive today if it hadn't been for you nagging me to death to get up out of my easy chair after my Mildred died. Honey, if I had the money, I'd give it to you quicker than I could spit at a rattlesnake. Now, tell me about this new singer man of yours."

"Sorry, Mr. Pitkins. Good try," she laughed. "Daniel isn't my 'man.' He's my boss." Mikaela reached over and gave the man a hug. "You are a sweet guy, Mr. Pitkins. I love you even if you are always sticking your nose into my business."

Mr. Pitkins smiled broadly, framing his pink gums. "The Lord might be seeing things differently. It's my thinking you'd better be praying on it."

"Forget your bottom teeth at home again this morning?" she asked, changing the subject.

"Oh Lordy, yes. Since my Milly passed over, I seem to be getting more forgetful. Just yesterday I put a roast into the oven and plumb forgot to turn the thing on!"

Mikaela leaned across the counter and gave the scraggly old cheek a kiss.

"Don't know why you bother with an old raccoon like me. But seeing the pretty likes of you in the morning gives a right good shine to my long days. I worry about you getting hurt over at that old settler's cabin. A sweet girl like you don't need to be spending all her hard-earned money on a firetrap like that. You find you a good strong man to marry and stay at home and raise a whole bunch of young'uns." His eyes suddenly twinkled. "Get them young'uns to do your cooking and cleaning so you can lie back and enjoy the easy life."

Mikaela couldn't help but laugh. She had heard it all before. Mr. Pitkins wasn't the only one who felt she should find a husband and raise a brood of children. There was the cashier at the grocery store, the Baptist minister, and of course Mom and Dad, who, although they lived in Florida now, regularly managed to give her their thoughts on finding a man.

But Mikaela was too busy right now to think about getting married. If she wasn't worried about it, she didn't figure anyone else should be either. Besides, God-fearing men were hard to find in a small community like Sugartree. Most men married young, or they settled in the big cities after attending college and finding out that there was much more to the world than a one-stoplight, one-church town.

There were a lot more important things to worry about at this time in her life. Saving the endangered species of the Great Smoky Mountains was her mission for the time being.

Mikaela opened the post-office door. If she didn't physically put one foot outside the building, sweet Mr. Pitkins would keep her commiserating for hours over all her lost chances for married bliss. "I've got to run on up the mountain now. I'm over an hour late for work, and I'm afraid the night nurse has already left. I shouldn't leave my boss alone for too long." She waved good-bye, then sidestepped out the door.

"Don't you go and forget to mail in that sweepstakes like you did the last two times. It says right there on the front you could be their next millionaire!"

"If life could be so easy." She shook her head as she buckled the seat belt firmly across her jeans. She laid the letters on the seat beside her. One fell to the floor. She chuckled when she picked it up and saw the return address: *Mr. Bartlet Bell.* Mr. Pitkins must have thought the name Bell referred to the local phone company, South Central Bell.

She shuffled through the rest of the mail, setting the bills aside. A small brown envelope caught her attention. The tastefully embossed return-address label read *Reverend Hanover.* Cynthia Hanover, the tall, thin girl who had wanted to grow up to be a nun.

She fought back the urge to open both letters right then and there. They were addressed to Daniel McFarland *and* Mikaela Davonport. She bit her lip and reminded herself that planning the reunion was intended to keep Daniel's mind off his writing slump. If she opened the letters now, it would spoil all the fun for him.

The last letter she looked at was the extralarge, extrapink, perfume-drenched envelope. She turned the letter over. She knew right away who the sprawling, elegant handwriting belonged to. This letter was addressed to Daniel McFarland only. Her blood pressure pumped up two notches. Gloria.

\\\\//

As Mikaela started walking from her Jeep toward the house, Theodore pounced from his favorite hiding place behind a large, scraggly mountain cedar. He leaped, big clumsy feet first, at a surprised Mikaela before she could sputter a quick, "Down, boy!"

The furry missile made contact dead center, waist high. The day's mail went up as she—yelling, "No!"—went down. Before she knew it, she was on her back in the tall, brown meadow grass, pinned down by a wiggling, drooling pup licking her chin.

"Theodore! You naughty boy," she scolded. Unlike his gentle parents, the pup didn't care one little bit about the tone in Mikaela's voice. He was determined to give her big, wet kisses no matter what the consequences.

Mikaela tried to push the rowdy pup off, without much success. First she began to giggle, then to laugh so hard she couldn't breathe. Her reaction delighted the wiggling Theodore. Finally she stretched her arms out beside her and succumbed to the rough, wet tongue.

A piercing whistle rang out. The pup stopped midlick, barked, and immediately hopped off Mikaela. He dashed toward the porch with all the intensity of a racehorse heading for the finish line, his great love of the moment left behind in the grass.

Mikaela wiped the dog slobber from her left eye and squinted into the sun. She leaned forward and shaded her eyes with her hand. The mail was strewn about her on the grass, stuck in the cedar tree, and poking out from under her now puppy-hair-covered jeans. She looked over at the back porch.

There sat Daniel in his wheelchair, trying to push a bouncing, barking ball of golden fur from his lap.

"When are you going to start training Theodore?" She stood up and brushed herself off, then gathered up the mail.

"You sure do look like you're in a better mood than when you left here yesterday. Whoo-whee, you scared me!" he exclaimed in mock horror. "I thought you were going to throw me clear off this mountain."

"I'm sorry. I've had a lot of things on my mind. I guess I was acting pretty childish."

"No, just human. I know I mess with you all the time, but you have to admit we've gotten pretty close these last few weeks. Shoot, you've seen me in my BVDs!"

She laughed, "Yeah? Only because you decided to hop from the wheelchair to the sink without calling for help. You should thank the Lord your elbow was the only thing you bruised when you hit the floor!"

"Hey, how come you're late? Mrs. Bloomgarten pushed me out here, ordered me to wait for you, and left without even a wave good-bye! Have you been hanging out with some other guy?"

She flipped her ponytail over her shoulder and went into the house, leaving Daniel on the porch looking puzzled.

"Talk to me, girl!" he called out.

"I don't want to talk right now," she called back.

Mikaela could hear the bumping his chair made as he tried to force it through the doorway. He could manage the French doors to the deck easily, but the narrow single door to the porch was another matter. The night nurse should never have pushed him out there.

She opened the refrigerator door and started taking out the stuff for sandwich makings. By the time she had laid everything on the kitchen counter, he still wasn't inside.

"Don't feel guilty for leaving me out here, OK?" he hollered. "I'd been praying for thirty minutes or more that the Lord would send my guardian angel home to rescue me. It's a good thing you're here. The wind is really picking up out here. I'm starting to feel like a frozen TV dinner." He paused for a response. "Ladybug?"

Now she was feeling guilty. Mikaela tried to look casual as she strolled out onto the porch. There was definitely an early winter quality in the brisk mountain air. Dark, distant clouds had begun loitering along distant Appalachian ridges, bringing with them ripples of cold air and threatening an early snow.

"It is pretty chilly out here. I think it would be a good time to get a fire going, don't you? I had better head out to the woodshed and split some wood."

Daniel's teeth chattered as he wrapped his arms around himself. "I got out here easily enough, but then I couldn't get this bulky chair back inside." He demonstrated by ramming his wheelchair through the door and wedging it against the doorjamb.

Mikaela looked closely at the man as he gave her the pitiful puppy look Theodore was famous for.

"Are your teeth really chattering? Oh, all right. Fetching wood can wait."

It took effort from both of them, and no help from a yapping, dancing Theodore, before the wheelchair squeaked through. Daniel cheered when he finally made it into the kitchen.

She threw him a thick wool sweater from off the hook beside the back door and went to put the kettle on to boil for hot chocolate. Despite his ruddy cheeks, Mikaela decided after a quick once-over that the man was none the worse for wear.

〜

Daniel watched Mikaela work. She moved quickly about the kitchen with simple, ordinary movements, fixing a plate of ham-and-cheese sandwiches smeared with Miracle Whip and mustard. She knew they were his favorite. *God, how can I thank you for sending Ladybug my way? She is an amazing woman!*

"I forgot to tell you. A guy called a little while ago and left a message on the answering machine. I couldn't pick up the phone because I was stuck on the back porch, but I did hear the message." He looked at her expectantly.

She didn't ask who called or what the message was, but he told her anyway. "The guy's name was Isaiah. He said you left something behind when you stopped by his place this morning."

"OK. And here's your mail." She handed him the letters.

Daniel held the mail in his hand and stared at her with a look of consternation. "You aren't going to tell me who Isaiah is, are you?"

\\\//

Daniel's plaintive question brought a smile to her face. The man was bothered by a call from Isaiah Pitkins! She should tell him not to worry. Let him know that the guy who left her a message didn't have an original tooth in his head and could tell you the stories his grandfather told him about fighting in the Civil War. But that could wait for later too.

When he saw that she wasn't going to tell him who Isaiah was, he looked down at the mail he was holding. She waited to see his expression when he saw that two of the letters were replies for the reunion. The big, pink, perfumed card had disappeared within the depths of the cedar tree during the wrestling match with Theodore. A childish act leaving it there, but she knew she would go dig it out in a while. It would have to wait.

"A letter from a Reverend Hanover." He didn't look up for a moment, but when he did, his eyes were as round as goose eggs.

He ripped open the envelope and took out an embossed card. Much to Mikaela's aggravation, he dropped the torn envelope on the floor. "You must be close relations with Charlie Brown's friend Pigpen. A mess whirls right behind you wher-

238

ever you go." She picked up the paper, wadded it into a tight ball, and hit the trash can dead center.

"Look at this, Mikaela. Cynthia Hanover has taken on a religious life!"

"I'm not surprised, really. Don't you remember? Back when she was a kid, she said she wanted to be a nun."

"I had forgotten about that," he said as he started to open up the gold-embossed card.

Mikaela leaned over Daniel's shoulder and read the return address out loud, " 'The United Anglican Church, Central Offices of the Bishop.' "

"Her Highness, little Miss Cynthia." Daniel said in an exaggerated tone.

Mikaela took a playful swipe at the top of Daniel's head. "Read the card!"

" 'Mail for Cynthia Hanover, Ph.D., is being forwarded through our office while she is working with the Chanuk Indian tribe along the Amazon River in Central Brazil. We are in regular contact with her via shortwave radio and have already forwarded your invitation on to her.' Yeah, right. Cynthia Hanover, master spy. Briefcase chained to her arm and a microchip hidden in her lipstick, trudging through the jungle to attend a secret meeting that will save the world."

"Very funny, Daniel! I'm going to have to tell Mrs. Bloomgarten to ban you from any more late-night spy movies on cable."

He looked at her in mock alarm.

She wheeled his chair beside the overstuffed leather couch, took the card from him, and sat down. "Your theory is off. A spy would never carry lipstick into the jungle—powder, maybe." Mikaela paused while she read the card over. "See, right here at the bottom it says, 'Missionary Hanover asked us to inform you that she will be returning Stateside within the week for a short furlough and will be able to attend the reunion.' "

"A missionary along the Amazon River. I never would have expected that!"

Mikaela smiled fondly at her boss. "That's the real fun of a reunion, finding out what everybody has been doing over the years."

He didn't say anything while Mikaela helped him onto the couch and propped his cast on a pillow on the coffee table. He leaned over and gently brushed a stray wisp of blond hair from her eyes. "Ladybug, what would I do without you?" Mikaela wanted to reach out and touch his cheek. Instead she went into the kitchen to see if the water was boiling for the cocoa. She spooned cocoa mix into two cups and went outside to fetch some logs for the fireplace.

A crackling fire was soon roaring in the huge stone fireplace. That accomplished, Mikaela carried in steaming mugs of hot cocoa and some sandwiches on a tray. After handing the tray to Daniel, she settled with a mug of cocoa and a sandwich into the overstuffed chair across from him.

"Ladybug, you are absolutely the best sandwich maker in these mountains. Mmmm." He leaned back and sighed as he took a second bite. They sat in comfortable silence as they ate, enjoying the sound, smell, and radiating warmth of the fire.

Daniel was the first to break the spell. "I don't know why, but finding out Cynthia is a missionary bothers me."

Mikaela could hear the agitation in his voice. "You should be happy, not irritated, that one of our friends has been called into the Lord's work. Don't you think you're overreacting a bit?"

He didn't answer. She gathered up the mugs and plates and carried them to the kitchen sink. While she rinsed them and placed them in the dishwasher, she thought about Cynthia.

Cynthia Hanover had been a quiet, sweet child. That is, until she started running with Gloria's crowd in high school. Mikaela always had the impression that deep down, Cynthia was only trying to find a place to fit in.

Cynthia's parents owned a successful hardware manufacturing business and were always jetting around the world on business, leaving her behind. The thin girl with the flip hairstyle needed to know she was accepted. Gloria's crowd must have provided the affirmation she needed. Even then, Mikaela had thought Cynthia seemed lonely.

"Ladybug?" Daniel called out from the great room.

Mikaela went in to see what he needed. He patted the seat beside him. "Do you have time to sit and talk for a while before you leave for your real job?"

She sank slowly into the softness of the leather beside him. He smiled and surprised her by reaching out and taking her hand. She could feel calluses on his fingertips caused by years of strumming a guitar. The gentle pressure of his large hand engulfing hers warmed her heart and strummed her soul. Being there with him, hand in hand, seemed like the most natural thing in the world.

"Thanks for being my friend these last few weeks. All my old buddies are too busy with their own lives and jobs to worry about me. It's meant a lot to me to have someone around who really listens."

She wanted to say something. She wanted to tell him that her feelings had been growing for him and that she had been running from them like an autumn leaf blown across the mountaintop by cold currents. She opened her mouth, but she couldn't find the right words, the right sentiment.

He sat silently holding her hand, his gaze toward the fireplace, where a big log hissed and crackled. Bursts of red-hot sparks shot upward, caught by a blast of cold air fighting its way down the warm chimney.

He finally released her hand and shifted around so he was facing her. She felt a brush of disappointment that she could no longer feel the warmth of his skin. In the short time she had come to know the adult Daniel, she already knew that the intent look on his face meant he was being serious.

She asked, "Why don't you tell me why you feel so uncomfortable about Cynthia Hanover being in the ministry?"

"Am I that transparent?" He took a deep breath. "A long time ago, during a chapel service at college, I told God I would give my whole life to him. I was nineteen at the time."

"I never knew that," Mikaela said, trying to keep the surprise out of her voice. Her brother and Daniel had roomed together in college, and she knew she would remember if Jonathan had mentioned it.

"I didn't tell your brother or anybody else about it at the time, and I don't really know why. I think I figured I was still young and had a whole life ahead of me to act on the calling. A few months after I dedicated myself to God, I kind of pushed him to the back burner."

"Didn't you go get advice from your pastor or one of your Christian teachers?"

"About a year later I went to visit my college pastor. I was into the worldly music scene by then. I told him that someday when I was more mature, I would work for the Lord." Daniel buried his face in his hands.

"What did he say?" Mikaela asked quietly.

"He said he would keep me in his prayers. I can still see the look on his face when I walked out of that church. He gave me the saddest smile I have ever seen." Daniel sighed.

"You weren't much more than a kid."

"I know. But that doesn't excuse my actions. When I think of the commitment I made back then and the path I chose, the old feelings of letting God down hit me hard. Seeing that Cynthia did what God wanted her to do makes me feel incredibly guilty."

"It sounds to me like you made a commitment to God without a clear sense of the job he'd prepared you for. Lots of people do that. Take me, for example. I first went into nursing in college, thinking that would be a really good way to serve God. But I discovered right away that my love was not sick people but animals and their habitats. I'm now working in an area that I believe God intended for me all along." Mikaela looked past Daniel and out over the mountains. She felt she could almost touch God's love when she looked out over the vastness of this beloved wilderness.

"Mikaela." The rich timbre his voice took on when he said her name brought a smile to her face. "I know what I'm doing now is right. I'm using the talents God gave me to their fullest, but I still feel guilty, wondering if I let God down in some way."

Mikaela leaned over and placed her hand on his arm. "God has blessed you in what you're doing. I think that should say something. I believe God meant for you to touch people's lives with your songs."

"Thanks, Ladybug." He gave her a sweet, dimpled smile. "I write to praise God. Wherever I go I tell people I love the Lord. I tell them that all my talents come from him."

The depth of gentleness in his warm brown eyes engulfed her. Mikaela could feel a new closeness, as though the sharing had spun a connecting cord between them. She wanted the moment to go on forever.

Daniel shifted, looking uncomfortable. Mikaela could feel the fragile cord slip away. The intensity of the moment was gone as quickly as if it had never been. They were back in the real world.

He ripped open another envelope and pulled out a two-page letter. "My old buddy Bart. The postmark's from Florida." He read the letter silently until Mikaela snatched the two pages from his hand.

"Hey! Give that back!" he yelled as he stood up and wobbled into his wheelchair. He landed with a grunt and didn't bother getting comfortable before coming after her.

"You were the one who said no fair reading the reunion letters alone." She made her getaway into the kitchen. "I penned the invitations and mailed them off. And if I'm not mistaken, the letter is addressed to both of us. You get it back as soon as you promise to read it out loud." She grinned down at him from the countertop, where she had jumped to get out of his grasp.

He tried to grab at the letter, but she held it high. "Out loud, Daniel." From her position on top of the kitchen counter, Mikaela waved the pages a few inches from his outstretched hand.

Finally Daniel raised his right hand. "I promise to read the entire missive *out loud* to Mikaela Davonport or be abused until my dying day by the previously named female."

"That's more like it." She hopped down from the counter and handed it to him.

" 'Dear Danny and Mickey,' " Daniel read. " 'I was so surprised to hear from you. It's been years since I've had any news from the old gang. I will be in Knoxville the week before the date of the reunion for a game, so I will be able to come! Did I mention I am now a coach for the Miami College Swordfish? (You may have heard of them. They're pegged to go all the way to the NCAA District One playoffs this year!) Can't wait to see you guys!' " Daniel waved the letter when he finished reading it. "He did it. Bartlet has a top-ranked college team. He's talked about wanting to do that since he was our star quarterback in high school."

"He wanted to be a coach like his dad. Remember that first reunion our parents had in the mountains? He came dressed in a University of Tennessee football uniform and wouldn't take his shoulder pads off all day." Mikaela smiled at the memory.

"And after a few hours he developed a horrible rash, and his mom started yelling at him because she had to leave the reunion early and take him to the doctor," Daniel added. They both laughed at the mental picture.

Daniel handed the letter to Mikaela. "Hang on to this letter. I'd like to keep it. Wow, a college football coach! That's quite an accomplishment."

Mikaela reached over and touched Daniel on the shoulder. She could feel the hardness of his muscles through his sweater. She held back the urge to push back a stray, soft curl beside his ear. "Daniel, you could teach a lot of us about reaching for our dreams." She felt a sense of pride for him.

"God has helped me achieve success doing something I love." He paused, and without turning, reached up and covered her hand with his. "But I don't think I've completely realized the extent of his plans for me yet."

*Lord, will I be able to realize* my *dream?* she prayed silently. Money—*I hate that word. Lord, why does seeing my dream come true have to hinge on money?*

"What more do you think God has for you to do?" Mikaela's hand had grown hot, but she resisted the urge to remove her hand from under his.

"Promise you won't laugh? I know I have a tough, independent image to uphold." He didn't wait for an answer. "I want to find the woman God has been saving for me. I want to . . . share my life with her." He let his voice trail off.

Mikaela pulled her hand away from his shoulder. Suddenly her mouth felt cotton dry. She had to have a glass of water. She started to ask him if the woman of his dreams was a beautiful country singer or a gorgeous model. He didn't give her a chance.

"That's it! I've confessed all my deep, dark secrets to you. Now it's your turn."

Now was her chance. She had just opened her mouth to speak when the phone shrilled an unwelcome interruption. Mikaela leaned over the kitchen counter and grabbed the receiver. A curt, female voice on the other end asked to speak to Mr. McFarland. Mikaela handed over the cordless phone.

A slow grin broke out across his face, arching from dimple to dimple, like the birth of a rainbow after a storm. He laughed out loud at the sound of the voice on the other end of the line, then pushed himself (with ease, she noted) to the far end of the great room. She stayed in the kitchen to afford him privacy. While he talked she put on a pot of coffee.

He had loads of women friends in Nashville, and all around the country, for that matter. They could call anytime. But why now, breaking the spell that had settled over them? Why now, when he had finally asked her to share her hopes and dreams? It was hard, downright hard, for her to open up to people, and now the moment was gone. Mikaela reached for the blue-willow coffee canister and managed in one smooth sweep to knock it over, spilling fragrant coffee across the tile counter-top.

She peeked around the corner and watched Daniel's animated face revel in the words of the woman at the other end of the line. Her cheeks began to burn at the sound of his voice. *Settle down, girl. He can talk to anybody he wants to and in any way he pleases. Daniel is your boss, nothing more.*

She couldn't come up with one good reason why there was a hot flush in her cheeks and her temples were throbbing painfully. To block out the rich timbre of his laughter floating from the other room, and to keep from acknowledging to herself that she was just this side of full-blown jealousy, Mikaela hauled the bag of dog food out of the pantry and carried it to the back porch. One sharp whistle with her fingers between her teeth brought the dogs running. The invigorating mountain air was cold enough to cool Mikaela's warm skin and give old Griffin an extra bounce in his step.

All three animals happily chowed down on the unexpected meal. "Hey, big guys. My blood pressure seems to be a tad elevated. Can you diagnose my condition? Do you think I'm in any danger of bursting a blood vessel?" Griffin gave her a fond glance and a good tail thump. Theodore looked up at her and gagged from bolting his food.

"Men. What do they know anyway?" When she sighed, Sally stopped eating and licked the back of her hand as if in agreement. "You are such a sweet girl, Sally. That man in there has my blood galloping through my veins." Sally came over and leaned warmly against Mikaela's leg. She got a scratch behind the ears and a treat from Mikaela's pocket as a thank-you.

Mikaela stood for a few minutes and watched a dark rain

cloud sneak quietly along the top of a distant peak. Before long the cold air would grab the few drops of rain and weave light, lacy snowflakes. Mikaela closed her eyes and turned her face to the last of the sun.

*Mikaela,* she chided herself, *despite past friendships, that man's personal life isn't any of your business.*

She slowly sucked in the invigorating coolness and sighed. They had had a close, warm moment, but that was all it was. It was time to get back to work and run some errands. There were more important things for her to be worrying about.

Mikaela let Sally in when she went back inside to see if Daniel needed anything from town. Looking over the tiled kitchen counter, she could see Daniel with the phone glued to his head. She hadn't seen him this exuberant, ever.

Mikaela had just taken a step into the great room when his voice suddenly took on a low, sultry tone. "I can't wait to get my arms around you!" He caught sight of Mikaela and smiled, not at all embarrassed that she had overheard.

"Gloria," he mouthed, winking.

Mikaela turned around and grabbed her purse off the counter. The fight-or-flight instinct filled her heart and soul. Fight or flight? Which should she choose? That was easy. She chose flight. Her mind a blur, she marched out. She didn't remember putting on her seat belt or starting the engine of the Jeep.

Gloria! Here she was, back in Mikaela's life once again. Granted, she, Mikaela Davonport, had typed the invitation for the reunion and mailed the thing to her. Since then Mikaela had dreaded the thought of Gloria's response. She honestly thought she had outgrown the feelings of insecurity and inadequacy that Gloria used to stir in her every time they were together. But here they were again. Feelings, like ugly weeds, began taking root in her heart. Suddenly she remembered the letter in the bush by the walkway. With a sigh, she turned off the engine and went to find the letter.

*God, why can't I handle the fact that Daniel enjoys talking with Gloria on the phone? I'm not handling these feelings well. Please help me. I can't do this alone.*

The drive into Sugartree was the quiet time she needed to talk to God. *Lord, help me to be more mature and give Gloria a break. Isn't it possible that the snobby teenaged girl who terrorized my younger years has matured into a fine, upstanding Christian woman? Anything is possible. So why don't I believe it?*

The more she thought about it, the more she wanted to kick herself for reacting so poorly to Gloria's call. She was stronger, more secure than that. A few miles outside of town she pulled the Jeep into a roadside lookout point and turned off the engine. *I can't deal with Gloria, but you can,* she prayed. *Please forgive me for the way I have been acting lately. Somewhere along the way my feelings for that aggravating, lovable lunk living up there on the mountain have grown, and I don't know what to do with them. I don't even know if I want to feel this way.*

᭙ᵐᵐᵐ

Daniel hung up the phone, then rolled into the kitchen. He hadn't been mistaken. A quick look out the back window confirmed that Ladybug had left. She hadn't said anything about leaving earlier. He hoped he hadn't said something out of line again. That woman was a complete mystery to him.

He sat by the kitchen window absently watching two squirrels play tag up and down a small tulip tree in the backyard. A fine mist was settling over the mountains where his ancestors had hunted and fished to survive. The distant shrouded peaks looking so like ancient Indian mounds weren't about to give up any of their secrets either.

Sally came around the side of the kitchen island, stretched, and sneezed. "Hey, girl!" Daniel said with delight. "I didn't know you were in the house."

Sally wagged her tail and placed her soft muzzle on her

master's good knee. Her soulful, big brown eyes gazed up at him. "You missed me when I sent you to live in the mountains, didn't you? I'm sorry, girl. I got kinda selfish there for a while. You know, fame and all." Sally continued to slowly wag her tail. "But you love me anyway, don't you, girl?" He played with her long, soft ears. Dog and master remained there for a long while, communing silently as only two old friends can.

The large golden dog broke the silence with a loving lick to her master's hand and a glance at the back door. "Need to go out for a while?" He smiled down at her. "Good idea. You had better check on that pup of yours. No telling what he's been up to."

He went to open the door to the back porch but paused briefly, lost in thought, before turning the handle. "You've been around Ladybug a while now. Do you understand her? Where does she go when she leaves here? Who does she see?"

Sally thumped her tail and looked expectantly at the door, revealing none of Mikaela's secrets.

"You women all stick together, don't you?" he asked as he opened the door. With an affirmative wag of her tail, Sally padded outside.

*Dear God, I keep making Mikaela mad, and I don't know why. Please open up her heart to come on back up here so we can work things out. She's beginning to mean a lot to me.*

Griffin barked from the back porch. When Daniel peered out the window, his heart jumped. Mikaela's Jeep was pulling up the drive.

# CHAPTER SIX

Two days later Mikaela stepped gingerly across the cracked boards on the slanting front porch of the old settlers' cabin. Everyone in town delighted in telling her what a fool she had been to buy the place. Most advised that she raze the old cabin and build something commercial in its place. A putt-putt golf course, a wax museum, an ice cream and fudge shop had been a few of the ideas.

She could no more tear down this wonderful old cabin than ride over a waterfall in a canoe. The history embedded in these old, worn log walls was almost palpable. She pushed open the squeaky door and startled a large wood rat standing on his hind legs. He squinted at the light intruding into his domain before scurrying through a hole in the plank flooring.

Mikaela stood and watched the swirling dust caught up from the floor, walls, and windowsills by a sudden gust of wind. She coughed and stepped inside. Here amidst the dust and dusk she envisioned the two-room cabin as it would look when she converted it into a nature gift shop.

The heavy, worn, ten-foot rafters would hold antique farm tools and implements like the ones used when the cabin stood on a working farm. The old heart-pine floor, newly restored, would give her customers a sense of the people who had lived and died within the cabin walls. She would patch the mud-and-straw chinking between the logs of the walls to keep out the cold mountain air. And last but not least, she would have the fallen brick chimney and fireplace rebuilt.

Karen Muldune over at the feed store had said she would donate the antique counters they had stored in the back after remodeling years ago. Mikaela planned to fill the shelves with birdhouses, birdseed, toy stuffed endangered animals for the kids, mountain rocks, plastic bugs and butterflies, and T-shirts and posters of forest flora and fauna.

She wanted to restore the feeling of the old place as close to the original as possible. The builder of the cabin had been Jedidiah Johnson, a member of the small first group of settlers in the area. He had married a Cherokee woman and had twelve children. Half the residents of Sugartree claimed they could trace at least one branch of their family tree back to Jedidiah.

The one-hundred-acre wedge of land directly behind the old cabin had been part of Jedidiah's original settlement. It was hard to imagine, looking out at the overgrown brush and thickets of laurel, what the farm must have been like when Jedidiah cleared and plowed the land to provide enough fresh produce for his wife and children.

Mikaela surveyed the area while mentally designing the layout of the stables, clinic, and nursery that would house injured endangered animals. Tourists would pay to bring children to see the animals and birds housed in their natural habitat. She would put the money she earned back into the sanctuary.

The loud slam of a car door broke her reverie.

"May I help you?" Mikaela asked the woman in the red silk suit, high heels, and overdone makeup. The woman was not from the Sugartree area, Mikaela was certain. The woman flashed a bright smile and hesitantly placed a red patent-leather shoe on the first step. "Let me come down to you,"

Mikaela said in alarm. "The wood on the steps and porch is rotten in places. You could injure yourself."

The woman backed away, looking relieved. "I am Rita Solei." The woman introduced herself with an extended, manicured hand. "I am with Sun Lake Realty in Knoxville."

Mikaela eyed the woman skeptically, then held back a sneeze brought on by the woman's strong perfume. "You're an awful long way from home, aren't you?" She regretted the tone in her voice as soon as the words were out of her mouth. Wiping her dusty hands down the sides of her jeans, she extended her hand. "I'm sorry if I sounded rude. You took me by surprise. My name is Mikaela Davonport. I am the owner of this cabin."

"I am here to meet with Harold Stone, the owner of the land behind the cabin. I am glad to meet you, Ms. Davonport." The look on her face said otherwise as she took in Mikaela's long ponytail, green-and-gray flannel shirt, and muddy hiking boots.

"The land behind the cabin is not for sale. That is, it's already spoken for."

The Realtor gave Mikaela a beauty-pageant smile. "That's not what I've been told. I spoke with Mr. Stone on Friday on behalf of a client who is looking for a piece of commercial property in this area. Mr. Stone offered my client this wedge of land, and she is anxious to acquire it sight unseen." She practically sniffed with arrogance. "In fact, my client is *very* positive about this particular piece of property." She ended her little speech with a dismissive wave of her hand, her red, samurai-sword fingernails glistening in the sunshine.

Mikaela was about to inform the woman that she was mistaken about *her* land when Harold Stone, the biggest landowner in that part of the Smoky Mountains, pulled up in his Land Cruiser.

"Mikaela Davonport! I've been trying to get ahold of you," he bellowed as he gave her a hearty clap on the back before grabbing the Realtor by the hand. "And this must be Rita

253

Solei!" With a theatrical bow, he kissed the back of the woman's hand.

"May I speak with you in private, please?" Mikaela grabbed his elbow and gave it a hard squeeze.

Harold Stone winced. "Please excuse me one moment, Mrs. Solei. It seems this young lady has an urgent matter. Read over this copy of the property survey, and have yourself a look around."

Mikaela stomped over to the large morning-glory bush next to the porch. Before she could sputter any more than, "What is going on here?" Harold Stone jumped right in.

"Hold on to your britches, little lady. I'll talk with you gentleman to lady, but you have to promise not to go off and slug me."

"Mr. Stone, you promised me that land and told me you would wait for me to raise the down payment. That property is crucial to the success of my animal sanctuary!"

"Slow down there, now. I know I said I'd sell you that piece of property a few months back, but I ain't seen no cash or collateral from you since. I'm a businessman, not the Goodwill."

"But you gave me your promise." She shook her head, partly in disgust and partly to hold back the tears.

"I practically *gave* you this charming log cabin and the surrounding acreage. You've got plenty of room here and more for what you need to do."

Mikaela clenched and unclenched her fists at her side. "This so-called charming cabin is a fire hazard as it barely stands now. I'll have to sink thousands of dollars and hours into it, not to mention blood and sweat, before it becomes a nature store. The property is a little over an acre. The additional one hundred acres are imperative if I want to give the animals a natural habitat in which to recuperate. You know that. You've had a copy of the plans at your office for almost six months now."

"Don't you raise your voice at me, young filly." He stabbed his thick, ringed hand in the direction of Rita Solei. "She has a wealthy client who is ready to sign on the dotted line and put cash on the table for that piece of property back there. You got hard cash you can lay on the table in the next few hours?"

Mikaela didn't know if it would be better to pummel the man's huge chest with her hands or chain herself to one of the large tulip-poplar trees out back. She slowly inhaled a deep breath of chilly mountain air in an attempt to calm down and spoke slowly and carefully. "Harold Stone. You gave me your word. It's taking time to raise that kind of cash." She wasn't about to tell him she had come up with only a minuscule twenty-eight hundred dollars toward the two hundred thousand she needed, mostly pledged by family and friends. "You promised me you would work with me on this."

The man looked anxiously over his shoulder at the Realtor. "That I did. OK, I'll give you until tomorrow to come up with a third of the total. And by the way, the price has gone up to $275,000 as of today. Tomorrow morning at eight o'clock, you hear me?" He flashed her one of his barracuda grins, turned, and walked away.

Numb. It was the only word to describe how she felt at that moment. It had been a long shot to think of coming up with a down payment on the original two hundred thousand dollars. How could she possibly raise what was needed plus an additional seventy-five thousand?

"I'm calling my lawyer the minute I get home. You won't get away with this!" She looked across the open field at the two already talking earnestly. "You'll see," she mumbled to herself as she slammed the door of her Jeep. She slumped into a black silence at the realization that she had never gotten the agreement with Harold Stone in writing. Even Jonathan, her lawyer and brother, couldn't help her out of this one.

The frustration she was feeling was numbing. *God, what do I do now? Please help me!*

# CHAPTER SEVEN

Daniel carefully placed his new walking cast on the floor as the physical therapist had shown him the day before. He checked the parking brake on the wheelchair, then slowly pulled himself into a standing position. He wanted to surprise Mikaela when she arrived. Where was she, anyway? He checked the clock on the far wall. She should have been here hours ago. Luckily he was now able to get around pretty well without much help.

He eased himself back down into the wheelchair. Waiting was making him antsy. He couldn't wait to see the look on her face when she saw him swing onto his crutches. Looking back over the last two days, it struck him that his life had suddenly taken a lurch forward. The doctor said his leg was healing nicely. The cast should come off before too much longer. He was also about to make some major changes in his life.

Daniel looked toward the back door. Had he heard Mikaela drive up? He pushed the chair over to the kitchen window. The driveway was empty except for a groundhog sitting on its haunches sniffing the air. Daniel sat there by the window in the silence of the afternoon thinking over the last two days.

Mrs. Bloomgarten had driven him to Knoxville Tuesday evening so he would be able to make his eight o'clock orthopedic appointment on Wednesday morning. He would have much preferred Mikaela's company, but she had said she had a problem to attend to in Sugartree.

Besides, there had been some business he needed to take care of in Knoxville, and it had to do with Gloria. It seemed that Gloria rubbed Mikaela the wrong way. Why? He had no clue. It must be one of those woman things.

When he met Gloria in Knoxville for dinner, he found she still had beauty, savvy ways, and a feisty mouth. But his fascination with the woman, which had tormented him from a young age, was no longer there, he had realized with a sense of relief.

Gloria had called him a couple of weeks back and offered to use her contacts and his money for a business venture. The woman had wasted no time in contacting her connections in Sugartree. Within a few days, she had called back, saying she had located a good piece of property that would help him benefit from the tourist boom in the area.

"I'm thinking a high-class hotel, a thousand-seat country-music concert hall, or maybe the largest water park in the South. You take your pick," she had told him over the phone. "I've got plans, Daniel, to make us lots of money. You don't have to worry about anything. I've already had the papers prepared for our venture. All you have to do is sign them."

Her ideas were not exactly what he had had in mind. He had been thinking about what Mikaela had said about saving the mountains for future generations to enjoy. Mikaela had also pointed out in her own gentle, perceptive way that God had given him a heart to help people. Even though he hadn't gone into the ministry, he could still use his God-given gifts for encouragement and shepherding. He had spent long hours praying about what he should do.

Within a few days, God's answer had come through loud and clear. The Lord had laid it on his heart to build a musician's retreat. A quiet, friendly place to work and share with others interested in country and Christian music. The retreat center would be open to any musician who needed the peace and tranquillity the mountains had to offer. It would be a place for creativity, sharing, and solitude. A place to glorify God.

He could envision small cabins in the surrounding woods, where musicians could live while they worked. Of course, there would have to be a large, comfortable lodge with a huge stone fireplace, and a long antique harvest table, where singers and writers could linger over coffee. His music-industry friends and contacts could teach seminars, share their successes, and offer encouragement to those trying to break into the music business.

He had thought of everything, except how to handle Gloria and her steamroller style. That could be a problem, her vision being much grander than his ever was.

When he had told her he was thinking of developing a place on a smaller scale than what she had in mind, she had answered, "Don't worry about a thing, Daniel. We can do that, too."

The thought of trying to dissuade Gloria from anything she had sunk her teeth into was troubling. *I'm a man of compromise,* he had assured himself. *To pacify Gloria, I will build an outdoor stage where the musicians can perform their works in progress for the tourist crowd. That should make the lady happy.*

On the trip home from Knoxville, he thought about his old friends from childhood. Gloria couldn't hold a candle to Mikaela. Mikaela had turned into a rare mountain beauty, in heart as well as soul. Mikaela was going to be so surprised when he told her he was going to stay in the mountains for good. He'd wait, though, until he had it all worked out.

Now here he was back home with a walking cast he wanted to show off and the knowledge that by this afternoon he would be the proud owner of a hundred acres down the road. And no Mikaela to share his excitement with.

Sally came into the kitchen and went to sit by the back door. She looked over at Griffin, who was patiently watching his master have a silent discussion with himself.

"Has your wandering son or our wandering lady finally come home?" Daniel asked, pushing the wheelchair to the door. As soon as the door opened a crack, the two golden retrievers raced down the drive. They stopped short of the gate and stood, noses pointed, necks strained, looking down the road leading to Sugartree.

The deep churning sound of a Jeep could be heard in the distance. It didn't take the dogs' excitement to tell Daniel who was coming. The forceful beating of his heart told him Mikaela was almost home.

\|\|\|/

The yellow buckeye, mountain ash, and black-cherry trees flowed with autumn colors, coursing from the highest elevations down through the valleys and coves of the Smoky Mountains. The sassafras trees mingled their yellow-orange hues in a delightful blend with the red leaves of the black gum and red maple. But for once, the hundreds of varieties of trees held no interest for Mikaela on the drive up the mountain.

She didn't notice the smoke from the great chimney of Daniel's cabin curling its lazy way above the trees as if sending smoke signals through the late-afternoon sky. She should be on her way to work at the ranger station. Instead she was on her way to confront a man whom, until now, she had been beginning to care about.

Harold Mason, a deacon in her church and a lawyer friend, had called an hour ago to tell her that her land had been sold. Gloria Sheraton had signed the papers just this morning.

Mikaela could feel the ball of anger inside her grow the more she thought about the situation. Daniel had been talking to Gloria daily for the past two weeks. She was sure he had known about Gloria's plans all along. How could he? *Settle down,* she told herself, but her anger was too far along.

She was driving too fast to see the ball of golden fur bound out from the forest floor and run toward the Jeep. The thump, followed by a loud yelp, snapped away the black cloud surrounding her heart and mind in a heart-stopping second. She slammed the brakes to the floor with all her strength. Through gritted teeth all she could say was, "No! No!"

Mikaela jumped from the Jeep and knelt down in the road. There beside the front wheel lay a still lump of dirty, golden fur. Mikaela reached out and touched a front paw streaked with the bright stain of fresh blood. *Theodore.*

She didn't feel the hardness of the blacktop chafing her hands and knees or the cold dampness of the mountain air left over from an early afternoon shower. She leaned down and carefully placed her ear against Theodore's chest. The fur wiggled at her touch. A blessed whine began deep in the pup's chest and rumbled slowly until it escaped his mouth.

Theodore tried to lift his head from the wet pavement. Mikaela gently took the fuzzy head in her hands, placed it in her lap, and began to soothe the frightened dog. A shaky Theodore gave her hand a weak lick and inched his battered body closer to his mistress. He didn't stop until he had his entire little, furry body nestled in her lap.

"I guess this means you don't have any spinal injuries!" She laughed with relief. But the next instant, tears fell unchecked down her cheeks. She cradled the shivering Theodore tenderly.

A crunching noise on the road behind her made her look over her shoulder. In a wheelchair rolling dangerously fast was a red-faced Daniel followed closely by two running, panting golden retrievers.

"Are you OK? What happened?!" Daniel yelled at the top of his lungs when he saw Mikaela hunched over on the ground beside the Jeep.

A quick thought crossed her mind. *How did he get off the porch with his wheelchair?* But there were more urgent matters.

"We heard the squeal of tires and the yelp all the way up at the house. Are you OK? Should I call 911?"

"Oh, Daniel, I've hit the baby! I've run over little Theodore." Tears began to cascade down her cheeks again. She didn't attempt to brush them away, she was so afraid to let go of the injured pup.

Daniel maneuvered his wheelchair as close to Mikaela as he dared. Griffin and Sally stood an uneasy distance back, unsure of the emotions of their masters. Mikaela watched the shock register in his eyes as he looked down at the whimpering puppy Mikaela cradled in her arms.

Without a word, Daniel took over. He pulled off the red flannel shirt he was wearing over long underwear and handed it to Mikaela to wrap around Theodore. He then pulled himself nimbly out of the chair and into a standing position. Before Mikaela could protest his actions, he was maneuvering a pair of crutches he had been balancing across his lap.

"What are you doing? I don't need you hurt out here too. Please! Sit back down." She spoke quietly, not wanting to send Theodore into a deeper shock. She pleaded urgently with her eyes.

He ignored her as he made his way over to the Jeep. "Do you have your cellular phone with you?"

"It's under the driver's seat," she whispered. She tucked the warm flannel around the puppy, being careful not to bump his broken leg, then gently lifted him. Daniel managed to pull himself and his cast into the passenger's seat of the truck to call Dr. Wally Arnet, the closest veterinarian, on the phone.

Mikaela carefully placed the now-quiet pup in his lap. She turned to get the wheelchair to throw into the back of the truck.

"Leave it be, Mikaela," he ordered. She turned the Jeep around and braced herself for the accusations that would surely come. She had almost killed Theodore. What the man beside her did next brought the tears flowing in a new torrent. Daniel McFarland, with his big, strong hands encasing the pup protectively, looked at her with his big, brown, kind eyes and gave her the sweetest, most encouraging smile she had ever seen.

# CHAPTER EIGHT

Mikaela looked down at the rumple of blankets. Daniel lay sound asleep. He mumbled softly in his sleep. The large cast rested on the far arm of the couch.

Theodore lay across Daniel's chest, eyelids fluttering in puppy dreams. His small pink tongue lay alongside his master's neck. The small, white cast covering his left front leg and paw lay cradled in Daniel's right hand. They both looked decidedly uncomfortable, but she wasn't about to disturb them in their exhausted sleep.

Mikaela shook her head and smiled as she sank into the large, overstuffed leather chair and took a sip from a steaming mug of coffee. She was glad Daniel had called Mrs. Bloomgarten from the veterinary hospital and told her to go home. Having to deal with the sitter too would have been more than she could handle. In the few moments remaining before the dawning of the new day, she watched them sleep. The anger she had felt toward Daniel the previous afternoon had taken flight to far distant places.

Mikaela's heart warmed at the sight of the soft rise and fall of the puppy's tummy. It was a miracle that Theodore hadn't been killed. "You are a lucky little fella to survive the accident with only a broken bone and four stitches under your chin. You are a puppy, Theodore, and puppies aren't allowed to go running in the mountains alone. There's cars and bears and other dangerous things out there. And," she finished, "you never, *ever,* run out in front of a car." She chided him, but only after the vet pronounced that the pup would survive.

Tears stung her eyes as she thought back a few hours to the way he had looked up at her with pitifully sad eyes and slowly wagged his tail, as though he were saying he had learned his lesson.

The whole terrible incident had certainly taken her mind, if not her heart, off the other major crisis in her life for a short while. She sat there listening to her softly snoring boys and the light crackling of split oak on the fire and thanked God. *Lord, thank you for these two guys you have placed in my life. They are a blessing to me.*

Mikaela pushed away the urge to reach over and brush a stray curl from Daniel's forehead. *And thank you, Lord, for showing me tonight that when it comes down to something we both love, Daniel and I work well together.* He had come right when she needed him. How he had managed to get off the porch and make his way down the road was still a mystery to her, but she was thankful just the same.

Daniel let out a snort, causing Theodore to raise his head. The puppy looked like he was considering moving to another spot, but when he realized he was in a safe place on his master's chest, he sighed and went back to sleep.

Why did this odd feeling stir in her heart every time she looked at Daniel sleeping with the puppy on his chest? It felt like a rosebud about to blossom. Was it because over the past twelve hours he had been an encourager to Theodore and a tower of strength to her? Not once had he left her side or blamed her for the accident. Instead he had sat quietly holding her hand as they'd waited in the outer office at the emergency animal hospital for word on Theodore's condition.

What had touched her most was the way he had insisted on staying up until Theodore stopped whimpering and finally fell asleep. Exhausted, she had finally gone home to try to get some sleep herself. But after a few restless hours she had given up and returned to the cabin.

Now she sat, in the gray of early dawn, in the big leather chair by the warmth of the fire with two beings who had become more precious to her than she ever would have imagined they could. Mikaela laid her head back on the soft, cool leather and thought through the problems in her life. In the stillness of the predawn morning, she could feel the tight knot that lay deep in the pit of her soul.

It wasn't the accident that had left the feeling there to smolder. The dread churned ever so slowly around until it was embedded deep within her heart. She needed to face the truth: She had not turned the sanctuary land over to God.

The soft sound of snoring males filled the silence of the morning as she prayed. *Dear God, I know you have a plan for my life. Show me what it is you want me to do. My lifelong dream is running through my fingers as fast and easy as the water in a mountain stream. If it's your will that I build this sanctuary, please show me the way. If it's not your will, dear God, direct me down the right path.* She was just mouthing *amen* when she felt something tap her on the head.

Daniel was watching her from between Theodore's fuzzy ears. "Praying always makes me feel better. For a person who looked like she was praying earnestly, you don't look very happy."

Mikaela pulled an orange guitar pick out of her hair. Had she been praying out loud?

"A guitar pick for your thoughts?" Daniel said softly so as not to disturb the worn-out pup.

Mikaela looked away. Should she inform him that she knew he was involved in taking the land that was rightfully hers? Just yesterday morning Mr. Pitkins had fussed at her when she stopped by the post office.

"You need to swallow that big pride of yours, girl. Go on and tell that singer feller you work for about your land troubles. I bet he'd be more than happy to help you out." If only it were that easy.

Here he was, the songwriter with a doctored golden-retriever pup across his chest, looking as innocent as the little towheaded boy playing catch with her brother. He had been kind then, too. She could still remember how he knew she hated to be "it," so in a game of tag he would always let her slip out of reach.

In a perfect world she should be trying to get the courage up to tell him she needed cash, and fast. In less than twenty-four hours everything had changed. Her world had come tumbling down. She couldn't, wouldn't, ask him now.

Let him see her heartbreak. She wanted to tell him that he and his friend Gloria had caused the earthquake that had shattered her dreams.

"Well, Ladybug?" Daniel gave her a kind look with his warm brown eyes.

She looked at the smoldering embers for a moment before answering. "There *is* something weighing me down," she finally admitted.

"Don't kick yourself for the accident, because that's what it was—an accident." He ran a big hand from Theodore's nose down to his hindquarters in one smooth stroke. The pup responded with a big yawn and a slobbery lick on his master's dimpled chin.

Mikaela couldn't help herself. She chuckled at the homey sight. There had been a brief moment yesterday when she thought she would never see such a sight again. It was hard to stay mad at a guy who smelled like a puppy and smiled in his sleep. Now wasn't a good time to talk to him about the land. Instead, she continued, "I've been wondering how you and your wheelchair got off the back porch and down to the driveway yesterday."

"Oh, that was easy." He lifted his cast in the air and admired it. "Thanks to this new walking cast, I was able to balance against the porch post, push the wheelchair over the edge, pitch the crutches down onto the ground, then bump down the stairs on my rear end."

"And that's all?" Mikaela shook her ponytail back over her shoulder. She wanted to scold him but couldn't bring herself to do it.

He smiled his sweet, dimpled smile that always managed to make her catch her breath. Theodore began to wiggle uncomfortably. Mikaela picked up the pup and carried him outside to the soft, brown grass beside the deck. Sally and Griffin came lunging around the side of the house with joy only parents could feel. With the two happily licking their offspring, Mikaela went back inside.

"Ladybug, tell Uncle Daniel what's been bothering you." He patted the couch beside him.

Mikaela sat down reluctantly. If she was ever going to confront him, it might be best to go ahead and get it over with now. "I received a distressing message yesterday from my lawyer."

He nodded encouragingly.

"My goal, no, my dream these last few years has been to open up a sanctuary for injured and sick endangered animals and birds."

"What a great idea!" He reached over and gave her hand a squeeze.

"I've bought an old settlers' cabin to convert into a gift shop to help support the place. The problem—" She chose her words carefully and calculatingly. "The problem has been buying the one hundred acres behind the cabin. Harold Stone owns the property. Months back he agreed to sell me the land and said he would hold the property for me until I could come up with the down payment."

Daniel suddenly sat upright and laughed. "Ladybug, this is amazing! I'm sorry for interrupting, but I have to tell you *my* news. I'm buying a hundred acres too. I'm staying in the mountains! The birth of my dream is happening as we speak!"

Mikaela sat there seething in silence. He wasn't listening to her. The anger that had dissipated over Theodore's accident was now having a Frankensteinian rebirth.

"You are buying a hundred acres." She fought hard to control her voice. "Are you and Gloria purchasing the land once owned by the first settler, Jedidiah Johnson?"

"That's it. How did you know?" Daniel obviously mistook the intensity of her expression for joy. He was grinning from dimple to dimple. "Gloria pulled it all together!"

Later she would not be able to recall all she said in those next few minutes. But she did remember her final stinging words before she ran out the door and slammed it behind her. "You, my good friend, have stolen my land and destroyed my dream!"

She got only as far as the front steps before the weight of her pain forced her to sit down. Her cheek rested against her knees as all the tension, pain, and heartache that had been building over the last twenty-four hours poured out in a torrent of tears.

"Ladybug?" Daniel stood behind her, leaning heavily on his crutches. "I'm sorry. I had no idea that piece of land meant anything to you. Please come back inside," he pleaded softly. "We need to talk."

Mikaela wiped the tears away on the sleeve of her flannel shirt, then stood. "We do need to talk, Daniel, but not now. I can't." She walked to her Jeep and opened the door. "I'm going to take some time off from work to think things through. I'll call Mrs. Bloomgarten when I get home and see if she can arrange for someone to come over during the day to help you out if you need it."

She glanced in her rearview mirror before turning onto the road. Daniel was leaning on the porch railing watching her go.

# CHAPTER NINE

Mikaela spent many hours over the next few days praying. She called her brother in London, confided in a neighbor, and even talked to Dr. Wally, the vet, when she took Theodore in for a checkup.

Mikaela had been coming up to the log cabin every morning around daybreak to check on the dogs. Each day she sighed with relief when Mrs. Bloomgarten came out to the porch and told her Daniel was still asleep. Yesterday the stern nurse had invited her in for a cup of coffee and she had not-so-reluctantly agreed.

Her eyes were drawn repeatedly to the silence of the great room and the empty couch there. Mrs. Bloomgarten informed her that she had told "The Leg" that with his new walking cast and crutches he was capable of making it to the bedroom under his own steam.

"You should talk to the man," Mrs. Bloomgarten said when Mikaela stood to leave. "It would make my job easier if you two would kiss and make up." The woman, for the first time Mikaela had ever seen, smiled. Daniel had gotten to her, too.

Mikaela listened to Daniel's urgent pleas on her answering

machine. He left a message every day, sometimes twice a day. The churning pit in the bottom of her stomach was beginning to feel less like heartache and more like guilt.

"I'm calling to say I'm sorry again. I really didn't know the land I bought was your sanctuary land. Can't we work this out? Ladybug, talk to me. Please come back. It's not right around here without you."

"Mikaela? It's me again—Daniel. The reunion's tomorrow. You've got to come back! I don't know where anything is, and the caterer called and asked me how much potato salad to bring. I've got no idea. I told her a pound ought to do it. Does that sound about right to you? I can't have the reunion without you. If you won't do it for *me,* please do it for our old friends."

She knew she needed to talk to him soon. But she felt like she needed a little more time to work through her feelings about everything.

She needed to talk to someone who cared. She decided on Sugartree's postman, whose sweet disposition and unconditional love would help her see things more clearly.

Bright sun spread across a clear blue, cloudless sky, warming the cool fall air around her. The heavy post-office door squeaked comfortingly as she pulled it open. She stepped inside, and at that moment, she knew something was wrong.

Behind the counter stood a woman she had never seen before. Stern eyes peered over a pair of reading glasses balanced on the end of her nose. "May I help you?" the stranger asked without emotion.

Mikaela pulled on the end of her ponytail in a moment of confusion. "I'm here to see Mr. Pitkins."

"I'm sorry, he is not available."

Not available? What did that mean? Of course the man was available. He had always been available when she needed him. "Has something happened to him?"

The woman's stiff shoulders visibly relaxed. "Is he a friend of yours?"

Mikaela nodded.

The woman walked around the counter and stood by Mikaela's side. "Mr. Pitkins collapsed as he was locking up yesterday. He was taken by ambulance down to the hospital in Pigeon Forge."

Noticing the stricken look on Mikaela's face, she added gently, "I'm afraid I don't know much about his condition, except that he had to have surgery. I'm sorry you didn't know."

For the second time in a week, Mikaela ran, but this time she was running *to* something, not *away*. The only thing she was able to whisper through a clenched jaw as she drove down the winding mountain road was, "Please, God, let Mr. Pitkins be OK."

The nurse at the front desk of the small hospital informed Mikaela that Mr. Pitkins had broken his hip in the fall and had undergone surgery the evening before. The hospital room was dark, and the curtain was drawn. Mikaela stood momentarily debating whether she should disturb her gentle friend.

"Is someone there?" a shaky voice called out.

Mikaela peeked around the edge of the curtain at the pale, wrinkled old man attached to lines of IV fluids and softly beeping monitors. He smiled an angelic smile that brought her quickly to his side. "Are you OK?" she asked with relief as she carefully hugged the old man and softly kissed his scratchy cheek.

"It's good to see you, child. Here, sit down, and I'll tell you all about it." With surprising gusto he proceeded to describe his dizzy spell, how he had fallen, how fifteen-year-old Morgan Mason had found him and called 911, and the exciting race down the mountainside in an ambulance.

"Mr. Pitkins, I believe you enjoyed causing such a fuss and being the center of attention."

The old man laughed with delight. "Now, girl, you have my story. Let me hear yours. What's been going on in your life that has your face all scrunched up so?"

Mr. Pitkins listened intently while Mikaela told him the whole story of how she had lost her land and the trouble with Daniel and Gloria. She ended by describing how she accidentally ran over poor little Theodore.

When she finished she sat back in her chair, exhausted from the effort.

"This whole mess is easily solved."

"How do you figure that, Mr. Pitkins?" Perhaps the surgery on his hip had temporarily affected his judgment.

"Give your troubles over to the Lord. He'll take care of everything. You're depending too heavily on that hard head of yours. God is trying to speak to you, but it's up to you to take the time to listen."

It was the same advice she had given Daniel only a few weeks ago when he didn't feel good about his life. Mr. Pitkins was right.

The nurse came in to take her friend down to X ray, so she gave him a kiss good-bye.

"One more thing, Mikaela. You have to experience true forgiveness for that Gloria woman."

"I have forgiven her, but I still feel angry."

"Honey, I'm not talking about the words *I forgive you*. I'm talking about the kind of forgiveness that Jesus showed us. Remember what the Bible says: 'If someone demands your coat, offer your shirt also.' Think about it."

*Lord, help me find and understand true forgiveness.* Mikaela drove away from the hospital that morning with a new resolve. She would not let her dream go. God had provided the cabin; she would let him take care of the rest.

The Jeep's engine whined in protest as she pushed the accelerator to the limit to make it up the last rise. She pulled on the emergency brake and grabbed her backpack, with the emergency supplies, water, and snacks she always carried when hiking.

After an hour of climbing, Mikaela reached the sun-warmed outcrop overlooking the seventy-five-foot Turkeywallow Falls. She watched a loggerhead musk turtle wobble among the rocks at the river's edge, hoping to snack on a stranded mud puppy. A current of mountain air surged from the bottom of the falls and blew a fine spray of mist upward. Mikaela was soon covered from head to toe with the chilly dampness.

The deafening noise of cascading water meeting the rocks below provided the soothing balm of nature Mikaela needed for her troubled heart. The crest of Balsom Mountain stood to the east, parading the impressive stands of red spruce and frasier fir that were found in the Smoky Mountains only at elevations over forty-five hundred feet. Far below her swirled the autumn colors of the pin cherry tree, the American mountain ash, and the mountain maple.

Standing on the rock outcrop, her face turned toward the cold, fine mist, she handed over the burden of pain, anger, hurt, the sanctuary land, Gloria, and Daniel to her Lord. Mr. Pitkins was right. She had to hold on to Proverbs 3:5-6, "Trust in the Lord with all your heart; do not depend on your own understanding. Seek his will in all you do, and he will direct your paths."

She began to feel the warmth of the sun through the cold mist of the falls. *Forgive me for my pride and for not depending on you, Lord.* She stood for a time and waited for God. The tears began to run down her cheeks, spilling quietly over her chin.

It came to her then, there on the mountain, in the stillness of God's whisper. She loved Daniel. She didn't love him like a friend, not like the childish crush she had had years ago, but with the full blossom of a God-given love. A love running so deep it had the strength of the waterfall crashing beneath her. Yet the love was also as gentle and soft as a newborn river otter.

She opened her eyes to see a rare, glorious sight. The sun still shining on the water, a sudden cold northern current captured the fine mist and began weaving each droplet of water into a tiny, lacy crystal.

Mikaela stood, reaching her arms skyward amidst the floating miniature snowflakes, and shouted, her voice echoing down the rock walls of Turkeywallow Falls, "To God be the glory!" For at that moment it became clear what she was to do.

# CHAPTER TEN

At the sight of Mikaela, Griffin growled and wiggled like a playful puppy. Sally nudged her hand and sniffed at the pan of Mom Davonport's famous reunion bread pudding that Mikaela held. Theodore hopped in a circle, disregarding his casted front paw. He thumped his tail hard against the ground and gave Mikaela a cheesy puppy grin.

"I've missed you guys," she said as she balanced the bread pudding in one hand and rubbed the dogs' heads with the other. "I'll let you in on a little secret. I may be back for good, if your boss will have me." She looked around at the unfamiliar cars parked in the driveway. Some of the guests had arrived early.

Mikaela would have to make her way around the caterers' van backed up to the back porch. On the way up, she had passed the appliance rental truck from the place she had called in town, so she knew the large-screen TV was already set up.

Despite everything that had gone on, Mikaela was glad she would be there with Daniel. It would be the highlight of the evening to hear his name announced if he won the award for

Songwriter of the Year. How would he feel not being there in person?

She had noticed a Toyota station wagon filled with car seats and a window sticker that said Baby on Board. It had to be Jessie's. There was no need to guess who the gold Mercedes 350 with tan leather interior belonged to; it had Gloria written all over it.

She laid her hand on Sally's big head. "Girl, with God's help, I'm going to march right in there and keep my feelings under control." She took a deep breath and smoothed down the Cherokee patterned gauze dress she had bought for the occasion. She nervously pushed back her long blond hair as she went up the steps. She didn't often let her hair hang down, and she hoped it didn't make her look too childish.

Griffin followed her up the steps, jealous that Sally had received the last pat. She gave him an extra scratch behind the ear. "Well, boy, wish me luck. And if you promise to keep this to yourself, I'll let you in on another little secret. I'm in love with your master. What do you think about that?" Griffin swung his tail in approval as she went inside.

"Mickey!" squealed a short, round, very pregnant woman with a pageboy haircut. Despite the circumference of her belly, the woman hugged with such enthusiasm that she almost knocked Mikaela over.

"Jessie?" was all Mikaela managed to sputter before she was grabbed by the hand and pulled into the great room, still carrying the bread pudding. The pregnant woman moved quickly despite her bulk. Mikaela found herself standing behind a couple whose arms were linked. They were admiring the largest TV she had ever seen.

"Gloria, Mikaela's here!"

Daniel swung around first and gave Mikaela a dimpled grin. He gave her long, loose hair and the dress a surprised look. He reached out his hand, but before she could react, Gloria had taken his hand in hers instead.

"Mikaela! It's so *nice* to see you again," Gloria said with a patronizing tone and a flutter of her eyelashes. "Daniel told me you were his hired help—or is the proper term *maid?* How nice of you."

Mikaela could feel her cheeks beginning to burn. An intense electricity seemed to shoot through her body and out her eyes. Forgiveness was momentarily forgotten. The pan of warm bread pudding suddenly felt heavy in her hands.

As though he sensed Mikaela's thought process, Daniel's smile disappeared. His cheeks took on an unbecoming shade of gray. He looked helplessly at a wide-eyed and fluttering Jessie.

"Gloria, I would like to say it's nice to see you, too, but—" Before Mikaela could finish the sentence, Jessie had taken the bread pudding from her and, with a firm hand on Mikaela's elbow, quickly ushered her back into the kitchen.

"Daniel was afraid this would happen," Jessie said, placing the dessert out of Mikaela's reach. "Here, have a glass of lemonade. Your cheeks are all flushed."

Mikaela took a long drink of the cool, sweet-and-sour liquid. With her heartbeat gradually calming, she looked around the room. The crew from Hog Heaven Barbecue had already set up tables in the great room. Trays of pork barbecue, buns, and baked beans and bowls of fire-and-ice salad, apple pie, and blackberry cobbler lined the counter dividing the kitchen from the great room.

She hadn't been here all week, but the month of organization and planning had paid off. The caterer silently moved about, getting pots of coffee brewing. Pitchers of lemonade and iced tea stood like sentinels on the counter beside the refrigerator.

"Feel better? Good. Ignore Gloria. You know she's always been like that." Jessie added as an afterthought, "I don't think she can help herself."

Mikaela smiled despite her desire to throw bread pudding in Gloria's perfectly made-up face. It was good to see Jessie again after all these years.

She looked down at the very pregnant and very concerned

Jessie. She sighed. "Don't worry, Jessie. I've prayed about this. I'll be OK." At the look of doubt on the woman's face, she added, "I promise."

Mikaela picked up a piggy-in-the-blanket and popped it into her mouth. Jessie smiled broadly. "I made those cute little tidbits myself. Aren't they sweet, all wrapped up in their little blankies?" With this last statement she blushed. "When I'm pregnant my maternal instinct gets stuck on superdrive."

Dispute her quirkiness, Jessie looked happy and settled. She noticed Mikaela looking at her stomach, and she reached out and placed the palm of Mikaela's hand on her bulging midriff. The sensation of the unborn child moving under her touch gave Mikaela an unexpected sense of joy.

"Feel that wiggling lump? I think that must be little baby Miko's knee. He's made it hard for me to sleep these past few months with all the jabbing he does."

Mikaela sensed someone watching her. She looked up to see Daniel standing in the doorway to the kitchen with an odd look on his face. Embarrassed, Mikaela quickly took her hand away. Jessie wasn't bothered at all. She marched right over to Daniel and grabbed his hand and placed it on her belly. He calmly patted the bulging midriff and said, "Hello, in there. I can't wait to meet you."

Mikaela was thinking about confronting Gloria as she went into the great room and stood in front of the radiating warmth of the roaring fire. The beautifully coiffured woman had planted herself in front of the big-screen TV, where she couldn't be missed by anyone entering the room. Mikaela turned around so she wouldn't have to look at the woman. She preferred the heat of the burning logs to the heat being put out by the flirting, fluttering Gloria.

"I have something I need to talk to you about when you have a moment." Daniel had come up behind her.

"I need to tell you something too," Mikaela answered. She was ready to lay everything on the line. "I'm free now if you want to talk."

They were interrupted by the doorbell chiming through the house. Before Daniel could make it to the door, a blond, sun-tanned Bartlet made an entrance with a woman on each arm. The woman on his right arm, dressed in a blue business suit and white collared shirt and wearing sensible shoes, he intro-duced as the Reverend Cynthia Hanover. The woman with pretty auburn hair, balancing a chubby blond toddler on her hip, he introduced as his wife, Elaine; the toddler, Devon. Laughter and greetings filled the air. Mikaela left her spot by the fireplace and joined in welcoming their childhood friends.

The reunion was running smoothly. Mikaela kept a con-stant prayer vigil for herself throughout the afternoon. She en-joyed her old friends' company and managed to stay away from Gloria.

Gloria and her possessive persona hung on Daniel's every word. She spent the rest of the time talking loudly about her investments and trying to be cute by sending little jabs Mikae-la's way.

As the afternoon progressed, Mikaela felt more and more out of place. She was the only one who had not left the Great Smoky Mountains and wasn't financially secure. Even Cynthia talked about investing an inheritance from her grand-mother and using the interest to build an orphanage in Hon-duras.

It didn't take long to see that Daniel didn't need her. Their friends gathered around him as he sat with his cast propped on a stool by the fire and listened intently to his stories of the country-music industry and his associates there. Daniel would look her way and smile occasionally, but he did not invite Mi-kaela into the inner circle. She watched from the kitchen as the group of old friends talked and laughed and shared their history.

Gloria ensconced herself on the edge of Daniel's chair, at times resting her blond head on Daniel's shoulder. Gloria's fawning and cooing were more than Mikaela cared to see. But worse, Daniel seemed to be enjoying the attention.

Daniel didn't need her. It was obvious that he was still smitten by the former beauty queen. It was getting late anyway. She decided it was time to go home. No one noticed as she quietly slipped out the back door.

An overwhelming numbness came over her as she stepped out onto the porch. She could hear the laughter as the reunion continued full swing. Mikaela sat down on the porch steps in the cold night air, and under a star-filled sky, she opened up her heart and gave God all the things she couldn't handle. Then she gave him all the things she had been handling on her own. *God, I tried to take things into my own hands again. Please forgive me. Show me the real meaning of forgiveness. I don't want to carry this anger I have toward Gloria anymore.* Griffin, Sally, and Theodore left the warmth of their spot under the porch and came to lie beside her as if they sensed that she needed them.

"I forgive you, Gloria," she whispered. God's peace surrounded her, and it was a peace like no other feeling she had ever experienced before.

*Daniel is yours, dear Lord, not mine. I want your will to be done even if it means I need to walk away for good. I love him, Lord. Please take good care of him and bless him with what he needs to be happy.*

She promised God she would do his bidding. She had dared to hope this afternoon that Daniel would tell her he really cared for her. But reality painfully painted the true picture. He was falling in love with Gloria. Mikaela loved him enough, she had to admit to herself, that she wanted him to be happy. *He can have my land, Lord. I want him to be able to follow his dreams, even if that means he needs to be with Gloria to make the journey.*

A shrill whistle pierced the air as she reached her Jeep. Mikaela's heart gave a big thump. She turned around to see Daniel's silhouette on the back porch. He was waving good-bye. No, he was yelling for her not to leave. "Ladybug, come back up here. I have something to tell you." His voice sounded like fine music strumming through the evening air.

Mikaela ran toward the man she loved. He reached down with a big, warm hand and pulled her up to the porch. He reached out and tenderly brushed her cheek with the back of his hand. For a moment she thought he might kiss her there, where his skin had momentarily touched hers.

"Gloria made you mad enough to run out on us, didn't she? Don't you worry about a thing, Mikaela. I told her to lay off with those wisecracks of hers. Listen. I've got great news! I'm going to make the show! There's a helicopter already on its way to the mountains to pick me up and deliver me to the award show." His smile was so tender she thought for a moment she would have to sit down on the rough boards of the porch before she melted away.

Then she heard him say what she had been praying to hear. "Mikaela, I need you."

She began to say, "I love you," but the loud pulsating whoosh of air from the helicopter swallowed her words.

He stood back as the thumping sound of helicopter blades filled the air. He was now yelling to be heard above the din of the rotating blades of the chopper as it prepared to land. "Thanks, Ladybug! You're the greatest! I knew you would come through for me! You've pulled this reunion together beautifully! Everyone here is raving about what a great job you've done, and your bread pudding was out of this world! I ate three bowls full!" He paused. Mikaela waited again for the words she longed to hear. "I hate to ask you this, as you were leaving and everything. But I need you to stay around a while if you would and act as host in my place."

She didn't answer. She couldn't answer. She stayed on the back porch a long time after the helicopter disappeared into the night sky. Then she, the good employee, with the angelic smile of the perfect hostess, went back into the house to rejoin the reunion.

# CHAPTER ELEVEN

The glowing embers in the fire mellowed into a deep orange as the fire burned low. The caterers from Hog Heaven Barbecue had cleaned up and left. The old friends sat in the big, comfortable, overstuffed furniture watching the big-screen TV. They sipped mugs of hot cider seasoned with cinnamon sticks and ate seconds of Mikaela's warm, fragrant bread pudding.

Mikaela sat on a stool by the kitchen counter with Theodore asleep across her lap. His casted paw rested on her knee. She had let him in after Daniel had gone. The cold night air wasn't good for a puppy on the mend, she had told herself. She didn't want to admit, even to herself, that she needed his warm little body to hug. She had been ready to give up her hopes and dreams for that man, and she guessed that, in a way she hadn't expected, she had. She sighed as she thought about the night's events.

Mikaela forced herself to watch the TV. Her heart filled with pride when the lady in a white sequined dress presented Daniel with the Songwriter of the Year award. The crowd in the great room cheered and clapped. Mikaela gave silent thanks to God. "Trust and obey," Isaiah Pitkins had told her yesterday. *Lord, I'm trusting you to know what's best for me.*

Mikaela hadn't noticed that the new Pepsi commercial had ended until the announcer boomed, "And now we offer, straight from the Great Smoky Mountains, your number one songwriter of the year, Mr. Daniel McFarland!"

The audience went wild. Whistles and shouts of "Go, Daniel!" could hardly be heard over the shouting and cheering from the people gathered around the giant-screen TV.

The camera panned the audience, then turned its focus to center stage. Daniel was now seated in a big chair, his casted foot propped on a stool, his guitar on his lap.

Gloria lifted her hand to her heart and said loudly enough for Mikaela to hear, "Look at that gorgeous man. He isn't going to slip through my fingers this time! Hi, honey. Hi, baby," she called out as she waved at the big screen.

Mikaela was sure she could feel the fault in her heart shift and widen. Daniel seemed to be staring straight out of the screen and into her soul, his big brown eyes full of all the tenderness and gentleness she had come to love.

"I am thankful for the talent my Lord has given me. I want to thank all of my fans out there for honoring me with this wonderful award. Tonight I am going to sing a new song I wrote in the beautiful Smoky Mountains. This song was written for an old friend. A person who makes me laugh. A person who makes me feel alive. A person who has taught me what it means to trust God."

Everyone in the room turned their eyes on a beaming Gloria. "That precious, zany guy," she cooed. She turned to find Mikaela. Despite the darkness of the room, Mikaela could feel her gloating eyes.

Theodore didn't notice when she stood. Still holding the sleeping pup, she hooked her purse with her free hand and had her hand on the doorknob by the time Daniel began to sing.

His strong, deep voice lifted high with the whoosh of eagle

wings. Mikaela could not move. The intensity of the words mesmerized her, even if they were meant for another. The melody seemed to take flight from the big-screen TV as it spiraled its way upward to the heavy oak rafters of the log cabin. They were words of love. They were beautiful words, declaring their very existence was a gift of God.

Daniel had rarely picked up his guitar while he was recuperating. When could he have written such a beautiful song?

She unsuccessfully fought back the tears of loss that mingled with tears of joy for the knowledge that he had finally been able to write again. Theodore woke up and began whimpering in concern as the tears escaped from her eyes, rolled down her cheeks, and spilled onto his fur.

The song ended to thunderous applause. Daniel laid the guitar beside his chair and looked into the camera. "I dedicate this song to the woman I love."

Gloria jumped up and squealed like a teenager. Mikaela buried her face in the comforting warmth of Theodore's fuzzy neck. She gently laid the pup in his basket in the kitchen. She grasped the doorknob again and was turning to go when she heard a soft, warm voice say, "Mikaela. My Ladybug."

She slowly turned. There he was via satellite, looking directly at her. The warmth of his eyes reached through glass, time, and space. "Ladybug, I love you. I've come to realize in these past few weeks that I don't want to live without you."

Mikaela dropped her purse and sank to the floor. Theodore lumbered into her lap and once again began to lick the tears streaming down her cheeks. A smile spread across Mikaela's face like the sun breaking across the horizon after a stormy night.

She smiled down reassuringly at the concerned pup and playfully tugged his fuzzy, oversized ears. "It's OK, little Theodore. It's going to be OK."

"There is something I planned on giving you tonight, but I had to leave before I had the chance. Go look in my Bible in Proverbs 3. I love you."

The screen cut to another Pepsi commercial. While their friends looked on silently, Mikaela walked to the bookshelf and took the big, worn Bible from its resting place. Inside, with her name handwritten under the word *owner*, she found the deed to her land.

# EPILOGUE

The soft twang of a guitar floated and intermingled gently with the sound of Daniel's words. The rich timbre of his voice filtered through the unfilled chinks between the log walls in the settlers' cabin. He was instructing the retreat's newest resident, Billy Synclair, on musical syntax.

Mikaela brushed a flyaway hair from her face as she looked about her with a sense of satisfaction. She groaned as she straightened into a standing position. All this cleaning was making her back ache.

The words of Daniel's latest number one hit, "Baby, You Are the One," followed her across the backyard to the newly built nursery. Mikaela entered the nursery with a joyful step and a feeling of accomplishment. She had released her first patient, a young falcon who had been shot full of BBs, back into the mountains this morning. The young bird had recuperated more fully than she had ever hoped. She had felt a deep satisfaction of motherly pride as she watched the beautiful bird take wing and circle overhead until he hooked a ride on an upward current and disappeared over the color-filled mountains.

She finished straightening up the medicine cabinet full of donated animal medical supplies. Next she read over the checklist of what she would need when Tom Mann, a park-ranger friend of hers, arrived with the newborn northern river otter twins he had found abandoned and starving.

"I seem to be starving, myself, all the time now," Mikaela said out loud. She paused for a moment to take a bite out of the Snickers bar she had been carrying around in the pocket of her blue-jeans overalls.

A large pair of warm hands surprised her when they surrounded her from behind and came to rest on her ever-expanding belly. "I guess the baby weighs about fifteen pounds right now, give or take a Snickers bar or two."

Mikaela laughed as she turned to face her husband. She gave Daniel a big, chocolate-caramel kiss. He enveloped all of her in his arms and buried his face in her long, sweet-smelling hair. "I love you," they whispered in unison.

Two human beings in need of love. Two dreams in need of becoming real. One God who fills those needs, one God who reaps those dreams, one God who blesses those who follow him.

# Recipe

\|\|\|

All five Duffy children—Aaron, Kristen, Adam, Andrea, and Katie—love traveling to Evansville, Indiana, for family get-togethers with their aunt Judy and uncle Jim. We all get excited when Aunt Judy pulls one of her famous steaming-hot bread puddings from the oven. The smell is glorious; the taste, even better! What makes Aunt Judy's bread pudding so extraordinary? The trick is to make sure the toast is buttered completely to the edges—including the crust.

Mix this with lots of hugs, sharing of all the latest news, and a roomful of love and laughter, and like all the Duffy children, you'll find this is the best bread pudding you have ever eaten!
—Jan Duffy

## Mom Judy Davonport's Reunion Bread Pudding

8 slices bread
butter
1 can evaporated milk plus enough 2 percent or whole milk to make 4 cups
1 cup granulated sugar
4 eggs
1 tbsp. vanilla
½ cup raisins
cinnamon

Heat oven to 350°. Make 8 slices of toast, and butter them completely out to the edges, including the crust. Tear the buttered toast into crumbs (approximately 4 cups). Place bread crumbs in an 8x8x2″ baking dish.

291

Mix together evaporated-milk mixture, sugar, eggs, and vanilla. Pour over bread, and let stand 10–15 minutes. Sprinkle with raisins, and dust top with cinnamon.

Bake one hour, or until knife inserted one inch from the edge comes out clean. Serve warm or cold with vanilla sauce. 6–8 servings.

## VANILLA SAUCE

¼–½ cup sugar
2 tbsp. cornstarch
2 cups water
1 tsp. vanilla
2 tbsp. butter or margarine

Mix sugar and cornstarch. Add water, and heat to boiling over medium heat. Cook, stirring, until it thickens. Remove from heat, and add vanilla and butter. Pour over Mom Judy Davonport's Reunion Bread Pudding. Enjoy!

## About the Author

Jan Duffy lives in Tennessee with her husband, two sons, three daughters, a white boxer, and a fat cat. She worked as a registered nurse in neonatal intensive care for a number of years and now works at home raising her children, the youngest two of whom were adopted from Romania in 1991 and 1993. Jan enjoys writing (including mysteries), buying and restoring old dolls, and spending time with her family. She is the author of a nonfiction book on adoption.

You can write to Jan in care of Tyndale House Author Relations, P.O. Box 80, Wheaton, IL 60189-0080.

# The Sound of the Water

## PEGGY STOKS

〣〣

For my six girls:
Jenna, Allie, and Rachel, mine by birth,
and
Ashley, Katie, and Vanessa,
whom I feed often enough to lay some claim upon

# CHAPTER ONE

Holly Winslow paused in the doorway of the Mukilteo Coffee Café and inhaled deeply, reveling in the fragrant mixture of fresh sea air and roasted coffee beans. This secret pleasure, losing herself in the unique combination of these two wonderful smells, was a ritual she enjoyed several afternoons a week when walking the two and a half blocks from her flower shop to the café along the charming Lincoln Avenue Courtyard.

Behind her, a queue of cars glittered in the Saturday morning autumn sunshine. Eager sightseers and tourists waited in their vehicles to descend the hill and drive aboard one of two enormous, white ferries shuttling automobiles and passengers to and from Washington's popular Whidbey Island. On this bright morning, the waters of Puget Sound were a sapphire compliment to the verdant island's steep white banks. The skies were unusually clear, rewarding residents and visitors alike with an unshrouded view of snowcapped Mount Baker.

The clamorous sound of seagulls faded as Holly stepped inside the café and took her place in line. Today she had come not for her usual double mocha and twenty minutes' break on a bench in the courtyard but to purchase a half pound of the shop's special blend of coffee for Jean Breck, her accountant and best friend.

This afternoon's visit had been planned partly for pleasure but mostly for business, as Jean was to be married in two weeks' time and wanted to have Holly's accounts in order before her wedding and honeymoon.

The women's friendship stretched all the way back to Mrs. Prizio's second-grade class—twenty years ago. Both girls had been good students, but Jean's predilection for organization and numbers had been evident even at that young age.

Every year, for as long as Holly could remember, Jean had converted the number of years of their friendship into a decimal equation. In third grade the studious blond announced that they had known one another 12.5 percent of their lives. By sixth grade the number had nearly tripled to 36 percent, and now, at the age of twenty-seven, they had been friends for 74 percent of their lives.

Holly's lips curved into a smile as she thought of Jean's ceaseless figuring and of Jean and Tim's upcoming wedding. No doubt Jean would present her husband-to-be, upon each of their anniversaries, with a similar tabulation of their time spent in wedlock.

"Holly? Is that you?"

A deep, familiar voice tickled her memory, making her feel seventeen years old all over again. It couldn't be. Not him. Not after all these years.

She had heard the café's door open and close behind her but hadn't paid any attention to the customer who had entered. Slowly, Holly turned. Less than a yard away stood Seth Glad, a captivating grin on his face. His brown gaze was fixed upon her, seeming to take in every detail of her appearance.

"Yes, it's me," she managed, replying in a light tone that belied the shock she felt at seeing him again after all these years.

"It's good to see you again, Holly. It's been a long time." His voice was warm, friendly.

What had it been . . . ten years since she'd seen him? During that long-ago spring of her senior year, Holly had fallen hard for Seth Glad.

He was the guy every girl would have died for in high school. It was as if all her dreams had come true when he'd asked her out—

"Are you still living in the area?" His expression was one of genuine interest, and for the first time, Holly noticed the wide, jagged scar that began above the lateral end of his left eyebrow and ran down the side of his face, ending in front of his ear.

"Yes, I . . . uh, live not too far from here." What had happened to his face? From reading the local papers, she'd seen stories about him from time to time and knew he'd played minor-league ball for several years. Could a baseball split open someone's skin like that?

He reached up and touched the scar, his smile changing to a wry grin. "I see you've noticed the visible reminder of my wild and wicked youth." The customer ahead of Holly was being waited upon, and they both took a step toward the counter. "I'm done playing ball," he volunteered. "I've been back in Everett awhile now, working for Griffin Construction."

"Oh," was all Holly could find to say.

"Mom and I are going to spend the day over on Whidbey," he continued, as much at ease with speaking to her as if they saw one another every day. He smiled again and checked his watch. "She's driving, and I'm in charge of getting the coffee and the tickets. She's raring to get over there and do some serious shopping."

"Next? Can I help you?" The customer ahead of them turned and walked away with a steaming cup, leaving a gap between Holly and the counter.

"A half pound of the Mukilteo Blend, please. Ground." Holly stepped forward, aware that Seth also stepped forward and was standing right behind her. His fresh, woodsy fragrance drifted to her, further disquieting her senses. Did he even remember going out with her? Considering the angry fireworks with which their second date had ended, he was being quite amicable.

Or was it that he didn't remember?

A lancet of pain spiked her heart at that thought. The waitress held the paper sack beneath the spout of the coffee grinder and turned the switch. What was going on inside her? Holly wondered, the noise of the machine filling the air. It wasn't as if Seth Glad mattered to her anymore.

But somehow just seeing him brought back the feelings of that wonderful—and terrible—spring, a full decade past. *Come on, Holly,* she told herself. *Ten years ago you were an immature high school girl with a crush on the high school baseball hero. Remember all the girls who used to flock around him? You were nothing special.*

They'd had two dates—only two—before Holly had told him she couldn't see him anymore. And she'd cried that whole summer for what couldn't be.

Setting her purse on the counter, Holly busied herself by slowly removing her money from her wallet. The café's side door opened, admitting a loud-talking knot of elderly women. Seth had fallen quiet behind her. She wasn't being very friendly, she knew, but feelings she had thought were long dead had resurrected themselves and were playing havoc with her heart and mind.

How could he still affect her this way? Was she no more emotionally mature than a seventeen-year-old girl? *Just go, Holly. Don't make a fool out of yourself again. He has one set of values, and you have another.*

"Sure you don't want a double mocha to go with that?" The energetic young woman behind the counter interrupted Holly's thoughts. Setting the bag near the register, she smiled. "You're breaking your routine today, flower lady."

"Oh, sorry, Monica. I didn't see you. . . . I'm just a little preoccupied this morning." Holly apologized and handed her a twenty, amazed at how smooth her voice sounded when every nerve in her body screamed that Seth Glad stood only inches behind her.

*Don't you remember how lovesick you were over him?* the inner voice chided. *Just get your coffee and leave.*

"Well, you're preoccupied, and it looks like I'm going to be occupied." Monica returned Holly's change and nodded toward the side door as several more patrons filed in from Lincoln Courtyard. "See you Monday, doll. Next?"

"Bye, Monica. Nice to see you again, Seth," she said with a glance and a quick smile at the tall, handsome man waiting behind her. "Good-bye." She made her farewell as brief as possible without being rude.

"Good-bye, Holly." Seth's smile had faded, she noticed, replaced by a contemplative expression. Without further conversation he moved aside and allowed her to pass.

*Whew! That's over with. What a fluke to run into him after all this time.* Hands trembling, she stepped out of the café into the sunshine and sea-scented wind. Starting toward home with a brisk step, she left Seth Glad and the coffee-flavored air behind her.

Or did she?

Maybe she was being ridiculous, but she had the strangest feeling a pair of coffee-colored eyes watched her until she was out of sight.

\\\\\/

Several hours later the sun began its descent in the western sky over Puget Sound. Leaving behind their spumous wakes, boats of all sizes skimmed over the sparkling blue water, giving wide berth to the ferries. Birds twittered in the tall evergreens of Old Town, the older section of Mukilteo, where Holly lived. A fresh breeze continued blowing off the water, carrying with it a slight chill that promised the coming cooler temperatures of autumn.

Situated just four blocks up the slope from the water's edge,

Holly's small 1920s house had been built to receive maximum benefit from its setting. A wide front porch and picture windows afforded breathtaking views of the Sound, while the kitchen in the rear of the house caught the warm rays of the morning sun.

Their business finished, Holly and Jean had moved from the kitchen table to the white wicker furniture on the front porch. Jean half sat, half reclined on the love seat's overstuffed blue-and-white-striped cushions, while Holly sat on one of two matching chairs. A pair of chocolate-smeared plates and forks sat on the low table in front of the love seat, mute testimony to shared female indulgence.

"You make the best brownies, Holly." Jean sighed with pleasure and took another sip from the large ceramic mug. A perfect blond bob framed her friendly, round face. "Coffee, too."

"Thanks." Holly's spirit had been heavy ever since her encounter with Seth Glad, but she made an effort to lighten up for Jean's sake. "Keep eating like that, though, and we'll have to wedge you into your wedding dress with a crowbar."

"Yeah, yeah. For your information, the dress fits fine," came Jean's retort. "Maybe I should ask how *your* dress is fitting?"

The friends shared a chuckle, as comfortable with one another as only childhood friends can be. A long silence slipped by while each woman was wrapped up in her own thoughts. Nearby, a squirrel chattered in a tree.

"I'm so glad your shop is doing well, Holly." Jean spoke with satisfaction, shifting in her seat. She took another sip of coffee and tucked her feet beneath her. "You deserve the success."

"I can't lay claim to any success. Max Sorenson spent twenty-two years building his business and reputation before I took over. I'm not doing anything special; I'm just running Maxie's Floral the way he taught me."

"Yes, but you could have run the place straight into the

ground. New business owners often do that. Your first year in business has been terrific."

"It's gone well." Holly curved her full lips into a smile, feeling the familiar hollowness inside. "I miss Max, though. The place isn't the same without him."

She had begun working at Maxie's Floral as a teenager, doing odd jobs; then, as time went on, she had become a designer. Max had been quick to spot Holly's talent for working with plants and flowers, her sense of color and eye for balance. Delighted with his discovery, the benevolent gentleman had taught her all he knew of the business.

When she'd gone off to college, she'd come home summers and continued working in the little shop near the ferry landing, located less than a ten-minute walk from where she now lived. Then her father had died suddenly of a heart attack the summer between her junior and senior years, and her mother was diagnosed with colon cancer just months after her graduation.

Instead of looking for a marketing job with her degree, Holly had come back to Mukilteo to care for her mother and had continued her employment at Maxie's Floral. Her only sibling, Denise, lived in Sacramento with her husband and young family, so the greater burden of caring for their mother had fallen upon Holly's young shoulders. It had been five long, hard years of ups and downs before Marion Winslow succumbed to the disease that had turned her into little more than a skin-covered skeleton.

She had died a year and a half ago; not long afterward Max had approached Holly about buying his charming, high-ceilinged shop. "It's time for me to retire," he'd begun without preamble. "I worked hard to make Maxie's a good business, and now my Sylvia and I want to do some traveling with the years we have left. You know the shop inside and out, Holly, and you have the same love for it I do. I'm guessing your parents left you a little money, and I want you to think about buying Maxie's from me."

So she'd bought Maxie's Floral. Once she'd sold her parents' home, she had also purchased the fetching little house in which she now lived. She loved living in Old Town, loved the view of the Sound, loved walking to work. Yet, for some reason, a hollow feeling in her chest stayed with her. It was grief, she supposed; it would just take more time for that feeling to go away.

Jean sat up and gave an unladylike snort. "I'm sure you're missing Max, but I wouldn't worry too much about him. I have no doubt he's enjoying his retirement immensely." Her voice softened then, her gaze seeking Holly's. "I'm a little worried about you, kid. Are you sure you're doing OK? Your last several years haven't exactly been easy."

"I'm fine." Holly mustered a smile, knowing Jean wasn't buying any of it. For some reason she'd withheld mentioning her chance meeting with Seth Glad, hoping it—and he—would fade from her mind. Instead, he'd been on her mind without cease.

"I've been meaning to ask you . . . ," Jean went on. "Well, I guess I'll just ask. Is Tim's and my wedding going to be difficult for you? I mean, with Kevin breaking off your engagement—"

"No, no. Please don't worry about that," Holly interrupted, touched at her friend's thoughtfulness. "I hardly think about him anymore. Kevin broke our engagement because he couldn't handle my mom's illness, which makes me wonder how he's going to weather the storms that are bound to arise in his life. Believe me when I say it's for the best I didn't marry Kevin Cowles. I'm looking forward to your wedding, Jean. And I'm honored that you chose me to be your maid of honor . . . and your florist."

"There's no finer florist in the area."

"Or accountant."

"Or brownie baker."

The friends shared a smile while Jean rose from her chair. "I'm so glad to have a friend like you, Holly. It means everything to have you in my wedding." An uncomfortable expression flashed across Jean's features, causing her smile to fade.

She sighed. "I have a confession to make. I hope you aren't going to be too upset."

"You've chosen another florist and can't figure out how to tell me?"

"Uh . . . no." The petite blond began to pace across the wide, painted planks. "But I did happen to run into someone last week. I know I should have mentioned it before now—"

"Seth Glad," Holly stated, somehow certain that that was the name Jean would give.

"How did you know?" Jean stopped pacing and leaned against the corner post near the steps, her eyebrows arching in surprise.

"Well, I can't think of anyone else whose name you'd agonize over mentioning in my presence." Holly was surprised to find her words sharp, and she hastened to soften her sarcastic tone. "I ran into him too," she admitted. "Just this morning."

"Really? Where?"

Holly held up her cup. "Getting your coffee. He came in right behind me."

Jean nodded with understanding. "Now I know why you haven't seemed like yourself today."

"Seeing him again was such a shock."

Jean smiled and hitched herself up to sit on the porch rail. "I know what you mean. Who would have figured him to come back and settle here? I thought he was destined for stardom in the major leagues. . . . I wonder why his career didn't pan out."

"Who knows?" Holly was quiet a moment, thinking of the past. It had seemed like a dream come true when Seth Glad had focused his attention on her.

Her parents had not wanted her to go out with him. Seth was the local sports legend, and tales of his fast living and bad-boy exploits were well known about the neighboring towns of Mukilteo and Everett. Good Christian girls just didn't date boys like Seth Glad. In her head, Holly had known her parents were right, but her heart hadn't been convinced.

It had taken only two dates for her to realize that their goals and values were very different, and difficult as it was, she had done the right thing and told him she couldn't see him any longer.

How she'd wished he desired more in his life than playing ball and pursuing temporal pleasures. When she'd attempted to share the gospel with him, he'd laughed and said in a scornful tone, "Who needs God? Look at all I have!"

To this day, Holly could honestly say she'd never known more elation or despair over a member of the opposite sex—including Kevin Cowles, to whom she had been briefly engaged three years ago.

"I bumped carts with him at the grocery store," Jean went on, seemingly unaware of the degree of turmoil within her friend. "And we had a really nice talk. He seems different from before. Nicer or something. Not so full of himself."

Holly remembered their meeting this morning, his warm smile and easy manner, and her heart did a little jig beneath her ribs. How could he still have such an effect on her? Heavens, he was every bit as good-looking as she remembered. Recalling how flustered she had become, she felt ashamed at the way she had thwarted his efforts to hold a pleasant conversation.

"He asked about you, Holly."

"Probably just because he remembered that you and I were friends. Funny how we've both run into him now." Holly strove to maintain a casual tone. "So was that your confession? That you saw Seth Glad at the grocery store and didn't mention it to me?" She shrugged. "It's no big deal. I doubt we'll see him again."

"Well, now comes the 'big deal' part of the confession." Jean looked uncomfortable, and she clasped her hands in her lap while maintaining graceful balance against the rail.

"What?"

"Well, we *will* be seeing him again. Both of us. I . . . uh . . . invited Seth to my wedding."

# CHAPTER TWO

Flowers. Dazzling assortments of blooms spilled from
vases at the altar of the small church Jean Breck's family
had attended since before her birth. Lavish bouquets,
tied with wide, ivory-colored satin bows, adorned the candles
at the ends of the pews and the arms of the three bridesmaids
making their way down the aisle.

The strains of Pachelbel's Canon in D filled the sanctuary,
mingling in the evening air with the delicate perfume of the
floral profusion. A soft breeze, invited to the ceremony by several partly open high-set windows along the west wall of the
church, teased scores of candle flames and provided blessed
refreshment for men fidgeting inside unaccustomed dress
clothing and women suffering the constraint of control-top
pantyhose.

Seth Glad was unaware of any physical discomfort as the
object of his interest passed by his seat, even lovelier than he
remembered in her summer blue dress.

*Lord, what kind of fool was I?*

No, he'd never forgotten Holly Winslow, nor the impas-
sioned verbal trouncing she'd given him that summer night a
full decade ago. Shifting in his seat to keep her in full view, his

lips were touched by a wry smile as he recalled the fateful evening he'd whisked her from the movie theater to the moon-lit water's edge.

One stolen kiss. A combination of testosterone and over-inflated ego had led him to believe any girl would be thrilled by his attentions. But not straight-as-an-arrow Holly. After she'd finished telling him what she thought of his behavior, she'd challenged his faith.

Not that he had any back then, except in himself. He still re-membered how she looked standing on the beach as she up-braided him, slender arms akimbo, dark blond hair gleaming in the moonlight. Impressive. And the way she spoke of Jesus . . . like she knew him. One part of him wanted to hear more, know more, but the bigger part of him scorned her words and what he viewed then as priggish self-righteousness. Holly the Holy.

If he hadn't been so incensed, first at her rejection, then at her rebuke, he might have listened. If only he'd possessed a modicum of maturity back then along with the physical tal-ents with which he'd been blessed. Absently, his fingers came up to trace the scar that snaked from temple to ear. The deri-sive "Who needs God?" he'd flung at Holly had come back to him countless times, always accompanied by her memory, un-til a ruined career and near-fatal motorcycle accident forced him to admit the truth: He did.

Seth Glad, washed-out party boy, onetime Double-A catcher, finally understood that apart from faith in Jesus Christ he was lost. Thanks to the ministering of a young, com-passionate hospital chaplain, he had learned of the Lord's lim-itless grace and forgiveness, and it hadn't been long before he'd humbly offered up his heart and life. And the funny thing was that he had hardly been able to wait to get back home and tell Holly.

While his bones and injuries healed, through every grueling session of physical therapy, the thought of seeing Holly again had spurred him on. He wanted to apologize to her. Thank her. Tell her he finally understood the wonderful truths of which she had spoken. It was probably crazy, but it was something he knew he needed to do.

After years of traveling the country with various minor-league ball teams and months of being laid up in west Texas after his accident, it was good to quietly settle back into his hometown. He could hardly believe the turn of events when he'd run into Jean Breck, Holly's best friend. His sense of hope, of expectancy, grew as Jean sketched out the events of the past ten years, mentioning that Holly was still single.

And then he'd seen Holly going into that coffee shop, her sun-kissed ponytail swinging with every step. If he hadn't known he'd see her again tonight, he'd have . . . he'd have what? She'd been polite but not overly warm. Reserve guarded the depth of her beryl blue gaze, a gaze he remembered flashing warmth and vitality and the passion of life itself.

The congregation rose to the unmistakable opening measures of Wagner's *Bridal Chorus* resonating from the organ, delivered with spunk by a white-haired matron in pink chiffon. All heads swiveled toward the rear of the church to behold the bride, flanked by her parents.

*Sorry, Jean. You're looking lovely tonight, but my eyes are for your maid of honor alone. Take plenty of time with the I-dos. . . . I have to step up to the plate and figure out how to right a ten-year-old wrong, and I need to make sure I don't go down swinging.*

\|||/

Holly managed to avoid Seth until the reception was nearly over, but she had a feeling it was only because he allowed her to do so. It wasn't until the wedding party and guests had seen the newly married couple to their garishly decorated car that he approached, an amused smile lighting his features.

*Oh no, here he comes.*

A part of her had known he would; she just hadn't known

311

when. She might as well have been seventeen years old all over again from the way she kept sneaking peeks at him. It was utterly immature, she told herself for at least the twentieth time that evening.

But during the ceremony and all through dinner, she'd sensed his searching gaze upon her. Why? His interest made no sense. Seth Glad could have any girl he wanted. *And probably had,* she thought with rancor, a wave of shame following the spiteful thought.

She'd tried in vain not to let his presence affect her, but she might as well have told herself not to breathe. Every nerve in her body felt as if it were stretched to the point of rupture. *Really, Holly? Is it just his presence? Be honest—you've been a wreck ever since you saw him at the coffee shop two weeks ago. Just keep your head now, and don't embarrass yourself. Be calm.*

"What a ruckus!" Seth had to nearly shout to make himself heard above the din of the honking car and spirited well-wishers. "Does this mean your duties as maid of honor are now complete?"

"I'm not sure—oh, my!" Her nervousness dissolved into unexpected laughter as the groom pulled his bride from the car and led her to the middle of the street. There, under the glow of the streetlights and the full September moon, he swept her into his arms, bent her backward, and laid an extravagant, passionate, and thoroughly crowd-pleasing kiss upon her. Amid the hoots and cheers, Holly couldn't help but think that unconventional Tim Doering was the perfect husband for Jean. Venturing a quick glance at the tall man beside her, she was somehow pleased to know that he appeared to be enjoying Tim's antics as much as she.

The crowd thinned quickly after the newlyweds' departure, but Seth made no move to leave her side. A sudden shiver caused her to rub her bare arms and wish she'd brought the shawl she'd left on the back of her chair. She wondered what she was supposed to do next. Say something, maybe? Clearing her throat, she forced a polite smile and prepared to speak.

But instead, Seth was first to break the silence between them. "I wonder, Holly, if you don't have any plans for the rest of the evening . . . well, I'd like to talk to you."

"About what?" His question roused even more curiosity within her, and she looked him full in the face. The cast of the streetlamps accented the lean angles of his jaw, and something earnest and tender shone from eyes as rich as cocoa beans. Unexpectedly, she felt her face grow warm.

"The past. And everything between then and now. Will you take a ride with me?" A small smile coaxed one of his famous dimples into appearing. "I promise, your virtue will be safe this time."

*So he does remember.* "I . . . uh . . . what did you have in mind?"

"Just a walk. Do you have any comfortable shoes, or do you need to stop home?"

"I think I've got a pair of running shoes in my backseat."

"Great. I'll pick you up out front here in ten minutes or so."

Eight minutes later Holly stood on the sidewalk and checked her watch, feeling ridiculous in her bridesmaid dress, shawl, and beat-up Nikes. What in heaven's name did Seth Glad want to talk to her about? And where was he taking her? Closing her eyes, she tried to picture him as she remembered, ten years past.

Bold. Brash. Talented. Full of himself to the point of conceit. Nowhere in her memory could she recall the considerate quality she'd seen in him tonight, the willingness to wait with patience for what he wanted. *But wasn't his devil-may-care attitude what attracted you back then? You knew his type was way off-limits, but didn't you have this silly idea that you could change him?*

"Are you too tired to go, Holly?"

She'd not heard his approach and was surprised to see a

late-model Ford pickup parked before her. "Oh. No. I was just . . . thinking."

He opened the passenger door and gestured. "About anything in particular?"

"Just that Jean was right." Somehow the words were out before she even thought about stopping them.

"Oh." His eyebrows arched with humor as the dimples on either side of his mouth gave way to deep grooves. "Am I supposed to know what Jean was right about, or is that privileged information?"

His hand was warm on her elbow as he helped her into the cab of his truck. "Well," she began, wondering why she seemed to be slightly out of breath, "she said that you seemed different than before."

His smile faded, replaced by a contemplative expression. "I hope so," he said quietly, closing the door.

While he drove, Seth kept the conversation light with amusing stories of his years in the minor leagues. Again, Holly noticed that he seemed as at ease with her as if they were old friends. That was strange, she thought, given their parting a decade before.

But even so, she found herself relaxing as he spoke, enjoying the gritty and outlandish accounts of his years on the road. The inflection of his voice rose and fell with all the grace of a master storyteller, his characters so real that Holly felt as though she knew them personally. Inhaling deeply, she became aware of the fresh, woodsy fragrance she'd noticed that day at the coffee shop, and she wondered how long it had been since she'd been in the company of such an interesting man.

Lost in the unexpected wonder of this interlude, she didn't immediately notice when the truck slowed, then turned to the left. The moonlight that had illuminated the cab and Seth's profile during their drive melted into deep shadows.

Puzzled, she leaned forward and took note of their surroundings. The truck moved forward at an unhurried pace, its headlights swallowed up by the thick stands of trees on either side of the road. Save the asphalt upon which they drove, it was as if all signs of civilization had disappeared. A second later, realization dawned upon her.

*Howarth Park.*

Holly was not able to prevent her shock, nor the gasp that escaped her lips and severed the companionable feelings they had shared for the past quarter hour. Turning toward Seth, who now sat silent beside her, she gave vent to the flare of anger that burst from some long-dead place within her.

# CHAPTER THREE

What do you think you're doing?" Her thumb popped the seat-belt buckle as she twisted toward him. "If you don't turn this truck around right now, I'm getting out." To prove her point, she reached for the door.

"Didn't you ever hear of returning to the scene of the crime?" Though his words were light, what she could see of his expression was earnest. "Holly, you don't have anything to be afraid of. I'm not going to hurt you. I just had an idea that a walk on the beach might break the tension between us."

"What tension?" she ground out.

"Look, Holly, we both know what a jerk I was, way back when—"

"A jerk? I'd say what you tried to do went beyond being a jerk. And then you made a fool of me—"

"All right, I was an arrogant jerk with poor impulse control. Does that work a little better for you?"

"A little." Against her will, she began to soften. "But if you want to apologize for mauling and mocking me, why don't you just say you're sorry?"

Pulling his truck to a stop in the wide lot at the end of the park drive, he sighed and turned off the ignition. The sound of the night wind rustling the trees added to the tentative chemistry in the cab. "I *am* sorry, Holly, very sorry. You were a really special girl, and I had no right to treat you the way I did." He was silent a long moment before adding, "I really liked you."

*I really liked you, too, Seth.* An answering sigh escaped her as the emotional pain of that long-ago summer came back to her. The wanting, the rejection. The knowledge that he was lost.

"Do you think you can forgive me enough so we can try it again? A walk, I mean. The moon is full, so we should have plenty of light, or I have a flashlight, if you'd like. And here." Reaching behind the seat, he pulled out a thick sweatshirt and laid it across her arm. "This will be warmer than that thin little thing on your shoulders."

"It's a shawl—and it was my mother's." The beginnings of a smile twitched her lips, and she shook her head. "You're certainly persistent."

"You'll be happy to know I've learned a few things about character. And manners, too—wait there."

Letting himself out of the truck, he walked around and opened her door, bowing. "Right this way, ma'am. I'll see if I can impress you with my good behavior this time around."

"I don't get it, Seth. Why come apologize to me ten years later?" she asked, stepping from the truck and slipping his sweatshirt over her head. "Why the trip back to Howarth Park?" *Bridesmaid dress, ugly old Nikes, floppy shirt. What an ensemble, Holly. I'm sure you've never looked more attractive.*

A white row of teeth gleamed at her in the moonlight. "It's part of the new me."

"What new you?"

In the clearing, it was easy to see the path that led westward, toward the beach. They began walking.

"Remember the old me?"

"Yes . . ." Her reply was cautious, her voice soft.

From beside her, his laughter carried to the treetops. "It's OK. You can say it. Prideful, pleasure seeking, immature, egotistical, self-destructive—"

"You were larger than life back then, Seth," she interrupted. "All that talent, and you were headed down the road to ruin."

"Don't I know it now . . . and you knew it then." His reply, initially colored with regret, continued in a teasing vein. "No, I had no question about where you stood on the matter, Miss Holly Winslow. Did you know I used to call you 'Holly Holly'?"

*Holly Holly.* She almost laughed at his nickname, except it was so far from the truth that she couldn't. She hadn't felt holy in . . . how long? She'd learned in Bible study that *holy* meant "set apart." But for what had she been set apart? Owning and operating Maxie's Floral, enjoying a double mocha every afternoon, and taking long walks along the beach whenever she could get away? What was holy in any of that?

The steps for the pedestrian walk over the railroad tracks rose before them. Seth allowed her to take the lead, and they began climbing. Overhead the chalky orb of the autumn moon illuminated the heavens and a thin, far-off bank of cirrus clouds. The waters of the Sound shimmered as always, the gentle sound of the waves both stirring and soothing.

Even though magnificent evidence of the Lord's creation lay before her, the last time Holly had been certain of his presence in her life was the day of her mother's funeral. Arising from her anguished prayers that morning, she had been blanketed within the warm, comforting folds of heavenly grace that whole difficult day through. There was no other way to explain it, she just *knew.*

But since then, it seemed God had been as distant as the sea was wide. It wasn't that she had stopped believing. She continued to pray and attend church and Thursday-evening Bible study. But this gulf, this emptiness, had stretched on for so long that it almost seemed futile to seek God anymore.

Shivering as she reached the top of the steps, she hugged her arms to herself, thankful for the way the thick sweatshirt insulated her from the crispness of the night air. The twinkling lights of Everett shone in the distance. A moment later, Seth fell into step beside her.

"Did I hurt your feelings?"

"No." He hadn't, not really. What hurt was facing the bleakness of what used to be a vibrant spiritual existence.

"Tell me about your store," he said, shifting the topic to one less personal. "Jean told me you've owned Maxie's Floral for over a year now."

They walked down the steps, and beyond to the smooth, wet beach. Seth asked several questions about the flower shop, showing genuine interest in the day-to-day operation of the business. Slowly Holly's disquiet receded. His friendly company and the calming sound of the surf almost made her forget she was taking a trip down memory lane with the man who had broken her heart like no other.

"Does this look like the spot?"

"What spot?" Holly looked about the beach, taking note of the distance they'd walked and the rugged appearance of several large rocks.

"The spot where I—"

"Oh. That spot." Holly was glad he couldn't see the pink heat that licked up her cheeks.

"Could you humor me and stop here for just a few minutes . . . please?"

"How come?" In the moonlight, Holly saw that Seth's expression was sober.

"I want to do this right. . . . I mean, I want—" Taking a deep breath, the tall man looked toward the sky for a long moment. "This is harder than I thought it was going to be," he said, flashing an uncertain smile in her direction. "As a girl of seventeen you had more courage than I have right now."

"What are you talking about?"

"Do you remember what you told me here?"

"'Take your hands off me'?" Why had she chosen such flip words when what he wanted to say was obviously serious?

"Yes, you said that," he allowed, his smile fading. "But do you remember what else?"

"Yes, I remember," she said quietly. She hadn't forgotten how her witness for Christ had been thrown back in her face.

"Holly, besides my mother and my sister, you're the only person who ever called me to account before God." Raking his hand through his short hair, he continued. "Mom was always a believer, but my dad never went to church. I guess I followed along in his footsteps, thinking there was no use for religion. They're divorced now. He left . . . for another woman."

"Oh, I'm sorry." The pain in Seth's voice was unmistakable, and Holly's heart went out to him. "How's your mom doing?"

"Pretty good, now. It was rough at first, but her faith is carrying her through." He sighed. "Holly, the Seth Glad you knew in high school only got worse. Life on the road was one big party, if you wanted it to be. Somehow I actually advanced to a Double-A club, but then I blew it. I'd never really had to work too hard at playing ball, and I didn't have any discipline. I guess I always figured I'd make it on my talent alone."

Holly remained silent, allowing him to speak.

"My career was already going downhill when I had the motorcycle accident. I was busted up pretty bad. That's where I got this scar—" he pointed to his temple—"and all the other ones you can't see."

Holly's pulse hammered at his words. He could have been killed. Studying his profile as he looked out to sea, she felt something twist inside her chest.

"While I was lying in that hospital bed, Holly, I couldn't stop thinking about what you said to me here, on this beach.

You told me I needed God, and I told you I didn't." A deep sigh left him. "It took a ruined career and nearly dying for me to see the light, but I finally saw it. I promised myself that once I got home I'd look you up and tell you in person that I surrendered my life to Jesus Christ." His admission made, he turned and took a step toward her, holding his palms in a supplicating gesture. "I also need to ask for your forgiveness for my insulting behavior toward you. Do you think you can forgive me?"

Holly nodded, stunned. Did things like this happen in real life? She knew several people from church who had undergone dramatic faith conversions . . . but Seth Glad? The image of the brash, swaggering adolescent athlete rose in her mind, out of accord with this humble man who stood before her.

"It's a lot to digest at once, I know. I'm hoping that when you have some time to think things over, you might consider having dinner with me. I owe you at least that much, plus I'd really like to talk to you now that we're both coming from the same place."

Seth Glad was a Christian *and* he wanted to have dinner with her? It was almost too much to take in.

His easy smile returned as he continued to speak. "My mom has been dying to meet The Girl Who Told Off Seth Glad ever since I let her know about you." He chuckled. "In fact, she was all set to jump out of the car along with me that day I saw you go into the coffee shop. I had to point out that one of us needed to stay in the car and drive it down to the ferry." As he talked, he began walking back in the direction from which they'd come.

Holly fell in beside him, noticing that the footprints they'd made earlier were now just shallow, water-filled depressions. The tide was coming in.

"So what do you say? You've been pretty quiet." Lightly, he touched her arm. "Don't tell me, after all this, that you've lost your faith, Holy Holly."

"No, I haven't." Her smile came with effort, her other emotions eclipsed by the sudden sweep of emptiness through her heart. How ironic. He had sought her out to tell her of his new birth, while she wallowed in some sort of spiritual dead zone. She felt like a fraud before him.

It was probably for the best if they parted company. What did they have in common anymore? She saw the peace in him, the joy. And she had watched him at Jean's reception, smiling and laughing and talking with his still-adoring public. She didn't fit in with any of that.

"I don't know about dinner, Seth," she began, carefully choosing her words. "But I'm really glad that God kept seeking you until you were finally ready to say yes to him—"

"Are you involved with someone else?" he interrupted, stopping midstride.

"Uh . . . no."

"Good." His grin was one she remembered, lazy and sure. "Then we'll just take it slow."

Holly wanted to protest, to tell him that she didn't think they should take things anywhere, but he had already moved ahead of her. Sighing, she strode forward, determined to squelch his misguided appreciation for the rebuke she had delivered a decade earlier.

But could she so easily suppress the deep-down longings she held in her heart for this man?

# CHAPTER FOUR

Three large, clear vases lined the stainless-steel work counter. Holly had "greened" each of the containers in assembly-line fashion and now added a balance of flowers in the same manner. Her movements were quick but not hasty, each bouquet gradually taking shape as she worked. A pile of cuttings grew on the floor about her feet, severed in deft motions by the sharp Swiss knife she wielded.

"How much is the lisianthus again?" asked Brenda Fahey, pricing an arrangement she had already completed. "Two fifty?"

"Two seventy-five." Holly smiled at the mother of three in her late thirties, who had begun working two days a week when her youngest child entered first grade last fall. Brenda was a good worker and a natural at designing.

"Someday I'll have these flowers figured out. I can't believe how automatic it is for you and Ellen to just whip these prices off the top of your head." Ellen Butler was the shop's only full-time employee. Hired by Max three years ago, she knew the business nearly as well as Holly.

"Well, Ellen's been here a long time, and don't forget that

I've been here since I was sixteen. You're doing a terrific job, Brenda, and we're glad to have your help," she encouraged.

Despite her cheery words, the hollowness in her chest persisted, as familiar as her beat-up Nikes. It had been more than a week since her moonlit walk at Howarth Park with Seth Glad, and she had not heard from him since.

She had firmly declined his dinner invitation that night, certain she was doing the right thing. They were from two different worlds, she and Seth. He was well known, a local sports celebrity, while she was just . . . *Be honest, Holly. His new-found enthusiasm for Jesus Christ scares you silly. You just don't want him to get close enough to find out what a rut you're in.*

Why, then, did a secret part of her hope he would call anyway? She couldn't forget the way he looked behind the wheel of his truck as he departed that night . . . strong, handsome, and somehow vulnerable. The image lingered in her mind's eye, aching and sweet.

*What's the matter with you? You never had feelings like this for Kevin. In fact, the only guy you've ever felt this way about has been Seth Glad.* Unbidden, the memory of Seth's long-ago kiss came back to her. Thrilling. Frightening. *Pure teenage infatuation. So what if Kevin never gave you a kiss like that? Mature love isn't supposed to pack such a wallop.*

Mature love? Was that what she and Kevin had shared? For a long time their relationship had been comfortable, amicable, so steady. No highs, no lows. Even when he'd asked her to marry him, she hadn't felt skyrockets go off inside her. But then her mother's cancer progressed, and she began to see less and less of him. Part of the reason was because caring for her mom required more of her time, but the other reason was that Kevin couldn't stand being around sick people. His petulance grew into resentment, resentment into anger, and finally he called things off.

"Do you want me to finish those for you?" Brenda's voice intruded into Holly's reminiscence. "It's already after two o'clock, and you haven't been over for your coffee yet. Either your inner clock is off or you snuck out and jazzed up on caffeine at lunchtime." Hazel eyes sparkled above a mischievous grin. "Although the way you're moving, you don't look very jazzed. You've been twiddling the same flower in your hands for five minutes now."

Holly checked her watch, then glanced at the spike of sweet-smelling stock she held, realizing she was doing more woolgathering than work. "I think I'll take you up on your offer." Flashing a rueful smile at her assistant, she set down her things. "Maybe I'd better make my double a triple today."

"Either that or chew a couple of those chocolate-covered coffee beans. Unless this is about some man, in which case no amount of caffeine will help." The mischievous grin widened at Holly's start of surprise. "Ah-hah . . . am I on to something?"

Pulling the sturdy green apron up over her head, Holly didn't make an immediate reply.

"Oh, my, I think I'm definitely on to something," Brenda continued. Whistling a series of cheerful notes, she stepped in front of the three vases. "But don't tell me anything if you don't want to, boss lady. Sometimes it's more fun to guess what's going on. . . ."

"Nothing's going on," Holly disputed, reaching for her purse. "There's no one, really."

"Sure there isn't." Satisfaction gleamed with Brenda's white teeth. "Go on, now, and get your coffee. I'll have these done and wrapped before Skip comes in for the afternoon deliveries."

Picking up a fat yellow mum, Brenda estimated the length she needed and cut its stem. "Now, how does that tune go? Seems like my kids are always singing it about someone." She spoke in an offhand manner, spiking the mum into the green foam material at the bottom of the vase. "Hmm, Holly and . . . Holly and . . . who? Holly and the mystery man. Oh, well, we'll just go with that." She began in cadence, "Holly and *someone,* sitting in a tree, k-i-s-s-i-n-g. First comes love; then comes marriage—"

Holly escaped the shop through its back entrance, flustered. Even as she reached Lincoln Avenue, her ears still rang with the ridiculous childhood singsong.

*Holly and* someone, *sitting in a tree, k-i-s-s-i-n-g . . .*

No, it was more like Holly and Seth, standing on a beach. Ten years later . . . ten years later . . . what? She couldn't think of a suitable rhyme. In fact, she thought, walking up the hill toward the café, she couldn't think of anything suitable coming from their acquaintance. The beach sounded good, though. A nice, long walk on the beach—by herself—was just what she needed to clear her head and give her a fresh perspective on things. The sound of the water was so calming, so soothing. . . .

Holly's thoughts were interrupted by the sight of Seth Glad waiting at the entrance of Lincoln Avenue Courtyard, holding a cup in each hand. Dressed in work-worn jeans and a navy blue T-shirt, his stance was casual. A warm smile lit his features when he saw he had her attention, and he stepped forward. "You're late," he called, inclining his head toward his wrist. "It's almost two-thirty. My source told me you were usually here by ten after."

Despite her wordless surprise at seeing him here, Holly felt her heart begin a crazy hammering, just as it had the first time she'd run into him. Only this was no accidental meeting. *But your meeting wasn't accidental the first time, either. He told you he was waiting for the ferry with his mother and saw you, remember? And what about those things he said to you at the beach?*

He was pursuing her, no question about it.

"One double mocha," he said, presenting her a tall paper cup. "Would you care to have a seat in the courtyard? I took the liberty of picking out a few treats your friend behind the counter said you might have trouble resisting."

"So Monica's your informant," she said, taking the cup.

Her voice sounded natural, but her insides felt far from it. She ran her hand through the wisps that escaped her ponytail, wishing at the same time that she'd freshened her lipstick.

"And a good one, at that," he replied with a laugh. "Come on, let's sit down. I worked all day without a break so I could take off early and meet you here. If you don't eat your goodies, I will."

"Where are you working?" she asked, following him to a small table. Normally, Holly drank in the beauty of the courtyard, the flowers, the view of the Sound. Today she barely noticed her surroundings. Seth Glad filled her senses instead.

"Griffin is putting up a couple high-priced homes on Goat Trail. Did you ever hear that bootlegging used to be quite a venture up there?" he asked, holding a chair for her. "One of the guys told me that during the depression, whiskey somehow got into the pipes that supplied water to the school. Just think of all those kids coming home looped."

"Did they really?" Taking her seat, Holly craned her neck to look up at Seth.

"Naw. They canceled classes till they got it taken care of." He chuckled. "You looked worried there for a minute."

When Holly glanced at her watch thirty minutes later, she couldn't believe so much time had passed. Seth was a witty and charming conversationalist, and she had to admit she'd enjoyed sharing coffee and pastry with him. Just as long as he didn't get too personal, which he hadn't.

"I've probably kept you away from your shop long enough," he said, also checking the time. "Can I walk you back?"

The waters of the Sound sparkled deep and blue in the afternoon sunshine as Seth accompanied her the few blocks to her shop, chatting idly about people and places. Rush-hour traffic had not yet begun, the pace of the small town appearing leisurely. But all too soon the Mukilteo Speedway would fill with Whidbey commuters yearning to be on the westbound ferry that would take them home after a long day of work.

"You own a great old building, Holly," Seth complimented, gesturing toward Maxie's Floral. "And I hear you run a good business."

"Let me guess—your 'source' told you that, too?"

"Careful, now, you're smiling." His grin widened as his gaze captured hers. Mocha brown, deep, bottomless. A long moment passed, and something changed between them.

Holly sobered at the intensity of Seth's gaze, an anxious tremor beginning in the pit of her stomach.

"I'm not going to beat around the bush," he began, stepping forward and taking her hand between his large palms. "I want to see you again. I want to have dinner with you. I want to know more about you, and I especially want to talk about your faith with you. In short, I want to catch up on all the things I missed out on when I was too young and dumb and stupid."

"Ah," Holly faltered, pulling back her hand. Alarm poured through her. "You don't have to try and make anything up to me—"

"This isn't about making anything up, Holly. This is about making a fresh start . . . the right way."

"What's the right way? And why me?" Holly was dismayed to hear how rapid her speech sounded, but she was at a loss to slow down. "I'm sure there are dozens of girls who are delighted to know Seth Glad is back in town."

"I don't care about dozens of girls, Holly. I'm interested in you." Hooking his thumbs in his pockets, he stepped back and regarded her with a long look. "Why you? If I said it was because you're a beautiful woman, I wouldn't be lying."

At his words, his perusal, goose bumps rose on the backs of Holly's arms.

"But mostly it's because I can't stop thinking about you." He shook his head and looked toward the sky. "I don't understand it, Holly. I really don't. All I know is that ever since I acknowledged my need for God, I keep feeling like I'm being pushed in your direction."

"So this 'divine' revelation—"

"I see your tongue hasn't lost its sharp edge," he interrupted, the lazy grin reappearing. "But I didn't say anything about a divine revelation. I can, though, if it'll make you feel any better. . . ."

"No . . . no." Growing more uncomfortable by the second, she shook her head and took a step back. "You probably think I'm being . . ." She couldn't think of a word to describe her emotions, her feelings.

He waited, warmth and patience emanating from his deep brown gaze. And somehow the unspoken message that she was worth waiting for made her feel worst of all. Because she wasn't. She wasn't any of the things he was expecting her to be, and it would be humiliating to have him discover what a spiritual midget she had turned into.

"I'm sorry," she whispered, her heart stirring with the same intensity of pain it had felt ten years before. Why were things destined never to work between them? "I need to go."

Reaching into his back pocket, he removed his wallet and handed her a card. "Here's my number. I don't give it to just anyone, you know." His grin was as engaging as ever, but tinged with sadness. "And I never tell people they can call me day or night . . . but I'm telling you."

Holly watched him depart through eyes filled with tears. What was it about this man that seemed to twist her heart right over? His gait was easy, his step sure, but she knew her rejection had hurt him. A profound sense of loss swept over her as he went around the corner, out of sight.

*Maybe, just maybe, if I can get myself together* . . . , she half thought, half prayed. But now, as usual, God seemed not to be listening.

331

# CHAPTER FIVE

S*ome Saturday night,* Seth thought as he took out the
trash and contemplated the best channel on which to
watch the news. Sensational stories and long-winded
weather prognostications preceded the sports on all of them;
maybe a guy ought to call it a night and skip TV altogether.

Hefting his bag into the Dumpster behind the complex of
townhouses in which he lived, Seth turned and walked along
the tidy concrete path back to his unit. Cool autumn air struck
his face and bare arms, and he couldn't help but think of how
he had hoped to spend the evening enjoying a seafood dinner
with Holly . . . while instead he took out the garbage.

*Holly.* She was on his mind so much that he was beginning
to wonder if he suffered an obsession. While he lay in the hospital, the idea of apologizing to her and telling her of his conversion experience seemed like a godly way to atone for his
poor treatment of her. But all his time spent thinking about
Holly had done nothing to prepare his heart for seeing her
again. He was sure his heart had jumped out of his chest and
landed on his sleeve when he'd seen her going into the Mukilteo Coffee Café that day.

Back in high school she'd been cute, but ten years had

changed the tall, impetuous girl into a lovely and graceful woman—and he found her irresistible. Instead of being satisfied with asking her forgiveness and saying so long, he now lived with a desire to know her better, to be a part of her life.

Locking the patio door behind him, he wondered why she kept turning him down. At different moments, he sensed her interest in him. He was sure of it. She didn't seem the type to play games, but he couldn't shake the feeling that something was causing Holly to balk where he was concerned. He could also swear he'd seen fear in her eyes.

Since he'd been back in town he'd learned of her broken engagement. Had that experience left her leery of men in general? He hadn't dated in a long time, and he hadn't dated at all since becoming a Christian. Maybe he was coming on way too strong, but there was something restless inside him, urging him to continue seeking her.

And she kept saying no. So what was he supposed to do?

Snapping off the living-room lights, he walked to the master bedroom and sank down on the bed. Far from drowsy, he opened his Bible to the Gospel of John and began reading. Somehow John's unique style of writing made him feel immediately connected to the reality of the living God.

Sleep must have stolen upon him more quickly than he thought. The next thing he knew, the phone was ringing and his foggy mind registered the fact that it was 4:15 A.M. The Bible had fallen sideways off his chest, and he had a crick in his neck from sleeping in a too-propped-up position for the past several hours.

Groaning, he reached for the telephone, wondering if it was his mom calling with bad news about some elderly relative, as she was wont to do. Instead, Holly's voice filled his ear, her words tumbling over one another, rapid and desperate.

"Hold on, Holly," he finally said, understanding only that her shop had been broken into. All tiredness had vanished the moment he'd heard her voice on the other end of the line. "Tell me everything you just said, only slower."

"I just got the call, and they want me to go down there," she said, sounding as if she had only a precarious grip on her emotions. "They said I need to make arrangements to board things up . . . and I don't know what to do. I would have called Jean and Tim, but they're still on their honeymoon. I know Max wouldn't mind helping, but he's on another trip." Her voice broke, and she was silent for a long moment. "I'm sorry to be calling you at this time of night," she finally said, her words somewhere between a sob and a whisper, "but I wonder if—"

"I'll be right there," he interrupted, already out of bed and impatient to be on his way. The need in her voice aroused all kinds of feelings in him: anger at whoever had dared commit this crime against her, a foreign yet intense sense of protectiveness toward her, and the poignant realization that she had called him in her time of need. And he had heard need in her voice, naked need. But what if she had called him only because she thought he would be handy to hammer some nails?

*Don't get your hopes up,* he told himself on the drive over, at the same time praying, *Lord, if this is the opening I need, I'll take it.*

⁂

A predawn glow hung in the eastern sky when Seth arrived in Old Town, pulling up behind one of the two police cars in front of Maxie's Floral. Holly's Toyota was parked across the street. Though he knew she was safe, he felt a fresh surge of adrenaline upon viewing her standing with an officer in front of her store. Light spilled from the shop's front windows, bright and unnatural on the otherwise darkened, deserted street.

Holly was not a petite woman, but she looked small and forlorn as he approached. "Thank you for coming," she said, offering him a weak smile as he joined the pair on the sidewalk. Blotchy eyes and a wadded tissue gave evidence of previous tears. Anger simmered inside him, and he found himself wanting to beat up whoever had done this to her.

The officer was busy taking down information in his notebook, his pen scrabbling across the small page. Job completed, he gave Seth his full attention. "So you'll take care of boarding up the window? Good. We're just about done here. Forced entry, rear window," he reported in spare fashion. "Cash register was empty, drawer open, so they thought they'd vandalize the place." He shook his graying head in disgust and reached into his breast pocket. "With the alarms, these guys know they have four to six minutes to get in and get out before we get here. You can't believe the things they'll do in those few minutes."

Pulling a card from his pocket, he wrote a few things down and handed the card to Holly. "Case number, badge number."

"Do you think you'll catch whoever did this?"

"We'll do the best we can, ma'am. If you talk to anyone along here who might have seen something, have them call the number on the card. An eyewitness is our best bet."

The other officer, a lanky man in his late twenties, came out the door then. "Once we get that window covered, we'll be secure. You the guy?" he said to Seth, indicating that he should come with him. "This shouldn't be any big deal. Just one window. You can see where they tried the door first, but they gave up and went the easy route."

Seth followed the policeman through the store to the back room, picking his way over dirt and broken glass. Green plants lay overturned and trampled, broken vases and dried flower arrangements littered the floor, and it appeared that someone had taken a baseball bat to the computer monitor and the clear glass doors of the large flower cooler on the show floor. A large amount of water from the containers that held cut roses, carnations, and several other types of flowers Seth couldn't identify added to the mess on the floor.

Senseless vandalism. His anger grew to the point that he

wasn't sure how much help or comfort he was going to be to Holly. He was glad he had made the call to his mother before he'd left home. She would know all the right things to say and do.

"This shouldn't take you too long." The cop pointed to the smashed rear window. Turning to leave, he paused and said over his shoulder, "Say, you gonna stay with the key holder for a while? She looks pretty upset."

"Yeah." Seth nodded. "I've got my mom coming to help out too."

"Glad to hear it. Try to have a good one," the officer quipped, walking away.

Seth measured the window opening and returned to his truck for his toolbox and some likely sized pieces of scrap lumber he had tossed in the bed of the pickup. Holly was still talking with the first police officer; only one of the squad cars remained. Just then, his mother's Honda turned the corner and pulled up behind his truck.

"Hi, honey. This must be the place," she called, getting out of her car and hefting a large canvas bag over her shoulder. Wide-hipped and full-bosomed, dressed in jeans and a sweatshirt, Barbara Glad looked like she was ready to roll up her sleeves and set right to work. Seth had no doubt that's exactly what she would be doing inside ten minutes' time.

"This is the place," he affirmed. Unable to resist ribbing her, he added, "What's in that suitcase you're toting? A five-course breakfast for the Mukilteo Police Department?"

"It's a thermos of coffee and some lemon poppy-seed muffins I made yesterday, funny boy. But if the officer would like something to eat, I'll feed him too," she finished loudly enough for the pair on the sidewalk to hear.

Almost a foot taller than his mother, Seth had to bend over to receive the hug and kiss she offered. Laying her cheek against his, she whispered, "She's the one, isn't she, Sethie?" He didn't have a chance to answer before she was down the sidewalk like a rock out of a slingshot, introducing herself to

Holly and enfolding her in a warm embrace. Sighing, he realized a good portion of his anger had melted away with his mother's arrival. No doubt she'd been praying ever since she'd received his call. Gathering the items he needed from the truck, he walked toward the group of people on the sidewalk. Officer Eckerd had just excused himself to write his report, but not before he took away a napkin and two large muffins.

Holly dabbed at her eyes, moist with fresh tears. "Thank you both for coming," she said, looking between them. "I can't believe you came out in the middle of the night, Mrs. Glad. You don't even know me—"

"It's Barb," the older woman interrupted with a gentle smile. "And sure, I know you, dear. Seth's told me all about you. Now, shall we get inside and take a look at things?"

Following the women inside, Seth chuckled as his mother exclaimed at the state of the shop and set down her bag, pushing up her sweatshirt sleeves with determination. He had underestimated her. Ten minutes was far too long to stand between Barbara Glad and a mess.

*

By eight o'clock, Holly couldn't believe the transformation that had occurred in her ransacked store, nor had it taken long to realize Seth's mother was an avowed enemy of dirt and disorder. With incredible efficiency, she had jumped into the chaos and begun setting things to rights. Once Seth had secured the back window, he joined their efforts, going to work with the garbage can, broom, and dustpan, taking care of the worst of the messes on the floor. The work had been hard, but the three had gotten along well, managing several laughs and a growing camaraderie.

"How can I thank you both enough?" Holly asked, surveying the show floor. "If I hadn't taken those Polaroids when I first came down, I would never believe we'd had such a disaster on our hands."

"You can thank me by letting me take you to breakfast," Seth replied, leaning the broom against the wall. "You, too, Mom."

"Breakfast? After all those muffins you ate? Besides, I'm in no condition to go anywhere." With both hands, Barb Glad gestured at her appearance. "Look at me!"

"So you're a little dirty. We all are. And I'm still hungry." His eyes met Holly's, and a slow grin spread across his face. "I don't know if we could take you into a restaurant, though. Those smudges on your face could keep us all out . . . but at least they match the ones on your T-shirt."

"Mind your manners, Sethie," his mother spoke, brushing off her own clothing.

Holly looked down at the grime on her top and threw him a look of mock exasperation. "Yeah, mind your manners, *Sethie,*" she said, swiping at her cheek.

"Other side," he mouthed, pointing and giving her a broad wink.

She pulled a face and wiped her other cheek.

*Careful, Holly, you're having too much fun with him. And his mom, too. She's really a neat lady . . . and godly. How did he ever get to be the way he was with a mother like this? She must have been overjoyed when he came back home a changed man. The parable of the lost son all over again.*

Her resistance to Seth Glad had been steadily melting away throughout the morning. Phoning him had been one of the most difficult things she'd ever done, but she had been so shocked to receive a call from the police in the middle of the night, telling her they needed her to come to the shop because of a break-in. For a long moment after hanging up, sitting in the dark bedroom, her mind had been blank. Who could she call for help, for moral support?

*Call Seth,* a voice inside her had whispered. *No! I can't!* she had argued with herself while hastily dressing and brushing her teeth. She didn't need to call anyone. She was a big girl now, a business owner, and she didn't require someone to hold her hand through her first robbery. But then the tears broke, and his name kept coming to her with such awful relentlessness that she had finally broken down and called him. The card he'd given her lay in her purse, right under her keys. Why hadn't she thrown it away?

*Three rings. That's it. If he doesn't answer in three rings, I'm hanging up.*

He'd answered on the second.

That he'd come so cheerfully after her rebuff—and brought his mother to help, besides—touched her deeply. Since Kevin had broken things off with her, she hadn't dated. Maybe it had been so long since a man had expressed interest in her that she was overreacting. Seth was undeniably interested in her, and she was finding him a lot of fun to be around. Who said things had to be serious?

Barb Glad interrupted her musings. "Why don't you both go home and shower and then come on over for breakfast? If we hurry, we can still make the late service this morning."

Seth feigned confusion. "Did you want us to shower together, or separately?"

"Separately—in separate houses!" Barb Glad tried, and failed, to maintain a stern expression. "Honestly, Seth Andrew Glad! You're going to scare the poor girl off."

"Aw, shucks, Ma, I already sent her runnin' once," he said in his best country-bumpkin imitation, tugging at imaginary suspenders. "She ain't likely to scare twice." Turning toward her, he inquired, "Miss Holly? Ma'am? Do you want to shower separately, in separate houses, and then have some victuals with my ma?"

"Well—," Holly began, more amused than shocked.

"She'd love to," he finished for her, turning to his mother. "Bacon and eggs?"

"Over easy. And orange juice and toast, my sometimes predictable son." Shaking her head, the older woman began packing the thermos and cups back into her bag.

"Do you want to come, Holly?" Seth asked, serious now.

340

"We could drive up to the Ice Caves after church. Do you like to hike?"

"I . . . yes," she said, surprising herself with her easy answer. Truth was, she didn't want this day to end. The long, solitary walk she had planned to take along the beach no longer had any appeal.

Seth picked up his toolbox and smiled, his dark gaze warm upon her. "Mom can give you directions, then. I'll see you over there."

# CHAPTER SIX

Pausing for breath as she stood in the rocky basin before the Ice Caves, Holly looked up at the tall mountains rising above the glacier. Patches of conifers dotted the steep landscape, adding color to the gray walls. She smiled as a Japanese family moved past her, pointing and exclaiming in their native language. The beautiful Sunday afternoon had attracted quite a few visitors to the park.

"How long has it been since you were here?" Seth asked from beside her.

"Four or five years, I think," Holly replied, remembering the long day of hiking she and Jean had taken.

"Longer than that for me. Have you ever wondered why people live by all these great places and never go to them? It's always the tourists."

"We'll just have to make it a point to do our civic duty and see the local sights, then, I suppose."

"Mount Rainier, next weekend."

Holly turned her head to gauge his expression. "Are you serious?"

"As a heart attack, baby." The coffee brown gaze met hers with challenge, and he grinned. "Are you kidding? Now that

343

I've got you convinced that I'm not some morally corrupt, depraved, predatory—"

"Hold on. . . . Who says I'm convinced?" She arched her brows and attempted to bite back an answering grin. "You've got quite a past to overcome, mister."

"You're telling me." His expression became rueful for a moment, then brightened. "You know, I like when you get a little sassy. It reminds me of this girl I knew about ten years ago." He took her elbow and guided her forward. "She was full of spit and vinegar, and I never quite forgot about her."

She shook off his hand. "You make me sound so . . . so cute or something. Don't forget that you were plenty mad at me. And I don't believe for one second that you went off to all your glory and fame pining away for Holly Winslow."

"Naw, I wasn't pining, but I never forgot you. And I think we both know the end of the story regarding the glory and fame." His smile flashed as a breeze came down the mountain, blowing over them with peculiar chill. "Feel that? The wind picks up the cold from the glacier. But back on that beach, what you said to me was even colder than this."

"Well, someone had to tell you off. You had an ego the size of—"

"So I had a teeny, tiny little problem with my self-evaluation. Sure, yuk it up at my expense," he exclaimed with mock indignation at the laughter that escaped her. "Here I am trying to be humble—"

"And completely truthful too?"

They shared a moment of humor while climbing closer to the "caves," the two dark openings in the glacier. The temperature steadily dropped as they neared the enormous chunk of compacted ice and snow. Gooseflesh erupted on Holly's arms, and she wished she'd brought a sweater.

"What do you say we take our peek in the caves and get back down where it's warmer? I forgot how cold it was up here," Seth said, rubbing his arms. Following a group of teenagers, they made their way to the glacier and began the descent back across the rock basin to the trail.

"Seriously, Holly," Seth began after a long, comfortable silence between them, "now that I look at things with my 'new' eyes, I see how great the temptations are for professional athletes. Especially the younger ones. They're at an age where they're more likely to be influenced by the money, the free time, and all the trappings of that kind of life. I know I was."

"This is none of my business, but did you make a lot of money?" She had no idea what minor-league ballplayers earned.

"Yeah, I did. More than your average lawyer or accountant, plus a signing bonus that would probably make you fall over. But I was a first-round draft pick—"

"I remember that. The papers carried stories about you for years, and then things kind of fizzled out. We didn't hear about Seth Glad anymore."

" 'Fizzled out' about sums it up." They had been able to walk abreast much of the way down the trail, for the number of climbers had now dwindled. "You know," he mused, "when everyone is always telling you how good you are, it's easy to become puffed up and believe what they're saying. Then you start making determinations of what's important and what's not based on your inflated view of yourself. Things really get distorted."

"How could your mom let that happen? She seems so . . . well, grounded."

Seth nodded. "She is. She was. But she was fighting uphill against my dad the whole way. And who's a strong-willed, arrogant kid going to listen to? The parent who does her best to keep him cut down to size, or the one who swells up his son's head right along with everyone else? Mom wanted me to go to college before signing with a ball club, but my dad insisted I sign. Of course, signing was what I wanted then, too."

"Don't you have an older sister? What did she think?"

"She was already out of the house, attending college back east, but she would have sided with my mom."

Holly thought of Seth's down-to-earth mother and of the breakfast they'd shared at her unassuming Everett rambler. It was hard to imagine serious struggles between her and her son, as it was nearly impossible to picture such a pleasant and loving woman embroiled in marital difficulties. "It seems like you two have a good relationship now."

"We do. I have to give her credit; she hung in there when I was my most awful. She never gave up or stopped loving me. And when I had the accident, she flew to Texas and stayed with me as long as she could." He paused, then added, nodding, "She's quite a woman. Not once did she say, 'I told you so.'"

"What about your dad?"

"He left my mom and moved in with his girlfriend about the time my career was seriously on the skids, and then he pretty much stepped out of my life. I disappointed him, he said."

Holly was quiet, digesting this information. They stepped around a couple who had stopped to change film in their camera. The air was fresh, smelling of pine and green, growing things. The farther down the mountain trail they walked, the warmer the afternoon felt, and a fine layer of perspiration clung to her chest and back. How had she ever thought the winds blowing off the glacier too cold?

"Mom got me hooked up with her church when I moved back home, and one of the parishioners was kind enough to offer me a job with his construction company," Seth continued. "I have a lot to learn, but I always liked to build, to make things with my hands. I know I have a lot to learn as far as God's concerned too." He chuckled. "If I do everything exactly opposite the way I used to, I'll probably be headed in the general direction of righteous living. You know," he added in a more earnest tone, "I often wonder where I'd be today if I hadn't finally called upon the Lord. I find myself envying people like you who have always known him."

At his words, Holly experienced the chill she had just longed for. Her relationship with God was at a standstill, and the feeling of being a spiritual fake swept over her once again. "Your mom seems to have a strong faith," she ventured, skirting the issue. "I liked going to your church today. Your pastor seems like a wonderful man."

"He is. For the next several weeks, his homilies will be coming from John's Gospel. The image of the vine and the branches today really hit me between the eyes. I can relate to that so strongly . . . Seth Glad was the branch trying to bear fruit all by himself. I can't even imagine how much different things would be if I'd been connected to the vine in the first place. When I think back, there were a fair number of Christian guys out there playing ball. I always made fun of 'em."

"And why doesn't that surprise me?" Holly asked in an arch tone, glancing up at him.

He threw back his head and laughed. "Touché, Holy Holly." His gaze lingered on her for several seconds, the expression in his dark eyes filled with amusement. "I guess I'm not going to be the one making fun anymore. . . . I'll be on the other end of the stick. Gee, doesn't that sound pleasant?"

"The rewards of living your life for Christ far outweigh the hardships." Her response was automatic, almost pat. She sounded like a regular church lady, which was what Seth expected her to be. *Do you believe that the rewards far outweigh the hardships, Holly? Can you honestly testify to a vibrant spiritual life?*

"That's what my mom tells me, too, so it must be true," he said, unaware of her inner distress. He clapped a friendly hand on her shoulder. "Come on, O wise one. I'll buy you supper at that little greasy spoon down the road."

\\\\/

The next few days flew by in a blur of insurance adjusters, repairmen, and the challenge of trying to carry on business as usual amidst the chaos in the small shop. Seth had been heavy on Holly's mind Sunday night, after their day together, but since then she'd scarcely had time to think about him, much less get out for her afternoon cup of mocha. Before they'd finished their fried-chicken dinner at the small restaurant he'd taken her to on the way home from the Ice Caves, he had pinned her down for a hiking trip at Mount Rainier the coming weekend.

Pausing from her row of arrangements to take a swig of tepid diet cola, Holly watched a bushy-haired worker take down the boards Seth had nailed across the back window. A quiver of emotion danced across her chest when she remembered how Seth had responded to her distressed, middle-of-the-night call.

"You got the five o'clock blues, or are you thinking about that tall, handsome dude, boss lady? You've got that 'lost in space' look again." Brenda grinned over the box of vases she carried. "And you said nothing was going on. I *did* happen to notice you and the mystery man talking on the sidewalk last week." She stopped in front of Holly, resting the edge of the box on the counter. "So what's his name?"

"What's *whose* name?" Ellen Butler chimed in from the show floor. At their insistence, both Brenda and Ellen had been working longer than eight-hour days to get the shop put back together.

"Just some awesome-looking guy Holly is trying to pretend she doesn't know anything about."

"Hol-ly!" Ellen's plump face appeared in the doorway. "I can't believe it! You're going out with an awesome-looking guy, and you weren't even going to tell us?"

"We're not really going out. . . . We're just . . . well, it's a long story. . . ."

"Let's just say Holly went out for an *extended* coffee break last week—" Brenda dished out the news, tabloid style—"and finally up the sidewalk she walks with Mr. Hunk. They talk for a while, and I notice he takes her hand—"

"And kisses her?" Ellen interrupted, having come completely into the back room by this time. She took off her glasses and peered at Holly with astonishment. "No kidding!"

"He didn't kiss her," Brenda said with disappointment. "But I'm wondering about the identity of this 'old friend' who came and boarded up the window Sunday morning. Could he and the mystery man be one and the same? Just think of the two of them, all alone in here during the wee hours. . . ."

"Oh, for heaven's sake, his name is Seth Glad, and he brought his mother with him!" Holly burst out, feeling her cheeks warm at her friends' jocularity.

"You mean Seth Glad, the catcher?" The bushy-haired man at the window spoke before Ellen or Brenda could respond, turning completely around to look at her. "Say, whatever happened to him, anyway? No one's heard nothing about him in a long time."

"He's back in the area again, working for Griffin Construction." Holly shot a *thanks a lot* look at Brenda as the worker continued to stare, obviously unsatisfied with her brief explanation. The enthralled gazes of the women were fixed upon her as well, and the roses in her cheeks bloomed all the brighter. "He had a bad motorcycle accident last year," she explained with what she hoped was a casual shrug. Sorting through the bundle of flowers and greens before her, she selected a Shasta daisy and added it to one of the vases.

"So that's it?" Brenda exclaimed after a long silence. "That's all you're going to say?" Pushing the box farther back on the counter, she used her hands to exaggerate her imitation of Holly. "'Oh, don't mind me. . . . I'm only dating this really cool guy who signed with some ball club right out of high school. Even though I haven't been out with anyone for a blue moon, I didn't think you'd be interested.'"

Just then the phone rang, providing a welcome excuse for Holly to turn her back on her audience. To her surprise, it was Jean. "Welcome home, newlywed," Holly said with a smile, her embarrassment fading at the delight of hearing her friend's voice. "Boy, have I ever missed you! How was San Francisco?"

"Good grief—have I been gone *that* long?"

"No, I suppose not . . . and don't give me some weird decimal equation about the amount of time you've been away." A deep sigh escaped. "Things have just been a little—"

"Uh-huh. Spill it, girlfriend. I've known you long enough to have a strong suspicion that something's up. You know, the whole time we were gone I couldn't get this thought out of my head that you've got a little romance cooking with Seth Glad. The last thing I saw as we drove away from the reception was you and him standing together under the streetlight."

"Oh, is that so?" Holly replied, dropping her voice. Glancing over her shoulder, she observed that everyone had gone back to their respective duties. Even so, she kept her voice low. "You must not have been too excited to begin your honeymoon if all you could think about was the state of your best friend's love life."

Jean's laughter flowed over her, warming her, bringing home the realization of how precious their friendship was. "Fishing for details? Well, you aren't going to get any."

"Tim's standing right there, huh?"

"You got it. Hey, the reason I was calling was to invite you to dinner tomorrow. I'd make it tonight and wring your confession out of you, but Tim's folks are having us over."

"Tomorrow's fine, but you don't want to be cooking so soon after getting home, do you?"

"Absolutely not. The place is a mess with trying to consolidate two households. I thought we could go to Ivar's."

"Sounds good to me. The shop should be back to normal by then. We were broken into Saturday night."

"Oh no! That's terrible!" Jean peppered Holly with questions about the extent of loss and damage. The worst of her curiosity satisfied, she insisted on picking Holly up at Maxie's the following evening so she could see the shop firsthand.

"And don't think I've forgotten about Seth Glad, either," she added just before hanging up.

Holly smiled, anticipating dinner with her friend. It would be good to have Jean's help in sorting out her tangled thoughts and feelings. Before she'd taken even one step, the phone rang again. "I got it," she said, automatically answering, "Maxie's Floral."

"Is this Maxie herself?"

"Hi, Seth." The peculiar quiver beneath her ribs started up again at the sound of his voice. She'd been wondering if she'd hear from him during the week.

"Thanks for the flowers, Holly. I just got home from work. You know, I don't believe I've ever seen a 'manly' bouquet before, but I really like what you did. Maybe it's the cattails . . . or the sunflower. Who knows? My mom got her flowers today too. She left me a message gushing about them. You didn't have to do that with everything else you've got going on."

"And you two didn't have to come out in the middle of the night and work your fingers to the bone, either. It's just my small way of saying thank you for your trouble."

"How have you been?" His tone was tender, concerned. "These past couple days must've been real killers."

"That's an understatement, but we're making pretty good headway while we try to carry on business as usual. As a matter of fact, the guy's here fixing the window right now."

"Tearing down my handiwork, I suppose," he joked. "So, would you like to take a break from the crime scene and have dinner with me? I can get cleaned up and be over there between six and six-thirty."

"Well—" The thrum of several butterfly wings in her belly momentarily tied her tongue.

"We don't have to go anywhere fancy. I'd just like to see you before this weekend." He chuckled, his voice warm in her ear. "Mom's talked to me twice since Sunday, wanting the two of us to come over to her place for dinner. I told her she'd have to hold her horses; she's not dating you—I am."

"Is that what we're doing?" The telephone receiver felt damp beneath her grip.

"Dating? I think so. Although it's been so long for me I can't quite remember."

Despite her nervousness, Holly laughed at his feeble-old-man impersonation. "Me either. I don't even know what I'm doing."

"You don't have to *do* anything, Holly." She imagined his grin on the other end of the line as he continued. "Just be ready for dinner by six-thirty. That's it. Nothing to do. We go; we eat; we talk. Should I come to your shop or to your house?"

Looking down, she checked her appearance. Not good. The unfinished arrangements on the counter beckoned, and Mr. Local Sports Fanatic appeared to have a ways to go on the window. "Uh . . . Seth, I don't know if I can get away by then."

"Not a problem. I'll just bring a pizza and keep you company for a while. Maybe we could walk down for an ice cream when you're finished."

Settling the issue of pizza toppings was surprisingly easy; they were both enemies of mushrooms and fans of pepperoni. Hanging up the phone, Holly turned back to her work, a mixture of nervousness and anticipation making her hands unsteady. *Careful, Holly, or you're going to slice your thumb wide open.* Taking a deep breath, she tried steadying herself. Was she really "dating" Seth Glad, as he had so casually mentioned? They had spent an afternoon at the Ice Caves and had plans to hike at Mount Rainier this coming weekend. Two outdoor activities; did that constitute dating? *And don't forget dinner tonight.*

In a rush, words Seth had previously spoken elbowed their way into her thoughts. *"Ever since I acknowledged my need for God, I keep feeling like I'm being pushed in your direction."* She remembered wanting to get away from him as quickly as possible the instant he'd said the words. How could he believe God was pushing the two of them together? On what basis could he make such a discernment? He was only a baby Christian, brand-new to the faith.

She didn't have any such perceptions about their relationship being God designed, and she'd had a relationship with the Lord a lot longer than he had. When she'd dated him as a teenager, she'd done so in disobedience to her parents' wishes—and that didn't line up with God's will at all. She'd just fallen for him so hard that she went out with him anyway.

*And look what happened.*

*But he isn't that kind of person anymore,* another part of her argued. *He's given his life to Christ. And he's still got that something about him that makes your heart pound like it wants to come out of your chest. You'd better watch yourself, Holly, or you're going to fall for him like a ton of bricks all over again.*

# CHAPTER SEVEN

S o you saw him last night too?" Jean took a sip of her iced
tea and met Holly's gaze over the rim of her glass. They
had placed their orders and were waiting for their plates
of seafood pasta to arrive.

"He brought a pizza over to the shop. I think Brenda must
have heard something of my phone call with him because both
she and Ellen managed to stay busy until he got there."

"That must have been something." Jean laughed, setting
down her glass. "I've only met Brenda a few times, but she
seems like she could be a real mischief maker."

Holly shook her head, an unwilling smile creeping across
her lips. "The guy installing the new window was the worst of
all; he hung around and pestered Seth with all kinds of questions. Ellen and Brenda stayed long enough to get a good look
at him, and then they left. I have to say that Brenda behaved
herself fairly well, but on her way out she told him to be sure
and make Holly glad."

"Make Holly *glad,* or make Holly *a Glad?*"

"Knowing how her mind works, she meant it both ways."

"What did he say?"

"He said, 'I intend to.'"

Jean's jaw dropped. "He wants to marry you, Holly?"

"No, no. I'm sure he didn't take it that way." A nervous laugh escaped her, and she took a bite of her hazelnut roll. "I'm sure he thought she was talking about making me the happy kind of glad."

"And then what happened?"

"We ate pizza, closed up the shop, and took a walk for some ice cream." Holly toyed with a hard pat of butter, remembering how Seth had tried to engage her in a spiritual conversation as they'd walked along the water's edge.

" 'Ho-hum, we got some exercise and plenty of calcium,' and that's it?" Jean's gaze was penetrating, direct. "Holly, you're acting very strange. You used to be wild about this guy, and now I can't even tell if you like him or not."

"Well . . . yes, I like him . . . but—"

"But what? Come on, what's going on inside that head of yours? You tell me all this stuff about his life and his accident and his conversion and about how he feels like God is pushing him in your direction—and you say it with all the emotion of someone delivering a news report. Where are your feelings? *What* are your feelings?"

"I don't know," Holly whispered, studying the light oak trim running around the edge of the table.

"You don't think there's any way God could have designed a second chance for you and Seth? I can't help but think how perfect it would be if the two of you—"

"Just because you're lost in some newlywed haze of love doesn't mean that I'm supposed to be too."

"Oh yeah? God's pretty funny sometimes. You've been hiding yourself away for years, and I wouldn't put it past him to set you two up again, this time the right way. I sometimes wonder if you forget how much he loves you, Holly—and you can bet he hasn't forgotten how much your heart used to desire Seth."

"But that was ten years ago—and I wasn't even supposed to go out with him."

"Tell me Seth Glad still doesn't make your heart go pitter-pat." Jean raised her eyebrows and leaned forward. "You know, if I weren't madly in love with Tim, Seth Glad might make *my* heart go pitter-pat."

"He scares me, Jean." She blurted out the words before she thought about saying them.

Jean nodded, thoughtful. "I don't think that's so unusual. You haven't been out with anyone since Kevin, and that's been a long time. More than 10 percent of your life."

"Your figuring seems a little loose," Holly commented lightly after a pause, deciding it was past time to steer the conversation in another direction. "Maybe your honeymoon short-circuited a few of those computer connections in your brain."

"Oh, you think so? Well, for your information, my figuring is as tight as ever. Twenty-seven into three makes 11.11 percent; in fact, the equation produces an infinite string of ones."

Holly smiled at the intense expression beneath her friend's smooth blond bangs. "Please. Spare me from the mental picture of little number ones marching on into infinity. I was only trying to change the subject. Tell me about San Francisco, the parts that aren't X-rated, anyway."

The hollowness in her chest came back, stronger than ever, as Jean shared the sights and sounds and flavors of the City by the Bay. Her love for her husband shone in her eyes and animated her speech, and Holly found herself wondering what loving a man with her whole heart and soul would be like. Even the plate of steaming, rich seafood pasta set before her did nothing to soothe the emptiness within her. She was wise enough to realize that her hunger had nothing to do with food, but what to do about it, she didn't know.

⫸⫷

A chilly fog pressed against the windows and blanketed the dark neighborhood. Weeks had passed since Holly's dinner with Jean, and she'd seen both Jean and Seth several more times since then. On the surface, things seemed to be going well, but deep down inside, Holly knew something vital was still missing within her.

Letting the bedroom shade fall back into place, Holly shivered and rewrapped the chenille robe more tightly around her. Five-thirty. She was tired, but she knew she couldn't fall back asleep. She tried to pray, but nothing seemed right. Nothing *felt* right. She hadn't perceived God's presence in such a long time that she was beginning to wonder if she ever had.

"What's going on, Lord?" she spoke into the darkened room after a faltering attempt at praise, an angry edge sharpening her voice. "Where are you? What am I doing wrong? What do you want me to be doing? And what's up with Seth Glad? Is this really all your idea, like Jean seems to think?" Stepping into the bathroom, she turned on the light and blinked, taking in her sleep-tousled image in the mirror. Abruptly, the anger drained from her, and she added softly, "Do you think you could please get my life straightened out? I'm getting awfully tired of living like this."

Neither heaven nor earth moved in reply, but Holly felt a little better after she showered and dressed. Even though she was prepared to face the world at this early hour, she was glad it was Ellen's turn to drive to the wholesale house to select the fresh cuts needed for the day. With her busy schedule, she appreciated the more leisurely pace of the two mornings a week her assistant made the trip in her stead. Her employees were fans of these days as well, for Holly often brought in freshly baked items.

Selecting a compact disc of Mozart symphonies, she loaded the turntable and pressed play. An instant later, the triadic melodies and crisp rhythms of Symphony no. 34 filled her small, neat home. Padding back to the kitchen to enjoy a steaming mug of coffee, she decided today was a good day to make scones. Everyone at the shop loved them, especially Ellen.

The previous owner of her house had updated the kitchen only three years earlier. Though not large, the room was laid out well, providing plenty of cupboard and counter space. Hardwood floors of satiny gold complimented the white wood trim and cupboard faces, while an understated fruit-and-floral wallpaper decorated the soffits and the walls in the breakfast nook. Coordinating valances and high-quality appliances finished off the room in grand style. Along with the location, this room had been the selling point of the home, no question about it.

Mixing together the dry ingredients, she cut in three-quarters cup of butter, as usual, and tried to figure the fat grams and calories of each scone. Astronomical. Anyone with half a brain knew that was why they were so melt-in-your-mouth good. Her friend Pam from Bible study had given her the recipe, admonishing her to be sure to use real butter and buttermilk for the best and lightest results.

Thoughts of Pam invariably led to memories of the wonderful times of fellowship she had shared with her Thursday-night small group. Laughter and tears, joy and sorrow. But for the past several months, she'd gradually taken on the role of a quiet student, becoming more and more distant and unfocused. Her work sheets were always completed on time, but the feeling of each lesson's holding something personal for her had long since faded.

She thought ahead to the upcoming weekend with Seth. Intent upon taking seriously her joking words about their seeing all the local sights, he had escorted her to several of the Seattle area's natural and man-made attractions over the past weeks. He had made plans for them to spend this coming Saturday on San Juan Island, something Holly hadn't done since she was a child.

Dropping large spoonfuls of dough on the cookie sheet, she reminisced about the past weeks with Seth, realizing what a wonderful companion he was. Aside from his good looks, he was witty and sensitive and engaging. Rather than dating, it almost seemed like they were doing things together as a pair of friends would.

*You can tell yourself that if you want to, Holly,* her inner voice spoke, *but you know Seth isn't going to be content with the two of you being sightseeing buddies forever. You've seen the look in his eyes, and you know he wants more.*

Placing the cookie sheet in the oven, she set the timer for fifteen minutes. Disturbed by the direction of her thoughts, she walked to the front door to retrieve the morning paper. With little interest, she skimmed over the headlines in search of the extended forecast for the weekend. Pleasant weather was predicted for Saturday, she was pleased to note, anticipating a sunny day on smooth seas.

She never would have believed how wrong she could be.

\\\\//

Saturday dawned clear. The chilly fog of the past few mornings was a distant memory as Holly stepped on the flagstones of her back patio and breathed in the warm undercurrents of an Indian-summer morning. Though her feelings toward Seth were no clearer than the mist that frequently settled over the coast, she was looking forward to spending the day with him. She hadn't been out to the San Juan archipelago for years.

With nostalgia, she remembered the last time her parents had taken her and Denise to San Juan Island. After spending some time in quaint Friday Harbor, they had rented a boat and gone around to the west side of the island in search of whales. It had been a family adventure of fun and laughter, with Dad taking the role of daredevil and Mom the halfhearted chastiser. Then a pod of playful orcas had surfaced near the boat, silencing them all with awe.

A wellspring of sadness opened for just a moment, and a deep sigh escaped Holly's chest. Dad and Mom were dead, and Denise was married, living in another state. Sometimes the changes that had occurred in the past years were hard to believe. But as blessed as she was with her friends, home, and successful business, the truth was she was alone in life.

Looking around at the overgrown flower beds bordering the patio and walk, she chided herself for dwelling on such aching thoughts when there were so many more things with which to concern herself. Several weeds sprouted from amidst the dahlias, and she bent to pull one, consoling herself with the fact that her parents were now in God's care.

*And so are you, Holly. You're not alone.*

Was that the voice of the Holy Spirit, she wondered, or just her own wishful thinking? So many long months had passed since she'd heard from God that there was no way to be sure. Walking to the spigot, she filled her watering can and began sprinkling her combination crop of flowers and weeds.

Today was not a day to ponder life's problems, she told herself, but one to be enjoyed. The heat of the morning sun struck her shoulders, and she glanced skyward, reassuring herself that no clouds lurked overhead. A day on the Sound would be perfect.

Seth appeared around the corner of the house making ridiculous chirping sounds while she filled her bird feeder. Turning to look at him, her heart leapt.

"The mountain's out," he announced with a cocky grin, referring to Mount Rainier's visibility on this clear morning. "Do I know how to pick a day or what? Are you ready to do San Juan and maybe see some whales?"

"Do you think it's too late in the season for us to see any?"

"My friend Todd tells me there are three resident pods of orcas in the San Juans. We'll stop at Whale Watch Park and take a look."

Holly smiled. "I was just remembering a trip my family took, years back. I thought my mom was going to faint when a whale rubbed against the underside of our boat."

"Did he roll over and stick his eye out of the water to look at you? The last time Todd took me salmon fishing, that happened to us. I think his dorsal fin alone was six feet." He laughed at her expression, his gaze as warm as the morning sun. "It's good to hear about your family, Holly. You don't talk about them very much. It must be hard for you to have them gone."

She nodded, blinking away the sting of sudden tears. "I was already feeling a little sorry for myself this morning for exactly that reason."

"Come here," he said, holding out his arms.

Somehow she found herself in his embrace, her cheek cradled against solid male chest, the coffee can in which she'd carried birdseed thunking quietly on the grass. The woodsy cologne he wore mingled with the fresh scent of his shirt, adding more ammunition to the assault on her senses. How long had it been since she'd been held in someone's arms . . . and had she ever been held in a pair of arms that felt this good?

One strong hand smoothed her hair with gentleness, and she felt him press a kiss against the top of her head. "Oh, Holly." He breathed her name with a sigh, his voice sounding like a rumble against her ear. "Do you want to go today? We can change our plans if you'd rather do something else."

"No, I still want to—," she began, looking up at him. Her breath caught in her chest at the expression in his eyes. "Go," she managed to finish.

Sightseeing buddies, indeed. It was time to break this clinch or completely lose her senses over this man. "We should probably leave, or we'll miss the ferry," she added, her voice sounding anemic as she took a step backward.

"As you wish. The whales are waiting, madam." He let her go with a wistful smile. "Let's go find them."

# CHAPTER EIGHT

Despite the promising weather, Holly was glad for the tunic-length, three-season jacket she had slipped on over her short-sleeved knit shirt and relaxed-fit jeans. A cool salt wind blew over her face as she stood before the enormous white boat and waited for Seth. Seagulls wheeled and screamed overhead, their cries competing with the deep noise of the ship's engines.

It was good that they had left her house when they did or they would have missed the 8:45 ferry and had to wait over two and a half hours for the next one. The sixty-or-so-mile drive from Mukilteo to Anacortes, the point of departure for the ferry to San Juan Island, had consisted of an odd mixture of friendly chitchat and not-so-comfortable silences. A line had been crossed with their embrace this morning, and Holly knew it was only a matter of time before the issue would be addressed again.

"Ready to board, matey? We'll be strolling the streets of Friday Harbor by ten-thirty." Seth held out two tickets and a pair of Styrofoam cups. "Here. I bought you a coffee that should shake off the cobwebs and put some hair on your chest."

"Just what I need," she drawled, accepting the cup and taking a sip of the strong brew. Once again they lapsed into silence while Seth led the way onto the ferry, to the outer deck. What was he thinking? Holly wondered. They had been conversing in fits and jerks all morning. The steady, comfortable patter into which they'd previously settled had evaporated with the warm embrace they'd shared.

Holly watched the green foothills of the Cascade Range fade away as the ferry left the dock and began its westward route through the sparkling waters at a speed that never failed to surprise her. The San Juan archipelago consisted of over 400 islands scattered across northern Puget Sound, 175 with names, mountainous in character and adorned with conifers. Their destination, the quaint town of Friday Harbor, lay on the east side of San Juan Island. To the west of San Juan Island was wide Haro Strait, then British Columbia's Vancouver Island.

"Washington is really a great state, isn't it?" Seth spoke several minutes into their departure, breaking the silence that lay between them. He took a sip from his cup and gestured in a wide motion, his hair blowing in the breeze. "God really knocked himself out. Where else can you find seawater, freshwater, mountains, forests, and even desert? There's something here to please everyone. It's another sad commentary on my life that I didn't appreciate living here until I *wasn't* living here anymore."

Snuggling into the polyester fleece lining of her jacket, Holly mulled over his words. "Sounds a lot like human nature to me." She curved her lips upward, searching his cocoa gaze for what might be hidden in its depths. "Even Dorothy from *The Wizard of Oz* said, 'There's no place like home.'"

"So now you're quoting L. Frank Baum?"

"I'm impressed," she said with a chuckle. "I didn't figure you as the bookish type."

"Trust your first instincts. I'm pretty much a video guy . . .

except for the Bible. I've read through it once. Right now I'm studying the book of John."

"If reading's too much trouble, I'm sure you can get it on tape," she bantered, wondering why he didn't smile in return.

After finishing their coffee, they retreated from the brisk outside air to a booth in the ferry's large, enclosed cabin. Their conversation during the remainder of the crossing continued in much the same vein as it had during their drive, bumpy and uneven.

"I say we pack in as much of this island as we can today," Seth announced upon disembarking, leading her along with purposeful strides. "So our first stop is up the hill at Susie's Mopeds for some wheels. I took her 'virtual tour' of the island on the Internet. The full excursion is forty-eight miles. Do you think you can handle it?"

"Can I handle it? What do you think I am, a wimp or something?"

"Nope. I think you're something else," he answered, his gaze warm upon her. Highlights of russet and gold glinted in his short-cropped hair, and an intense expression flickered across his face. "Hey, don't look now, but we're almost having fun again," he quipped, lightening what could have been another awkward moment.

Susie Campbell, the owner of the business bearing her name, greeted them with a big smile and made short work of outfitting them with mopeds, helmets, safety tips, and a map of the island. "Stay single file on the right side of the road," she instructed, her blond curls blowing in the breeze. "Wear helmets and eye protection at all times, don't exceed twenty miles per hour, and watch your mileage—the bikes only run sixty-five miles on a tank of gas. Now go out and have some fun!"

Their second stop was for a fully packed picnic lunch, which Seth purchased and set into the large wire basket on the back of his moped. Armed with their map, island itinerary, and delicious food, they set out south on Argyle Road toward the American Camp area on San Juan's southern tip.

It was a perfect day for such a tour of the island, and they took turns leading and following one another. Since it was late in the season, the roadways weren't at all crowded. Holly gave herself over to enjoying the scenery—and, after a time, to being in Seth's company. The uneasy feeling that nagged her whenever she thought too hard about their relationship faded with each mile they traveled.

After hiking a mile through a self-guided tour at American Camp, they remounted their mopeds and continued riding to South Beach, where they stopped for lunch. The sun was warm but not too hot, tempered by the fresh sea breeze. Only a few visitors wandered about the beach, no one near them.

"God's creation is amazing, isn't it?" Opening the European-style basket, Seth spread the linen tablecloth across the picnic table. Plates, napkins, and silverware were set out next, along with the food. After arranging the generous spread, he gestured at the spectacular scenery. "Did you ever think about what it says in Genesis, that God just *said* and things were created? Look at all this . . . the sky, the water, the mountains, the trees, the wildlife."

"It's beautiful," Holly agreed, turning around in a circle to take in the complete vista.

"And so are you," he pronounced, causing her to falter in her rotation. "Come and sit down, Holly. It's time to talk."

Sudden anxiety filled her, replacing the comfortable, well-worn feeling she had allowed herself to fall into. A quick glance at his expression confirmed that he meant business. His gaze was dark, unreadable. Her legs felt as though they were traveling through molasses as she made her way to the table and perched on the seat.

*Here it comes.* Swallowing hard, she noticed there was no moisture in her mouth.

"Do you want a cranberry spritzer or raspberry?" he inquired, holding up two bottles.

"Are you sure I don't need a blindfold and a cigarette?"

"Oh, Holly." A faint grin turned up one corner of Seth's mouth as he took a seat across from her. "This isn't an execution."

"Then what is it?" Her heart beat faster.

"Let's call it an execution of honesty." Twisting the cap from his sparkling juice, Seth took a sip and looked directly into her eyes. "I've tried all kinds of ways to reach the Holly I remember. Today I'm probably going to tick you off good, but I'm determined to break through this plastic barrier you've been hiding behind."

"Plastic barrier? Excuse me?" Holly felt the stirrings of defensiveness and, as he had just predicted, the lick of quick anger.

"Don't pretend you don't know what I'm talking about." He set the partly empty bottle on the table harder than necessary, making the pink liquid fizz. "Why won't you let me in, Holly? I'm as patient as a man can be—maybe more so—but enough's enough!"

"What do you want from me, anyway?" Her anger grew at his incisive words, words she knew were right but didn't want to hear.

"I want the truth! I want you to tell me what's really going on in your head, not what you think I want to hear. You know, for a while I thought you might be depressed, but you just don't fit the picture of someone suffering clinical depression—"

"Hold your diagnosis right there, Dr. Laura," she interrupted, her voice drowning out his. She launched herself to her feet, anger coursing through her. "I didn't know they handed out amateur psychology degrees along with the amateur baseball uniforms."

"I think you're suffering something else." He went on as if she hadn't spoken, but the edge in his voice told her her blow had landed. "You've grown stagnant, Holly. Every time I bring up the subject of faith, you duck it or change the subject or throw out some trite saying. I want to know what happened to Holy Holly with the fire in her eyes and the convictions of Saint Paul himself."

Coming to his feet, he planted his hands on the table and leaned forward. "I want in, Holly. I want to know what you're thinking. I've been waiting and waiting, hoping you'd trust me enough to share whatever—"

"Whatever what?" Frustration spiraled upward from her belly. "There's no deep, dark secret lurking inside me."

"What is it, then?" he nearly shouted. "Why do you keep going out with me if you have no intention of ever venturing past this point?"

"And what point do you want to venture past? Are things getting a little too dull for you as a Christian?" From where in her heart had those vituperative words come? Oh, mercy, it was too late to take them back.

"Are you talking about sex?" His brows drew together, darkening his countenance even further.

She took in a great, shaking breath, giving voice to a ten-year-old question. "If I'd been willing, Seth, how far would you have gone with me that night on the beach?"

He looked out to sea, quiet for a long moment, before meeting her gaze. "I don't know," he answered, throwing his arms up in frustration. "I just don't know. Probably not as far as you think, but I can't say." He sighed. "You did right by putting a stop to things. God's timing is always—"

"Don't give me this stuff about God's timing. You're just a brand-new Christian with stars in your eyes. Let's give it some time and see what happens." A cauldron of wrath bubbled within her. How dare he speak to her this way?

"Well, if you're an example of mature Christianity, then I might as well go back to my old ways." Chests heaving, they glared at one another before Seth spoke again. "I haven't heard you profess one heartfelt thing about your faith since we've been going out. Whenever I open the door, you slam it right in my face."

"Maybe I don't feel like talking about God."

"Why not? The girl who stood on the beach at Howarth Park was passionate about Jesus Christ."

"Well—"

"Every time I look in the Bible, Holly, I learn more about how deeply the Lord loves me and what my response to him ought to be. Being the old, experienced Christian that you are, can you say the same thing? It's like you've withered on the vine. What are you holding on to? What *aren't* you holding on to?"

He paused for her response, and when she made no reply, he continued. "Can you say you don't have any feelings for me? I think you do." His gaze didn't waver. "I want you to know that after my accident, I couldn't wait to have the chance to talk to you again, to tell you how you affected my life . . . and my decision to start fresh."

"You said all this before," she volleyed, arms akimbo.

"But I didn't tell you how I felt the first time I saw you again. You took my breath away."

At his statement, something like a fist pushed against Holly's diaphragm, cutting off any retort she might have made. Overhead, a seagull screeched. The sound of the water against the shore was the only steady thing within her scope of awareness. How could it be that his feelings had echoed her own?

"And I haven't told you that I've fallen in love with you." He held up one hand to silence her, an unnecessary motion. "Don't say anything right now; just hear me out. I'm going to lay my heart on the line, as premature as it all seems. I want to connect my life with yours—"

"What are you talking about?" Her words were strangled. The fist pressed tighter.

"I love your smile, Holly, the way you laugh. I love the sparkle in your eyes when you tease me and forget to keep up your guard. I love everything about you from your intelligence and creativity to your long, tanned legs." He walked around the table and stood before her. "And I love the memory of the girl who used to stand tall for God. I know she's still in there somewhere."

"Just leave me alone," she cried, taking a step backward. The pressure on her chest was suddenly gone, leaving in its place shards of stabbing pain.

"I wouldn't be spending all this time with you if my intentions weren't serious. And lately I've been wondering what it would be like to be married to you, to see you in the morning with your hair sticking up, and to have a bunch of babies with you. Holly," he murmured, placing his hands on her shoulders. "I find you incredibly attractive, but when I became a Christian, I made a decision for renewed chastity. I'm far from perfect—my thought life could often stand a good cleaning, cuss words still slip out of my mouth, and my pride wants to rear its ugly head more than you would ever guess. Until recently I haven't led a very good life, but I'm serious about the commitments I've made. And because of them, I'm scared to touch you."

Slowly, he bent his head toward hers and pressed a featherlight kiss upon her lips. His hands slid upward from her shoulders, framing the lines of her jaw. "I love you, Holly Winslow," he murmured, "and I'm waiting for you to trust me."

Closing her eyes, Holly gave herself over to the warmth of his hands for just a moment, pondering his words. Could Jean have been right? Was God behind this after all? But what about those other things he had said to her? *Depressed . . . plastic . . . withered.* Even if he was right, it wasn't any of his business—it was between her and God.

"I trust you, OK?" she said, breaking away. "Let's just have lunch."

"And what neat compartment are we going to whisk this conversation off to, Holly? Do you realize what I just did?" His voice grew harsh, the scar on his face stark white against his heightened color. "I just told you I loved you and said I hope you might be my wife someday." Jamming his hands into his pockets, he faced her with hurt and anger written across his handsome features. His next words were low, hard to hear. "And you just threw it all back in my face. You patronized me."

Swift shame clutched her. "Seth, I didn't mean—"

"Save it, Holly. I guess I was wrong about you after all. The girl on the beach doesn't exist anymore. My mom told me that you probably—"

"Your mom!" Anger frothed up and over her regret. "You've been sitting around psychoanalyzing your stagnant girlfriend with your *mom?* Isn't that rich! Why does everyone seem to think the state of my spiritual life is their business?"

Seth's voice continued low and hard. "Oh, I don't know. Maybe because it's such a shame to see a great person go to waste. But do it your way. Do it all by yourself, and be sure not to ask anyone for help. Especially those who are willing to do just about anything for you."

A terrible hollowness gripped her vitals, but she couldn't stem the flow of her pride. "Why don't I leave and just go waste away somewhere else, then?"

"Your choice, Holly." He shrugged. "I thought you were the kind of woman who would rise to a challenge, but I guess I was wrong."

"I guess you were." Turning on her heel, she left behind her untouched drink, a fat pastrami-and-rye sandwich, and the man who had just offered her his heart.

# CHAPTER NINE

Sheets of rain beat against the large front windows of Maxie's Floral. The gray skies and steady downpour hastened the approach of twilight, and Holly toyed with the idea of closing the store early. Both the shop and the phones had been slow all day, and she'd let Ellen go home at three o'clock.

Running a soft cotton cloth over a shelf she'd emptied, she dusted and replaced each item. The building was silent, save the mournful sound of the rain, for she'd turned off the radio soon after her employee had gone. A vanilla-scented candle burned behind the counter, releasing its mellow fragrance into the air.

Almost three weeks had passed since the morning Seth had taken her to Friday Harbor. And still, fifty times a day, if not a hundred, Holly played the South Beach scene over in her head. She knew she had treated him horribly. But still she made no move to contact him, apologize, or set the record straight. If anything, she'd slipped deeper into the spiritual slough in which he'd accused her of wallowing.

In response to Holly's desperate plea, Jean had driven to Anacortes to pick her up the day she'd returned alone from

Friday Harbor and had quietly listened to Holly's emotional explanation of the turn of events. Once home, Holly had made hasty arrangements with Ellen and Brenda, packed a bag, and driven up to the mountains to spend a week at an isolated chalet.

Hiking. Praying. Fasting. None of it had helped. It almost seemed like the harder she tried to run toward God, the farther away he moved. Punctuating her gloom were episodes of anger—anger at God and anger at Seth for saying the things he had. Once back at work, she'd assumed a cheerful, albeit brittle exterior, but inside she was empty, hurting, aching.

She avoided Jean, making excuse after excuse for not calling or spending time with her, especially after Jean confessed to calling Seth when Holly went to the mountains. "I knew he would be worried sick about you when you took off like that," her friend had defended herself. "I only let him know you were safe." Resisting the urge to demand to know what else they'd talked about, Holly had promptly changed the subject.

"What are you going to do, Holly?" Jean had persisted. "Even if you don't care about Seth—and I know you do—he deserves better than what you've given him. If I understood you correctly that day I drove you home, you were upset that he had figured out you were holding back from him because you've been feeling spiritually lost. That sounds an awful lot like pride to me, and I think you're looking at things all wrong. Here you've got this man—this dreamy, hunky, gorgeous man—who walked away from a life of sin, gave his life to the Lord, and wants to live righteously. He tells you he's falling in love with you and that he even thinks about marrying you. Now, correct me if I'm wrong, but wasn't this the guy you cried your eyes out over all summer before you left for college, the guy you wanted in the worst way but couldn't have? Holly, the only problem I see with any of this is you!"

Annoyance flickered through Holly as the bell over the shop's front door tinkled, jarring her from her thoughts. Who would want to buy flowers on a day like this? Setting down her dust cloth, she turned toward the customer struggling with a large tote bag, a dripping umbrella, and an equally drenched raincoat.

"Hi, honey," Barbara Glad's warm voice greeted her. "I had to drive down to Edmonds today and thought I'd stop on my way back. The shop's looking good," she complimented, walking toward the counter, having shaken off the worst of her wetness. "You'd never know it was such a mess once."

"Yes . . . well . . . thank you." Holly was at a loss for words, an anxious thrumming beginning in her chest. Had Seth sent her? What was she going to say?

"I need to have a flower arrangement made up," the older woman went on. "The bouquet you sent me earlier this fall was so lovely that I couldn't imagine using any other florist."

"Th-thank you," she repeated, remembering to ask, "When do you need it?"

"I was hoping you might have some time right now." A rich, familiar gaze searched her own. "In case you're wondering if Seth sent me, the answer is no. I'm sure he'd be quite upset if he knew I was here."

"How is he?" Holly queried softly, dropping her gaze and fumbling about for an order form. The bottom of her stomach felt as though it had dropped away, so rapidly did her heart beat.

"He's fine. Sad, but fine. He fell hard for you, Holly." Her words were truthful but without reproach.

A pen . . . finally she located one in the drawer beneath the counter. "Uh . . . what type of arrangement would you like me to make, Mrs. Glad?" A dam of tears was building behind her eyes. "Something formal? Casual? Any particular look?" Her last words were strangled; she could barely talk.

"Something romantic, I think." Barb Glad spoke as though she hadn't noticed Holly's distress. "Blues and pinks and purples, nice and full." She smiled and pointed to the shelf behind the counter. "In one of those pretty, round glass vases."

"It'll be just a few minutes." Her words were rushed as she escaped to the sanctuary of the back room. Tears had already escaped her eyes and trickled down her cheeks as she entered the small, walk-in cooler and began to select blooms and fillers. *Oh, Seth. Oh no. What did I do?*

"Was I right in figuring you'd need a hug about now?" Barb Glad stood in the doorway of the cooler, arms outstretched, on her face an expression of extreme compassion. She had shed her wet outer garment, the soft folds of her blue knit top drawing Holly's attention and, strangely, causing her undoing. A noisy sob escaped her as she stood in the chilly room, fresh tears blurring her vision.

"Oh, honey." Gentle hands took the flowers from her and set them aside, and then those soft, warm arms enfolded her. "Just rest your head and let yourself cry."

And Holly did just that, for longer than she would have ever imagined, while Barbara Glad stroked her hair and whispered words of comfort and assurance. Despite the pain in her heart, a sea of sweet solace enveloped her, and she realized she'd forgotten what it was like to receive such mothering. As the storm of tears abated, Holly began noticing little things. The cadence of the older woman's breathing. The faint, mingled scents of laundry detergent and elegant bottom notes of her unfamiliar floral fragrance. She shivered.

"It's time to get you out of this icebox. Here, I've got the flowers, dear. Come on." The warm arms guided her from the cooler to the stool near her workstation, then pressed a thickness of tissues into her hand. "Will you excuse me for just a minute?" she asked, with one last comforting squeeze.

It seemed that only a few moments later a steaming cup of apple cinnamon tea was set before her, and Holly accepted the drink with gratefulness. Its spicy warmth made her realize she hadn't eaten since breakfast. "Do you always travel with food?" she asked, managing a small smile. She took a sip and felt her stomach rumble.

"Just about always. Before I left my friend's house in Edmonds, I made up a fresh batch of tea because I had a hunch it might hit the spot here. I brought some zucchini bread, too, if you'd like a slice." Before Holly could reply, Barbara Glad had reached into her bag and produced a napkin bearing a generous slice of the sweet, homemade bread. Once again tears filled Holly's eyes.

"My goodness, it is a wet day, isn't it?" Seth's mother remarked with a quick squeeze of Holly's hand. "Here, take a bite, dear. I doubt you've been eating enough to feed a sparrow."

While Holly obediently ate her snack, Barb Glad selected her desired vase from among the neat assortment of glassware arranged in the open cupboards. Pulling a tall stool over from the other work station, she sat opposite Holly, poured herself a mug of tea, and began separating flowers and filler.

"In the months before my husband left me," she began in a subdued tone, "I experienced a long dry spell in my relationship with the Lord. And when Bob walked out, I felt utterly abandoned. My faith, which had always provided me with comfort, seemed empty and dead."

"What did you do?"

"I'm sure I tried everything. I wondered what I was doing wrong; I cried out for mercy; I got angry; I tried to fix things myself."

Holly nodded, feeling her pulse pound. Barb Glad had gone through such a lonely and barren time herself? How had she gotten through it? Popping the last bite of zucchini bread into her mouth, she almost forgot to chew.

"And then one day I realized I wasn't the only person in the desert—that there were lots of us there together, and I saw many folks making an effort to help others and be cheerful even though they were suffering the same terrible dryness. It wasn't that they were being dishonest or denying that their experience was really happening; they had just purposed to do the best they could despite the drought. What also separated these people from the others was that they felt comfortable enough to say what was in their hearts." She pushed the vase toward Holly, along with the red-handled Swiss knife.

"One particularly wise woman taught me that we can be filled with the Holy Spirit and not *feel* a blessed thing. She said that we ought to consider the dryness, the lack of feeling, a blessing because it moves us toward contemplation. God doesn't abandon us during these quiet times; he uses them, ultimately, to draw us closer to himself."

"But it doesn't feel that way," Holly burst out, using her frustration to begin greening the vase. "I'm not close to him at all anymore."

"Ah, feelings. They will tell you all sorts of things." Nodding, Mrs. Glad took a sip of tea. "On what is our faith founded, Holly? Moods? Feelings?"

"No . . . it's founded on truth," she admitted, beginning to see where she'd faltered.

"Our whole lives through, God works on purifying and perfecting us. You can imagine yourself being the clay on the potter's wheel, or a vine being pruned by the Master Gardener. However you choose to view things, the truth is that these experiences don't usually feel good or helpful or useful. They're painful."

"No kidding."

Larkspur, freesia, stock, and pale yellow roses joined leatherleaf and Italian ruscus in the vase. The design took shape as the women shared a relaxed silence, with Holly occasionally asking the older woman's color and style preferences.

"I'll leave the decisions up to you," she deferred. "I can't believe how lovely it is already."

Holly eyed the bouquet, deciding a lavish amount of baby's breath and wispy caspia would give it the romantic look Mrs. Glad had asked for. She worked quietly, thinking about the past year and a half of her life.

"Holly, I'd like to ask you something."

"Yes," she said, a deep sigh escaping. The issue of Seth lay between them, undiscussed. She knew she had hurt him badly, and in the process, no doubt, this fine woman too.

"Can you generously and willingly accept what God gives you?"

There was nothing more to her question. Holly was silent a long moment, surprised at what the older woman hadn't asked. She set the vase into a small box and began packing newspaper around its sides.

"Until this point in my life," she ventured, "I wouldn't have hesitated to say yes. But since my mother died . . . ," she trailed off, tears threatening once more. "Since Mom died and God became silent, I've been moving farther and farther away from him. Now I look at myself and see that for a long time I've just been existing, not really living. I've let myself become so numb that I've cut myself off from him . . . and I haven't been thankful for anything."

A tear slipped down her cheek as she silently begged forgiveness. Ripping a length of sturdy green-and-white-print paper from the roll, she paused. "I forgot to ask; did you want to fill out a card? There's a selection right over here."

"Yes, I believe I do."

Dabbing at her eyes with another tissue, Holly waited to staple the package closed until Mrs. Glad had sealed the small envelope and handed it to her. "Thank you so much for stopping by today," Holly said, a rueful smile curving her lips. "I was just about to close the store early, go home, and hibernate. You've given me a lot to think about."

She was enfolded once more in the comforting arms. "Sometimes it just helps to know you're not alone. If you ever need to talk, dear, please call. Now how much do I owe you?"

Naming a price well under the usual charge, Holly busied herself with tidying her work area while Seth's mother repacked her thermos and cups into the oversized tote and wrote out a check. "Take care now," she said with a gentle smile, leading the way back to the showroom.

"I will," Holly replied, her spirits feeling more buoyant

than they had in longer than she could remember. Watching Mrs. Glad don her raincoat, she remembered the bouquet. "After all this, you forgot your flowers!" she said, turning to retrieve the package. "Let me—"

"I didn't forget anything, honey," the older woman replied. Adjusting the folds of her raincoat around her ample figure, she looked full into Holly's face, tenderness shining from her rich brown gaze. "They're for you."

"Me? I . . . Why? How come?" she stammered.

"Let's just say they're a small token of my gratitude to you," she said enigmatically, strolling toward the door with her umbrella and tote. The bell tinkled, a gust of damp, chilly air entering the shop as she exited. "I'll keep you in my prayers," she called with one last smile and a nod of her head.

The silence of the shop pressed around Holly as she contemplated what had just happened. She turned the OPEN sign on the door to CLOSED and walked back to the counter, switching off the lights. Barbara Glad's words mingled in her mind with Jean's words, and then, to top it off, her explosive interchange with Seth at South Beach jumped in to join the party. It was too much, just too much.

Her throat closed spastically as she sank to her knees, hot tears spilling from her eyes. But instead of feeling isolation, pouring forth along with her tears was the assurance that her sorrows were not unknown to the Lord.

"Thy will be done, Father," she hiccuped her prayer. "I haven't done a very good job of accepting anything from you lately. I'm sorry. . . . Please, will you forgive me?" Fumbling for a tissue, she blew her nose. The worst of her tears were over, and she found it easier to speak. "Jean thinks I'm being prideful and stupid. Seth tells me I'm withered. His mom says I'm taking a trip through the desert. I don't know what's going on, Lord, but I'm deciding to trust you with whatever you've got in mind."

In her mind's eye she saw Seth standing on South Beach, his powerful shoulders framed by the blue waters of Puget Sound and, far behind him, the spectacular view of the Olympic Mountains. *"I wouldn't be spending all this time with you if my intentions weren't serious. . . . I love you, Holly Winslow, and I'm waiting for you to trust me."*

A profound sense of longing burst free from deep inside her, its warmth spreading throughout her entire body. *Seth.* She wanted him, wanted to trust him . . . wanted to express her love for him. Ten years ago they were no kind of match, but now there was nothing standing in the way of their pursuing a relationship—not anymore.

With awe, she bowed her head. "Thank you for loving Seth so much that you spared his life and gave him a second chance. And thank you, Father, for bringing him back into my life. If your plan for my life includes Seth Glad—" A thrill shot through her vitals while a slow grin curved her lips. She rose to her feet. "Then who am I to say no?"

Suddenly light of heart, she walked to the back room to retrieve her purse. Sitting on the counter remained the neatly wrapped floral arrangement she'd made for Barb Glad, the sight of it prompting an offering of thanks for the woman's visit. Holly's curiosity overcame her as she remembered the card, and she worked open the paper just enough to slip in her fingers and pull out the envelope.

A wet gust of wind beat its fist against the new window, drawing her attention for a moment. The sky beyond the glass was black, but a glow of brightness enveloped her spirit. Withdrawing the card from the envelope, she read: *Dearest Holly, No matter what happens between you and Seth, you will always hold a special place in this mother's heart for your part in saving my son. God bless you. Barb.*

She exhaled, a good amount of euphoria escaping with her breath. Oh, the things she'd said to Seth that day out at South Beach, realizing she might very well have blown any chance of continuing a relationship with him. The days since they'd spoken had now stretched into weeks, and he'd had plenty of time to think things over. Plenty of time for regrets. Considering the circumstances under which they'd parted, she wondered if he would even agree to speak with her again.

"So what are you going to do, Holly?" she asked herself. "Shy away from the pruning shears some more? If God sent Seth to trim away the deadwood in your heart, you might as well let him finish the job." With a poignant chuckle, she recited one of her mother's favorite sayings. "It's bound to either kill you or cure you."

Tucking the card into her purse, she closed down Maxie's Floral, tucked her package of flowers under her arm, and went home to ponder her best course of action in the matter of Seth Glad.

# CHAPTER TEN

In recent history, Saturdays had become either very good or very bad, Seth thought, recalling several wonderful outings spent seeing the local sights in Holly's company. The Saturday of their San Juan visit had begun with great promise, but the minute he'd closed his arms around her that morning, things had changed.

Maybe it wasn't that things had changed, he amended; rather, their embrace had served to bring to the forefront issues and emotions that could no longer be ignored. Like the fact that something was deeply affecting her spiritual life and she refused to talk about it . . . and that he'd given her every chance and encouragement under the sun he could think of to do just that.

Not that he necessarily had any answers. Holly had been right; he was just a baby Christian beginning his spiritual walk. An off-color word escaped his lips as he struck yet another mistaken set of numbers into the accounting program of his home computer, and he breathed a quick apology with frustration. Balancing his checkbook on the computer was a great idea, but until someone figured a way around this blasted data entry . . .

Pushing his hand through his hair, he sat back in the chair and closed his eyes. Data entry wasn't his problem. Waiting was. Just as surely as he had sensed God's hand pushing him to pursue Holly these past few months, he now knew he was supposed to withdraw and let her take things where she would.

He still couldn't believe half of what he'd said to her at the beach. His only intention had been to bring into the open her avoidance of all spiritual topics. Telling her he loved her while she was—while they both were—in the grip of anger was about as far from romantic as things could get. And then he'd talked about marriage. What a fool. Why did he forever play his hand too soon where Holly Winslow was concerned?

But he knew she had feelings for him. He'd seen her start at his words. And then she'd stormed away from him, just like she had ten years earlier. Only this time, he couldn't console himself with the fact that there were other fish in the sea. The only woman he wanted was Holly. The only woman he loved was Holly.

How long was he supposed to wait for her? As often as his heart cried out the question, there was still no answer. In fact, he had no assurance she would return to him. But at least he'd provoked her anger. Aside from the flash of ire he'd seen when he took her to Howarth Park after Jean's wedding, she had only shown him a placid facade of her deep emotions.

*Yep, at South Beach you broke through that plastic barrier, all right.* He couldn't stop his wry grin as he recalled the barbed words, the high color in her cheeks, the dangerous glint in her eye. Now *that* was the Holly he remembered. Passionate. Earnest. Full of life.

Jean had given him a little encouragement when she'd called to tell him she'd driven Holly home from Anacortes that day. "I know she cares about you, Seth," she'd said, carefully walking the line of loyalty. "And I'll tell you that I can't seem to get to the bottom of whatever's going on with her either. I guess we need to just give her over to God's hands and let him help her."

The phone rang, tugging him back from his thoughts. Pushing back his chair, he reached for the receiver on the wall and nearly lost his balance when Holly's voice greeted him on the other end.

"Hello, Seth." Her voice was strained, subdued.

"Hi, Holly," he replied, his heart leaping. He wanted to ask her a million questions. *Let her take the lead, Glad. Be patient.*

"I was wondering if we could talk."

"I'd like that."

"It's . . . uh . . . I'd rather not do this over the phone, if that's OK."

His soaring hopes did an immediate one-eighty. Do what over the phone? Break it off for good? Tell him to get lost? *Adiós? Sayonara? Auf Wiedersehen?* "What did you have in mind?" he responded, managing, somehow, to sound normal, even agreeable.

"Do you think you could come to Howarth Park at five o'clock or so?" She paused briefly before continuing, nervousness straining her voice. "It seems like an appropriate place to meet."

"Today?" he queried, stalling for time, for more information. For any shred of hope. Five o'clock wasn't long before dark in November, so whatever she planned to say to him obviously wouldn't take long. *Give me a little more to go on, Holly—please!*

"Today," she affirmed, falling silent.

"I'll be there."

The remainder of the afternoon dragged its feet while Seth tried to occupy his mind with first balancing his checkbook, then leafing through the pile of books he'd brought home from the library. He prayed. Nothing seemed to make the passage of time any less agonizing, so he tossed swim trunks and a clean towel into his gym bag and went to the YMCA to work off what nervous energy he could.

The temperature was in the midfifties when he stepped out of the Y at twenty minutes to five. His skin was still damp, the breeze against his face fresh and bracing. He'd swum, sat in the sauna, showered, and, for good measure, shaved for the second time in eight hours. Pausing before he started his truck, he prayed for help accepting whichever way Holly chose to let him down.

Her dark blue Toyota was the only vehicle in the lot at Howarth Park. At least there wouldn't be an audience to witness his humiliation, he thought with a sense of fatalism. The air was cooler near the Sound, making him shiver as he stepped out of his truck, and he was thankful he'd had enough presence of mind to grab his fall jacket on his way out the door.

The autumn sun dropped steadily toward the horizon as he made his way along the wooded path to the stairs of the pedestrian walk, his left knee groaning in protest as he began climbing. Another reminder of his accident.

Reaching the top, he paused with curiosity. A lone figure, far down the beach, hunkered over a small fire. Holly? What was she doing? He strained his eyes, trying to make out the items near the fire. Blankets? Camp chairs? . . . A cooler?

She didn't notice him until he was nearly upon her. A stiff breeze off the Sound challenged her little blaze, but it appeared that she was gaining the upper hand over the elements. Unmatched plaid blankets lay side by side, overlapping, their corners pinned with rocks. A pair of canvas camp chairs had been set before the fire, separated by a cooler and two grocery sacks. She must have worked like a mule to haul everything out here.

"Seth!" she cried, turning. "You're here." Quickly, she pushed herself to her feet, brushing the sand and debris from her hands.

"Didn't you think I was going to show?"

Her cheeks were flushed pink from the wind and her exertion. "I wouldn't have blamed you if you didn't come." The beryl gaze was steady, but the emotions in the greenish blue depths were hidden.

Silence expanded between them while Holly dropped her gaze and took a deep breath. "Seth," she said, taking his hand. She looked up, tears brimming in her eyes. "I think I've loved you ever since twelfth grade—"

"You don't have to say anything more," he said hoarsely, crushing her in his embrace. He felt her arms wind around his back as she whispered words of apology and asked his forgiveness, squeezing him with a depth of feeling rivaling his own.

"It's gone now," she spoke into the side of his neck. Fumbling through the pockets of her jacket, she pulled out a crumpled tissue and wiped her eyes.

"What's gone?" Unwilling to let her go so soon, he pulled her back into his arms, raining kisses on her forehead, her nose, her salty cheeks.

"That terrible emptiness . . . like I was all hollowed out inside." He felt her muscles tense against him as she spoke. "At first I thought it was just grief from my mom dying. And it probably was, to start. But the longer I walked through the 'dead zone,' as I used to call it, the more I pulled away from any intimacy with God. I was just playing at being Christian. I couldn't bear for you to find out," she concluded, "so I hid behind my . . . my—what did you call it?"

"Your plastic barrier?" He grinned. "With the way I put the rush on you here after Jean's wedding, I can understand why you felt like you had to hide. I didn't leave you much room to be anything but perfect, Holy Holly." With his fingers, he lifted her chin and tilted her face toward his. "I'm sorry, darlin'. I sometimes have all the tact of a freight train."

"Well, it's not like I never do anything headlong. I still can't believe I left you on San Juan Island the way I did."

"Speaking of that . . ."

"Yeesss?" She winced as though expecting the worst. Seth took the opportunity to drink in the planes and angles of her face, revel in the feel of her next to him.

"Susie says she'll give us a deal if we come back and finish our tour of the island."

Holly giggled. "She will, huh? Are you sure you want to try that again?"

"There are a lot of things I'd like to try with you, Holly Winslow," he said earnestly, cutting short her laughter with a slow, gentle kiss. "And I hope to spend the rest of my life doing just that."

The sound of the water lapping against the shore was steady and sure. Taking his hand, she led him toward the dinner she had prepared. "I can't think of anything I'd like more," she whispered in reply.

# RECItPE

ılılı

*If you're in need of a serious dose of chocolate, these brownies
will do the trick. I've also learned that they can be frosted
while still warm—or even out-of-the-oven hot. They're one
of my daughters' favorite snacks, as well as a big hit with
the nurses on my hospital unit. When I took them to work
one weekend, a certain person (sorry, Molly!) exclaimed,
"Man! Would you look at that? Don't you wish you could
just lie down in the pan and roll around in all that chocolate?"*

*I don't know if I'd take things quite* that *far, but this is the
richest, most flavorful brownie recipe I've ever found. Using
high-quality cocoa will improve the brownies all the more.*
—*Peggy Stoks*

## BROWNIES
¾ cup cocoa
⅔ cup shortening
2 cups sugar
4 eggs
1½ cups flour
1 tsp. baking powder
1 tsp. salt

Melt cocoa and shortening together, either on the stove top or
in the microwave. Cool slightly. Mix in sugar, eggs, flour,
baking powder, and salt. Batter will be thick. Spread in
greased 9x13˝ pan and bake at 350° for 30 minutes.

## ICING
1 cup sugar
¼ cup milk

¼ cup butter
¼ cup cocoa
pinch of salt
1 tsp. vanilla
1 heaping tsp. peanut butter

In a small saucepan, mix together sugar, milk, butter, cocoa, and salt. Heat to boiling, stirring constantly. Then boil for one minute. Remove from heat and add vanilla and peanut butter. Beat until thick; then pour over brownies, tilting pan back and forth to cover evenly.

## ABOUT THE AUTHOR

Peggy Stoks lives in Minnesota with her husband and three daughters. She has worked as a registered nurse for nearly twenty years. She has published two novels as well as numerous magazine articles about child care and pediatrics. In addition to her novella for *Reunited,* she has written novellas for Tyndale's Christmas anthologies *A Victorian Christmas Tea* and *A Victorian Christmas Quilt.*

You can write to Peggy at P.O. Box 333, Circle Pines, MN 55014.

## Current HeartQuest Releases

- *Faith*, Lori Copeland
- *Prairie Fire*, Catherine Palmer
- *Prairie Rose*, Catherine Palmer
- *Reunited*, Judy Baer
- *The Treasure of Timbuktu*, Catherine Palmer
- *The Treasure of Zanzibar*, CatherinePalmer
- *A Victorian Christmas Quilt*, Catherine Palmer
- *A Victorian Christmas Tea*, Catherine Palmer

- *With This Ring*, Lori Copeland
- *June*, Lori Copeland—coming soon (spring 1999)
- *Prairie Storm*, Catherine Palmer—coming soon (spring 1999)
- *The Treasure of Kilimanjaro*, Catherine Palmer—coming soon (spring 1999)
- *Finders Keepers*, Catherine Palmer—coming soon (fall 1999)
- *Hope*, Lori Copeland—coming soon (fall 1999)

## Other Great Tyndale House Fiction

- *The Captive Voice*, B. J. Hoff
- *Dark River Legacy*, B. J. Hoff
- *The Embers of Hope*, Sally Laity and Dianna Crawford
- *The Fires of Freedom*, Sally Laity and Dianna Crawford
- *The Gathering Dawn*, Sally Laity and Dianna Crawford
- *Jewels for a Crown*, Lawana Blackwell
- *The Kindled Flame*, Sally Laity and Dianna Crawford

- *Like a River Glorious*, Lawana Blackwell
- *Measures of Grace*, Lawana Blackwell
- *Song of a Soul*, Lawana Blackwell
- *Storm at Daybreak*, B. J. Hoff
- *The Tangled Web*, B. J. Hoff
- *The Tempering Blaze*, Sally Laity and Dianna Crawford
- *The Torch of Triumph*, Sally Laity and Dianna Crawford
- *Vow of Silence*, B. J. Hoff

## Heartwarming Anthologies from HeartQuest

*A Victorian Christmas Tea*—Four novellas about life and love at Christmastime. Stories by Catherine Palmer, Dianna Crawford, Peggy Stoks, and Katherine Chute.

*A Victorian Christmas Quilt*—A patchwork of four novellas about love and joy at Christmastime. Stoires by Catherine Palmer, Debra White Smith, Ginny Aiken, and Peggy Stoks.

*Reunited*—Four stories about reuniting firends, old memories, and new romance. Includes favorite recipes from the authors. Stories by Judy Baer, Jeri Odell, Jan Duffy, and Peggy Stoks.

*With This Ring*—A quartet of charming stories about four very special weddings. Stories by Lori Copeland, Dianna Crawford, Ginny Aiken, and Catherine Palmer.